Changeling Press, LLC
**ChangelingPress.com**

Intergalactic Brides Vol. 5

Jessica Coulter Smith

# Intergalactic Brides Vol. 5
## Jessica Coulter Smith

ISBN: 978-1-60521-827-4

Publisher:
Changeling Press LLC
315 N. Centre St.
Martinsburg, WV 25404
ChangelingPress.com

Printed in the U.S.A.

Editor: Crystal Esau
Cover Artist: Karen Fox

The individual stories in this anthology have been previously released in E-Book format.

# Table of Contents

# Haven and the Alien Mechanic
## (Intergalactic Brides 13)
### Jessica Coulter Smith

When the IRS claimed her parents' home and all of their possessions, Haven lost everything. She was plunged into an unforgiving world she'd never been prepared for. Pregnant and alone, she's not sure how much more she can handle, when her car breaks down in a parking lot. Good thing for her it's a auto repair shop.

Dryden has always wanted one thing. A mate. When the brides being sent to his world barely spared him a glance, he moved to Earth to see if he could find a mate on his own. Little did he realize the perfect woman would fall into his lap. Her rotten luck was the best thing that ever happened to him.

When the true facts about the baby Haven is carrying come to light, her world is turned upside down once more. But with Dryden by her side, she knows that anything is possible... even true love and a happily-ever-after.

# Chapter One

Haven bashed her hands on the steering wheel as her car coasted to a stop just inside the nearest parking lot. While she was definitely having some rotten luck lately, it seemed angels were watching out for her tonight. Her car might have broken down on a busy street, but the parking lot she'd pulled into belonged to a car repair place. *Dryden's.* She'd never heard of it, but it wasn't like they could break the damn thing since it was already broken.

She pulled herself out of her car, shivering a bit when the winter air hit her. Not that her car was toasty, since the heat was broken, but at least the chilly breeze hadn't been cutting right through her. She left the keys in the ignition as she headed toward the shop to see what, if anything, could be done for her poor car. Truthfully, she just needed a new one, but she couldn't afford it. Once upon a time, she'd had everything. A nice house. A fancy car. She could have shopped until she dropped every day of her life. Then the IRS came along and said her parents hadn't paid taxes in ten years. They'd taken nearly everything.

Pulling open the glass door, she stepped inside the empty reception area. There was a beat-up couch, a scarred counter, and three doors. One was clearly marked as a restroom. The large glass window next to the second door showed it went to the shop area. And the third she was guessing was an office. There wasn't a bell on the counter and there hadn't been one over the door.

Haven walked over to the large window and banged on the glass. A gasp slipped past her lips when a tall, hunky Terran slid out from under a car, shirtless with smears of grease here and there. And damn, but wasn't he sexy? She'd seen several Terrans around town before, but this one had shoulder-length hair, shorter than what seemed to be the norm for his race. And was that an earring in his left ear? Her stomach fluttered, and she wasn't sure if it was attraction or the little being she'd found out about a few months ago. If nothing else, her predicament served as an icy cold shower, reminding her where wayward hormones would get her.

On the other hand, it wasn't like she could get knocked up again.

The door opened and Mr. Sexy stepped inside, an easy grin on his face.

"May I help you?" he asked, his gaze skimming over her.

"My car broke down in your parking lot. I wondered if you could take a look at it?"

He nodded. "Just let me grab a shirt."

Pity.

He stepped through the third door and returned a moment later, wearing a long-sleeved tee. Haven went outside to her poor car and waited for the alien to follow her. When he came outside, she'd have sworn the temperature rose a few degrees. Or maybe it was her overactive sex drive making her warmer than usual.

"It was driving fine and then just started shimmying and shaking. Right when I neared your shop, it sputtered and died. I managed to coast to this spot."

"It's hard for me to say what's wrong with it just off a description. Mind if I push it inside and take a better look?" he asked.

"No, I don't mind. How much does it cost to diagnose the car?" she asked, thinking of her dwindling bank account.

His gaze skimmed over her again, a half-smile on his face. "Why don't I take you to dinner and we call it even? I was close to finishing up for the night."

Her cheeks warmed. It had been a while since someone had asked her out. Haven hadn't exactly been popular at college, and then she'd dropped out and her social circle had shrunk even more. Especially since she hadn't told her friends why she was leaving. She'd been too embarrassed. And then everyone else had abandoned her when the money went away.

"You really want to go to dinner with me?"

His smile grew a little. "You seem surprised. If you tell me you've never been asked out before, I won't believe you."

"I've been on dates before," she said. "Just not in a while."

"So, you're not seeing anyone?"

"No. And I'd love to have dinner with you."

"Why don't you go back inside where it's warm? I'll push your car into the nearest bay and take a look at it."

Haven followed his instructions and went back into the shop. She sank onto the beat-up leather couch. She shivered a little, still cold from being outside. Her coat wasn't that warm, but she hadn't been allowed to keep the expensive one her parents had bought her. All of their designer clothes, jewelry, shoes... all of it was gone. Everything had been auctioned or sold. There were times she missed it, but mostly she missed the comfort of having a roof over her head, knowing where her next meal would come from, and not having to worry about things like money.

She'd been allowed to keep her iPhone, but now she had to pay the monthly fees herself. Pulling it out of her pocket, she played a game and checked her social media accounts while she waited on the hunky mechanic to finish looking at her car. She hoped it wasn't anything serious, or she wouldn't be able to get it fixed right now, and if she didn't have a car, she couldn't look for work. Not that anyone seemed to want to hire a spoiled ex-socialite.

The minutes ticked by on her phone and finally the mechanic appeared again, shirtless once more to her delight. But the grim set of his mouth told her it wasn't good news. He wiped his hands on a rag and tossed it onto the counter before crossing his arms over his chest.

"How much do you love that car?" he asked.

"Is it bad?"

"You'd be better off buying a new one. It's probably going to cost about four thousand to fix everything wrong with it. When's the last time maintenance was done on it?" He held up a hand. "Let me rephrase. Has maintenance *ever* been done on it?"

"I bought it used, so I don't know."

"I think you were sold a lemon. Any chance the dealership would take it back and refund your money?" he asked.

"I bought it from an individual off Craigslist."

He winced.

"I needed something cheap," she said. "He assured me the car was in great running condition."

"You were lied to. Your engine needs to be rebuilt. Your transmission is leaking. The fuel pump looks like it's about to go. And your fan is cracked. There's more, but those are the big things."

"All of that only costs four thousand?" she asked skeptically.

"I may have discounted the price a bit."

Haven sighed. "I appreciate you taking a look at the car, but I can't afford to have all that taken care of right now. I'll just have to figure something out."

He moved closer and sank onto the couch next to her. "I'm going to get cleaned up and take you to dinner, then you're going to tell me exactly how much trouble you're in. I can't promise to have a solution, but I'd like to help, if you'll let me."

"Why are you being so nice to me?" she asked. No one ever did anything out of the kindness of their heart, not anymore. The alien had to want something from her, but she couldn't figure out what.

"Maybe I'm a sucker for a damsel in distress."

Well, that was certainly her at the moment. She watched as he disappeared into the office and shut the door. It sounded like water was running and fifteen minutes later, he reappeared in clean clothes with his wet hair brushed back. He had a shower and spare clothes in his office? How often did he go on dates with customers?

"I don't believe I introduced myself earlier. I'm Dryden," he said, holding out his hand.

"Haven."

He smiled. "Beautiful name for a beautiful woman."

She wondered if she said that to every woman who

walked through the shop door. The humor and kindness in his eyes made her trust him at least a little. But she didn't know anything about him. For all she knew, he was a player and had a different woman on his arm every night.

Dryden escorted her outside, stopping long enough to lock up his shop and set the alarm. Then he motioned toward a large, black truck across the parking lot. It figured he would drive something big. He easily stood over six feet tall and he was rather broad through the shoulders. Her five-foot-three felt rather dainty next to him.

Dryden opened the passenger door and helped her up onto the seat. While she buckled, he walked around the front of the truck and climbed behind the steering wheel on the driver's side. In the confined space, she could smell the spicy scent of his soap or cologne. She tried not to lean closer as she breathed him in. The way men smelled had always been her weakness.

Dryden pulled into a steak place not far from his work. The Lone Steer. Haven hadn't heard of it before, but the parking lot was fairly packed. It seemed to be well-liked by the community so she was more than willing to give it a try. Besides, it had been a while since she'd had a juicy steak, and her baby hadn't had a good meal in a while.

Inside, everyone was talking and laughing and throwing peanut shells on the floor. She crunched her way to the hostess stand, passing a massive barrel full of the nuts. The kitchen had a long window almost the length of the wall, where everyone could see their food being prepared. The hostess smiled at them, giving Dryden an appreciative look.

"How many?" the woman asked.

"Two," Dryden said.

Her gaze flicked to Haven and her look clearly said she didn't understand why they were together. Haven smoothed her hair back behind her ear, feeling self-conscious. It had been a long time since anyone had made her feel out of place. Her sweater hugged her curves under her poorly put together coat, and her jeans might have been secondhand but they were name brand and fit her well. She'd thought she looked nice.

The woman showed them to a table and left menus with them. Before she walked off, she gave Dryden a flirty smile. Haven tried to shrug it off. It wasn't like she had a claim on the alien. He'd asked her to dinner, but one dinner didn't mean they were dating. If he wanted to flirt back with the hostess, she'd just get up and leave. It wasn't too far to her motel.

"Sorry about that," Dryden said. "We either get that kind of reaction from humans, or they can't stand us."

She blinked and looked from the hostess' retreating back to him again. "People flirt with you everywhere you go?"

"And not just women."

She smiled a little, trying to picture the hunky alien getting hit on by men. The way he'd handled the hostess, she'd imagine that he was nice about it. Maybe she'd misjudged him. Just because the college guys she'd been dating were jerks, didn't mean all men were. And she'd never been on a date with Terran before. Maybe they followed a different set of principles than human men.

"If you want her number, it won't hurt my feelings," Haven said.

"No. I'm right where I want to be." He smiled. "Order anything you want, and then we'll talk."

A waiter came by and took their drink orders while they decided what to eat. When he returned, they placed the order for their meals and then they were left in peace. Except Haven didn't know how much she should tell Dryden. It wasn't like they were best friends. She didn't normally open up to strangers, but she was short on friends these days. When she lost her money, she lost her friends. It seemed they only liked her when she could go do things with them, or buy them things.

"Why don't you start by telling me why you had to buy a cheap car off someone you don't know?" Dryden said.

"Do you know the name Henry Fordham?" Haven

asked.

"The CEO of Fordham Enterprises who was recently incarcerated for tax evasion?" he asked. "It was all over the news and papers the last few months. That happened like three months ago, right?"

She nodded. "Henry Fordham is my father."

"And when his possessions were taken by the IRS, whatever car you had was taken too," he said.

"Yes. I lost everything, even though I wasn't to blame. Just because my dad had his name on everything."

"Didn't I hear your mom checked herself into rehab to avoid jail time?" he asked.

"Yes. She's had a drinking problem for a while, and the D.A. offered her the chance to get clean. Mom's lawyer argued that if she hadn't been under the influence, she might have questioned whether or not her husband was paying taxes. Dad shared the business with Mom, so her name is all over everything too."

"So, you're all alone now?"

"Yes. I had some money in my savings account the IRS couldn't touch because it came from my grandparents, but it wasn't enough to sustain me indefinitely. I bought a cheap car, picked up some clothes at the secondhand store, and I've been staying at the Lazy Daze Motel."

"And you don't have enough left to repair your car?" he asked.

"I do, but it won't leave me much for living expenses. I've tried finding work, but no one wants to hire me. I don't have any job experience and I dropped out of college. And thanks to Dad, none of the bigger companies around town will hire me. My name is tainted."

Dryden studied her a moment. "What about your friends? And why did you have to leave college? Tuition too expensive?"

"My friends vanished when the money did. And I stopped going to school right before the scandal hit. I went to a party and got too drunk about four months ago. I only remember bits and pieces of the night, but I found out a month later I was pregnant, and I hadn't been seeing anyone. So, I know it had to have happened that night."

Dryden sat back. "What about the baby's father?"

"I have no idea who it is. I know that sounds horrible, but it's the truth. I'm not a big drinker. I'd just aced a test and my friend talked me into celebrating. I guess I celebrated a little too well."

"So, you're pregnant, running out of money, and don't have a home or a car. What exactly do you plan to do?" he asked.

"I don't know. If the car was still running, I could keep searching for jobs. I've already checked all the places within walking distance of the motel. No one would hire me. Not even the diner."

"Did you think about signing up for the Terran bride program?" Dryden asked. "You'd have to move to my world, most likely, but they would pay you to consider a mate there."

Her cheeks flushed. "I looked it up online at the library. It says they aren't currently accepting pregnant females or single moms. I guess they must have had a lot of them apply."

"So, you're willing to mate with someone like me?" he asked. "You'd consider living on another planet?"

"There's nothing for me here," she said. "But I can understand why your people don't want an influx of human children on your world. If they wanted to marry someone already carrying a baby, they could just move here and live among humans, right?"

"Several of my kind have made their home here."

"Why did you ask about the bride program?" she asked. "Trying to marry me off already?"

"If you're open to accepting a Terran mate, I had thought perhaps you would consider me."

Her eyes widened. "Wait. You want me to marry you? I've known you an hour, if that. You can't just take a woman to dinner and expect her to marry you."

He smiled a little. "I hadn't planned to rush you right to

my council for an approved mating. We could go on a few dates and get to know one another. I've been here long enough to know humans date. Terrans do to some extent, but we usually know when the right woman comes along. And divorce isn't possible on my world. So, if you decide to marry me, it would be forever."

"It doesn't bother you I'm pregnant with someone else's child?" she asked.

"No. Not as long as you agreed to have at least one or two more in the future. It's time for me to start a family, and I will gladly accept your baby as my own. I would treat them no differently than I would my own child. Just think about it."

Haven nodded. Their food arrived and she tried to steer the conversation in another direction. It wasn't that she wasn't attracted to the alien, because she was, but love at first sight didn't exist and she'd always said she would marry for love. Getting married because she was out of options didn't seem like the smartest thing to do. What if they found out later they didn't get along? What if he grew to hate her?

"What are your parents like?" she asked.

"My father works with the military. He's not a soldier, but he handles their weapons testing and training. He's one of a small group with that responsibility. My mother keeps their home. I was their only child so it's been hard for them to accept that I spend so much time on Earth, but they understand. Finding a mate on my world, even with the bride program, is hard. The competition is high and those with better jobs and better social standing usually get chosen first."

"There's nothing wrong with being a mechanic," Haven said. "It just means you're good with your hands. I mean… " Her cheeks flushed.

Dryden threw back his head and laughed. "What's that Earth saying? You're good for my ego?"

"You know what I meant."

"I do, but teasing you is fun. I like watching your

cheeks turn pink."

"What will your parents do if you move here permanently?" Haven asked.

"I'm not sure. They love living on my world, but they might consider having a home here too. The council would pay for them to stay in a hotel if they wanted to visit for a week or two here and there. Or they could buy a small home, but then it would sit empty part of the year."

"You said you don't have a home here. Do you stay at the hotel when you're on Earth?" she asked.

"Yes, I stay at one of the hotels my council pays for, and if my bride decides she wishes to remain on Earth, then I will choose a home here at that time. I would probably sell my home on my world. Then when the children are older, and better able to handle such a journey several times a year, I could look at buying a small home on my world again. Or we could stay with my parents while we're there."

"We?" she asked.

He smiled. "Well, whatever family I have at the time."

"It doesn't bother you? Who my parents are? You aren't worried I'll run off with your money?"

"No, I'm not worried. Just because your parents tried to game the system doesn't mean you're cut from the same cloth. You have an honest face, and your eyes tell me everything you're thinking or feeling. I don't think you could lie and cheat even if you wanted to."

"You're the first person to say that to me. I half expect people to move to the other side of the street when they find out who I am."

"It's their loss if they don't want to take the time to get to know you. From what I've seen so far, you're sweet and charming. And you're honest. You didn't have to tell me who you are or that you're already expecting."

They finished their meal and Dryden left a stack of cash on the table. He rose to his feet and held out a hand to Haven, helping her stand. Her belly was only slightly curved from the baby, but he slowly reached out and placed his hand there. She held still, her heart hammering in her chest at that slight touch. Dryden stared into her eyes and for a moment she thought he might kiss her. Instead, he pulled away, taking her hand and leading her back outside to where he parked.

"I'm at the Lazy Daze Motel," she reminded him, "if you don't mind dropping me off. I'll try to make arrangements for my car tomorrow."

"Do you have the title to it?" he asked.

"Yes. It's at the motel in the safe."

"If you'll sign the back of the title, I'll see if I can find someone who will buy it as either something to part out or a project car. I can't promise you'll get much for it, but it might give you a little more room financially."

"Thank you," she said softly. "I appreciate any help you're willing to give."

Dryden reached over and took her hand, lacing their fingers together. She stared at their clasped hands for a while, trying to decide if the flutter she felt was from his touch or indigestion. Heartburn was a bitch when you were pregnant, as she'd discovered. They arrived at the motel all too soon and she told him to drive around the back to room thirty-seven.

He pulled to a stop in front of her door, but it didn't look right. She'd left a lamp on and light was streaming around the door, as if it weren't completely shut.

"Stay here," he told her, sliding out of the truck.

He approached the door and she watched as he pushed it open. She couldn't see much around his large frame, but she saw enough to know her room had been tossed. Despite his words, she rushed out of the truck to the open motel room door. Her clothes had been shredded and left everywhere, her shoes were gone… and the safe stood open.

"No!" She pushed past him and ran to the safe, falling to her knees in front of it. Tears streaked her cheeks as she saw that the cash she'd stored in there was gone, along with the title to her car.

Dryden knelt by her side, pulling her into his arms. "Take a breath and remain calm. Everything will be fine."

She blinked up at him. "Nothing will ever be fine again. I've lost everything."

"Not everything," he said. "You haven't lost me."

## Chapter Two

Dryden held Haven as she cried, and tried to decide what to do. She had nothing, as she said. Her clothes and shoes were gone, her cash was gone. And without the title to her car, he couldn't sell it for her. She needed his help, even if she didn't want to accept it. He wasn't rich compared to his friends. Even on his world he was working class, but he was doing well enough financially that he could take care of her.

He rose to his feet and lifted her into his arms, carrying her back out to the truck. He buckled her in and pressed a kiss to her forehead before returning to her motel room. He gathered all of the destroyed clothes and shoved them into the trash can, then packed up her bathroom items and carried them out to the truck along with her empty tote bag. He got the room key from her before driving around to the front office, where he handed the key over and informed them she was checking out, as well as informing them her room had been broken into.

"Where am I going to go?" she asked when he got back in the truck.

"First, we're stopping at one of those twenty-four hour stores and getting you a few clothes and another pair of shoes. You need something to get you by for a few days while we decide how to replace your belongings. Then you're coming home with me."

"You don't have a home," she said softly, staring out the passenger window.

"My hotel room has two bedrooms. You can have the one I'm not using. You'll have your own bathroom so you don't have to worry about sharing."

Her gaze swung his way, her expression tired and wounded. "I don't have money for clothes. I need to save what I have left in the bank to find a new place to live."

"Haven, I'm not asking you to purchase anything tonight. I'm going to take care of you, and I'd appreciate it if you wouldn't argue about it. I have the means to replace your wardrobe, and you can stay with me free of charge for as long as you need to. Any meals sent up to the hotel room are covered by the council. I just have to inform them I have a houseguest and get a room key for you."

"Why are you going to so much trouble to help me?" she asked.

"Maybe it's my way of showing you I'd be a good mate."

She smiled a little and looked back out her window. The drive to the store was quiet and he observed her when he could. She seemed subdued and he wondered if she was stressing over her situation. He'd told her he would take care of her, but Dryden wasn't certain she understood what he meant. He'd told her how he would help right this minute, but not that he meant to do it long-term. If he thought she would accept, he would offer once more to take her as his mate. But she hadn't seemed that interested at dinner. Almost horrified, in fact, that he might want to marry her so soon after meeting her. He would give her all the space she needed, but he planned to keep her in his hotel suite for as long as possible. Sooner or later, she would see that he would make a good mate.

At the store, she moved slowly, almost as if she were in pain. He stopped her before they reached the women's clothes. "Are you all right?'

"My back hurts a little. I did a lot of standing today when I went hunting for a job. I'm sure once I get some rest, I'll be fine."

Dryden pushed the cart over to the women's clothes and hunted until he found things for expectant mothers. Haven tried to look at the tags, but he covered her hand with his.

"Don't worry about price. Find something that's comfortable."

She nodded and went back to searching. A half hour later, she had a few outfits and two pair of pajamas. Haven hesitantly went to the intimates department and selected a few bras and a package of panties. Her cheeks were an adorable pink as she added them to the cart. On the way to the shoe department, Dryden threw in a package of socks, thinking she might need them.

The tennis shoes on her feet were cute, but he wondered if they had enough padding in them. He'd seen commercials for inserts for shoes to make them comfortable and when they reached the shoe department, he picked out two of them and added them to the cart. He hoped they were the right size, but Haven wasn't paying much attention to him as she walked up and down the aisle.

Dryden didn't know anything about women's shoes, but he picked up a few pairs of boots and checked them out. Some had no padding inside, and some were so stiff that they had to make the wearer miserable. He found a soft black pair of ankle boots that had a lot of cushion inside.

"What about these?" he asked, handing her one.

Haven looked the shoe over and smiled a little. "If they have my size, I'll try it on, but this one is three sizes too big."

He looked from the shoe to her small foot. "What size do you wear?"

"A six and a half."

He put the shoe back and rummaged through the boxes until he found a pair in her size, then handed them to her. Haven sat down and tried them on, a sigh escaping her as she walked the length of the aisle.

"They feel amazing," she admitted.

"Then get them."

Dryden looked at other shoes in that same brand and showed them to her, encouraging her to pick at least one other pair. When they were finished and had checked out up front, he loaded the sacks into the backseat of his truck and drove them to his hotel. Dryden carried everything inside for her and went straight for the elevator.

"I thought you had to let someone know I was staying here," she said.

"I'll clear it with my council once you've gotten settled for the night, and then I'll get you a room key so you can come and go as you please."

"You won't get in trouble for bringing me home?" she

asked.

"No." He smiled. "It's not like I'm a wayward child who will be reprimanded by his parents. I just need to inform the council I have a guest so they can approve it with the hotel. I don't foresee any problems with you staying here."

When the elevator let them out at his floor, he led the way down the hall to his suite. Dryden slid the keycard into the lock and when the light turned green, he pushed it open. Warm air greeted them. Not too hot, but just right, in his opinion. If Haven was too hot or too cold, she could adjust it however she pleased. He carried her packages and toiletries into the spare room and set everything on the dresser. Turning, he found her in the doorway, checking out the room.

"It's bigger than I thought," she said.

"There's not a TV in here, but you can watch whatever you want in the living room. Would you like to take a bath and relax while I contact my council? I shouldn't be gone more than thirty or forty minutes."

She stepped further into the room and looked around the corner of the bathroom door. "I think this bathroom is nicer than anything I've seen at a hotel before. A separate tub and shower?"

"It's the master bedroom, I believe, so the bathroom is a bit bigger than the other one."

She turned to face him. "You didn't give me your room, did you?"

"No. I took the smaller room when I got here. It was more than adequate for my needs. Please, make yourself at home. Enjoy your bath, and if you decide you're hungry when you get out, there's fruit in the kitchenette and juice in the fridge. Help yourself to anything you want."

Haven nodded and stepped into the bathroom, closing the door behind her. Dryden pulled her bedroom door shut behind him, made sure he had his keycard, and then went to contact the council. The hotel had been updated with a Vid-Comm in one of the smaller conference rooms, but it was presently not working. Dryden drove the short distance to the Terran Station, hoping he'd been correct and the council wouldn't make him toss Haven out of his hotel room.

The receptionist smiled at him as he passed her desk and went straight back to the conference rooms that held the Vid-Comms. All but one was in use and he quickly claimed it before someone else could. Pressing the appropriate buttons to call on the council, he hoped someone would be available on the other end. A sound filled the room, telling him his call was being rerouted. A moment later, Borgoz appeared on the screen, his small daughter in his arms.

"I'm sorry to bother you at home, Chief Councilor."

"Arabella couldn't sleep so I've been walking with her. What is it you need, Dryden? Everything all right on Earth?"

"I've found a potential mate and I've moved her into my hotel suite. I know policies have recently changed and I need the council to approve her with the hotel so I can get a keycard for her. We only met today so she claims it's too soon to get married, but she needs my help."

Borgoz nodded. "What seems to be the trouble?"

Dryden explained about Haven's parents and what happened to her, mentioning her unplanned pregnancy and that she was completely alone, without transportation, and low on funds.

"Someone had broken into her motel room while she was gone today. I couldn't leave her there," Dryden said.

"I understand," Borgoz said. "I'll make sure the hotel knows she has permission to stay with you, and a keycard will be ready for her sometime tomorrow. As late as it is there tonight, it's impossible for me to set it up right now. Enjoy your time with her, and don't rush her into marriage. We Zelthranite males have a way of knowing when we've met the right woman, so if you believe she's meant to be yours, she probably is. Just give her some time to come to the same conclusion."

"Do you still plan to tell Earth that we aren't really called Terrans?" Dryden asked. "The word is out around the station and our people are concerned it could end badly for those who have made their homes here."

"I have a Vid-Comm conference with the Earth world leaders in three days. I will tell them the truth, and why we lied about the name of our world and what our people are called, and let them decide how we should proceed. If they think it's best for us to remain Terrans, then that's what we'll do. Panic is the last thing we want."

"Understood. Thank you for taking my call. I hope Arabella can sleep soon."

Borgoz looked over his shoulder at the rising suns. "She doesn't have long to sleep before breakfast. I may just enjoy this time with her, and wake my mate when it's a little later in the morning. Charlotte has had trouble sleeping lately."

"I hope it's nothing serious."

"I'm sure she'll be fine. I scheduled an appointment for her at the clinic this afternoon just to be safe. Go be with your Haven, and don't hesitate to call again if she should decide she wants to be your mate."

Dryden cleared his throat. "Her current pregnancy won't be an issue, will it? She said she looked online at the bride program and it said we weren't accepting anyone who was pregnant or already had a child."

"We've had a big rush of applications from expectant mothers and single moms. There's nothing wrong with taking them as mates, but we needed to thin them out a bit. I asked the Terran Stations to stop accepting them as brides for the time being, just to widen our bride pool a little. I'm hoping more countries will start participating as well. So far, the majority of our brides are Americans. Not that there's anything wrong with that, but it would be nice if some of the other places would send more our way."

"Thank you, Chief Councilor."

Borgoz ended the call and Dryden drove back to the hotel. When he entered his room, he found Haven sitting on the edge of her bed, dressed in her pajamas, and crying. Worried that she may have hurt herself, he rushed to her side and knelt at her feet.

"What's wrong? Did you fall getting out of the tub?

Does it hurt anywhere?"

"I'm fine." She sniffled. "The ache in my back got sharper and I tried to lie down, but it hurt too much."

"Can you lie on your stomach still?"

She nodded.

"Stretch out on your stomach and I'll see if I can make your back feel better."

Haven crawled to the center of the bed and stretched out. Dryden placed a knee on either side of her hips and slowly lifted the back of her shirt. He could see the muscles tightening and winced at how painful it must be for her. Rubbing his hands together to warm them, he placed them on her soft skin and began to massage her tense lower back.

Haven sucked in a breath, but after a few minutes, she began to relax. Dryden fought to think of anything but how silky her skin was, and failed miserably. He made sure to keep his weight off her, and his growing erection away from her delectable ass. If she knew how turned on he was, she'd probably throw him out of her room, and possibly leave the hotel altogether.

The muscles under his fingers began to ease and loosen. When he moved away from her and stood beside the bed, Haven rolled onto her side and looked up at him, her gaze catching on the tent forming in his jeans before skimming over his chest and up to meet his eyes.

"Thank you," she said softly.

"Feel better?" he asked.

She nodded. "Dryden, can I ask you something?"

"Anything." *Preferably not about the current state of my cock.*

"Is selecting a mate more of a sexual thing?"

Her question surprised him, though it shouldn't have considering his erection. "There has to be sexual attraction there in order for us to have children at some point, but no, it's not just a sexual thing. Not all females who want to mate with Terrans are selected. There are other things we look for besides a physical attraction."

"Like what?"

"Kindness. Honesty. Faithfulness."

"And how did you know I possessed any of those qualities after knowing me for less than an hour? Have you asked many women to be your mate?"

Dryden eased on the bed and reached for her hand. "I've never asked a female to be my mate before tonight. I haven't been a saint. There have been women in my bed since coming to Earth, but none were worthy of standing by my side. You have a pure soul, and it shines through your eyes for the world to see. I asked you to be my mate because I knew you would make me happy, and I hoped I would be able to make you happy."

"Thank you for telling me."

Dryden nodded and stood. "If you don't need anything else tonight, you should probably get some sleep. I'm just across the living room if you need anything. I'll have my door closed, but don't hesitate to knock."

Haven squirmed until she was under the covers and her eyes were closing as he shut the bedroom door. Leaning his forehead against the wood panel, he had to wonder whether having her in his hotel suite was the brightest thing he'd ever done. She was going to torment him with her sweet curves and charming smile. He pushed away and went across to his bedroom. He closed the door and began stripping off his clothes as he headed into the bathroom.

Dryden started the shower, turning the hot water all the way on with just a little cold to keep it from being scalding. Steam billowed out from behind the curtain and he stepped over the edge of the tub, letting the water pelt him. He jerked the curtain closed and shut his eyes as he tried to clear his mind of everything. Normally, he used his shower time to do a sort of meditation. Tonight, that wasn't working out so well. His thoughts were filled with Haven.

His cock was still hard and pointing straight up at him. He glared at it, wishing he hadn't gotten so excited rubbing Haven's back. She probably didn't think much of him right now, and he wouldn't blame her. Just touching a woman had never made him hard before, not even the Hollywood types he'd seen while visiting the Terran Station in California. Haven was beautiful, but that wasn't the only reason he was attracted to her. He hadn't lied when he'd told her why he wanted her for a mate.

Squirting some shower gel into his palm, he gripped his shaft and gave it a firm stroke. It felt good, but he knew without a doubt that Haven's small, soft hands would feel so much better. It was doubtful she was touching his cock anytime soon, though. He gave it another stroke, twisting his hand a little. Dryden widened his legs and cupped his balls with his other hand. A groan slipped past his lips as he quickened his pace. His balls sizzled and his lower back tingled a moment before he came all over his hand and the shower wall. He bit his lip to keep from crying out and braced a hand on the wall.

The release felt good, but it wasn't enough. It had been a few months since he'd been with anyone, but now that he'd met Haven, he knew that not just any woman would do. The second he'd seen her standing in his shop, it was like the world had stood still. Nothing had mattered in that moment, but hearing her voice, learning her name, and asking her out. He'd have fallen to his knees the minute she looked at him, but he'd held strong. For the most part.

He'd read the human fairy tales and watched the animated movies about love at first sight. The princess who danced in the woods with a prince and fell for him instantly. The peasant girl who went to a ball and fell madly in love with the prince. He'd never understood how someone could instantly know they wanted to spend the rest of their lives with someone, until meeting Haven. She was his princess, his wish upon a star, and he was going to do whatever it took to make her his.

He dried off and pulled on some loose pants before picking up his phone. Pulling up his contacts, he sent a message to his shop manager, asking him to cover the place for a few days and do whatever it took to get Haven's car running and safe. She might be upset when she found out what he'd done, but he couldn't leave her without transportation, and he didn't think a new car would go over well. If she became his mate and decided she didn't want her car anymore, they would request a replacement title and trade it for something else, but until then, he'd know that she was safe while driving around town.

Setting his phone down, he stretched out on the bed and placed his hands behind his head. He stared up at the ceiling and listened for any signs Haven might be up. The suite was quiet and still. It was a good thing because it meant she was sleeping. He doubted she'd had many good nights of sleep since finding out about her parents. No matter what he had to do, he was going to give her peace of mind. If it meant claiming her as his mate, he would gladly do so. And if she wanted more time and a place of her own, he would respect her wishes.

He'd never realized how complicated women could be, until he found one he wanted, who was determined to stand on her own two feet. It would have been so much easier if she'd let him take care of everything, claim her, and give her everything she could ever want or need. But then, if she gave in that easily, she wouldn't be Haven. And he was finding her rather intriguing. He wanted her, and the child growing inside of her. With a bit of luck, they would be his family before too long. Everything he'd ever wanted was within his grasp. He just had to figure out how to make it happen.

# Chapter Three

Haven stretched the next morning and smiled at the sunlight streaming through her window. She'd had the most delicious dream about Dryden and felt more rested than she had in months. Her hand smoothed over her small baby bump and she marveled at the fact he wanted her, baby and all. She had no doubt that he had his choice of women. He was a Terran and females flocked his way, like the hostess at the restaurant, but he was also kind and charming. And when he smiled it made her knees weaken and her heart skip a beat.

She got out of bed and rinsed off in the shower before pulling on one of her new outfits. She left her socks and shoes off, preferring to be barefoot when she was home. Not that a hotel room was home, but she supposed in a way it was for now. Opening her bedroom door, her jaw dropped a little at the service cart laden with food. Pancakes, muffins, fruit. She even smelled bacon.

"Good morning," Dryden said, rising from the couch. "I hope you don't mind but I ordered breakfast. I thought you might be hungry when you woke up. My friend's mate seemed to eat more than usual when she was carrying their child."

"I am hungry."

"I didn't know what you'd want so I tried to get a little of everything. I ate the eggs when they started to get cold. If you'd like more, I can have some sent up."

She shook her head. "This is more than fine."

Haven picked up a short stack of pancakes and drizzled syrup over them. Putting her plate down on the small dining table, she went back for bacon and a blueberry muffin, then grabbed the orange juice from the fridge and poured a glass. When she had everything she needed, she sat down to eat, smiling when Dryden claimed the seat across from her, a banana nut muffin gripped in his hand.

"Still hungry?" she asked.

"I thought I'd keep you company while you ate. As for being hungry, I can always eat."

Her gaze skimmed over his chest and what she could see of his abdomen. The T-shirt he was wearing was tight and showed off every muscle he had. If he was constantly eating, she didn't know where he was putting it, unless it just automatically converted to muscle mass. He wasn't bulky like a bodybuilder, but in her opinion, he was just right.

"Did you have plans for today?" Dryden asked.

"Just job hunting, but I can't really do that without a car."

He nodded. "I called into my shop manager and asked him to cover the place a few days. I wasn't sure if you would need my help with anything and didn't want to leave you alone until you have a keycard for the room."

"You weren't able to get one last night?" she asked.

"No. I did speak with the Chief Councilor and he approved you staying here, but he said he wouldn't be able to get a message to the hotel until sometime today. I thought we could go to a movie this afternoon."

"I haven't been to a movie in a few months. It sounds like fun. Anything good playing?"

"There's an action movie that looks like it has lots of explosions, a romantic comedy, an animated movie that looks cute, and I can't remember the other two."

She smiled a little. "You watch animated movies?"

"Sometimes. I like that they usually have a happy ending, there's always a lesson to be learned, and you leave the theater just feeling good in general."

"Then we should see that one. I used to have a DVD collection of every animated movie I loved as a kid. I lost it along with everything else. They wouldn't even let me keep the locket my grandmother had given me before she died. They said if I wanted it, I had to buy it. Then they asked for a ridiculous price, no matter how much I wanted to keep it."

He reached across the table and took her hand. "I'm sorry you lost so much. It must have been hard to have the world at your feet and then have it all snatched away, and all because of something someone else did. It must have felt very unfair."

"It did, but I'm learning to cope with it all. I'm not doing so great taking care of myself, but then I've never had to before. I lived at home with my parents when I wasn't in school. I've never paid rent, had a car payment, or even had to pay off my credit cards. Mom and Dad took care of everything."

"It sounds like they didn't do you any favors. By giving you everything, they didn't prepare you for living on your own."

"How ridiculous is it that I'm twenty and other than my savings account, I've never had to balance a bank account before? My parents always put my monthly allowance in my checking account and if I ran out of funds, they'd just add more."

"With this baby, you have a chance to do things differently. You can teach him or her early on the value of a dollar, that you have to earn the things you get. And when they're older, maybe they won't flounder when it's time to set out on their own. I'm not saying never give them things, but just... don't give them everything."

Haven nodded. "I agree. I don't want to make the same mistakes my parents made. For one, I'm always going to pay my taxes. Well, if I ever have a job to earn money."

"I'm sure you'll find something. Or you may decide you'd rather be a stay-at-home mom when the baby is born."

"And how am I supposed to pay rent and buy food?" she asked, smiling a little. "I doubt I'm getting those things for free."

"Maybe you'll have help," he said softly, and she knew he meant him.

"Maybe."

She wasn't ready to agree to be his mate, but after the tender way he'd taken care of her last night, his obvious arousal at touching her, and then her hot dream, she was starting to think that maybe being Dryden's mate wouldn't be so bad. She still didn't want to marry a stranger, though. But there was no reason she couldn't get to know him while she was staying here, and then make an informed decision when the time came.

Haven finished most of her breakfast before pushing away what was left. If she ate another bite, she'd explode. Dryden rose and began placing her plates back onto the trolley and then pushed it out into the hall. There was still quite a bit of food left over and she hated they'd wasted so much. She rose from the table, rubbing her belly, then collapsed onto the couch. The TV was on, playing softly, and she watched the ticker scroll across the screen as the news came on.

"You can change it," Dryden said. "If anything important happens that affects my people, we're sent a notice."

"I grew to hate the news when every station played my family's drama nonstop," Haven said. "I haven't watched it since the trial. They portrayed me as the poor little rich girl and were rather nasty with their comments. Everyone seemed to think I should have known what my parents were up to and they blamed me as well."

"Anyone who met you couldn't have thought poorly of you," Dryden said. "It's obvious you were an innocent in the whole affair."

She shrugged and began flipping through the channels until she found an old Scooby Doo cartoon. She'd loved the classic ones growing up, and didn't much care for the newer versions that'd come out in recent years. Dryden smiled a little when he saw her choice and he settled back to watch.

Haven didn't know how much time had passed before he stood and stretched. She watched the muscles bunch and flex in his back and arms, and absently wiped her chin to make sure she wasn't drooling. When he finished and sat back down, Haven curled her legs under her and leaned a little closer in his direction. The tang of his cologne had her taking a deep breath and smiling in appreciation. He didn't seem to notice, or if he did, he was pretending not to.

Haven placed her hand on the cushion between them. She didn't have to wait long before Dryden reached over and laced their fingers together. Biting her lip to hold back a smile, she tried to focus on the cartoon on TV and a little less on the alien holding her hand. When the cartoon marathon ended and talk shows came on, Dryden clicked off the TV and rose to his feet, pulling her with him.

"Why don't you put on your shoes and we'll go check out the theater? We can get our tickets and maybe have time for lunch, unless you prefer the food there? They have hot dogs, pretzels, and popcorn. And, of course, candy."

Haven smiled. "I've always loved a good salty pretzel smothered in mustard. And Cherry Coke! That's a must."

"Then movie food it is. I'm just going to make a quick call and check on the shop and then we can go. I'll meet you back here in the living room in a few minutes."

Haven nodded and went to her bedroom to get her socks and shoes on, then she brushed out her hair and put on a hint of blush and lip gloss. Her make-up was the one thing she'd been allowed to keep, at least the used items. She'd never been one to go all out with make-up unless it was a special occasion, but she had everything she'd need for an afternoon out on the town. Movie first, and then who knew where they would end up.

When she walked back into the living room, Dryden was waiting for her. He'd changed into a navy shirt and had donned a black leather jacket. He looked sexy as hell, and every inch the bad boy with his jeans molded to his thighs and the black boots on his feet. He gave her one of those smiles that she felt all the way to her toes and held out his hand. She closed the distance between them, clasping his hand and letting him lead her down to the lobby and out to his truck in the parking lot.

The movie theater wasn't far away and it only took Dryden a moment to purchase their tickets. There was a showing in a half hour so it gave them plenty of time to visit the concessions and find a good seat. The theater parking lot wasn't very full so Haven hoped the best seats would still be available -- in the middle of the cinema. He ordered Haven a salty pretzel with mustard and a large Cherry Coke, then got two hot dogs and a Dr. Pepper for himself. The girl behind the counter loaded everything onto a disposable tray and handed it to Dryden.

There were a lot of children present when they went to find their seats, but most were sitting in the lower rows. Her favorite seats were already taken, so they went up two more rows and sat in the middle. Dryden pulled up the armrest between their seats and pulled her tight against his side before handing her the pretzel and her drink. She'd never cuddled with someone during a movie before, not since she was little and snuggled with her dad. The few boyfriends she'd had had never been interested in cuddling. They'd taken what they wanted from her and given little in return.

By the time the movie was starting, they'd finished their food and Dryden set the tray on the seat next to him. He wrapped an arm around her shoulders and held her close as they watched the animated princess go on her quest for true love. Well, more like a quest to save her people, but of course she found true love along the way and in the most unlikely of places. It was a feel-good story and exactly what Haven needed right now.

She watched as the princess and the blacksmith's son went on their journey, making new friends along the way, and falling more in love as the days passed. When it got to the end of the movie and they shared true love's kiss, Haven couldn't help but sigh. She wanted a happy ending like theirs, to find someone who would love her no matter what. Glancing at Dryden out of the corner of her eye, she wondered if perhaps she'd already found him.

Love at first sight only existed in the movies, but it didn't mean they couldn't have a happily-ever-after together. She rested her head on his shoulder as they watched the credits roll and listened to the music until the last strands faded and the lights came up. Dryden gathered their trash and she followed him down the steps. He tossed everything in the trashcan on the way out and reached over to take her hand.

"What did you think?" he asked.

"I always love a happy ending."

"I know you aren't ready for a permanent happy ending with me, but it doesn't mean I can't give you happy-for-now. Is there anything else you'd like to do today? We can go anywhere you'd like. Although, as cold as it is, it's probably best if we don't go somewhere that requires us to be outside for any length of time. We might freeze."

She laughed and thought about where she might want to go. "Could we go to the mall to walk around and window shop?"

"We can do that. Or we can do actual shopping if you see something you want."

He was generous, but she wasn't going to ask him for more than he'd already given. The clothes and a place to stay were more than enough. It still baffled her that he'd been so ready to start a new life with her, and even when she'd turned him down, he'd still taken care of her when she'd had nowhere else to go. It just proved that he was the kind of man you kept, the kind you married and raised a family with. And he was hers for the taking. So, why wasn't she grabbing hold with both hands and never letting go?

At the mall, Haven took a deep breath near the leather store, loving the smell of the purses and coats. They passed the perfume store and she ducked inside to let Dryden smell her favorite scents. He bought her a bottle of Masaki Matsushima, despite her protests, then treated her to a new purse from Macy's. She didn't think mechanics made anywhere near enough to spend that kind of money all in one day and didn't want him wasting it on her.

When he tried to buy her a new sweater and a pretty long-sleeved dress at an upscale maternity store, she put her foot down. "It's too much."

"Do you like them?" he persisted.

"Of course, I like them, but that doesn't mean I have to have them. You're spending too much money on me."

"I want to buy them for you, Haven. I want you to have nice things again. You deserve to be pampered."

"But… "

He placed a finger over her lips, then pulled out his wallet, taking a folded piece of paper out of it. He opened it and showed her his last banking receipt. The balance in his account made her gasp and look up at him with wide eyes.

"You're a mechanic. How do you have that much?"

"I'm poor compared to the warriors and scientists on my world. I can't afford for you to buy expensive things all the time, but I can pamper you a little today if you'll let me. You need some nice things, and this maternity store is busy enough that I'm guessing the items are quality. If you like the sweater and the dress, get them. If you see something else you like, get it too."

She leaned in close. "How does a mechanic who is poor on his world have nearly half a million dollars in his account?"

He smiled a little. "Your Earth government was very generous with the exchange rate between my currency and yours. I transferred half my money to an Earth bank, plus I still get income from the shop. I have very little overhead cost because I paid for the shop and tools in cash."

"You have more money on your world?" she asked.

He nodded.

"Then I guess I won't feel as guilty letting you buy me a few things. But no more extravagant purchases after today. I appreciate everything you're doing for me, but if you keep spending money on me, I'm going to feel guilty."

"Pick out a few outfits while we're here. You're going to need them. The few things you purchased at the store last night won't hold you for the upcoming months. Get at least three or four to get you through the cold months, then we'll come back when the weather turns."

She looked around the store and picked up the dress she'd liked, along with the gray sweater. She selected a pair of black pants, then grabbed some jeans and an aqua sweater. Carrying everything into the fitting room, she tried them on to make sure she'd picked up the correct sizes. Everything fit perfectly and she thought the dress even made her look sexy, baby bump and all. After she'd put her clothes back on, she carried everything to the register.

A silver necklace and matching bracelet fell on top of her items and she looked up at Dryden. "What are you doing?"

"You don't have jewelry. Women like shiny things."

"Dryden, put them back."

He looked like he might argue, but he picked them up and returned them to the shelf. He pulled out his bank card and paid for her clothes, carrying them out along with her other packages. He tried to stop at two other stores, but Haven nudged him along and back to the parking lot. Dryden placed her things in the backseat and she went up on tiptoe to brush a kiss against his cheek.

"Thank you for my new things."

"I'd have gotten you more, but you didn't seem to want to spend my money."

"Dryden, if there's anything I've learned in the last few months, it's that things don't make people happy. Yes, there's a moment of happiness when you wear a new outfit or buy a new pair of shoes, but in the end, it's the people in your life that make you get out of bed in the morning."

"You're very insightful for someone so young."

"I've had to grow up a lot recently."

He pulled her closer and reached up to caress her cheek. "So, who do you have in your life who makes you happy?"

"Until yesterday, no one. My friends abandoned me. My parents are both locked up. Mom may be in rehab, but they aren't letting her out anytime soon. She might as well be in jail with Dad. Until you came into the shop to greet me last night, I had no one. The money left and they did too."

"I'm not leaving you, Haven. Not even if you push me away."

"I know," she said softly. "And that's why you don't have to buy me so many things. I don't need them. I just need you."

He leaned down slowly, as if to give her time to move away, and pressed his lips to hers. Haven wound her arms around his neck and leaned against him. The kiss was sweet and light, and full of all the promises Dryden had made to her. Even if they never got married, she knew she'd found a friend, and that was worth more to her than all the money in the world.

# Chapter Four

Dryden lay across Haven's bed, her body tucked in close to him. Her long, silky hair was down, and he twirled the ends around his fingers as he watched her sleep. She'd changed into her pajamas, and after he'd changed as well he'd stepped into her room to say goodnight. He'd found her lying on top of the covers, curled on her side. There had been something in her eyes, the way she looked at him, that had drawn him further into the room. She'd scooted over and patted the bed, asking if he'd hold her for a little while. He hadn't intended to stay the entire night.

The sky outside the window was lightening, but he couldn't bear to let her go yet. She felt so right in his arms, her heart beating against him, as the soft puffs of her breath fanned across his bare chest. Her head nestled perfectly under his chin and every time he inhaled he could smell her sweet scent. It was both torture and heaven. She shifted, moving closer. Dryden tightened his arms around her and pressed a kiss to the top of her head.

Haven murmured something in her sleep and her hand crept up to settle on his chest. Her touch was light but it sent a jolt through him. He'd been hard for hours, wanting her, and yet satisfying himself with the knowledge she'd wanted him close. He'd had a good time with her yesterday, possibly the best day he'd ever had with a woman. Not once in all his years had he ever held a woman at night. The females he'd been intimate with had served a purpose, but they hadn't been the type of woman you cuddled and talked to after sex. He wanted that, and he thought he could have it with Haven.

Slowly, her eyes fluttered open and she gave him a sleepy smile.

"You stayed," she said softly.

"There's nowhere else I'd rather be than right here with you."

"It's not just your looks that attract the women, is it?" she asked. "They get a taste of how sweet and romantic you are and they want more."

He smiled a little. "You think I'm sweet and romantic?"

"You know you are, so stop fishing for compliments."

He smoothed his thumb along her jaw. "You're beautiful in the morning."

"Thank you. I'm sure I have dragon breath though. I should go brush my teeth."

He leaned forward and placed his lips against hers. Haven resisted only a moment before her hand crept around his neck as he deepened the kiss, holding her tight against his body. Dryden wanted her, desperately, but he was trying to satisfy his craving with just a taste. Her fingers curled in his hair and her thigh slid up over his hip. He rolled them so that she lay under him, her body open and responsive to his every touch.

It would be so easy to open the buttons on her pajama top and spread the material to expose the breasts he longed to see. His hips fit perfectly between her splayed legs, and had they been naked, he could have easily slid inside of her. He could feel the heat from her pussy even through the layers of their pajama pants. Her hands slid across his chest, down his arms and back up around his neck, as if she wanted to touch every inch of him.

His hand cupped her breast through the material of her top and he felt her nipple pucker against his palm. Haven moaned a little as she squirmed beneath him. He gazed into her passion-filled eyes. Her body might want him, but that didn't mean he should take things further. The last thing he wanted was for her to have regrets. When he made love to her, he wanted to know that she wanted him every bit as much as he wanted her, that it meant something and wasn't just convenient. Dryden already felt more for her than he had for anyone else.

"Make me yours," she said. "I want you."

"Will you be my mate?"

She hesitated, but it was telling enough. He wanted her, but he could control himself and give her pleasure without claiming her body as his. When his cock was inside of her, he wanted to know that it was forever. Meaningless sex had lost its appeal long ago, and he could never think of Haven the same as the previous women in his life. She was so much more than a meaningless one-night stand.

Dryden pulled away long enough to remove her pajamas and the pink panties underneath. He swallowed hard when her body was bared to him, tracing the slight swell of her belly with his hand. Knowing there was a baby growing inside of her left an ache inside of him. It might not be his child, but he wanted it to be. He wanted a family, and he wanted that family with Haven. She was everything he'd been searching for.

Settling between her splayed thighs, he marveled at her bare pussy. She was pink, and wet, and so damn sexy. He lapped at her silken flesh, her taste exploding on his tongue. Dryden shifted his hips to ease the ache of his cock pressing against the mattress. His shaft pulsed with need, and he wanted to sink into her tight channel until she was screaming his name.

He circled the bundle of nerves silently begging for his attention, making her gasp as she threw back her head and gripped the sheets tight. Her hips undulated, as if seeking something more. His tongue flicked out and gathered her cream before teasing her again. He gently gripped her clit between his teeth as he lashed it with his tongue. Haven's body tightened, her thigh muscles clenching.

"Yes! Yes! Dryden!" she called out.

Her back bowed and her pussy gushed as she found her release. Dryden lapped up her cream before kissing his way up her body. She lay replete, blinking up at him as if in a daze. She'd come so hard it was a wonder she hadn't passed out. Dryden stretched out on his side and pulled her into his arms.

"No one's ever done that to me before," she murmured against his chest.

"Made you come?"

He felt her smile against him. "Well, that or put their mouth down there. I liked it."

He fought back a laugh. "I could tell."

"Why didn't you finish? Don't you want me?"

"More than my next breath, but now isn't the time."

She studied him a moment. "It's because of me, isn't it? Because I didn't agree to be your mate."

"Haven, I'm not going to push you into something you don't want or that you're not ready to accept. You wanted time to get to know me, and I'm going to give it to you. I thought we could go on a date today. Starting with breakfast at one of those pancake house places."

"So, you're not saying never, just not right now?" she asked.

"I'm giving you what you wanted. I refuse to group you in with the past women in my life and have sex for the sake of sex. When I finally make love to you, it's going to be because you're mine and I'm yours."

"What if it's not what I need? What if what I want and what I need are two very different things?" she asked softly.

He smoothed her hair back from her face. "Haven, you're beautiful and sweet, and I will give you anything you want and everything you need. But I think if we took things further right now, you would second-guess yourself later, maybe even regret what happened between us, and I don't want that to happen."

She reached up and traced his lower lip before kissing him.

"Go shower," he said. "Then put on something warm and we'll get something to eat."

Haven got out of bed and disappeared into the bathroom. Her scent lingered in the room even after she shut the bathroom door. Dryden went to his own room before he was tempted to climb in with her. He showered quickly and pulled on a black tee and jeans. Using a towel to dry his hair, he then brushed it before cleaning his teeth. He'd noticed Haven liked his cologne, so he spritzed some on. Staring at his reflection, he wondered what she saw when she looked at him. He'd adopted some of the human practices since moving to Earth. He'd cut his hair, pierced his ear, and had even contemplated a tattoo. Was he too human? Was that why she resisted?

He didn't think he'd assimilated too much. At heart, he was still a Zelthranite, or Terran as humans called his race. While he might not be warrior status, his job was important to his people. He kept their shuttles and aircraft running so their brides could be delivered, and their warriors could protect their planet. He stared at his hands, rough from the hours he spent working on engines, both human and alien. His touch hadn't seemed to turn her off, even though others had complained in the past.

Dryden leaned his hands on the counter and stared hard at himself. He wasn't as handsome as most from his world, but Haven had seemed pleased with his looks. He'd seen her pulse flutter when he'd first met her. He stayed in shape, even though he wasn't bulky with muscle. No, he didn't think his looks had anything to do with her resistance, and he'd treated her like a lady, so that couldn't be it. Maybe she was just scared. She'd been abandoned with a baby in her belly, and that had to be scary, especially as young as she was.

He pushed away from the counter and went to see if she was ready yet. He found her standing uncertainly in the living room, looking small and lost. There was a hesitance in her eyes that hadn't been there before and he blamed himself. Dryden moved closer and reached for her.

"I'm sorry," she said, tears gathering in her eyes.

"Haven, you have nothing to be sorry for."

"You're offering me everything I ever wanted, and I'm too damn scared to take it. I'm too worried that I won't be enough for you, that you'll come to resent me for having a baby that isn't yours."

He dried the tears that slipped down her cheeks. "Haven, the child you carry is a gift, one that I would treasure every day for the rest of my life, just as I would you. Don't you realize that I think you're perfect just as you are?"

She sniffled a little and hugged him.

"We're a pair," he said with a smile. "Here I was worrying that I wasn't enough for you, and you were worried you weren't enough for me."

"So, where does that leave us?"

"It leaves us with a day to enjoy together. And later tonight, we'll see where things go. No expectations."

"You're so good to me."

"Come on, beautiful. Let's go get breakfast and then we'll figure out what else we're doing today."

They gathered their coats and went down to his truck. On the drive to the restaurant, he noticed she smiled a lot, even if she didn't say much. He wanted her to be happy. Maybe he should have told her that. Or maybe he'd seen one too many happily-ever-afters in the movies and he was too much of a sap. One woman had called him a hopeless romantic, and maybe he was. He hadn't thought there was anything wrong with that.

At the restaurant, he requested a table by the window. Haven slid into the booth across from him and picked up her menu. He could hear her stomach rumbling from hunger and hoped they didn't have to wait long to place their order. As if his thoughts conjured their waitress, she appeared, pad in hand.

"What can I get for you?" the woman asked.

"I'll take the breakfast special with a side of pancakes," Haven said. "And a glass of sweet tea."

"Make it two," Dryden said, folding his menu.

The woman scribbled down their order and disappeared.

"So, you mentioned you were in college before," Dryden said. "Do you think you'll go back?"

"It's hard to get a decent job around here without a degree, but now that I'm pregnant, I don't see me going back for another year of college. Not unless I can take classes part-time and online. This baby changes a lot of things for me."

Dryden could understand that. She no longer just had to take care of herself, but she had a child on the way. He hated to think of her on her own while juggling a job and a baby, but if she didn't agree to be his mate, then it was out of his hands. It didn't mean he couldn't help her though.

"Speaking of jobs," she said. "Shouldn't you at least check on things at the shop? I know you said someone was watching over things, but is it typical for you to not go in to work?"

"It's Friday. My shop manager works Friday and Saturday so he can have Mondays off. I've never asked why, figured it was personal."

"So, you're off until Monday?"

He nodded.

"Good." She smiled. "I like spending time with you."

"I'm actually scheduled to work off world next week. You'd have to get clearance from the clinic, but would you want to go with me? You could see my world, and while you couldn't walk around without being mobbed by males wanting a mate, I could take you out to see the sights when I wasn't working. You could even meet my parents and spend the day with them, if you'd like."

"You'd let me meet your parents?"

He bit his lip and studied her a moment. "I'm still hoping that maybe one day you'll agree to be mine, and they'll be your parents too."

"But we could still live here on Earth, right? Or would my human baby be accepted there?"

"We're a very accepting people," he said with a smile. "Your baby would be more than welcome, especially if it's a girl."

"Then yes, I'd like to go with you and see your world."

"We'll stop by the clinic later today and let Xonos check you over. Make sure it's okay for you to make the shuttle trip."

Their food arrived and Haven ate as if it were her last meal. When they were finished, Dryden paid the check and escorted her back outside. He knew exactly where he wanted to take her next, and drove there without giving her any hints as to where they were going. She seemed accepting and didn't question him.

When they pulled up to the zoo, she laughed a little. "I thought you said we should do indoor things."

"There are some indoor exhibits, and I'm sure they had some outdoor heaters spread throughout the area. If you get cold, we'll leave."

"I haven't been to the zoo since I was a little girl. This will be fun."

As far as Dryden was concerned, doing anything with Haven was fun. They looked at the elephants and zebras, moved on to the large cats, and checked out the lizards and snakes for a reprieve from the cold. Haven seemed to be tiring, so Dryden escorted her back to the front.

"We can come again some other time," he said. "Maybe this spring when it's warmer."

She nodded and climbed into his truck, shivering a little. Dryden cranked the heat and soon her face had lost the rosiness from the cold. As they neared the Terran Station, he wondered if he should have called Xonos ahead of time. He'd never needed an appointment at the clinic before, he didn't know the rules when it came to potential mates. He knew she'd need a check-up before he could claim her, even though it was apparent she was able to have children.

"The doctor won't do anything that hurts, will he?" Haven asked as he pulled into the parking lot.

"I don't believe anything will hurt. Have you seen a doctor since finding out you were pregnant?"

"I went for a blood test to make sure I was really pregnant, but then I lost my insurance when my parents were dealing with the IRS."

"Then it's a good thing we're going today. I'll see if Xonos will agree to be your doctor until the baby is born. I'm not sure if he'll be allowed to though. The council prefers that he only treat humans who are mated or related to Terrans."

"I understand."

They went inside and passed the receptionist. Dryden led her down hallways until they reached the clinic. The wall of glass showed that no one was sitting in the waiting area. He pushed open the door and ushered her inside. There was a bell on the counter and Dryden smacked his hand on it a few times. Xonos came out of the back and smiled when he saw them.

"I haven't seen you in a while," Xonos said.

"I've kept busy. This is Haven. I'm trying to convince her to be my mate, but she's a stubborn one." He smiled to soften his words. "She would like to travel with me to Terran next week for work, but she's expecting and I thought you should check her over first. Make sure it wouldn't harm the baby."

Xonos nodded. "Come on back. I don't have anything scheduled today and it's been quiet."

They entered one of the exam rooms and Xonos pulled out a hospital gown, handing it to Haven, then he motioned for Dryden to follow him into the hall, giving her privacy. Dryden liked Xonos all the more for that small kindness. It wasn't like Dryden hadn't had his face in a very intimate place not but a few hours ago, but it didn't mean Haven would be comfortable changing in front of him.

"So, a mate," Xonos said. "You've wanted one for a while."

"With some luck, Haven will agree to be mine. How are the kids? I haven't seen them in a while."

"Evie is learning to drive. She received her driver's permit the other day. Gryl and Taffy are both handfuls, but at least they're both in school this year."

"What's Victoria doing with her time? Did she decide to work?"

Xonos shook his head. "She tried to come here and help with files and such, but it didn't work out. She decided to stay home in case the kids needed her, and she volunteers at the elementary school a few days a week."

"Haven talked about needing to work when the baby comes. She was in school, college, but had to stop going when she found out about the baby. I wish there was a way for her to finish her degree. It seems to mean a lot to her."

Xonos clapped him on the shoulder. "If she agrees to be yours, there's no reason she can't take classes online while the baby is small, and by the time your son or daughter starts school maybe she could put that degree to use. Unless you use the daycare here at the station. I've heard it's decent now that the harpy who denied Lily entrance has been removed."

The exam room door opened a crack and Haven peered out at them. Xonos smiled at her reassuringly and they both entered the room. She climbed onto the table and fidgeted while she waited to see what Xonos would say or do. Dryden wished he could ease her fears.

"Haven, do you know how far along you are?" Xonos asked.

"About four months."

Xonos nodded and began pulling out different medical instruments. Dryden watched as Xonos did a bio scan, listened to her heart and lungs, took some blood, checked her blood pressure, and then did a full-body scan just to be safe. As Xonos studied the results of each test, Haven seemed to grow more and more nervous.

Dryden stepped closer and took her hand in his. She smiled up at him gratefully, and they waited together for the results. It made Dryden wish all the more that he really was waiting for news of his son or daughter, but until Haven agreed to be his, she was just a friend who was having a baby. It was damn hard though not getting emotionally invested in her pregnancy.

"Everything looks good," Xonos said. "The baby is healthy and strong, has a good heartbeat and growth rate. Your blood pressure is a little higher than I would like, but it's not life-threatening. Just try to take it easy. Whatever you're stressing over, try to put it out of your mind for a while. If it gets worse or doesn't seem to drop, then we can discuss medication."

"Could you tell if I'm having a boy or a girl?" she asked.

"Not yet. The baby is turned the wrong way, so we can try again in two to three weeks. We should be able to see something then. I have one of the human ultrasound machines if you'd like a picture of your baby."

"I'll wait until I can find out the sex," Haven said.

"Very well. Then you can get dressed and you're free to go. I didn't see anything medically that would keep you from travelling on Monday. If you're concerned about your blood pressure, you can always stop here before meeting the shuttle and I'll check it again for you."

Haven nodded. "Thank you."

Dryden and Xonos left the room so she could get dressed. The doctor leaned against the wall and studied Dryden. It looked like there was something he wanted to say, but for some reason, Xonos held back.

"What is it?" Dryden asked.

"You know how in-depth my scans are."

"Of course. Was there something you saw that worries you about the baby?"

"Has Haven discussed the father with you?"

"She doesn't know who the father is. Haven said she was drinking too much at a party and a month later she found out she was pregnant."

Xonos nodded. "The baby is only half human. It's part Traxian. I'm not certain how she would have come into contact with one. They tend to stand out."

"I doubt she knows, and I'm not certain how to bring it up. If I can think of a way to work it into conversation, I'll try. I don't want her to be blindsided when the baby is born, but it's not something I want to blurt out either."

"Let me know if you'd prefer that I talk to her. I could mention it Monday, or even now if you think that would be better."

"I'll tell her as soon as possible."

Haven opened the door and stepped out of the room, a smile on her face. Her stomach rumbled, and Dryden realized it was well past lunch. Even if they had eaten breakfast a little late, as an expectant mother she needed to eat more often than he did. Or so he'd learned from his friends when their mates were pregnant.

"Come on," Dryden said. "Let's feed you. If you'd like, we can eat here at the station. There's a food court."

"Really? Do they serve cuisine from your world?" she asked.

"Yes, although most places serve human food. You can have whatever you want," Dryden said.

Xonos led them back to the front of the clinic. "It was nice meeting you, Haven, and it was good to see you again, Dryden. Stop by any time if you have questions or concerns. Haven, as long as you're a potential mate, I'm allowed to treat you."

"It was nice meeting you too," Haven said.

Dryden led her through the maze of hallways to the food court and let her explore each option before ordering their food. He selected a table away from the few people taking a lunch break, intent on talking to her about the baby in her belly. If he waited, he worried he might chicken out of telling her. He wasn't certain how she would react. To him, a mixed race child wasn't a big deal. A baby was a baby, and he would love that baby regardless of its race, color, or sex. He just hoped Haven believed him. He'd learned that humans could be prejudiced when it came to different races. There wasn't a difference to him between a half-Terran child or a half-Traxian one.

As she took her first bite of Terran cuisine, he tried to think of the best way to bring it up. She seemed so happy, and he didn't know what her reaction would be. The last thing he wanted to do was upset her. Maybe he'd give it a few days and see if he could figure out the best way to break the news to her. Since she didn't remember the father of her child, he didn't know if discovering it was an alien would be upsetting to her.

Why couldn't anything ever be easy?

# Chapter Five

Monday morning came all too soon, and Haven found herself packed and waiting at the Terran Station for the shuttle. They'd arrived early and were enjoying breakfast in the food court. Haven was pleasantly surprised that the Terran food tasted so good. She'd been expecting something strange and unusual, but the meat tasted almost like ham, and the blue-and-orange vegetable-looking things tasted like bell peppers and onion. She glanced at Dryden and knew there was something on his mind, but for some reason he was keeping it to himself.

"You're quiet," she said.

"Just thinking."

"Anything good?" She smiled. "You look almost worried."

"Are you sure there's nothing you remember about the party you went to the night you became pregnant? Any unusual people there?" he asked.

"Unusual like different from me but human, or unusual as in alien?" she asked.

"So, there were aliens there."

She nodded. "Some college-aged guys were there. They were in town for something happening at the Terran Station and I guess someone invited them to the party. One looked like a tiger, another was blue with black hair, and one was red with fangs. I remember seeing a Terran or two there as well. Why?"

"I need to tell you something about your baby, but I'm not sure how to do it. I don't want to upset you."

She placed a hand over her belly. "The baby is healthy, right? Does it have a birth defect? Xonos didn't mention anything, and when he checked my blood pressure this morning he said everything looked good."

The good doctor had done more than that though. He'd also given her an implant behind her ear that would translate other languages for her. She would be able to understand everything said on Terran, as well as anywhere else in the galaxies or on Earth.

"No, nothing like that. But it's not going to look human either."

She set her fork down. "I slept with one of the aliens?"

He nodded. "A Traxian. And if they were present for an event at the Terran Station, I can find out who those males were and we can narrow down who the father is. If you want to know. Even if I were to take you as my mate, if the baby's father found out later that he had a child, he could try to take the baby from us. I think it would be best to get him to waive his rights. Or come up with another solution."

Haven stared at her food a moment, trying to process everything. She'd slept with an alien, and from what she'd heard, they wanted babies in the worst way. Why would the Traxian give up his rights? And if he didn't, what did that mean for her? Would she be forced to marry him? Her stomach rolled and nausea welled in her throat. Tears misted her eyes and Dryden reached across the table to take her hand.

"We'll figure this out," he assured her. "When we're done eating, I'll speak with someone about gathering the names and contact information for the males who were here from that world. There couldn't have been many of them."

"I don't think I can eat anymore."

Dryden squeezed her hand. "Think about the baby. You need to finish your food. Don't worry about the baby's father."

Haven nodded and took another bite. It didn't taste as great as it had before, but she knew the food hadn't changed. By the time she'd finished her meal and Dryden had thrown away their trash, her nausea had doubled. What would she do if the father of her baby tried to take it from her?

Dryden led her down several hallways before approaching what looked like a conference room. A large screen was on one wall and he began pressing buttons. When the screen lit up, it showed a room with four Terrans sitting around a table. Dryden waited until he had their attention.

"Dryden, is there a problem with the hotel?" one of

them asked. "Chief Councilor Borgoz requested a key for your mate."

"I haven't checked with the front desk yet," Dryden said. "But we may have a situation that can't be resolved with a call. Haven is pregnant, as I mentioned to the Chief Councilor, and Xonos ran some tests the other day. We've discovered that the father of her baby is a Traxian."

"How could she not know the father was Traxian?" one of the men asked.

"I had too much to drink at a party," Haven said. "There were a few alien races present and I think I must have slept with one of them. But I don't remember doing it."

The men talked amongst themselves for a moment.

"Dryden, we'll contact the Traxian government and see if they can help us locate the father of the child. I'll ask Xonos to send any data he has about her pregnancy in case they need the information. How far along are you?" the man asked her.

"Four months."

"Traxian pregnancies run about the same length as a human pregnancies. Which means we have some time to locate the father and figure out what to do."

"Larimar," Dryden said. "What if the father wants to claim the child? Haven doesn't want to give up her rights."

"The Traxian government will not allow the baby to be separated from the mother, but they can demand that the father be allowed to visit whenever he wishes."

Haven breathed a little easier. That didn't sound so bad. As long as they didn't try to send her baby to another world, she could live with anything else. Visitation rights didn't sound so horrible.

Dryden thanked the men and ended the call.

"So, he won't take my baby away?" Haven asked.

"It doesn't sound like it. I wouldn't put it past him to try to convince you to mate with him though. Especially, since you're carrying his child. If I were in the same position, I'd do the same thing. But just because he asks, doesn't mean you have to say yes. You can turn him down, or if you want time with him to see if things could work, then I'm sure he would stay on Earth for you to date."

She glanced up at him. "And you would be okay with me dating someone else?"

A muscle in his jaw ticked. "No, but I have no claim on you. I want you for my mate, but you're free to do as you please. If you think the Traxian would make you happy, then I will try to be content with your decision."

Haven smiled and reached for his hand. "I don't want the Traxian, even if he's super nice. Now, I believe we have a shuttle to catch. I'm anxious to see your world and meet your parents. If you still want me to go."

Dryden kissed her softly. "Of course, I want you to go."

"Then let's catch that shuttle."

Dryden led the way, stopping to leave her bag with someone, before showing her to the docking station. She climbed the steps to the platform and then entered the shuttle, Dryden right behind her. There were a handful of potential brides in the front row and a smattering of people in the other seats. Dryden helped her into a seat near the window and then he claimed the one next to her. He helped her buckle the harness before fastening his own.

A few more people drifted in and claimed the seats around them. Dryden shook hands with another Terran on the flight and they talked for a few moments. Haven stared out the window and tried to settle her nerves. She'd been on airplanes before, but she'd never taken a shuttle to another planet. Her stomach rolled a bit and she fought back the nausea. Dryden seemed to sense her unease and reached over to take her hand.

"You'll be asleep for most of the journey," he told her. "When you wake up, we'll be on my world."

She nodded and gave him a reassuring smile. The last thing Haven wanted was for him to worry about her. Dryden continued to talk quietly with the other Terran and Haven closed her eyes. She opened them when she heard the shuttle hatch being locked into place.

"Is it time?" she asked.

"Everything's going to be fine, Haven. Xonos wouldn't have allowed you to come on this trip if he thought it would harm you or the baby."

She nodded and tightened her grip on his hand.

A voice filtered through the shuttle. "Good morning, everyone. I'm Captain Kijaro and I'll be taking you to Terran today. The beginning of our flight might be a little bumpy but within a few minutes we'll break through the atmosphere and everything will smooth out. As we leave Earth behind, masks will pop down. I want you to place them over your mouth and nose and breathe deeply. The gas that will be administered will put you to sleep until we reach my home world. You'll be awakened when we get there."

Dryden leaned over and kissed her cheek before tightening both of their harnesses. A loud rumble filled the cabin and Haven's stomach dropped as the shuttle lifted into the air. The captain had been right; it was a bumpy ride for a few minutes. As the ground got further away, and then the planet began to get smaller, everything evened out and her nerves settled a little. The view out of her window was spectacular and she was a little in awe.

The masks dropped down in front of them and Dryden helped Haven put hers on before donning his own. The tang of the gas filled her nose and her body began to feel heavy. Her gaze fastened on a shrinking Earth until everything went black. The next time Haven opened her eyes, the shuttle was still and people were departing. Dryden was already awake and out of his harness.

"We're on Terran?" she asked, her voice still thick with sleep.

Dryden nodded. "How do you feel? Should we stop and see the doctor at the clinic before I take you to my home?"

"I'm fine. Still a little groggy, but I'll be okay. I'm anxious to see where you live."

He bit his lip and looked away a moment. "My home isn't as large as you might be expecting. On my world, I'm not very wealthy. I'm worth far more on Earth than here."

"Dryden, I don't care how much money you have or how big your house is. Have you not gotten to know me at all in the last few days? Do I seem like the type of person who cares about those kinds of things?" she asked.

"No," he said softly. "I just don't want to disappoint you. I know you come from a wealthy background and I live in a small apartment on my world."

"Just take me home. To your home. I don't care where it is or how big it is."

"As you wish."

Haven couldn't help but smile. "You like *The Princess Bride* too?"

"I tend to like movies with a happily-ever-after."

Dryden held out his hand to her, helping her to her feet.

"I guess we should get my bag," she said.

"I've already had it sent ahead. They'll leave it outside my place. No one will bother it. We don't have theft on my world. We actually live in a society of very little crime. It's been a long time since anything bad happened here that was caused by my people."

The suns were bright as Haven exited the shuttle. She saw a large group of Terrans gathered nearby and a few aliens who were black with white markings. They were striking, if a bit unsettling.

"Who are they?" she asked.

"Large groups form whenever new brides come to my world. The black-and-white warriors are Bentares. Some of them have formed a warrior bond with our Terran warriors. Any woman accepting one of them will have to accept both. They've had a hard time finding brides though. Most people think taking them on is fun, but not something they want to do long-term."

"That's rather sad."

They made their way through the streets of Terran Prime and Haven took in all the sights and sounds. There were human women walking around, a few who were obviously pregnant. The Terran males they passed watched her in curiosity and she inched a little closer to Dryden, remembering his words about unmated women on his world. The last thing she wanted was to be followed by men wanting to claim her as a mate.

They neared two tall buildings that were made of some sort of glass, passing a pool area where Terrans, women, and children splashed and had a good time. From what she'd seen of his world so far, she liked it. They approached one of the buildings and he entered a code to go inside. The lobby was different from anything she'd seen before and she stared in wide-eyed fascination. An elevator took them up to the tenth floor and she followed Dryden down the hall. He stopped outside a door and entered another code, pushing the door open. He picked up her bag and set it inside the door.

"Welcome to my humble abode," he said, motioning for her to step inside.

The apartment opened to a small living area with a padded bench along one wall with pillows tossed along the back. There was a small table, and a large Vid-Comm screen opposite. A small kitchen was to the left, full of gadgets she didn't recognize. Dryden pushed open the closed door next to the kitchen and she followed him into a bedroom. No, *the bedroom*, as in there was only one.

"If you don't want to share the bed, I can sleep in the living room," he told her.

"We can share." Her cheeks flushed. "It's not like you haven't seen me naked."

"The bathroom is through there," he said, pointing to another door. "It's small."

Haven looked around. "I like your place, but I'm curious. How are you supposed to raise a family here?"

"Once I'm mated, I'll be given a raise in salary. It won't be much, but it will allow me to purchase a small home. We could never have a large family, not unless we moved in with my parents. Despite the fact I'm an only child, they have six bedrooms in their home. They'd always wanted a large family, and even when they realized more kids weren't coming, they kept the house."

"You wouldn't mind living with your parents?" she asked.

"No. It's not looked down on in my society. We're very family-oriented."

"When do I get to meet them?" she asked, feeling both nervous and excited about meeting Dryden's parents.

"Why don't you get freshened up, and we'll meet them for breakfast."

"Breakfast?" she asked, looking out the window. "But we had breakfast before we came here."

"It's nighttime on Earth now, which means it's daytime here. The shuttle ride took about eight hours."

"Then breakfast sounds nice."

He nodded. "There's a human-owned restaurant in town that serves Earth cuisine. Why don't we eat there? My family likes going there from time to time, and after that trip you probably aren't ready for more Terran food."

"I could really go for an omelet or something."

"I'll contact my parents while you do whatever it is women do after long trips."

She pressed a kiss to his cheek. "I won't be long."

He backed out of the bedroom, pulling the door shut behind him.

Haven turned on the light in the bathroom and stared at her reflection. Her hair was a little messy and her clothes were wrinkled. She went to retrieve her bag and then ducked back inside the bathroom to clean herself up a bit. If she was going to meet Dryden's parents, she wanted to look her best. Despite the new development with her baby, she still was seriously considering marriage to Dryden. He was kind, smart, funny... and she'd never met anyone so inclined to romance before.

When she was ready, she stepped back into the living room and fidgeted until Dryden looked up at her.

"Ready?" he asked.

"I think so. I'm a little nervous."

Dryden came over to her, taking her hands in his. "Don't be. My parents are going to love you."

She nodded and followed him out of the apartment. The entire way to the restaurant her stomach was tied in knots. Just because he assured her that his parents would like her didn't mean they really would. What if they hated her on sight? She didn't remember ever being so scared before. Taking a deep breath, she let Dryden lead her into the restaurant and she steeled herself to meet her possible future in-laws.

# Chapter Six

Dryden smiled when he saw his parents. He hadn't had a chance to visit with them on his last trip home, and he noticed the sheen of tears in his mother's eyes. They really had been the best parents, and still were. He felt Haven's hand tremble in his and wished he could reassure her. He had no doubt that his parents were going to love her, and would probably ask about their mating. They'd always wanted grandchildren, and the fact Haven was pregnant would just be a bonus to his parents even if the baby was half-Traxian. He just wished he'd gotten a chance to speak with them more before meeting with them today. They would no doubt jump to conclusions.

"Mom. Dad. I'd like you to meet Haven," he said, tugging her forward. "Haven, these are my parents. My mom, Tilia, and my dad, Harvol."

Haven clung to him. "It's a pleasure to meet you both."

His mother smiled widely and rushed forward to hug Haven. When she stepped back, her gaze dropped to Haven's stomach and her smile widened even more.

"You're expecting!" Tilia said excitedly.

"Mom. Calm down."

"Why didn't you tell us you were seeing someone?" his mother asked.

"The baby isn't Dryden's," Haven said. "I was pregnant when I met him."

Tilia's smile dimmed a little. "But the two of you are together now, right? That's why you're here?"

"Mom, Haven wanted to come see our world and I offered to bring her with me. I'm here for work."

Tilia deflated even more. Harvol wrapped an arm around her waist and motioned to the table where they'd been sitting.

"We should sit and eat," Harvol said.

"Mom, I know you want to see me settled, and it will happen in time. I care about Haven, but she has a lot going on in her life right now. I told her she can have as long as she needs."

Haven looked at his parents uncertainly. "I don't want you to think that I don't like your son. I think he's really great. But the baby I'm carrying is a Traxian's. Your council is trying to locate the father and I don't know what's going to happen when they find him. I was already at a low point when I met Dryden, and it doesn't seem very fair to drag him into my mess."

Tilia's gaze softened. "If I know my son, he would gladly take on any burdens you bring with you to a mating. But it's sweet of you to worry."

Haven slid into the booth and Dryden claimed the seat next to her, with his parents sitting across from them. A digital menu was on the table and everyone was able to place their own order. When the total was presented, his father swiped his arm across the machine, paying for their meal.

"How did you do that?" Haven asked.

"Everyone on Terran has an implant. It's how we pay for things and how most buildings are accessed. In the last few months, The Towers were given access codes so potential brides wouldn't have to get implants if they decided not to live here," Harvol said.

"Potential brides stay in the apartment buildings?" she asked.

"They're given suites without kitchens as temporary housing. It's encouraged that they spend their mealtimes with potential mates," Harvol said. "Those who find a mate are given an implant and anything they purchase is paid for with credits their mate earns. Or mates plural in the case of some of the warrior pairs."

"Does the implant hurt?" she asked.

"The doctor would put you to sleep long enough to make an incision with a laser, insert the implant, then seal the opening. It doesn't take long and there's a slight ache the first day after the implant goes in, but there's no real pain involved," Tilia answered.

"Mom, I wondered if you might take Haven around and show her Terran Prime while I'm at work today. I have to work on a shuttle today and one of our battleships the next two days. I told her it would be best if she weren't alone outside of my apartment," Dryden said.

Tilia smiled brightly. "I would love to show her around. Maybe we can do a little shopping too. With all the human brides joining us, quite a few Earth-like stores have opened around town. One carries clothes for pregnant women."

He was glad that his mother was so accepting of Haven, but then, he'd known that she would be. His father had never been much of a talker, but even he opened up around Haven. She fit in so well with them. He wondered how she felt about his parents. Since he had to work after their meal, he wouldn't get a chance to ask her until later in the day. He hated that he had to essentially abandon her with strangers, but he knew his parents would take good care of her. No doubt his mother would take her to his childhood home after their shopping was finished.

Their food arrived and he looked at Haven's plate in curiosity. The omelet he recognized, and the pancakes, but he had no idea what the white stuff was on her plate. It looked very unappetizing, all lumpy with something yellow and watery covering it. Haven took a bite and closed her eyes as she hummed in appreciation.

"What is that?" Dryden asked.

"Grits," Haven said. "Want to try?"

She scooped some up and offered it to him. Dryden leaned forward and accepted the bite, surprised by the buttery flavor. At least he now knew what the yellow stuff was. He still didn't have a clue what a grit was, even if they were tasty.

"They're good."

Haven smiled and went back to eating her meal. He could tell his parents wanted to ask questions about her, but weren't certain if they should. He tried to draw his dad into a conversation, but both his parents were too enthralled with Haven. Dryden couldn't really blame them.

"Haven, I know a lot of women on Earth work. Do you have a job?" his mother asked.

"No. I was a full-time student at the college, but when I found out about the baby, I withdrew from my classes." She bit her lip. "My parents had some financial problems and had to go away. When Dryden found me, I was running out of money and was about out of hope."

"Away?" Harvol asked. "Where did they go?"

Haven's face lost some of its color and she stared at her plate. Dryden reached over and took her hand, giving it a reassuring squeeze. He knew his parents wouldn't blame her for her parents' problems.

"Haven's father was put in jail for not paying taxes, and her mother was sent to a rehab place because she had a drinking problem. She's alone in the world."

"Taxes?" Harvol asked. "I don't understand. They didn't pay tax on items they purchased?"

"On Earth, you have to give the government a percentage of your earnings. Haven's parents didn't file their tax returns and kept all of the money, so the government took their home and belongings, and put her father in jail. If her mother had not gone to rehab, she probably would have been jailed too."

Harvol nodded. "Now I understand. I'm very sorry you had to go through that, Haven. It must have been scary. You seem young, and I'm assuming you lived with your parents."

"Yes, I did. And I'm twenty. I know there's a bit of an age difference between Dryden and me, but I've had to grow up fast in the last few months."

Tilia smiled. "I think you and Dryden make a striking couple. We haven't seen too many human females here with your color hair. It's such a beautiful color, like the sunset."

Haven's cheeks flushed. "Thank you."

"You know, since Dryden is going to be busy the next few days, you should come to our house in the morning. I can make breakfast for all of us, then we can spend time together while Dryden and his father go to work," Tilia said. "I know we're strangers and you may not feel comfortable around us, but I'd really like to get to know you better."

"I'd like that," Haven said softly, a smile curving her lips.

Dryden wondered how long it had been since someone tried to mother her. If what she said was true, and her mother was an alcoholic, he doubted there had been a lot of bonding going on between them. And from what he'd learned about her father from the newspaper, the man was all business all the time. Haven might have had every financial need met, but he wondered if her emotional needs had ever been met by her family, or by anyone else.

As she spoke with his parents, he observed her. She seemed genuinely happy to have met them, and even appeared excited about spending time with his mother. When his parents asked about the baby, she grew quiet and he worried they might have upset her. But she bit her lip, took a breath, and opened up more with them than she had with Dryden.

"I'm scared," Haven confessed. "I was scared before, when I thought the baby might be human, but knowing it's half Traxian worries me. Not because I'll love the baby any less, but when the father is located, I don't know how he'll react or what he'll want from me. I don't want to lose my baby, and I don't want to be forced into a mating with the father either."

Harvol frowned. "Traxians are having a hard time procreating even when they do find brides. Your baby is going to be a miracle to them, and I think they'll want to keep you happy. But I won't lie. The fact you're unattached could pose a problem. They could pressure you to accept a mating with the father and ask you to move there."

"I don't have a problem living on an alien world," Haven said, "but I don't want to marry a stranger. It's why I haven't accepted Dryden's proposal yet. It isn't because I don't like him, because I really do, but I'm worried we don't know one another well enough for that kind of commitment, especially since divorce isn't a thing here."

Tilia reached for her hand. "I would love to have you for a daughter-in-law, and because of that, I'm going to make a suggestion. Over the next few days, why don't you see what it would be like to live on our world? Get to know the people, get to know us, and maybe get to know Dryden a little better. You may see him in a different light when he isn't surrounded by all of your Earth things. From what I've learned of your Earth, things move quickly there. Our pace is much slower on Zelthrane-3, even though we are far more advanced in technology and medicine."

"Zelthrane-3?" Haven asked.

"It's the true name of our world," Harvol said. "When it was decided we would reach out to Earth, we thought calling ourselves Terrans would make us seem less frightening. But we're Zelthranites, and we're a proud people. I think Tilia has the right idea. Experience all our world has to offer, spend more time with Dryden, and perhaps you'll be mated before the Traxians find the father of your child and send him here, or to Earth if you're no longer on our world."

Haven nodded and seemed to accept their suggestions. He'd known that she was worried about the baby's father, but he hadn't realized just how scared she really was. Not that there was a lot he could do. He could be her friend and give her support, but unless she agreed to mate with him, he wouldn't be able to stop the Traxian from making demands Haven might not like. And at the same time, he didn't want her to accept his offer just as a way of avoiding a mating with the Traxian. He wanted her to want him because she truly cared about him.

There were times when she looked at him that he wondered if she might have feelings for him. Since the morning he'd pleasured her, they'd shared a handful of kisses and nothing else. It was torture keeping his hands to himself, but in the end it would be worth it. When they finally joined together, he wanted it to be special, to mean something and not just be for a quick release. He could have that with anyone. What he wanted with Haven was so much more.

"Breakfast was wonderful. Thank you, Father," he said

as he stood. "I need to report for work. Haven, my mother will take excellent care of you. I'll stop by my parents' place to pick you up when I'm finished this afternoon."

Harvol stood as well. "I need to report for duty. There are some new weapons that need to be tested. I should only be gone a few hours."

As Dryden and his father left, he glanced back one time and found Haven watching him. She offered him a smile before turning to face his mother. It was just a smile, something she'd done a hundred times in the last few days, but this one seemed different. Or maybe it was wishful thinking.

* * *

Haven took a sip of her drink as she listened to Tilia. The woman was a chatterbox, but Haven was enjoying every minute of it. She didn't know if Terrans -- no, Zelthranites -- had photo albums, but if they did, she wouldn't put it past Tilia to drag them out and show her every embarrassing picture of Dryden. The woman was proud of her son, anyone could see that, and she wanted only the best for him. For some reason, she seemed to think that was Haven.

"When Dryden was little, he would follow his father everywhere. We thought he might choose the same career path as Harvol, but as he grew older he lost interest in the weapons testing and seemed more focused on how things worked. There wasn't a single device in our house he didn't take apart and put back together."

"I hope he put them back correctly," Haven said with a smile.

"Oh, there were a few things that never worked the same again." Tilia laughed. "I remember when he pulled the food processor from the wall. Harvol and I had gone out with friends and when we came home, the processor was in pieces all over the kitchen floor. Oh, Harvol was so mad. It took Dryden three days to put it back together, but I'd swear the thing worked better afterward."

"That's kind of how we met, because of his ability to fix things. My car broke down and I managed to coast into the parking lot of his repair shop. He was the only one there and offered to take a look at it."

"I bet it's running better than ever," Tilia said.

"Actually, I told him not to fix it. There was a lot wrong with it and it would have cost more than the car is worth. I'm not sure what I'll do for transportation. If Dryden and I don't get married, I won't be able to stay with him forever. I'll need a job and a way to get there."

Tilia patted her hand. "I don't think you'll have to worry about it. My son lights up when you look at him, and I've seen the look in your eyes when you're watching him. You may not want to admit it to yourself for whatever reason, but you have feelings for him. Deeper than you think. I'd even go so far as to say you love him, and I can tell he loves you."

"He loves me?" Haven asked softly.

"Yes, he definitely loves you. I don't know why the foolish boy hasn't admitted it to you. Sometimes males just don't make any sense. When Harvol courted me, I thought he only wanted me because of who my father was. I come from a long line of important warriors. I didn't think he wanted me for me, and the stubborn man never let on how he felt about me. Not until I told him I couldn't see him anymore. I could see the near panic in his eyes, and he stumbled over his words before finally admitting that he loved me. We've been together ever since."

Haven sighed. She'd always loved a good romance, and she wanted the same kind of lasting love that Tilia and Harvol had. Was Tilia right? Could she have that with Dryden? Did she already, and she was just too blind to see it? Part of her was still hesitant about moving too fast. Tilia had made some good points though. She could take the next few days and get to know more about Zelthranites and their way of life, get to know Dryden more, and see where things ended up. She was curious if the Dryden of this world was different from the Dryden she'd gotten to know on Earth.

He claimed to be common here, poor compared to the riches he had on Earth. Would that change who he was? Or would Dryden remain the same sweet romantic that she'd come to know so far? She could lie to anyone but herself. Haven knew she was falling for him. Tilia seemed to think she was already in love with Dryden, but if she were would she be so hesitant to take that leap?

"Are you ready for some shopping?" Tilia asked.

"I don't want to spend Dryden's money," Haven said. "And I don't have any."

Tilia smiled at her warmly. "Today is on Harvol and me. The man hardly spends any of the credits he earns. Even my shopping sprees here and there don't put a dent in his account. Besides, this is the first time I've had a potential daughter-in-law and I want to celebrate."

"Maybe one or two things, but I really don't need anything right now. Dryden just bought me some clothes and shoes. My things were ruined when someone broke into my motel room. He was nice enough to buy me enough clothes to last a week or more, and several pairs of shoes."

"A woman needs more than a week's worth of clothes. We'll go to that cute shop I was telling you about for expectant mothers. And I won't take no for an answer."

Haven smiled and grudgingly gave in to Tilia. The woman really did seem excited about their shopping trip. Since she hadn't had any daughters, and Haven was Dryden's first potential mate, it was no wonder the woman wanted to have some fun. Although, Haven's own mother hadn't been interested in spending time with her, unless it was to project a certain image for society. Haven had learned to hate those outings, but something told her hanging out with Tilia would be fun.

As they walked through the streets of Terran Prime, she gazed at everything in wonder. Vehicles that looked almost like flying cars passed overhead and Haven wondered where they were going. She hadn't seen any parked on the streets, and she hadn't noticed any parking garages either. She pointed to the sky.

"Where are they going?"

Tilia shielded her eyes from the suns and looked up.

"Most are going to the other Terran cities. Terran Prime is our main hub and by far the largest. Some people live in the outlying cities and come to Terran Prime for work or to visit family. It's too far to walk to those other cities. Our planet is much smaller than Earth, and our people aren't as plentiful. Although, now that our younger males have a way to find mates, more and more children are being born every day."

"Your generation was the last of the females born?" Haven asked.

"Yes," Tilia said. "And with so many males being born, families who normally would have had five or more children stopped at two or three. And then there are couples like myself and Harvol who were only able to have one, or in some cases, weren't able to have any at all. I think mixing our people with others is a good thing. Even though the newest generation isn't purely Zelthranite, blending our societies has brought so much to our world. We have shops and restaurants that never would have existed before. The pool near The Towers was added after the agreement with Earth. Parks were added. We opened more clinics. Our world has changed a lot over the last ten years or so, and I think it's all for the better."

They stepped inside a shop filled with maternity clothes, body pillows, nursing bras, and so much more. The outside had been deceiving, making Haven think it was a small place, but the space inside was quite large. She wondered how many pregnant mates were on the planet currently for there to be such a large selection available.

Tilia helped her pick out several outfits and the shopkeeper started a fitting room for her. By the time Haven was ready to try on clothes, she felt like Tilia had put half the shop in there. It took her an hour to try everything on, and at Tilia's request, she made a pile of things that fit and looked nice and a pile that were a definite no. When she emerged from the fitting room, she couldn't even lift the pile of things she'd liked, but there was no way she was letting Tilia buy all of them.

"There are too many," Haven said.

Tilia flipped through the items Haven had liked and started pulling several out. She didn't stop until she'd selected ten outfits. The shop clerk carried the items to the register with Tilia following in his wake. Haven didn't understand the currency of Zelthrane-3, so she had no idea if her purchases were extravagant or not.

"Please have everything sent to Dryden's home," Tilia told the male as she swiped her wrist over a pad by the register.

"Of course. If there's anything else I can help you with, please let me know. I should receive new items in a few days."

Tilia thanked him and ushered Haven out of the shop. They went two doors down before she stopped again, this time at a baby store.

"Tilia, I can't buy baby furniture. I don't have a way to get it home."

"Indulge me," Tilia said. "I won't purchase anything, but I would like to ask them to hold it for a few days. If you haven't decided to become Dryden's mate by the time you leave our world, then I won't purchase the items. But if you decide you love him and can't live without him, I'll buy the things to have at my home for when the baby comes to visit."

"We haven't really discussed where we'll live if we were to get married."

"I know Dryden has a business on Earth, and he's wealthier there than here. I would understand it if he chose to make his permanent home there, but he still has responsibilities on our world, and you could visit once a month with the baby."

Haven sighed, knowing this wasn't an argument she would win. Tilia was determined that Haven would have her happily-ever-after with Dryden. She helped the woman pick out a bed and changing table, then they couldn't help but fall in love with some of the bedding choices. She had to admit that shopping for the baby was fun, even if she wasn't actually buying anything. The baby clothes were adorable, but since Haven didn't know if she was having a boy or a girl, she couldn't really pick anything out.

Tilia clucked her tongue at her and picked up a onesie that was white with yellow ducks printed on it. Haven had to admit it was adorable, and it would easily work for a girl or a boy. She let Tilia buy the outfit, then practically dragged the woman from the store before she could buy anything else.

"Are you getting tired?" Tilia asked. "Are you hurting?"

"My back and feet are a little sore," Haven admitted. "I'm not used to doing much walking, but it seems to be your main mode of transportation here."

"We believe in staying fit and healthy, so we walk everywhere we go around town. Well, as long as we're close enough to the shops. The homes on the outer edge of town are a different story. Harvol and I live nearby though, so we're lucky. Are you ready to see our home?"

Haven nodded, wincing a little as the muscles in her back pulled again. She wondered if Dryden would be so nice as to rub her back like he had several nights ago. His hands had been like magic, and it was the most relaxed she'd been in a long time. She didn't want to be selfish and ask for his help, though, especially after he'd had a hard day of work. Maybe if she rested for a little while the pain would go away.

Tilia led her back the way they'd come, and past the pool. There was a residential area tucked back off the road. The homes were large and beautiful, and different from anything Haven had seen before. Tilia approached one made of chocolate-colored stones with copper accents. She swiped her wrist over a panel beside the door and it opened.

"Welcome to my home," Tilia said. "Let me give you a quick tour and then you can stretch out in one of the bedrooms and rest if you'd like."

"I don't want to be a bad guest and take a nap."

Tilia waved off her concern. "You're an expectant mother. You need more rest than I do. I can keep myself busy while you take a nap, and when you wake up, I'll fix something for us to eat for lunch. Have you had food from our world before?"

"Before we got on the shuttle we ate at the food court inside the Terran Station. I tried some then. It was good, even though I couldn't identify any of it."

Tilia smiled. "I'll make something special for us."

She led Haven through the house, pointing out the family room, kitchen, dining room, and the six bedrooms which each had their own bathroom. There was also a sun room on the back of the house that overlooked a small garden, and a bonus room that was completely empty.

"This was Dryden's playroom," Tilia said. "As he got older, the toys changed to books, and then things he wanted to take apart and put back together. When he grew up and moved out, I emptied out the room and it's just sat here. Waiting."

"Waiting for what?" Haven asked.

"Grandchildren. I'll make it a playroom again when I get my first grandchild. I'm hoping Dryden will be luckier than Harvol and I were and will have many children. He's always wanted a big family. Even though he never complained, I know he wished he had siblings."

Haven rubbed her stomach. "What if this baby is all I'm able to have? What if something goes wrong?"

"Then Dryden will love the baby you give him and will be content with the one. I've found that the universe doesn't always give us what we want, but it does give us what we need. It brought you to Dryden when you needed someone in the worst way. And maybe he needed you just as much." Tilia took her hand. "Dwelling on what could go wrong, or what might happen, isn't going to change anything. Life gives us unexpected surprises along the way, and we grow and learn from them. But the secret is to find the happy moments along the way and hold on tight to them."

Haven's eyes misted. "I wish my mother had been more like you."

Tilia led Haven to one of the bedrooms and urged her

to take off her shoes and lie down. "What's your mother like?"

Haven stared up at the ceiling a moment. "She's hard. Cold. She never does anything unless it will benefit her in some way. The only times she took me to the park was so she could brag to the other mothers. She didn't take me shopping unless it was to flaunt her money. I don't remember ever getting a hug from her, except for the few times in public, when she was trying to convince everyone she was a great mother."

"That sounds like a lonely childhood."

"It was. I was an only child so I didn't have siblings to play with. I wasn't allowed to have friends unless the connection would benefit my parents in some way. When the money went away, all of my so-called friends did too. Once I couldn't buy them things, or go to the country club with them, they lost interest."

Tilia looked out the window before focusing on Haven once more. "May I say something you might not want to hear?"

Haven nodded.

"You've spent your entire life surrounded by people who wanted something from you. Perfection. Money. Connections. Dryden is very different from the people you're used to dealing with. None of those things mean anything to him. The only thing Dryden wants from you is love and a chance at happiness. And I think that scares you. Not because you don't want the same things, but because you've never had them. I think you're afraid to fail."

Haven swallowed hard and blinked the tears back. Tilia wasn't wrong. She was afraid. Terrified, in fact. Dryden was everything she'd ever wanted, the Prince Charming she'd dreamed about since she was a little girl. But her life had taught her that fairy tales didn't exist, and happily-ever-after was just for the movies.

"What if I love him and it all goes wrong?" she asked, her throat tight with unshed tears. "What if he wakes up one morning and realizes he made a mistake, that I'm unlovable, and that my baby is unwanted?"

Tilia sat on the edge of the bed. "Do you really think that would happen? Knowing Dryden the way you do, can you honestly see him thinking any of those things?"

Haven bit her lip. "Maybe not."

"I'm going to let you rest, but think about something while you're lying here. Has knowing Dryden made your life better? And I don't mean in a material way. Has he given your life meaning that wasn't there before? Has he made you hope for something you'd thought you'd never have? When you think about the future, does it hurt to imagine him not there?" Tilia stood. "I think once you answer those questions, you'll have a better understanding of your feelings, and you'll be able to release some of those fears."

"Thank you, Tilia. You really are a great mom."

Tilia smiled and stepped out of the room, letting the door shut behind her.

Haven stared at the ceiling, and pondered Tilia's words. There was still so much she didn't know about life, the world, or herself. But Dryden's mother seemed wise, and while Haven knew it was Tilia's love for Dryden that urged to speak out, she felt that Tilia wouldn't lie to her. Maybe Tilia saw things in Haven that she herself was unable to see.

As Tilia's words played over and over in her mind, she closed her eyes and willed her body to sleep. Perhaps the answers she sought would be found in her dreams.

# Chapter Seven

Dryden tightened the last bolt on the shuttle and put his tools away. His hands ached, but it was the good kind of hurting. The kind you only get from an honest day's work. He stretched out his back and cracked his neck. Being hunched over the shuttle engine for the last few hours had given him a few twinges. He pulled a rag out of the back pocket of his jeans and cleaned his hands off before tossing the rag into his toolbox.

The captain of the shuttle started her up and Dryden smiled. The engine was running better than ever, and he knew it was thanks to his magic touch. There were other mechanics on his world, but his services were always requested first. He might not have a high-paying job, but at least he was considered the best at what he did. He took pride in his work, no matter how small or large the task.

The engine shut off and the captain exited the shuttle. "It's running perfectly. Thanks, Dryden."

"Just doing my job, Sentir. If you don't need anything else today, I think I'll go home. I brought a potential mate with me and she's been spending time with my mother. Knowing Tilia, she's talked Haven's ears off by now."

Sentir laughed. "Go rescue your bride. I think the shuttle is in good shape for now. If anything else breaks, you'll be the first one I call."

Dryden stored his tools in his designated area before heading for his parents' house. He wasn't sure if his father was home yet. He'd missed his parents while he was on Earth, but if he hadn't opened his repair shop in the small Kentucky town, he never would have met Haven. He wondered what she thought of his world, and if she would want to live here. He could either sell his business on Earth, or make monthly trips there and leave the place in his manager's hands. He'd often thought about what would happen when he found a mate.

At his parents' house, he waved his wrist across the pad and unlocked the door. His mother greeted him, and pressed a finger to her lips.

"Haven is still sleeping. She took a nap before lunch, but I must have worn her out too much. I checked on her a few times, but she hasn't moved."

Dryden frowned. "Are you certain she's all right?"

"She's breathing evenly, but she seems to be in a deep sleep. Has she not been getting enough rest?"

"Xonos checked her over before the flight and said everything looked good, but then we talked about the baby. I called the council on the Vid-Comm before we left and asked them to search for the child's father. Maybe it was too much stress for her to handle combined with the trip here."

Tilia nodded. "Why don't you go check on her? You're welcome to stay for dinner, but I'll understand if you'd prefer to go home. You haven't had much time with her today."

"I'll try to wake her and see what she wants to do. She may want to go back to my apartment and sleep some more. I know the shuttle ride here can be taxing on my body and she's carrying another life inside of her. Maybe she'll be more rested tomorrow."

"Bring her by before you go to work, unless she'd prefer some quiet time to herself. I don't want to push myself on her."

Dryden smiled a little. "You like her, don't you?"

"Yes, I do. I think the two of you are well matched and I'd like to see the two of you mated. Haven and I talked a little today. I think she's scared. She told me about the world she comes from, the society she was raised in, and it's vastly different from what you're offering her. She has a big decision to make, and she's worried she'll make the wrong choice. Not because she doesn't want to be miserable but because she's worried you'll be unhappy."

"Idiot," he muttered. "And I mean that in the nicest way. The woman is going to drive me crazy. I would give her anything she asked for if she would only agree to be mine. I've known from the moment I saw her that she was the one. Convincing her of that has been damn near impossible though."

"I think she'll come around."

Dryden kissed his mother's cheek. "I'll go wake the sleeping princess. Thank you for spending time with her today."

"It was my pleasure."

Dryden searched the rooms until he found the bedroom where his potential mate was sleeping. He eased open the door and stepped inside. Haven had curled onto her side with her hands tucked under her chin. She looked so innocent, and she really was. Not innocent in a virginal way obviously, but there was still a childlike wonder to her sometimes. And he loved that about her.

Hell. He loved *her*. But he had a feeling if he told her that, she'd run as fast and as far as she could.

"Haven," he said as he gently shook her. "It's time to wake up."

She murmured in her sleep and curled her body around him. Dryden smiled and rubbed her back, but his smile quickly turned to a frown when he felt the muscles pulling and contracting in her lower back like they had done at the hotel on Earth. How long had she lain here in pain without saying anything? He reached under her shirt and began working the tense muscles as best he could from the odd angle. If she was hurting, he didn't want to wake her just yet.

Dryden massaged her lower back until he felt the muscles loosen. It worried him that this had happened twice now. He didn't remember his friends mentioning such a thing happening with their pregnant mates, and he wondered if the pregnancy was too hard on her body. If something like this was happening when she was barely showing, what would happen when she gained more weight?

He smoothed her hair back from her face and knelt beside the bed. He leaned down, placing his cheek against the bedding, his nose brushing hers. Trailing his fingers down her cheek and through her hair, he tried once more to wake her. A smile curved Haven's lips and her eyes fluttered open.

"You're home," she said, her voice heavy with sleep.

"I am. You had me worried."

"I didn't mean to sleep so long. I should have been well-rested after that eight-hour nap on the shuttle. I've been a horrible guest. Your mother is probably sorry she asked me to stay with her today."

Dryden traced her lower lip and kissed her softly. "My mother is completely in love with you already. If anything, she thought she was too hard on you after such a long trip. Don't feel bad for falling asleep."

"I think I must have walked too much. My back was hurting, but it feels better now."

"Your muscles were contracting when I came to wake you up. I rubbed your back for a few minutes. Haven, I'm worried that this has happened to you twice now. Maybe you should see the doctor while we're here."

She frowned. "But it happens all the time, whenever I exert myself. I'm sure it's just part of being pregnant."

"No, I don't think it is. Not this soon in your pregnancy at any rate. I've seen pregnant women rubbing their lower backs, but they're usually much further along than you are. I know Xonos said everything was fine, but what if it's not?"

Her hand rubbed her belly. "You think the baby is in trouble?"

"I think the pregnancy is too hard on your body. Will you please let me take you to the clinic? We can go now."

"If it will make you feel better, I'll go."

He kissed her again. "Thank you."

He helped Haven stand and then went in search of his mother. She was watching something on the Vid-Comm, but looked their way as they entered the room.

"Is everything okay? You look worried," she said.

"I'm taking Haven to the clinic. She keeps getting back spasms and I don't think that's normal for this stage of her pregnancy, or any stage for that matter. Even though Xonos said she was in perfect health, I think something is going on."

Tilia nodded. "Would I be in the way if I came with you?"

Dryden looked down at Haven, taking her hand. "If you want it to just be the two of us, she'll understand. But I'm all right with her coming along if you'd like for her to be there."

"I'd like for her to come with us."

Dryden nodded and the three of them set off for the clinic. It was several large city blocks, probably close to two miles, and he worried about the strain on Haven's body. When they reached the clinic, her face was pale and her features pinched, and he wondered if her back was spasming again. He reached for her, casually placing his hand there, and he felt the muscles contracting.

Zaylon, the clinic's assistant, was in the waiting area when they arrived. He smiled in greeting, then quickly frowned when he saw the state Haven was in.

"What's wrong with her?" Zaylon asked.

"We were hoping you could tell us," Tilia said. "She's in pain and it's still early in her pregnancy."

"Let's get her to a room. Are both of you going back with her?"

Dryden nodded.

They followed Zaylon down a long hallway and into an exam room. The doctor's assistant helped Haven into the chair used for full-body scans. He made sure she was comfortable before starting the machine. When it was finished with the scan, Zaylon helped her onto the padded table.

"I'm going to take some blood and do a few more scans. I'd also like to get a good look at your baby. The body scan will show us how healthy the child is, but it doesn't let us see the baby like you would in one of your Earth pictures. We have a new machine that will do that for us. Similar to your ultrasound machines on Earth."

Haven nodded and lay back on the table. Zaylon took several vials of blood, ran two more scans, then checked on the baby. His eyebrows shot up. "Interesting."

"What's wrong?" Dryden asked. "We were told the baby is a Traxian."

"Well, that's partially true. Did she see Xonos while you were on Earth?"

"Yes. He assured us everything was fine with the baby."

"The baby is perfectly healthy from what I can tell, but it's not Traxian. Not completely anyway."

"Then what is it?" Haven asked.

"The baby is a Traxian hybrid if I'm judging the facial structure correctly, and you're probably further along than you thought."

"It's been four months," Haven said.

Zaylon nodded. "And with a Traxian/human coupling, that would mean you had another six months to go. But this baby... there's no way to know for sure when you're going to deliver. I've never seen a combination like this before. If I had to guess, I'd say your baby will arrive in about two to three months. It's small now, but fully formed."

"I don't understand," Dryden said. "If it's not fully Traxian, what is it?"

Zaylon tucked his hands into his lab coat pockets. "If I'm reading the imaging correctly, your baby is a Traxian/Kuliki hybrid."

Dryden's jaw dropped a little. "But... the Kuliki people are thought to be extinct. Their planet was destroyed and no one has seen one in decades. The Traxian male Haven saw looked close to her age, and she said he was tiger-striped. The council was looking into the matter as we had several Traxians at the station during that time."

"It seems that some have survived. It's possible the Traxian traits would have been dominant and the father of the child may not have possessed any visible Kuliki characteristics."

Haven held up a hand. "I'm sorry, but what does a Kuliki look like?"

Zaylon pulled out a handheld comm unit and tapped on the screen until an image appeared. Dryden looked at the rather striking alien. Brilliant turquoise eyes stared back at them from a light green face. Black hair framed features that were damned near perfect in every way. Pronounced cheekbones. A long, straight nose. But it was the shape of the eyes that really drew attention to the alien. Large and almond with tipped up corners. All of that could have described other alien races as well, but the Kuliki people had four round bumps across their foreheads in a pearlescent white that would glow when their psychic abilities were active.

"And my baby looks like that?" Haven asked. "How do you know it's a Traxian/Kuliki hybrid?"

Zaylon showed her the image of the baby and Dryden peered down at the screen. The child was tiger-striped, but its skin was a soft green with black striping, and it bore the four bumps across the forehead. None of which would have shown up in the scans Xonos did. But Dryden didn't understand how the Kuliki DNA wouldn't have shown in the same test that determined the baby was part Traxian. His confusion must have shown on his face.

"Your baby has signs of being part Kuliki, but I'm guessing the Traxian genes were dominant in the father, which means the DNA that Xonos pulled would have shown Traxian with only faint traces of human and Kuliki. If he didn't know to look for it, he could have easily missed it." Zaylon put the comm unit back in his pocket. "Your body is reacting to this pregnancy as if you were eight months pregnant by human standards."

"But you said the baby was small," Dryden said. "Is it too small to be born healthy?"

"No. The child is nearly fully developed. I don't know why Xonos didn't say more when he did the exam on Earth. The baby could even be born a few weeks early and still survive. The unusual mix of human, Traxian, and Kuliki seems to have had some unexpected results. If I had to guess, I would say your baby is a girl. Would you like me to take another look and see if we can find out?" Zaylon asked.

"It's not too soon?" Haven asked.

"No. Considering you're getting close to your due date, we should be able to tell something. If the baby cooperates. I may have to push on your stomach to shift the baby into another position. I promise it won't hurt."

Haven nodded her consent and waited patiently while Zaylon performed the imaging test again. He smiled broadly as he froze the image on the screen and showed it to them. "I was right. You're having a girl. Kuliki females are small and dainty. I wouldn't be surprised if she never reached your height, momma."

Haven's eyes misted as she stared at the picture on the screen. "That's really my baby?"

Zaylon nodded.

"She's beautiful."

"Yes, she is," Dryden said.

Tilia wiped away tears as she stared at the image and Dryden knew she'd be out tonight buying little girl baby clothes. Even if Haven never agreed to be his mate, his mother had decided she was family. And once Tilia decided something, she made it so.

Haven bit her lip. "My baby isn't going to be accepted on Earth, is she? She's too different from everyone else. I mean, Earth is getting used to seeing different types of aliens, but no one will look like her."

"Since humans have never seen a Kuliki before, I'm not certain how they would react," Zaylon said. "I can say with certainty that if you made your home here, our people would welcome her with open arms."

Haven nodded.

"She's been getting back spasms when she does a lot of walking," Dryden said. "Should she limit her amount of exercise?"

"Walking is normally good during a pregnancy, but I think the baby is a bigger strain on her body because of its mixed heritage. Very little is known about Kuliki pregnancies except duration. I wouldn't say their people were secretive, but they kept to themselves." Zaylon smiled at Haven reassuringly. "I think the baby will be just fine, and as long as you don't overdo it, you shouldn't be in any pain. If the spasms start again, get someone to rub your back or place a hot compress on the area."

Dryden shook Zaylon's hand. "Thank you."

"If you have any other questions or concerns, come back and see me. If I'm not here, Banchek should be around."

They left the clinic and walked back to his parents' house. Haven rubbed at her back and he knew it was bothering her again, yet she didn't utter a word of complaint. She seemed almost happy after having seen her child. But one thing was certain. They had just narrowed down the list of possible fathers for the baby. Dryden doubted there were many Traxian/Kuliki hybrids. More than likely, there was only one. Which meant Haven was going to meet the father of her child sooner rather than later.

* * *

Haven stared out the window as she waited for Dryden to return. Shortly after they'd arrived back at his parents' home, he'd left to meet with the council. Since her child was so unique, there would be no question of who the father was. She had to admit she was anxious about meeting him. Well, she'd obviously already met him, but she didn't remember much about that night. All she could recall were vague flashes of the party with several aliens in attendance.

If the Traxian was mixed with a race thought extinct, would that mean he was more likely to want the baby she now carried? She had hoped that they could discuss visitation rights, and the baby would remain with her. But now she had to wonder if that would be the case. He'd looked like the other Traxians she'd seen, from what she could recall. The picture Zaylon had shown her didn't look anything like any of the aliens she'd ever seen. Her baby though… Her daughter was beautiful.

Tilia gave her a cup of something steaming that smelled faintly of mint.

"It will sooth your nerves," Tilia said. "It's similar to your Earth tea."

Haven took a sip and smiled her thanks. The liquid was hot, but whatever was in it made her calm almost instantly. Maybe she should ask how to make it. Something told her she'd be needing a lot of it in the upcoming months. As if having a baby wasn't a big enough deal, she had to have a special baby. Her hand smoothed over her belly. She already loved the child, more than she'd ever thought possible. And now that she'd seen her precious little girl, she loved her even more.

"Everything will be fine," Tilia told her. "Worrying isn't going to do you or the baby any good."

"I know. I just hate not knowing what lies in store for us. Now that I know my baby is unique, and so is her father, what if he demands custody? What if they force me to mate with him?"

Tilia took her hand. "Whatever happens, know that we'll be here beside you every step of the way. I know your home is on Earth, but have you considered staying here? At least until everything is resolved."

"Dryden said he had to return to Earth in a few days."

"You're more than welcome to stay with Harvol and me. And I'm sure Dryden could make arrangements to extend his stay if you want him here too."

"You're really sweet to offer, but I'd feel like I was imposing."

"Nonsense. In fact, I insist that you stay here for the rest of your time on our world. Dryden can bring your things and his over here. No point in the two of you staying in that cramped apartment if you don't have to."

Haven finished her drink and handed the cup back to Tilia. It was a very tempting offer. She genuinely liked the Zelthranite woman. But Dryden had obviously moved out of his parents' home for a reason, and she wasn't so certain he would want to move back. He'd talked about living with them if his mate wanted a large family, but would he be happy with such an arrangement?

As if her thoughts conjured the alien himself, Dryden strode into the room. He looked anxious, which didn't help her nerves in the slightest. Claiming the seat next to her, he reached for her hand.

"Whatever it is, just tell me," she said.

"When I shared with the council about your baby's heritage they immediately contacted the Traxians. They knew right away who the father is and they're sending him on a shuttle tonight. Depending on his departure time, he'll arrive late tomorrow, so you probably won't see him until the day after."

"What do you know about him?" Haven asked.

"His name is Tryval. He's half Traxian and half Kuliki, just as Zaylon predicted."

"Do you know anything else about him?" she asked.

Dryden shook his head. "The Traxians thought it best if Tryval met with you for a private conversation. They did assure us that he's well-mannered with females and you would have nothing to fear from him."

Great. She hadn't even thought to fear for her life, but now that he'd planted the idea in her head... A noise filtered through the room the Vid-Comm on the wall lit up. Tilia moved in front of the screen to accept the call.

When Haven saw the Traxian on the screen, she couldn't stifle her gasp. Though her memories from the party were fuzzy, she did remember the male. He'd been kind to her and made her laugh. And now she knew what her baby's father looked like, but why was he calling? Had he decided not to come after all?

"My name is Tryval, and I was hoping to speak with the human called Haven."

Tilia glanced at Haven over her shoulder, as if asking if Haven wanted to speak with the alien. Even if she refused to talk to him now, she'd still have to see him when he arrived. *If* he arrived. She still held out hope he'd changed his mind and was calling to say he wasn't coming. Standing, she moved across the room to stand next to Tilia.

"I'm Haven," she said, smoothing a hand over her baby bump.

Tryval smiled, a genuinely warm smile that reached his

eyes. "Of course you are. It's good to see you again. I hear we have much to discuss."

Haven nodded, not trusting herself to say much.

"My flight has been delayed due to mechanical issues. I won't be able to leave until the morning and it's a day's journey if there's no trouble along the way. I'm anxious to see you again. I had hoped after our night together that I would hear from you, but my elders informed me that you don't remember much of that night."

Her cheeks warmed. "I'd had too much to drink. Until the doctor did a scan of the baby, I didn't know who the father was. I'm sorry."

"All that matters is that I know now." He glanced from her to the others in the room and back again. "Are you on Zeltrane-3 as part of the bride program? Are you seeking a mate there?"

"I'm not part of the program, but I have been considering one of them as a mate. I came to meet his family."

"I see." He looked displeased with her news. "We'll discuss it more when I get there. I look forward to seeing you again, Haven."

He winked at her before signing off.

"What's that Earth phrase?" Dryden asked. "Cheeky bastard."

Haven gave a bark of laughter hearing the alien use that phrase. "Yes, he is. I only hope he's a reasonable one."

"I guess it would be rude of me to suggest that we have the council bless a mating between us before he arrives."

"I somehow don't think they would agree to that," Tilia said. "As much as we may not like it, Haven will have to hear out Tryval. He seems nice and even charming. There was no cruelty in his eyes."

Haven almost wished he'd been an evil bastard, then her decision would have been even easier. She was now torn between her growing feelings for Dryden and wanting to give the charming alien Tryval a chance. He'd seemed nice, and from what little she remembered, he'd been kind to her.

If he asked her to be his mate, it might be hard to say no to him. Her baby deserved to know her father, but did that mean she had to marry him? She looked at Dryden, conflicted.

"If you pick him, I'll understand, Haven."

"I'd thought earlier I was ready for a mating with you. And now I feel lost and don't know what to do. If I choose you, then Tryval loses the chance to be a part of his daughter's day-to-day life. And if I choose him, then I lose someone who's become my best friend."

Dryden moved closer to her, cupping her cheek. "Haven, you're not going to lose me. Even if you don't become my mate, I'll always be a part of your life in any way that you'll allow. I care about you a great deal."

"Harvol will be home soon," Tilia said. "I'm going to make dinner. Are the two of you staying or would you prefer to be alone tonight?"

"I'd like to stay," Haven said.

"Then I'll go get our things from my apartment. Keep my mother company and I'll return shortly." Dryden pressed a kiss to her forehead and it made her eyes mist with tears. Just a few short hours ago, that kiss would have landed on her lips. Why couldn't anything in her life go right? Ever since the scandal with her parents, it had been one bad thing after another.

When Dryden left, Tilia tugged her toward the kitchen. "You don't have to help, but you can keep me company. I think you could use a little... what's that Earth term? Girl talk?"

Haven smiled. "I could use some of that about now."

"May I make a suggestion?" Tilia asked.

"Elope with Dryden before Tryval gets here?"

Tilia laughed. "No, but I would be quite happy if that were possible. I was going to suggest that you meet with Tryval with an open mind. I want you for my daughter-in-law, more than you can imagine, but I also want you to be happy. Tryval seems like he would be a good mate to the right woman. I'd like to believe that woman isn't you, but maybe it is."

"So, you want me to give him a chance even though you want me to marry Dryden? You've been quite adamant about the fact you believe your son loves me. Wouldn't that doom him to a miserable life if we're supposed to be together?"

"I want you to do what's best for you and for your baby, whatever you think that might be. Do I want you do be with Dryden? Yes. It would make me, and him, extremely happy. But I want you to follow your heart. The way you watch Dryden leads me to believe you love him, or at least care for him deeply. But maybe I'm wrong."

"You're very confusing, Tilia."

"I'm a mother and a female. It's allowed."

"What if I can't choose?" Haven asked. "What if I like them both?"

"I'm afraid Dryden isn't into sharing."

Haven sighed. Not that she'd really thought about taking on both of them as mates. Even she wasn't that crazy. One man was more than enough for her. She was almost certain that Dryden was meant to be hers, and she would have gladly mated with him if it weren't for Tryval. So maybe the real question was why she was even considering Tryval. Just because he was charming and the father of her child didn't seem like a good enough reason to spend the rest of her life with him. Plenty of mothers had babies without marrying the father. Earth was full of mixed families.

"You look like something important just occurred to you," Tilia said.

"Tryval is the father of my child, and I would never deny him if he wanted to see her. But having a baby together isn't reason enough to get married. We may have spent one night together, a night I don't even remember, but we're still complete strangers. A nice smile and a baby do not a happy marriage make."

Tilia stopped what she doing to sit beside Haven. "So, what are you going to do?"

"I'm going to meet with him, hear him out, and then I'm going to ask how to best make it work so that he can see his daughter without us being married. I'm going to make sure he understands there's no chance of a mating between us. I want Dryden."

There was a sigh behind her. "You have no idea how happy I am to hear that."

She looked over her shoulder and saw Dryden standing in the doorway, a smile on his handsome face. Haven stood and ran to him, throwing her arms around his waist. She felt free now that she'd made her decision, as if a weight had been lifted from her. In that moment, she realized that it had never been a matter of choosing between Dryden and Tryval, it had been her upbringing of always doing what society deemed as the right thing demanding that she make a choice. Once she focused on her feelings and not what she *should* do, the answer was easy enough. Dryden was who she wanted to be with.

"You're my best friend," she said. "And I want to spend the rest of my life by your side. I'm sorry it took me so long to realize that we belong together. I was close to telling you before we found out about Tryval."

"My council won't approve our mating until you meet with him. But knowing you want to be with me is good enough for now."

Haven bit her lip. "Even if we aren't officially mated, do you think we could share a room like we'd planned to do at your apartment?"

"Nothing will keep me from your side."

"Except work," Tilia said. "One of the captains is heading up our walkway."

Dryden groaned and looked toward the door. "They have the worst timing."

"I'll answer it and stall for a moment while you tell Haven goodbye," Tilia said. "I have a feeling you're going to be gone until after dinner. Maybe longer. If they're coming for you and not just any mechanic will do, then it must be a big issue."

Haven brushed a kiss against Dryden's lips. "Go take care of your job. I'll be here waiting when you're done."

Dryden held her tighter and kissed her again, his tongue flicking against her lower lip until she opened to him. He took his time exploring her mouth and making her toes curl before he pulled away. Giving her that sexy smile that made her knees weak, he caressed her cheek, and left to meet with the captain at the door.

When Tilia returned a moment later, Haven didn't even hide the smile. She was grinning from ear to ear and didn't care who knew how happy she was. Now that she'd chosen Dryden, she couldn't wait to make things official. She didn't care what Tryval had to say. He might be her baby daddy, and perhaps over time he could be her friend, but that was all that would ever be between them.

"Dinner is almost finished. Want to help me set everything out?" Tilia asked.

"Put me to work," Haven said. "And maybe next time you can teach me how a Zelthranite kitchen works. I have a feeling it might be something I need to know."

Tilia snorted. "Don't even attempt to make anything in Dryden's kitchen. His apartment is definitely meant for an unmated male. You should probably talk to him about looking at houses. The baby is going to need a room soon."

"I think he's worried he won't be able to afford one large enough. We want more children, and so do I, but he said he could only afford a small place."

Tilia stopped what she was doing and faced Haven. "I don't even have to ask Harvol before offering. The two of you, and any children you may have, are more than welcome to live here. Even with Dryden and you taking a room, there would still be four bedrooms."

"I'll talk to him about it, but I don't want to intrude on your privacy. I'm sure Harvol likes the peace and quiet when he's home from work, and a houseful of children would be anything but."

Tilia smiled. "We would welcome the noise from any grandchildren you give us. I was unable to have more children after Dryden and we've always wanted a house full. Believe me when I say all of you would be welcome here."

Haven nodded. "Thank you, Tilia. I'll talk to Dryden about it and we'll let you know."

Tilia smiled and handed her a dish full of food. By the time they had set the table, Harvol was home. Haven glanced toward the door but knew it could be hours before Dryden returned. She'd looked forward to a family dinner in his childhood home, but it seemed she'd have to wait one more day.

Still, even with Dryden off working, the night was just about perfect. She was surrounded by warmth and love, something that had been missing from her life for as long as she could remember. Finally, she felt like she belonged. And now that she'd found happiness, she was going to grab it with both hands and hold on tight. Nothing was going to take her away from this loving family or the man she'd decided to call hers.

## Chapter Eight

The suns had set long ago, but the heat of the day lingered. Lights at the shuttle station allowed him to work long into the night, whether he wanted to or not. Dryden was more than a little frustrated. He'd replaced rods, hoses, had done a tune-up on the engine, even removed a few parts that looked worn. Still the damn shuttle wouldn't start. The captain tried to turn it on again, the engine clanking and grinding but not turning over, and Dryden studied every part looking for some clue as to what was wrong. Three hours after he'd started he was no closer to figuring out the problem.

The captain exited the shuttle, sealing the door behind him. "Dryden, you've been working nonstop since I came to get you, and I know I called you away at dinnertime. Whatever is wrong with the shuttle can wait until tomorrow. Go home and get some rest."

"Maybe a good night's sleep will refresh me enough I can figure it out tomorrow," Dryden said. "I'm sorry I didn't get it running tonight, Keylon. I know you have a trip planned for the morning."

"I'll either take another shuttle or the trip will be delayed. I was taking two brides home who didn't find mates. Giving them one more day on our world won't hurt anything. Maybe they'll pair off with someone after all."

Dryden nodded. He started to turn away, but paused. There was one thing he hadn't yet checked. Pulling out one of his gauges, he hooked it up to the shuttle and asked Keylon to try starting the engine again. There was a slim chance that the spark that propelled the fuel to the engine wasn't happening. It was a small part to replace, if a bit difficult to reach.

The gauge mocked him, showing that it was working fine. He drummed his fingers on the shuttle as he stared at the engine some more. Pulling the panel off the fuse box, he tested each one. None appeared to be fried and all were working properly. If the shuttle was getting fuel, all of the fuses were fine, and the engine was in excellent condition, he didn't know what the hell was wrong with the thing.

Or was it getting fuel? Just because the spark was there didn't mean anything was actually happening. What if the fuel wasn't getting to the engine because the pump had gone out? The part was at the back of the shuttle, underneath, and behind two steel plates and a ton of wiring. It definitely wasn't a job he could handle tonight.

"I'll come back in the morning. There's one more thing I want to check before I call in someone for a second opinion," Dryden said.

"She'll be here whenever you're ready," Keylon said. "Enjoy the rest of your evening."

Dryden cleaned up and went home, feeling exhausted. Despite scrubbing his hands, there was still grease under his nails, but then there usually was. His hands ached from holding his tools the last few hours while he tried to solve the puzzle of why the shuttle wouldn't start. He tipped his head from side to side, getting his neck to crack and relieve some of the pressure building there. It had been a long-ass day and he was more than ready to get home.

The hunger pains he'd felt off and on were back full force and he couldn't wait to see what his mother had made for dinner. He missed her cooking now that he no longer lived at home. The house was dark when he approached the walkway, and he wondered if Haven was already in bed. He quietly let himself into the house and went straight to the kitchen. There was a covered plate on the counter, exactly where his mother had left his meals all the times he'd been called out before moving into his own place.

The food had grown cold, but he didn't care. He ate quickly, then put his plate into the cleansing unit. The four empty bedrooms were dark with their doors open. His parents' room had the door shut and no light shone underneath. Haven had been given her choice of the empty rooms and she'd chosen the room at the end of the hall, the farthest from his parents, and the door was partially open. He peered through the darkness and saw her lying on her side, hands tucked under her cheek.

Dryden closed the door and went into the bathroom, pushing the door shut before turning on the light. The male staring back at him in the mirror looked tired and filthy. A good night's sleep would cure the tiredness, and a shower would fix the rest. He stripped out of his clothes and turned on the water. It didn't take him long to get clean, and he shut out the bathroom light before going into the bedroom.

Fatigue pulled at him and he didn't bother with pajama pants, even though he'd packed some. Now that he knew Haven was his, keeping covered around her wasn't as important. She would eventually see all of him. He lifted the blankets and slid into bed, pulling her against his tired body and breathing in her sweet scent. Haven turned and curled against him, her hand sliding around the back of his neck as her other landed on his chest.

"You're home late," she said softly.

"I'm sorry. I can't figure out what's wrong with the shuttle. I'll have to go back tomorrow."

"Did you eat?"

"I found the plate my mother left out."

He felt Haven's lips curl against his skin. "Tilia didn't leave it. I did."

Dryden brushed a kiss against the top of her head. "Already taking care of me."

"Tilia offered to teach me how a Zelthranite kitchen works. She also offered to let us stay here as long as we want. Even permanently."

Dryden pulled back a little and looked down at her in the darkness. "You want to live here? On my world and in my childhood home?"

"You said if you made your home here again you would need to live with your parents in order to have space for a large family."

Dryden's hands stroked her back. "How large?"

"I think at least three or four children," Haven said. "It sucked being an only child. I want this baby to have lots of siblings. I have a feeling she's going to need a protective brother or two when she gets bigger."

"I can't think of anything I'd like more. Are you certain you don't wish to return to Earth?"

"I'm positive. There's nothing for me there. All I need is you, and your job brings you here just as much as your work on Earth. I guess I'll need to go back and pack my things, but I brought most of my clothes with me."

"I'll take care of it," Dryden said. "I'll need to return to Earth for about a week to get everything set up, then I can cut back to monthly trips to check on the shop. I don't think I want to sell it just yet, in case you decide after a year or two that you'd like to return to Earth."

"Dryden?"

"Hmm?"

"I don't know if you've noticed, but we're in the dark. Alone. In a bed."

He smiled. "It hadn't escaped my attention."

"Now that I've agreed to be yours, there's no reason for us to wait, is there? You said you wouldn't make love to me until I'd made my decision, and now I have."

The thought of having her under him, of her wet heat welcoming him, was enough to nearly jolt him wide awake. He shifted and reached for the pajamas she'd put on before getting into bed. In under a minute, he'd stripped her bare and tossed the covers aside. Moonlight filtered through the window, giving him just enough light to see her beautiful curves. Even without the light, he still remembered what she looked like.

"What do you want, Haven?" he asked, willing to give her anything she desired.

"Kiss me. Make me yours."

His mouth pressed against hers, his tongue flicking out until she opened. He kissed her hungrily, his hands caressing the lush curves of her body. He cupped her breasts, the soft mounds swelling against his palms, as he leaned down and took a rosy peak into his mouth. He tongued the bud until Haven squirmed beneath him, her nails raking his shoulders and back. Dryden lavished the other nipple with attention, gentle nips and long, hard sucks, making Haven cry out in the darkness.

He licked and sucked his way down her body, stopping to delve his tongue into her navel and leaving a love bite on her hip. The scent of her drove him crazy and he couldn't wait to have her sweet taste on his tongue again. He spread her legs wide with his shoulders, feeling her body tremble beneath him. Haven gripped the bedding tight as her body lifted, begging him to touch her.

The moment his tongue touched her pussy, lapping at her cream, she melted. His grip on her hips tightened as she relaxed in his hold. His tongue dipped inside her tight channel before swirling around her clit. Her sweet nectar flowed over his tongue like honey and he did it again. Dryden teased her clit. Circling. Flicking. Then he sucked the bud into his mouth, drawing on it long and hard until she cried out and bucked beneath him. Her cream coated his tongue and dripped down her thighs, and Dryden licked up every drop.

Rising above her, he stared into her passion-glazed eyes. She was so beautiful, so his. His cock brushed against her and with a flex of his hips, he was buried inside of her. Her pussy squeezed him tight, damn near making him come. She was all silken heat and perfection, wrapped around his steely shaft. Dryden pulled back, then eased back in, taking her with slow, gentle strokes. Every thrust felt like he was entering heaven, only to retreat and plunge back into her welcoming body.

Sweat slicked his skin as his control neared the breaking point. He wanted the night to be special for her, to be perfect, but he was barely holding on. Haven's hands gripped his biceps as her legs came around his waist, opening her farther to him, and he slid in a little deeper.

"More," she begged. "Harder."

His control snapped and Dryden growled softly as he took her hard and fast, every stroke a little wilder than the one before, until he lost his rhythm and could do little more than feel. Her pussy fluttered around him, the little pulses urging him on. As Haven cried out her release, Dryden gave himself up to the pleasure. Haven lay panting beneath him as he spilled himself inside of her tight sheath. His orgasm left him damn near breathless and his arms shook from the effort to hold himself up.

Pulling from her body, he rolled to his side and wrapped his arms around her. Haven snuggled against him, letting out a contented sigh. Dryden stared at the moons through the window as his heart began to slow. The woman in his arms meant everything to him, but he'd never said the words to her. And as much as he wanted to confess his love, part of him wanted to hold back a little longer. If he said something now, she might wonder if it had more to do with the intimate moment than true feelings. She would meet with the father of her child in a day or two, and once things were sorted with Tryval, then he would tell her how he felt.

"As much as I would love to lie here with you all night, I'm sticky," Haven said. "Do you think we could rinse off in the shower?"

"This house has larger bathrooms than most. The unit will comfortably hold two."

Dryden released her and they both went into the bathroom, leaving the door open as he flicked on the light. He started the cleaning unit, making sure the water was a comfortable temperature. When he was certain it wouldn't scald Haven's skin, he helped her into the unit and followed behind her, letting the door shut. Steam fogged the glass wall and door.

"It's like a shower," she said, smiling as the water soaked her hair.

"Almost. It can be programmed so that the water has a cleaning agent in it, but most homes with human brides just use plain water. We've noticed that human females like soaps that are scented in a way that suits each of them."

She nodded. "I was always partial to strawberry-scented stuff, but anything girly will do."

"I noticed your soaps and shampoo were in here when I showered earlier, so I left the cleaning agent out of the water."

"What does the cleaning agent smell like?"

"It's unscented, but leaves your skin and hair clean. Until humans began living here, we didn't have things like scented lotions or hair conditioners. Most of us have found pleasure in some of the human things our shops now carry."

"I've noticed males here wear black leather pants and either nothing on the top half of their body, or some wear a black leather vest. Is that the only clothing on your world that isn't human?"

He slowly soaped her skin. "The leather pants and vest are what most wear. Our Chief Councilor tends to wear white flowing clothing. It sets him apart as our leader, but similar clothes are available for those who prefer something less constricting."

"Do you dress in the leather attire when you're here?" she asked.

"Most of the time, yes. I didn't have time to change this morning after we landed so I kept on my Earth clothes. I packed a mixture of Zelthranite and human clothing. Our world is very warm, so the leather can be hot if I'm out in the suns a long time."

Haven smiled. "Maybe you should make shorts and tank tops a trend on your world."

Dryden laughed. "I don't even wear shorts on your world. A female's legs are nice to look at, but a male's legs just aren't attractive."

She leaned back and looked down at his legs. "I think it's a matter of opinion. I happen to like yours."

"We'll have to agree to disagree."

Haven took the shower gel from him and began soaping his body. "If I could find a reason to touch you every second of every day, I would die a happy woman. Your arms are so strong. I love the way they feel when they're around me."

He flexed. "It comes from lifting heavy machinery. Warriors are much larger, though. I'm considered small on my world."

"No, you're perfect. There is such a thing as too much

muscle. I think your body is just right. You're tall, far taller than me, so I don't see how they could call you small."

Dryden smiled. "My ego doesn't need stroking, but thank you."

Haven yawned and blinked up at him sleepily. Dryden shut off the water and helped her dry before tucking her back into bed. Neither of them bothered with pajamas as they cuddled together under the covers. Haven curled against his side, her even breaths soft against him as she drifted back to sleep. Dryden had gone from exhausted to fully charged when Haven had asked him to make love to her, but now his energy was fading once more. He yawned and closed his eyes, willing his body to relax enough for sleep to claim him. As much as he'd love to be with Haven tomorrow on the off chance Tryval arrived, he needed to fix the stubborn shuttle.

With thoughts of fuel pumps, ignition switches, and fuel pump relays filling his head, he started to drift off to sleep. *Fuel pump relay*? He bolted upright in bed, suddenly far more awake than he'd been all day. He felt like a complete and utter idiot. Easing out of bed so as not to wake Haven, he pulled on a fresh pair of jeans and a tee before tiptoeing from the room. By the front door, he put on his boots and stepped back out into the night.

Walking to the shuttle station was no more dangerous late at night than it was during the day. There was little to no crime on Zelthrane-3 and he reached his destination without incident. Dryden flicked on the lights and grabbed his tools before opening the belly of the shuttle. He had to remove a panel, a steel plate, and push some wires out of the way, but once he found the fuel pump relay he reset it.

The shuttle keys were stored in a cabinet along the wall and he found the right set. Entering the cockpit, he took a breath, said a prayer, and turned the key. The engine roared to life on the first try and he gave a triumphant cry. All the damn work he'd done on the blasted shuttle and all it needed was to be reset. He'd blame being tired for his stupidity. After turning off the shuttle and returning the keys to the cabinet, he left a note for Keylon.

Maybe he wasn't losing his touch after all. He'd started to wonder when he couldn't figure out what was wrong. Apparently, he needed the release he'd found in Haven's arms to get him thinking clearly again. Whatever the cause for his sudden clarity, he was thankful the job was completed. Now he'd have tomorrow free, unless he was called out on another job.

By the time he reached his parents' house, the sky was lightening as the suns began to rise. He wouldn't have long to sleep before breakfast was ready, but a few hours would be enough to keep him going all day. He quietly entered the home, removing his boots before creeping back into the bedroom. Haven hadn't moved and he quickly stripped out of his clothes before sliding into bed and pulling her back into his arms. Now that the shuttle repair wasn't hanging over his head, he was able to clear his mind and finally relax. As his eyes closed, his mind began to drift, as if he were floating on a cloud, and with his future mate in his arms, he fell asleep.

# Chapter Nine

The next day passed without word from Tryval, but Haven could feel the tension in the air. Dryden had been called out on another job, and he'd looked worried as he left. She knew he was concerned about her meeting with Tryval on her own. Not that he thought the alien would harm her, but he knew she was nervous about meeting with him. By the second day, she was nauseated and she didn't think it was from the pregnancy. Then the third day arrived and there was still no word from Tryval.

"You need to eat something," Tilia said.

"I'm worried it will come right back up. How long does it take to get here from Traxia? He said the journey took a day, but it's been more than a day. The waiting is killing me."

"I'm sure he'll be here soon," Tilia said. "Maybe his shuttle was delayed again."

"Wouldn't he have called? He called the first time."

Tilia rubbed her back. "Try not to worry so much. It can't be good for the baby. Do you want some *fuzba*?"

"Is that the tea stuff you made me that tastes like mint?"

"I believe I've heard humans describe it that way. It will calm you and ease your worries."

"In that case, do you serve it by the gallon?"

Tilia smiled at her and went to the kitchen to make the drink. Haven stared out the window into the back garden and wished that Dryden were with her. He'd wanted to be by her side, but it was time for his return trip to Earth and she'd assured him she would be fine. Now she was wishing she'd kept her mouth shut and let him remain with her. She didn't know how long he would be gone, but she missed him already, and he'd only left a few hours ago.

When her soon-to-be mother-in-law returned with the *fuzba*, she accepted the cup and sipped at it. Haven had to admit that Tilia had been right to suggest it. Only a few swallows and she could already feel herself relaxing. If the Zelthranites sold this stuff on Earth, they'd make a fortune off mothers alone, not to mention overworked business persons. She took another swallow and closed her eyes, letting the calm flow through her.

"Better?" Tilia asked.

"Much. Thank you." Haven smiled at her. "I miss Dryden, but I'm really glad Harvol and you are here with me. I never knew what it was like to have parents because mine were so unattached. You've given me a taste of what a family is supposed to feel like."

Tilia wrapped her arms around Haven. "You're the daughter I never had, and you are a most welcome addition to the family. I'm sorry your mother couldn't see you for the treasure you are. It was her loss."

"Thank you, Tilia."

Tilia bit her lip and looked like she wanted to say something. The woman hadn't hesitated to voice her opinion thus far. Haven waited, knowing eventually she would say what was on her mind. She didn't have to wait long.

"You're going to be mated to my son as soon as the issue with Tryval is settled. Would you consider calling me Mom or Mother?"

"I would be honored to call you Mom." Haven hugged her tight.

"I know Harvol isn't here to say so, but he'd love it if you called him Dad or Father. We already think of you as part of the family."

Haven's eyes misted with tears. She'd never felt like she belonged anywhere, but Dryden's family made her feel wanted. Her car dying in his parking lot was the best thing that had ever happened to her. She'd felt hopeless and lost before she'd met him that night. And if she had the rest of her life with him, it would never be enough time to show him what he meant to her.

"Mom, I want to do something for Dryden, but I don't know what."

"I could teach you how to make his favorite dessert," she offered.

Haven was thinking something on a larger scale, but

she'd always heard the way to a man's heart was through his stomach. Maybe the same held true for aliens. She smiled and nodded, then followed Tilia into the kitchen. Tilia opened the equivalent of a refrigerator and pulled out several types of fruit, each one looking stranger than the first.

"It's called Starkist pie," Tilia said. "We have to clean and slice the fruit, then set it aside with some sweetener drizzled over it while we make the crust."

Make the crust? Haven had always thought you just bought a pie crust. For that matter, she didn't even know where the Zelthranites got their food. Did they have a grocery store? She hadn't seen one, but that didn't mean it didn't exist. There was much of Terran Prime she had yet to see.

Tilia pulled out something that looked like purple flour, along with some dark blue eggs that were far too large to belong to any birds she'd ever seen, and some type of cooking oil. Tilia showed her how to mix everything together, then helped her roll out the crust, which she placed in a pie-shaped baking dish, cutting off the excess.

"Now you empty the fruit mixture into the dish," Tilia said. "Then we'll make the top of the pie."

Haven looked at the leftover dough. "Could we do a lattice top? I always thought those were pretty."

Tilia frowned. "I'm not sure what that is."

"You crisscross the dough over the top of the pie so it makes a lattice."

Tilia smiled. "I understand. Yes, we can do that. It will be different from my usual way and a nice surprise for Dryden, if he returns in time to eat it. If he isn't back before the pie has to be eaten, we'll make another when he gets home."

Haven hoped he wouldn't be gone too long, but she knew tying up loose ends could take a while, as well as packing up the hotel suite. She missed him horribly and almost wished she'd gone with him. But then she might have missed Tryval and would have had to wait even longer for things to be settled. And she definitely wanted the mating between her and Dryden to move forward as quickly as possible.

Tilia showed her how to actually bake the pie, which was easier than she'd thought. A Zelthranite oven looked similar to a large microwave, with a specific sequence of buttons that had to be pushed to cook different dishes. Then Tilia explained how the food processor worked in the kitchen, and showed her how to program certain meals, which would slide out on a tray when they were finished.

"I don't understand," Haven said. "If the processor can cook everything from pushing a few buttons, and you don't even have to insert ingredients, why do you need to bake the pie?"

Tilia smiled. "Because the pie is made with love. The food processors weren't always here. When I was a little girl, my mother had to make everything from scratch. Processors didn't come around until I was nearly in my teen years."

Haven found everything about Zelthrane-3 to be fascinating and wanted to learn as much as she could. "Do you have libraries here? I haven't seen many books on your world."

"Most of our reading is done on handheld comm units. They can be used for more than just communication, but not everyone has one. Since bringing humans to our world, a library has been opened here in Terran Prime. There are books there in many languages. We can go sometime if you'd like."

"I'd love that. I've always enjoyed reading, but I won't understand any of the books that aren't in English."

"Most of them are in English as the majority of our brides seem to come from America. The other countries seem hesitant to participate even though we have Terran Stations in every major city on your world. It's our hope that the longer the program is open the more diverse the candidates will be."

"What about other worlds? Surely humans aren't the only ones compatible with your people."

Tilia smiled. "No, they aren't. There are other worlds that enter negotiations with our warriors from time to time, but there isn't a bride program in place on any of them. If a warrior goes to one of those worlds and sees a female he wishes to claim, then he makes a declaration to her people and terms are agreed upon. You won't see many wandering Terran Prime, though."

"So it's rare for a warrior to select a mate not of Earth?" Haven asked.

"Not so much rare as that the women seldom wish to leave their worlds. A lot of our warriors have joined the military forces of other planets in order to take a mate. The Bride program with Earth has kept that from happening as often. But as I mentioned, the pool isn't very diverse. Not that there's anything wrong with Americans. We just wish everyone would participate."

Haven could understand that. Eventually, America would run out of women who wanted to consider marrying an alien. And even if they didn't, there were so many alien races out there who needed females as badly, if not more so, than the Zelthranites. Already she'd seen several other races in her small Kentucky hometown. She could only imagine who she'd see in places like New York or London. She found the different aliens to be fascinating, but only one had captured her heart.

"The pie will be ready shortly. You look tired," Tilia said. "If you'd like to take a nap, I'll pull the pie out when it's ready. I'm sure the baby is draining some of your energy the closer you get to your due date."

"I'm worried if I go to sleep, I'll miss Tryval's visit."

"Perhaps we should contact the council and see why he hasn't arrived?" Tilia suggested. "He seemed most eager to reach you, and now he's all but vanished. Something doesn't seem right."

Haven had to agree. "Could you contact the council for me? Or show me how to use the Vid-Comm?"

"I would be delighted to show you how it works."

Tilia led her into the living room, then showed her the

sequence of buttons to turn on the Vid-Comm and dial the council. A room appeared on the screen with a group of males surrounding a table. One was dressed all in white and she assumed he was the Chief Councilor based off Dryden's earlier description.

"Good morning," the chief councilor said. "You must be Haven."

"Yes, sir," Haven replied.

"My name is Borgoz. Did you need something?"

She licked her lips, suddenly feeling nervous. "An alien by the name of Tryval was supposed to come here days ago to meet with me. I haven't heard from him and to my knowledge he hasn't arrived. I wondered if the council knew anything about his whereabouts."

Borgoz frowned. "I'm familiar with Tryval. He was very anxious to meet with you and I find it odd he hasn't met with you or contacted you."

"He called on the Vid-Comm four days ago saying his shuttle had been delayed, but he'd planned to leave the next morning. That was the last I heard from him."

"Let me make some calls and see if I can locate the shuttle he was supposed to be on. As soon as I hear of anything, I'll contact you, Haven. I'm sure you have nothing to worry about. There could have been another delay for shuttle maintenance."

"Thank you, Borgoz."

He smiled and signed off.

"See, he's going to take care of it," Tilia said. "He's very good at his job and if Tryval has been delayed, the chief councilor will find out quickly. Borgoz has been known to be stern in the past, but since finding his mate he's softened a bit."

"Is she like me?"

"Human?" Tilia asked. "Yes, and she's American. But Charlotte is different from most people. She has a hard time hearing and reads lips to understand what people are telling her. There's something she wears in her ear that lets her hear a little. Their daughter is completely deaf, so Borgoz has asked that we learn sign language, not only to communicate with his daughter, but to open up the possibility of accepting brides with the same affliction. Charlotte is able to speak in a way that we can understand, even if her voice is different, but from what I understand not all deaf people can communicate that way."

"Was it a love match between them?" Haven asked.

"Oh, yes. He loved her so much, he would have been willing to give up everything for her. The Chief Councilor isn't allowed to leave our world because of the dangers, but he informed the council members he was leaving anyway. Charlotte was facing a pregnancy on Earth that could have been fatal and he wanted to be by her side."

"That had to be scary for her, but it's so sweet he rushed to her side."

"Why don't you rest and if the council calls, I'll be sure to wake you?" Tilia asked.

"I don't think I could rest if I tried. Is there anything you need help with around the house?" Haven asked.

"One of the human brides has a housecleaning business. She comes by once a week and cleans for me. It was a present from Harvol. I have an idea. With the influx of humans on our world, in the last year our... I believe you would call them technology experts, have managed to pull a handful of movies from Earth's libraries and load them so we have access through the Vid-Comm units. Would you care to watch something with me?" Tilia asked.

"I love watching movies."

"I doubt we have anything new from your world."

"Sometimes the best movies are the older ones," Haven said. "I think my favorite movie is *Rebel Without a Cause* with James Dean. He was such a cutie."

Tilia smiled. "I'll see if it's available. If not, we can put in a request. They add a new movie every few weeks. It's not as simple as tapping into one of your satellites; they have to convert the files to a format that will play on our technology."

Haven nodded. "That makes sense. If it were as easy as

popping in a disc I'm sure the brides would have requested hundreds of DVDs and Blu-rays by now."

"After the movie, we can go to the library if you'd like. I don't know if there's a limit on how many books you can have at one time. Or maybe we could put in a bookshelf while Dryden is gone and ask him to bring books home to you. Is there a certain type you like?" Tilia asked.

"Romances. Any type of romance. I read everything from historical, to paranormal, to the racy BDSM books."

Tilia smiled. "I didn't understand some of that, but I'm sure Dryden will know what to search for. He won't reach Earth for a while yet, but we can have a message waiting for him. Let's call the Terran Station in your hometown."

Tilia moved over to the Vid-Comm and pushed a series of buttons. Haven paid attention in case she needed to place a call there in future. When someone appeared on the screen, Tilia smiled.

"Greetings, Myska. I would like to leave a message for my son. He'll be arriving there in about four Earth hours."

The alien called Myska nodded. "I will be happy to deliver a message for you."

"Please tell him to bring back two boxes of romance books for Haven. She said any kind would be fine."

Myska made a note and placed it in an envelope, writing Dryden's name across the front. "Anything else?"

Tilia looked at Haven. "He can bring back anything you'd miss about your world. As long as it can travel approximately eight hours."

"I have a lot of music on my iPhone, but no way to charge it here. I've seen solar chargers on my world that would allow me to charge my phone here. Could he find one for me?" Haven asked. "I know I can't use the phone to call anyone, but I really do love music. I even have some books and movies downloaded to it."

Myska's brow furrowed. "There are solar-powered charges that would allow humans to use Earth devices on our world?"

Haven thought about it a moment. "Anything that

could be charged off a USB plug would be able to charge from the solar charger. So, not all Earth devices would work, but I bet quite a few would. They would just have to preload them with the books, music, and movies before bringing them to your world."

Myska's eyebrows arched. "And not a single bride has mentioned one of these chargers before, that I know of. My parents own one of the Earth shops there. I'll send a box of the chargers to them in case other brides would like one. Thank you!"

Haven smiled as he made a note for both himself and one for Dryden.

"So, with the solar chargers, any of those Earth devices would work, as long as the material was pre-downloaded," Myska clarified. "Which means if I bought some tablets and loaded them with movies, my family could sell them on my world? We used to have a way to download Earth books on a unit similar to our handheld comm units, but the scientist who made the technology possible is no longer on our world, and the devices have stopped working with your Earth e-books."

Haven nodded. "I'm sure they would be really popular. I've heard they aren't reliable for long-term use, but once some are brought here, maybe your inventors could create larger community solar-charging stations around Terran Prime."

"It's possible," Myska said. "Thank you, human. You've been most helpful."

Tilia patted her back. "Haven is incredibly smart. She chose Dryden after all."

Myska smiled. "I'll see that he gets your message when he lands. Enjoy your day!"

Tilia signed off. "I wonder why none of the previous brides have mentioned these solar chargers. Are they not common on Earth? We use solar energy for most everything here, but don't have the proper outlets for your devices. One inventor looked at the possibility of added Earth outlets to some of the homes, but then he discovered there was more than one kind depending on where on Earth the bride came from, and it would be difficult to get the needed amount of supplies here from your world. They tried to design something similar using our materials, but it shorted out the device."

"There are different types of USB-charging cables, but as long as the humans brought one with them that worked for each of their devices, there's no reason the solar-power chargers wouldn't work. I would imagine you would have more brides willing to move to this world if they could bring a bit of Earth with them. They wouldn't have to give up everything they know."

Tilia hugged her. "You are incredibly smart, Haven, and have given my people much to consider. I'm sure Myska is already on a call with the council to discuss the possibilities with them."

"Most devices have Wi-Fi on them. As long as Dryden keeps an account on Earth with a bank card attached to it, he could easily take my iPhone with him and download new material for me. It might not be as easy for all brides, but maybe there could be some sort of service provided for them in future?"

"Myska will give you credit for the idea. I'm sure the council or the inventors will reach out to you before long. Make a note of anything you want to mention to them. Our council will be open to any ideas to make our current brides happier, and those ideas may help other women decide to join the program."

"Eventually all of your males will have mates. What will become of the bride program then?" Haven asked.

"Even with the current generation giving birth to females, there may be males who prefer an Earth bride in future generations. The program may slow down and become more selective, but I don't think it will disappear altogether. And even if Zelthrane-3 no longer uses the program, it can be adapted for other worlds. Already there are negotiations for other races to use the program. We aren't the only one with a lack of females. The Traxian and his companions you met at that party are a prime example."

"I've seen the black-and-white Bentares warriors mingling with your people. Do the warriors ever form bonds with other races?"

"The Bentares live the closest to our world, but in the past other races have formed bonds with Zelthranite warriors. There's a Zorlon-Zelthranite pairing and a Skuriu-Zelthranite pairing that I know of currently. We don't mingle with other races often because we're not on a direct trade route. Only those who go off-world mingle with others. Sometimes we have visitors, but it's not that common."

"How did the Zorlon and the Skuriu come to be here?" Haven asked.

"The Zorlon crashed in the wilds of our planet and our warriors went to investigate. He was badly injured in the crash and was here for months as he healed. The bones in his legs were crushed and the healers worried he wouldn't be an effective warrior, but he proved them wrong. His name is Django. The Zorlon people are seafarers on their world and love the water, but Django formed a bond with one of the warriors who rescued him and decided to remain here."

"What do the Zorlons look like?" Haven asked.

"They're a medium aqua color with almost lime-green hair, to better blend with the waters on their world. They're quite beautiful to look at."

"What about the Skuriu? How did he come to be here?" Haven asked.

"Plivarian was actually freed from a slave market. His partner, Sumari, discovered him when his warship refueled. He'd been captured during a raid by pirates. When Sumari found the proud warrior, he purchased him and offered him freedom once they were off that horrible planet. Plivarian said he owed Sumari a life debt and they became a warrior pair. If you see Plivarian around town, the Skuriu is hard to miss. He's bright, lemon-yellow with small black spots, like one of your wild cats, and has jet-black hair. He's very striking."

"I'd love to meet him sometime."

Tilia smiled and pulled up a list of movies on the Vid-Comm. "As you can see, we don't have many options right now. Only about fifteen. You'll get tired of watching the same ones over and over."

Haven looked over the list and picked one of her childhood favorites. "I love *Labyrinth*. Could we watch that one?"

"Of course."

Tilia showed her how to start the movie, then they got comfortable. It hadn't been on fifteen minutes before a weird sound came from the Vid-Comm and the movie disappeared to be replaced with the councilors. Borgoz looked worried, as did the others. Haven's stomach pitched.

"We have received word of the ship *Excessia*. Tryval asked for a ride from them when shuttle repairs were going to take several days," Borgoz said.

"And where is the *Excessia* now?" Haven asked.

"Raided and blown up. The ship's identifying marks were found in the wreckage. It is believed if there are any survivors they have been taken as slaves." Borgoz looked grim. "I'm sending three ships to the planets closest to the wreckage in hopes of finding your Tryval at one of the slave markets. It's possible he is lost to us."

Haven thought she was going to be ill. She might not have wanted to spend the rest of her life with the alien, but she also didn't wish him harm. He was the father of her child. Her hand shook as she pushed the hair behind her ear.

"You're going to do everything you can to find him, though, right?" Haven asked.

"I'll make sure my warriors scour the galaxy for him."

"Thank you, Chief Councilor," Tilia said. "I know Haven will worry until Tryval is found. Will you keep us updated for any new developments?"

"Of course."

The screen went back to the movie, but Haven didn't much care to see it now. "We need to call Dryden. He needs to know what's going on."

Tilia nodded. "I completely agree. Why don't you go relax in your room and I'll call the Terran Station in Kentucky? I have a feeling Dryden will make a quick return trip."

"No, he should remain there and take care of things on Earth. As much as I would love for him to be here, he has important things to do, and rushing home won't make them find Tryval any faster."

"Very well. I'll convey your wishes to him, but I can't promise he'll abide by them."

Haven kissed Tilia on the cheek before making her way to her room. She stared out the window, looking up at the sky, and wondering where Tryval was, and what was happening to him. What if he'd been killed during the raid and the body had been blown up with the ship? If they couldn't find Tryval, would the council delay her mating with Dryden indefinitely? Not that she only wanted him found in order for her to get married. She was genuinely concerned for him. Being abducted by space pirates didn't sound like much fun.

Staring up at the suns, she said a prayer for Tryval, hoping that wherever he was he was safe and healthy. Then she prayed for the warriors who would be looking for him, wishing them a safe journey and the best of luck in finding the father of her child, along with any other survivors of the *Excessia*. Zelthrane-3 might be a peaceful world, but this served as a reminder that there was ugliness out there, and much closer to home than she'd have liked.

# Chapter Ten

Dryden stood in the middle of the Terran Station and stared at the notes in his hand. He'd only been gone eight hours, but it seemed a lot had happened in such a short time. His mother's message said Haven was adamant he remain on Earth to do whatever was necessary, but at the moment, all he could think was his daughter's biological father was in trouble, and his mate was worried.

He walked to the nearest department and picked up the phone off the counter. Zwyk stared at him with a raised brow, but didn't say anything as he made his call. It was damn near ten o'clock at night, and he hated to call so late. Thankfully, he had his manager's home number memorized. Floyd picked up on the fourth ring, just as Dryden was about to hang up.

"This better be important," Floyd griped. "I was damn near asleep."

"Floyd, it's Dryden."

"Sorry, boss. What can I do for you?"

"I just landed a few minutes ago, but I won't be able to stay the week like I'd planned. I need you to take care of things a little longer for me. When I'm able to come back, we'll discuss a raise for you, along with more responsibilities. If you can handle things for me another week or two, I will make it worth your while."

"I hope everything's okay, boss. It's not like you to take off right after getting here," Floyd said.

"I have a family emergency, but I'm sure everything will be fine. Thank you, Floyd. If you have any questions, please come use the Vid-Comm at the Terran Station and get a message to me."

"Yes, sir," Floyd said.

Dryden hung up and handed the phone back to Zwyk.

"Family emergency? Everything all right with your parents?" Zwyk said.

"Tilia and Harvol are fine. My future mate is worried. The father of her child is in trouble. Who do you have at the station who has a fast ship? We only have shuttles docked on Earth and I need something that can move a lot faster."

Zwyk tapped on his computer. "We have a Sketaline6000 docked that belongs to a Purlane warrior. His crew remained on board, but I'm showing there are ten of them. There's also a Rumigar2000 docked that's owned by a Markisite warrior pair. They reported a crew of six."

Dryden drummed his fingers on the counter. "Have either asked for repairs?"

Zwyk shook his head. "Just fuel."

"The Sketaline6000 is faster and the crew is larger. Do we know why the Purlane warrior is here? Would he still be in the building?" Dryden asked.

"The report says he's here for entertainment purposes. He landed four hours ago and his ship has already been refueled. It's doubtful he remains in the building."

"Who would know of his plans?" Dryden asked.

"You can ask reception. She's human and single. If he's not mated, it's possible he stopped to flirt with her."

"Thank you, Zwyk. I owe you one."

Dryden took off toward the front of the building at a run. Everyone got out of his way as he sped past them, skidding to a halt at reception. The woman blinked up at him. He couldn't remember her name, as she was fairly new.

"There was a Purlane warrior who landed a little while ago," Dryden said. "Do you know where he was going?"

"Which ones are the Purlanes?" she asked, her brow furrowed.

"Bright pink skin and dark turquoise hair. They're usually quite tall."

She smiled brightly. "He stopped by here on his way out. Asked where the best places were in town to meet eligible females. I sent him to the Blue Oyster."

Holy hell. This time of a night on a Friday the place would be packed. On the upside, even in a crowd it shouldn't be too difficult to find someone with hot pink skin. He thanked the receptionist and ran to the parking lot, pulling out his keys as he went. His truck fishtailed as he sped out of the parking lot and drove across town to the strip of bars and clubs. The neon lights of the Blue Oyster glowed in the dark and he cursed at the long-ass line waiting to get inside.

He parked half on the curb and barely remembered to lock the truck before he bolted for the front of the line. A bouncer who looked like he doubled as an MMA heavyweight threw up an arm to block him.

"There's a line," the bouncer said.

"I need to locate someone inside," Dryden said. "It's an emergency. There's a Purlane warrior I was told came here tonight, and I need access to his ship. Someone's life is in danger."

The bouncer sighed and let him inside, whether he bought his story or not. Dryden paused at the edge of the dance floor and scanned the crowd. On the opposite side of the room, he saw the warrior, a head above everyone else in the room. Shoving his way through the gyrating bodies, he fought his way to the warrior's side. The Purlane didn't even notice him, he was so intent on the female in front of him. Dryden stepped between them, careful not to knock the female to the ground.

"I need your help," he screamed over the techno music pounding through the speakers.

The Purlane frowned. "I'm busy."

"Please. I'll pay you. I'll... Hell, I don't have much to offer, but I have an emergency and need you take me somewhere."

The Purlane motioned for Dryden to follow him. They stepped into the back hall, which was much quieter, even if it did smell like piss and smoke.

"My name is Warlyn," he said. "Now what is it you need with my ship?"

"There's a woman I wish to mate on my world, who is pregnant with another's child. The father of that baby has been taken by pirates in a raid. I need to find him and take him to Zelthrane-3."

"And where was he last seen?" Warlyn asked.

"I don't know. The message I received didn't give the

details, only that the ship he was in had been blown up and it was believed pirates had enslaved all those on board."

The Purlane sighed. "Very well. Let's return to the Terran Station and find out more details about that ship."

"What do you want in return?" Dryden asked.

Warlyn looked out toward the dance floor. "A mate. Convince your council to give me time here so that I may find a mate. I don't need access to their bride applicants, just permission to be on Earth. I can take care of the rest."

"Done."

Warlyn followed Dryden to his truck. On the way, the Purlane used the telecommunication device on his wrist to contact his ship and ask them to be prepared to take off within the hour. At the station, Dryden went straight to one of the conference rooms and dialed the council on the Vid-Comm. It was still early enough in the day that someone on his world should be available.

"Dryden," Larimar said when he came on screen. "I take it you've heard the news."

"Yes, Councilman. I would like to join the search for Tryval and this Purlane warrior has agreed to help me. What can you tell us about the situation?"

"The *Excessia* was last reported having docked at Vrylon9 yesterday. It was a few hours after they disembarked that reports of debris in the Falian galaxy near Prilian were reported. Further investigation proved it was the remains of the *Excessia*. There were some... parts among the wreckage, so it's possible Tryval is gone. We didn't want to worry Haven more than necessary."

Dryden felt sick knowing the male might be dead, and all because he'd wanted to see the mother of his child. The pirates needed to be stopped, but they were like Earth's plague of locusts he'd read about. They devoured everything in sight and multiplied almost overnight.

"If Tryval cannot be found, what will happen with Haven? I know the council wanted this meeting between them before agreeing to our mating."

Larimar sighed. "If Tryval is not located within the

month, we will approve your mating. It wouldn't be fair to Haven or you to make you wait indefinitely for a male who may very well be dead. With some luck, survivors will be found who can tell us more."

"Do you know if any of the worlds in the Falian galaxy have already been checked for survivors?" Dryden asked. "I'm assuming warriors were dispatched."

"We sent out three ships. One is checking Prilian, one is checking Krylox, and the third is investigating the space station Jeron5. There's a lot of territory to cover and it could take days if not weeks. Are you sure you want to join the search? We would understand if you wanted to return to Haven's side," Larimar said.

"I can do more for her by locating Tryval. In exchange for his assistance, Warlyn has asked that he receive permission to return to Earth in order to search for a bride. He prefers to find his own instead of using the bride program," Dryden said.

"I will agree to those terms. Make sure any fuel used is charged to the council."

"Thank you," Dryden said.

"Good luck, Dryden. I have a feeling you're going to need it."

Dryden ended the call and went straight to Tyril's office. The Terran seemed surprised to see Dryden.

"I didn't realize you were back on Earth. Did you need help with something?" Tyril asked.

"I'm about to go on a rescue mission. I need some weapons in case there's trouble."

Tyril frowned. "You're not trained as a warrior."

"Even I know how to point and shoot," Dryden said.

"Very well. Thrace is on duty. I'll page him to meet you at security. He'll give you whatever you need."

"Thank you."

As Tyril accessed the intercom system to page Thrace, Dryden and Warlyn walked to the security office at the back of the station. Thrace was waiting for them when they got there.

"It's good to see you, Dryden," Thrace said. "But why are we meeting at security? Is there an issue?"

"I need weapons," he said.

Thrace looked him over before unlocking the security office. He accessed a panel on the far wall and Dryden watched as the wall slid open, exposing the armory. Thrace browsed the selection before selecting two small laser guns and a *glyk*. He handed them to Dryden, then strapped a holster around Dryden's waist.

"Is this problem you're facing on Earth?" Thrace asked.

"No. In the Falian galaxy."

Thrace nodded. "If you should get into trouble and need help, call for me."

Dryden thanked him and followed the Purlane to his ship. The crew gazed at him in curiosity when they boarded, but Warlyn made the introductions, then beckoned for Dryden to follow him to the front of the ship. Warlyn claimed the captain's chair and issued the commands for takeoff, while entering their coordinates into the system.

"We're on a rescue mission," Warlyn told his crew. "Take us to the Falian galaxy. We'll stop at each space station and planet until we find the male we seek. If any of you would prefer not to accept this mission, I can leave you at a station along the way and you can request another ship to pick you up."

There were murmurs amongst the crew, but they stuck with their captain.

Dryden found an empty seat and made himself comfortable. As the ship exited Earth's atmosphere the crew began to buckle.

"We're going to fold space," Warlyn said. "There's a little-known wormhole not far from here that should drop us out near the Falian galaxy."

"So, you're saying the trip that should have taken more than a day will take how long?"

"About five hours, give or take. It will depend on if we run into meteors or pirates. There are two empty crew rooms on board. You should probably get some rest in case we run into trouble and need all hands."

Dryden wasn't certain he could sleep, but he thought it was the Purlane's way of subtly asking him to get out of the way. Now that Warlyn knew he wasn't a warrior, he doubted the Purlane would want him underfoot. The crew on board would have been trained in combat. Dryden escaped to the crew quarters and stared out the porthole. Time seemed to stretch forever, and with each passing minute, his unease grew. By the time they reached the Falian galaxy and the first space station, Dryden had decided this was a bad idea. It was like... what was that Earth saying? Finding a needle in a haystack? He hadn't understood the expression until he'd actually seen a haystack.

"We've reached Seeton Prime," Warlyn said over the comm. "Meet me in the airlock."

Dryden made sure his weapons were ready before making his way to the airlock. Warlyn and two other warriors were waiting for him.

"While you were in crew quarters," Warlyn said, "I contacted your council and asked for a picture of the Traxian. My crew has also seen the image and we're ready to help you. Stay close to one of us at all times. I don't wish to send you back to your mate in several pieces, or have to explain that you were captured by pirates."

Dryden would have been insulted, but he knew the warrior had a point.

He followed them into the airlock and waited for the outer doors to open. When they stepped off the ship, the stench of unwashed bodies assailed Dryden's nose. He followed the Purlanes into the market place, where locals hocked their wares and pirates paraded flesh in front of eager buyers. It disgusted him that people were so eager to embrace slavery, and he wished there was a way to wipe it out completely.

They paused at each slaver's station and examined all the bodies being auctioned to the highest bidder. They saw two Traxians at the fourth station and Dryden paused. Neither were Tryval, but it was possible they'd been on the

*Excessia.* While he wasn't a wealthy man, he knew the council would pay him back for any monies spent in an effort to locate the hybrid.

The first Traxian was brought out, a ferocious glare on his face as he studied the crowd. As the bidding began, Dryden listened to the numbers go higher and higher. It slowed when the bid reached 10,000 marks.

Dryden lifted a hand. "Eleven thousand marks."

The slaver pointed to him. "Eleven thousand to the Zelthranite."

There were murmurs in the crowd, but no one bid against him. After a moment, the slaver banged a gavel.

"Sold to the Zelthranite in the back. You may either come pay for your purchase now, or wait until you're finished bidding. I have another Traxian who may interest you."

Dryden nodded and folded his arms, trying to look like he belonged amongst the bloodthirsty lot. When the second Traxian came up for bid, Dryden won and went to pay for both males. They looked confused, as everyone knew it wasn't customary for a Zelthranite to purchase slaves. He gave them a subtle signal he hoped they would understand. The last thing he needed was them asking questions out in the open.

They stopped at several more slave stations, but didn't find more Traxians. They had already been sold or were never there. Dryden and the Traxians followed the Purlanes back to the ship, and once they were on board he finally breathed a sigh of relief.

"I know you're confused," Dryden told the Traxians. "I purchased you with the intent of freeing you, but first I must ask if you were on board the *Excessia.*"

"Yes," the first one answered. "We were captured along with most of the crew and several passengers."

"Do you know if Tryval was among those captured?" Dryden asked.

They shared a long look, and Dryden hoped they weren't about to share bad news. The last thing he wanted to tell Haven was that the father of her child was dead. He waited for them to speak.

"Tryval fought against the pirates when they boarded us. He's young, but he's skilled with most weapons," the first Traxian said. "That last we saw of him, he was battling with two pirates near the airlock as they paraded the rest of us onto a ship. If he was captured, he wasn't held with us in the cells below ship."

That didn't sound promising. Dryden stepped back as the Purlanes showed the Traxians where they could stay and fetched clean clothes for them. Dryden followed Warlyn to the front of the ship with two other crew members.

"The fact they didn't see him doesn't mean he's dead," Warlyn said. "It's possible they kept him in nicer quarters if he fought well, in hopes of keeping him in good shape."

Dryden's stomach sank. "The gladiator games on Luresta?"

He supposed it could be worse. Tryval could have been taken to the Karvikian death rings. No one came out of there alive, and there would be no way to get Tryval out. The Karvikians would not accept payment and would likely capture all of them and force them to fight to the death. Once you entered the ring, there was no escape. Even if you lived to fight another day, eventually your luck would run out.

Warlyn nodded. "We need to contact at least one other ship and go check out Luresta. If your Traxian is still alive, I bet that's where he's been taken."

Dryden nodded and gave him the names of the three fastest Zelthranite ships, in hopes those were the ones used for the search. When the captains answered, he was relieved that he'd guessed correctly. Once everyone had been given the information, they all changed course and headed for Luresta. Dryden just hoped they could make it onto the planet without getting caught and kept for the games. He was far smaller than the others, but the Purlanes would make excellent gladiators.

It only took two hours to reach Luresta and then they waited while the other ships docked as well. Everyone met on board the Purlane ship and left together, in hopes of finding Tryval. Their group was larger and they garnered more attention than Dryden liked, but no one seemed too anxious to mess with them.

"You asked the other ships to meet us so we'd be too formidable for anyone to fuck with us, didn't you?" Dryden asked.

Warlyn smiled. "Of course. We're completely safe as long as we stay together."

Plivarian and Sumari had joined Kijaro's ship, and Dryden was thankful for their presence. Everyone within five galaxies knew you didn't mess with the duo. They were known for gutting you first and asking questions later. While they may have been just the types the leaders of the games were looking for, he trusted Warlyn when the alien said no one would mess with them.

The coliseum loomed before them and they made their way to the dais where the leaders sat and surveyed the games. The roar of the crowd filled his ears as they made their way up the winding staircase. Four leaders sat on bronzed thrones wearing flowing white clothes.

"What is the meaning of this interruption?" the eldest looking one asked.

"We've come seeking a friend," Warlyn said. "A Traxian who was captured by pirates a few days ago. His name is Tryval."

The leaders murmured amongst themselves before the only female smiled in their direction. "We are familiar with Tryval. What is it you want with him?"

"We wish to purchase his freedom," Dryden said. "He's important to my mate and she would be devastated if anything happened to him."

The female focused her attention on Dryden. "And why should we care if your mate is upset?"

"Please. She's expecting and I don't want her to feel more stress than necessary. It would mean a lot to us if Tryval could leave Luresta and come back to Zelthrane-3 with me. I'm sure you have cages full of gladiators. What's one less?" Dryden asked.

The leaders murmured amongst themselves again.

"Very well," another said. "You may have Tryval if your Skuriu and Zelthranite warrior pair remain here for three days to compete in our games. No money will be necessary. All we care about is having a good show."

Plivarian and Sumari looked at one another before agreeing.

"You don't have to do this," Dryden told them. "There must be another way."

Plivarian smiled. "Nothing will happen to us. We'll kill our opponents slow enough to keep the crowd entertained and in three days we'll return home. I'm sure Kijaro will wait for us."

Kijaro nodded. "I'll ask for accommodations for me and the crew. I believe it would be best if the two of you remained out of the cells."

The female stood. "Only the best rooms for our guests. I'll have a contract drawn up and once all parties have signed it, I will release Tryval into your care. A copy of the document will be given to you in good faith. If we break the terms of the agreement, your council can send ships to retrieve your warriors."

"We won't break the terms," the eldest said.

The leaders ordered food and drink for everyone as a contract was created in order to free Tryval. The ship captains reviewed the terms, conferred with the council via handheld Vid-Comms, and signed away three days of combat for the warrior pair in exchange for Tryval's freedom. When the Traxian hybrid was brought to them, the relief in his eyes was apparent.

Before the leaders could make any other requests of them, they took their leave, with Kijaro and his crew remaining behind. Instead of boarding with Warlyn, Dryden and Tryval decided to travel back to Zelthrane-3 with Keylon. The ship was cramped, but anything was better than what the hybrid had been through over the last several days.

Dryden contacted the council once the ship had lifted

from the planet and jetted out of the atmosphere. As Luresta became smaller and smaller, the unease in the pit of his stomach lessened. The council appeared on the Vid-Comm screen.

"We have Tryval," Dryden said. "The games leaders kept their word and Privlarian and Sumari stayed behind to fight. I'd like to request that something special be done for Warlyn and his crew. If it weren't for them, we never would have found Tryval."

"I'm sure we can come up with something," Borgoz said. "Warlyn requested time on Earth for himself to seek a mate, but perhaps his crew would like to be included. I'll also see that some Earth credits are waiting for them at whichever Terran Station they choose."

"Thank you," Dryden said. "We're on our way home."

"You should call your mate. She's been worried, especially since learning you went after Tryval," Borgoz said.

"I'll call her next. Thank you for your support in the search for Tryval."

Borgoz nodded his head and the Vid-Comm went dark. Dryden dialed his parents' home and waited for someone to answer, but the call was never picked up. He wasn't worried because he knew how much his mother loved to shop, especially if she was worried about something, and she'd have taken Haven with her. The trip home wouldn't end soon enough. He longed to hold Haven in his arms again.

Stretching out on one of the beds in the crew room he was using, he folded his hands behind his head and allowed himself to relax for the first time since receiving the messages from home. It had been a full day, but it had ended well, and that was all that mattered.

Now the only thing he had to worry about was Tryval stealing his mate. Not that he thought Haven wanted anyone else, but it wouldn't stop the hybrid from trying. Facing possible death changed a male, or so he'd heard. What if it had made Tryval more determined than ever to mate with Haven? It wouldn't be long before he found out. Dryden just hoped for the outcome he wanted most -- Haven by his side for the rest of their lives.

## Chapter Eleven

Haven was still sniffling long after Dryden had come home. When she'd gotten the news that he was joining the search for Tryval, she'd worried that he too would be taken by pirates. It had ended well, for everyone except Keylon's crew. She worried about Plivarian and Sumari, but had been assured they were the best fighters within five galaxies. She hoped they would return home soon.

The council had put Tryval up in The Towers in a small apartment similar to Dryden's. From what she understood, he was allowed to stay as long as he wanted. Haven worried a little about how he would take the news that she had no intention of mating with him. Even though Tryval and Dryden had been on Zelthrane-3 for hours, she had yet to see him. She could only imagine how traumatic it had been to be captured by pirates and sold. He'd probably thought he would spend the rest of his life in the gladiator games, however long that might have been.

Dryden pulled her into his arms and kissed her softly. "Everything is going to be fine. Tryval seems to have survived the ordeal just fine and is probably resting. I doubt he slept much the last few days. He'll come see you before the end of the day."

"You're awfully calm about the entire thing," Haven said. "What if he tries to claim the baby and me?"

"Then we'll tell him you're both mine and he can have visitation rights. I'm sure he's a reasonable sort. While looking death in the face changes people, he seemed to have retained some of the humor we saw in the Vid-Comm chat you had with him."

Haven nodded.

"Why don't you go get ready and I'll call him and let him know we're going out for a while. Maybe he'll join us along the way. How does lunch at the Earth diner sound?" Dryden asked.

"I'd like that," Haven said.

She'd already showered for the morning, but she went to brush out her hair, added a little lip gloss, and changed into one of the summery dresses Tilia had purchased for her. All of her maternity clothes from Earth were for winter, but there was no such thing as winter on Zelthrane-3. The coldest it got was seventy degrees, and Haven was loving every minute of it.

She slipped on a pair of sandals Tilia had purchased as well, and met Dryden by the front door. She'd assumed Tilia would be with them, but her future mother-in-law was absent. Haven looked around, but didn't see nor hear Tilia anywhere in the house.

"Mom isn't coming?" she asked.

"She had some errands to run and said she would let us have some fun on our own. I'm supposed to invite Tryval for dinner when we see him. I was able to reach him on the Vid-Comm and he said he would meet us at the diner in an hour."

"Where are we going until then?" Haven asked.

"There's a new store that opened this morning. I believe you call them pet shops. One of the brides was lamenting over the fact she hadn't brought her pet with her, so the council agreed to opening a pet shop. Normally, our pets are raised in someone's home and later they find a loving family. I think this is an experiment that may not stick around for long."

"Are they just Zelthranite pets or did they bring in some from Earth?" she asked.

"I believe it's a mixture. Some from my world, some from yours. In future, they may carry pets from other galaxies. It will depend on what they eat and how easy it is to stock their food supplies."

Haven nodded. "I'm anxious to see the shop. I've always loved animals, but I was never allowed to have a pet."

"Then maybe we should get one."

"Or maybe we should wait until after the baby is born." She smiled. "I've heard babies are a lot of work."

"Whatever you want to do. We can just look today. Maybe they'll let us play with some of the animals."

Haven took his hand and they headed toward the main strip where most of the human-like shops were located. The pet shop was easy to spot, as there was a line out the door and halfway down the block. Dryden was going to move on to something else, but Haven really wanted to see the animals.

"Do you have a zoo here?" she asked.

"You mean those parks where wild animals are kept behind bars or glass?" he asked.

Haven nodded.

"Not exactly. We have Fendrix, who is like a zoologist from your world. He takes care of any wild animals that are injured and in the case of some of our rarer species, he keeps breeding pairs in captivity long enough for them to safely have offspring, and then he sets them free again. He rotates the breeders out so the herds stay diverse and aren't populated by only one set of parents."

"Can people visit the area where he keeps the animals?" Haven asked.

"I suppose. I don't believe anyone has ever asked before. Remind me after the baby is born and I'll call to ask. His home was on the outskirts of town and it would be a far walk. He doesn't allow vehicles near his home for fear of frightening the creatures."

"That's understandable. I look forward to possibly seeing them." She smoothed a hand over her belly. "After this one is born."

"Have you thought of a name for the baby?" Dryden asked.

"I had thought about giving her an Earth name," Haven said. "Would you be all right with that?"

Dryden pressed a kiss to her cheek. "You can name her whatever you want. I just want a healthy daughter."

"So, you'd be all right with me naming her Amelia?"

"Amelia?" he asked.

"My favorite woman in history was Amelia Earhart. She was brave and adventuresome. She was an aviator who flew solo across the Atlantic Ocean. She tried to fly around the world, but her plane vanished somewhere over the Pacific Ocean in 1937. There's still a lot of speculation over what happened to her."

"She sounds fascinating," Dryden said. "Perhaps our library has a book about her, and if not, we could request that one be added."

"I'd like that. There are a lot of great women in the history of my world. I'm sure some of the brides would enjoy learning more about them."

"I'll mention it to the librarian and he can put the request in with the council. The council funds our library so any purchases have to be approved by them. Barstoc is allowed to accept donations if anyone wants to bring books from Earth and give them to the library, but that doesn't happen often."

"Well, I'm greedy and want a bookshelf of my very own at home, but maybe on some of your trips you could pick up some new books for the library. Could we afford to do something like that? You mentioned travelling to Earth once a month to check on the shop. Maybe a handful of books each month wouldn't cost too much," Haven said.

"I will be happy to donate books to the library, after we have your own bookshelf stocked. I noticed my father has already started building one."

Haven smiled. "He started it the moment Tilia said I wanted one. When we found out you'd joined the search for Tryval, I told him there was no rush on building it, but he insisted."

"Sounds like my father."

The line moved forward and they were now within a few people of being able to go inside. Haven hadn't lied when she told Dryden she'd always wanted a pet. Her mother had claimed that animals were nasty and dirty and didn't want them on her furniture. In all fairness to her mother, their furniture had all been light colors and would have gotten dirty easily, but who didn't love animals? She hadn't even been allowed a hamster that stayed in a cage because she was told they were nasty rodents that stunk.

As the line moved again, Haven could finally see inside. She heard birds chirping and could see glassed-in areas where kittens and puppies romped and played. There were no lizards or fish, but she saw some unusual animals she knew had to have come from Zelthrane-3. One was blue with fuzzy fur and two sets of eyes, with small antennae on its head. A black tongue flicked out to lick its snout and she heard it make a chirping sound.

"What's that?" she asked, pointing to it.

"Vardril. They're quite amusing and move quickly. You have to watch them though because they like to stay close to their owners and can trip you."

"What about that?" she asked, pointing to a green-and-orange creature with fur and feathers. Its yellow eyes seemed to glow and it had a beak instead of a nose.

"Santor. They tend to nip and can be very loud, but they make loyal pets," Dryden said.

When they were motioned inside, Haven didn't know where to look first. She checked out every pet in the store, stopping to play with all but the Santor. It snapped its beak at her several times, so she kept her distance. The Vardril was adorable and ran around its glass cage, following her with its eyes. She came back to it, reaching inside to scratch the creature on the back of its neck.

"He likes you," Dryden said. "Are you sure you wish to wait for a pet? If we bring him home before the baby arrives, he should bond with her and be quite protective."

"You think I should get a pet so close to my due date?"

Dryden shrugged. "I will leave it up to you, but if you want the Vardril, I will be happy to purchase one for you. I can assure you my parents won't mind having a pet in the house. I had a Cartoo when I was younger."

"What's a Cartoo?" she asked.

"They're bright pink and dark purple. Their fur is really soft and they make purring noises like your Earth cats. They are hard to find though as they aren't from our world. There was a breeder here when I was little, but he has since moved away and took his Cartoo mated pairs with him. I believe they come from a distant galaxy, but they enjoy eating the fruits we have here on Zelthrane-3."

Haven smoothed her hand over the Vardril's fur and it rumbled at her while closing its eyes in contentment. Dryden reached into the cage and lifted it out, handing it to her. It had six legs that kicked at the air until Haven wrapped her arms around it and held it close.

Sistin came over, a smile on his face. "Did you find a pet you want to take home?"

"I like this one," Haven said, as the Vardril licked her cheek.

"I see that he likes you too. He's only a few months old and won't get much bigger. I'll get some food for you. Will you need anything else for your pet? The room through the archway has bedding, bowls, toys, treats. I tried to stock a little bit of everything, but hope to add more if the shop is a success," Sistin said.

Haven smiled. "We had to wait a while to get in here. I think you can call it a success. I'll take a water dish, food dish, and something for him to sleep on. What types of toys would he like?"

Sistin rubbed his chin. "We've never had toys for pets on our world, but he might like those squeaky dog toys I supplied for the puppies. His teeth are sharp, but I don't believe they will tear up the toys too quickly."

"Then I'll take two toys as well," Haven said then looked at Dryden. "That's all right, isn't it?"

"Of course. Sistin, we're meeting someone for lunch and I don't want Haven to overdo it too much. Would you hold the Vardril and his new things until we're finished? We can come back and pick him up in about an hour or two."

Sistin nodded. "I will move him to a cage in the back so no one else will try to buy him."

Haven reluctantly let go of her pet, but not before kissing it on the head. Then Dryden led her out of the pet shop and toward the human diner. Tryval was already seated at a booth waiting for them. He smiled when he saw Haven, but to her, it didn't look like the smile reached his eyes.

She slid into the booth across from him, with Dryden scooting in next to her.

"You look beautiful, Haven," Tryval said. "The pregnancy is going well?"

"I haven't really had any problems. My blood pressure was a little elevated on Earth, but it seems fine now. Dryden and his family have been taking excellent care of me."

"Good." Tryval glanced at Dryden. "I have heard that you wish to claim Haven as your mate."

"Yes. I tried to convince her on Earth to become mine, before we discovered you were the father of her child."

"You were willing to accept a baby as your own without even knowing what race it might be?" Tryval asked.

"If Haven were my mate, her baby would be mine, regardless of the color of her skin or how many eyes she had. A child is a gift, regardless of race." She felt Dryden's thigh clench under her palm. "Do you have a problem with me raising the child as my own?"

Tryval smiled a little sadly. "No. I'm actually happy to hear that you would watch over her like a true father would. My time with the pirates has shown me that perhaps my daughter would be better off with someone a little less adventuresome than myself."

"I don't understand," Haven said. "Anyone could have been attacked by pirates. It was just bad luck. Are you saying you're giving up your rights to your daughter because you were captured?"

"I'm saying that fighting the pirates was exhilarating. Yes, I was captured and I could have spent months or years stuck in the gladiator games. But it made me realize that my skills would be better put to use trying to fight piracy than sitting at home being a father," Tryval said. "I took out six pirates on my own before they captured me. Just think of the good I could do!"

Haven's brow furrowed. "Honestly, I had thought I would have to fight harder to keep custody of our daughter. You seemed so excited about the baby."

"I am. Truly. She's a gift that I will treasure always. I just think it would be better if I treasure her from a distance and send gifts every now and then." Tryval smiled. "I've already made arrangements for the *Pertvada 5* to pick me up in the morning. I'm joining their crew for the foreseeable future."

"So, I have your blessing to marry Dryden?" Haven asked.

"Yes. You would have been a wonderful mate and I'm sure you will be an excellent mother. My daughter is in good hands with both of you," Tryval said.

"The baby is due in about four weeks," Dryden said. "Do you think you could make arrangements to be here for the birth? I know it would mean a lot to Haven to have you here."

Haven's eyes misted with tears at how thoughtful Dryden was. "Please say you'll be here."

Tryval smiled, a genuine one this time. "I will return in three weeks and stay until my daughter is born. I'm sure as she gets older she will notice that she's different from either of you, but you don't have to call me her father. Dryden will be her true father."

"There's no reason she can't have two," Haven said.

Tryval nodded and the discussion came to a close. They ordered their food and enjoyed light conversation until it was time to part ways. Haven felt better, knowing that Tryval wouldn't try to take her daughter away, but she had to admit that she would worry about him while he was gone. Chasing after pirates and slavers seemed like a dangerous job. For her daughter's sake, she hoped Tryval was able to keep his promise and return in a few weeks.

After lunch, Dryden took Haven back to the pet shop where they collected her Vardril and went home. Tilia and Harvol were both waiting for them. If Dryden's parents were surprised they were bringing home a pet, they didn't show it. Tilia helped Haven find the perfect place for the Vardril's new belongings and they laughed as he scampered around the house checking out everything.

"You seem happier," Tilia said as Haven curled up on the padded bench to watch a movie, the Vardril in her lap.

"Now that I know we have nothing to fear from Tryval, my mind is at ease, even if I am worried about his safety."

Tilia patted her hand. "He'll be fine. I've heard of the *Pertvada 5* and they have a formidable crew. He will be joining a dedicated group of males who watch each other's backs. I'm sure he will return here safely for Amelia's birth."

Dryden walked over to the Vid-Comm and stopped the movie. After punching in some buttons, the chief councilor appeared on the screen.

"Pardon the interruption, Chief Councilor, but after meeting with Tryval, I would like to formally request a mating between myself and Haven."

Borgoz smiled. "I heard from Tryval after he met with the two of you. I'm aware he's given his blessing, and as I knew you wanted Haven as your mate, I already started the paperwork. It's merely a formality at this point. Consider yourselves married."

Haven set the Vardril aside and joined Dryden in front of the Vid-Comm. "Just like that? All that waiting and worrying, and all it took was one meeting with Tryval and now we're mated?"

"I apologize for making you wait, Haven. We needed to be certain that Tryval would accept your pairing with Dryden. Now that he's met with both of you, he feels confident you will give his daughter a good life, and you apparently made it clear you expect him to visit," Borgoz said. "I've assured him that he's welcome on our world whenever he wishes to stop by and see his daughter. And should he later decide he'd like to use the bride program to find a mate, it will be open to him."

"Thank you, Chief Councilor," Dryden said.

"You're welcome, Dryden. I'm glad you were able to find happiness. If there's anything further we can do for you, please let the council know."

Borgoz ended the call and Dryden pulled Haven into his arms, kissing her softly.

Haven leaned in close and whispered in his ear. "We have a few hours until dinner. Should we celebrate our mating?"

Dryden smiled down at her. "I'm sure my parents would understand if we were to retire to the bedroom for a while."

Tilia picked up the Vardril and started heading toward the kitchen. "Harvol and I will feed your pet and take him out into the garden for a while. We'll understand if we don't see you until dinner."

Haven's cheeks flushed, knowing that her mother-in-law knew exactly what they were about to do in the bedroom. Dryden took her hand and led her back to their room, closing the door behind them. Dryden quickly removed his clothes and impatiently pulled at Haven's. She smiled at his eagerness and let him tumble her to the bed. His nose trailed along her neck as his tongue flicked out to taste her, making her shiver in the best of ways.

Dryden kissed the hollow of her throat as his hands cupped her breasts. The mounds plumped against his palms and Haven arched into his touch. His lips traced a path down the valley of her breasts before closing over a rosy peak. Her nipple hardened further against his tongue as he laved and nipped at it.

"Dryden," she murmured, her hands reaching for him.

His teeth grazed the sensitive tip before moving to the other nipple, giving it just as much attention. Her pussy was slick with need and she widened her thighs, cradling his body. The head of his cock brushed against her wet folds and Haven's hands slid down to his ass, trying to pull him inside of her.

"Impatient, aren't we?" he asked, kissing her breast before claiming her lips.

"It feels like it's been forever since we were last together."

"Not that long, Haven, but I understand. Every second that your body isn't beneath mine is agony. I want you more than I've ever wanted anyone before."

"I love you," she said softly.

Dryden stilled and met her gaze. "I love you too. I have almost since the moment we met."

"Then make love to me. Make me yours. We're mated now. Consider this our honeymoon."

He smiled. "I've heard of that Earth custom. I can't think of anything I'd like better than days of keeping you wrapped in my arms, my cock filling your sweet pussy."

With a flex of his hips, he entered her. Haven cried out as pleasure zinged through her body, her nails biting into his skin. Dryden took her slow and deep, every thrust making her whimper and beg for more. Her legs wrapped around his waist, holding him, urging him to move faster, harder. His strokes quickened, every thrust making her toes curl.

Dryden claimed her lips in a searing kiss that fanned the flames of her desire, making her climb higher and higher, until she shattered. She cried out, calling his name, as her pussy clenched on his cock. He surged into her again, muffling his cries against her neck, as he spilled himself inside of her. Sticky and covered in a light layer of sweat, they lay joined together as they tried to catch their breath.

"Every time with you is just as amazing as the first time," Dryden said. "I hope it's always like that."

"It will be because we belong together."

"Let's get cleaned up and visit with everyone until it's time for dinner. Then I plan to wear you out all night long once we retire for the evening."

Haven smiled and kissed him. "I can't think of anything I'd like more."

# Epilogue

Haven gritted her teeth and bore down as Amelia fought her way into the world. She'd been in labor for hours already and worried that the baby would never leave her body. As the contraction eased, she breathed and tried to focus on the men on either side of her. Dryden held her hand, taking as much abuse as she wanted to heap on him. Tryval stood on her other side, looking both worried and excited.

"Almost there, Haven," Vyrex said. "Just one more good push and her head should clear."

Haven gripped Dryden's hand tighter, noticing his wince as his fingers turned a darker shape of purple. She bore down for all she was worth, not even stopping to take a breath until she heard Vyrex's cry of delight.

"The head is through. Another push and the shoulders will be out. After that, it's easy," Vyrex said.

Haven wasn't certain how much she believed any part of this birth would be easy, but she did as the doctor said. When her baby was finally held in the doctor's hand and was screaming for all she was worth, Haven finally relaxed into the pillows stacked behind her.

"Is she healthy?" Haven asked.

"Amelia seems perfect," Vyrex said. "I'm going to have Zaylon clean her up while I deliver your afterbirth, and then you can hold her."

Haven watched as the doctor's assistant carried her baby out of the room. By the time Amelia returned, swathed in a diaper and a cute pink shirt Tilia had sent to the clinic with Dryden, Haven was so tired she could barely keep her eyes open. She reached for her baby and held her close, looking at her beautiful daughter.

"She's stunning," Tryval said. "You did an amazing job, Haven. Thank you for my daughter."

Dryden pressed a kiss to her sweaty brow. "I would have to concur with Tryval. She's gorgeous and you were amazing."

"Would her daddies like to hold her?" Haven asked, fighting a wave of fatigue. "I think I need a nap."

"If she gets hungry, we'll give her a bottle," Vyrex said. "You mentioned you didn't want to breastfeed so Dryden would be able to bond with her during feedings as well. The formula we have will give her just as many vitamins as your breastmilk would have. She won't lack for anything."

"Thank you," Haven murmured as she fought to keep her eyes open.

She watched sleepily as Dryden and Tryval took turns holding her and even feeding her. At some point, Tilia and Harvol entered the room, cooing over Amelia. Haven would doze for a minute, then jolt to alertness long enough to take in everything going on around her before dozing off again. She felt a kiss on her cheek and opened her eyes to see Dryden looking at her with so much love in his eyes.

"The doctor said your body needs to rest before we try for another one," he said.

"Can we hold off a year before having another one? That was exhausting."

Dryden smiled. "I'm afraid birth control doesn't work very well with my kind. But we can abstain for as long as you like."

Her eyes shot open wide and she jerked upright in bed. "Abstain? As in no sex at all?"

"Well, Vyrex seemed to think you'd need about six weeks to recover. Any time after that will be up to you."

"If birth control doesn't work, does that mean we're going to have twenty children?" she asked.

Dryden laughed. "Once you're certain you don't want anymore, one of us can get sterilized. I've been told the procedure is fairly painless with a quick recovery time. But we can discuss it more at a later time. Right now, I think Amelia wants to see her mommy."

Haven reached for her daughter, cuddling her close.

"I love you, Amelia, and I will be the best mom ever. You have two wonderful daddies and grandparents who already adore you. Just you wait and see. You'll have everyone falling at your feet in no time. And one day, some special boy will come along and steal your heart, just like Dryden stole mine."

"Let's hold off on the heart stealing," Tryval said. "Any male who wishes to claim her has to go through me."

"And me," Dryden said.

"And us," Tilia and Harvol said at the same time.

"You have a room full of protectors," Haven told her daughter. "And unlike your mommy, you will never go a day without feeling loved. I promise to do everything right, no matter what it takes."

Dryden kissed her softly before brushing a finger down Amelia's cheek. Haven didn't know how she'd been lucky enough to break down in Dryden's parking lot, but she would be forever grateful. Without him, she would only be partially living her life. He'd given her so much, but most importantly, he'd given her the one thing she'd wanted most in her life -- a family.

# Abbie and the Alien Official
## (Intergalactic Brides 14)
### Jessica Coulter Smith

Abbie prides herself on being a strong, independent woman. Having been on her own since she was seventeen, she's taken care of herself, doing whatever was necessary to keep a roof over her head and food on the table. But when she loses her job, her car, and her apartment, she begins to think maybe it's time to admit defeat and ask for a little help. Even if it means becoming the bride of an alien and living on another world.

Councilman Larimar has only wanted one thing since he reached adulthood. A mate. But his duties have kept him from seeking a wife, no matter how many tempting humans enter the bride program. They're all attractive, and certainly any of them would do. Then he meets Abbie. The moment he sees her, touches her soft skin, he knows he wants her more than his next breath.

Despite Larimar's reservations when it comes to Abbie, he finds he can't keep his hands to himself, and the only place he wants her is under his roof and in his bed. When she accidentally ends up pregnant, he knows he has to do whatever is necessary to make her his, and not just because she's carrying his child. Even if it means studying human mating customs, or inviting her crazy mother to live with them.

One way or another, Abbie will be his.

# Chapter One

Abbie Carson pushed back her bangs as she surveyed the items on the curb. Or maybe she should say, what was left of the items on the curb. She grabbed one of the boxes, dumping out the crap inside, and began filling it with her treasured possessions and some clothes. Her heart ached for the loss of some of her mementos, but at least her favorite music box hadn't been snatched yet, nor her stuffed bear she'd had since she was little. She dug a little deeper and found her family photo album, shoving it into the box. When she'd gathered as much as she could, she hefted the box into her arms and began walking.

She'd applied for the bride program at the Terran Station, but that had been weeks ago and she hadn't heard back. Now that she was homeless, jobless, and carless she didn't have much of a choice but to go to the station and ask about the status of her application, in hopes she'd maybe slipped through the cracks or they'd been unsuccessful in reaching her. It was a long walk to the station and her feet and back began to ache before she was even halfway there.

Dropping her box to the sidewalk, she collapsed beside it, pressing her forehead to her bent knees. A shiver raked her body, the air only slightly warmer in February than it had been at Christmas. She'd hoped for an early spring, but it seemed she wasn't going to get her wish. A limo pulled to a stop in front her, her jaw dropping a little when a hunky Terran stepped out.

He crouched in front of her, hands clasped and a look of concern on his face.

"Do you need help?" he asked.

"I was on my way to the Terran Station, but I had to stop and rest."

A frown marred his face. "You were walking?"

"I don't have transportation and I didn't have cash for a taxi or a bus pass."

He glanced at the box next to her, reaching out to shift a few things aside. His expression turned grim when he saw the clothes bunched up with her keepsakes. Her cheeks burned with embarrassment, even though she knew she'd have to explain things when she got to the station. She'd been standing on her own two feet since she was seventeen, and it hurt to know that she'd failed now.

"Come on," he said, standing and holding out a hand. "I'll give you a ride. My name is Bancheck."

"Thank you," Abbie said, rising from the sidewalk and dusting off her jeans. Bancheck picked up her box and placed it into the limo before helping her inside.

"Do you live on Earth full-time?" Abbie asked, thinking he was rather sexy.

"Yes. Is there a reason you were going to the Terran Station?"

"I applied to the bride program a few weeks ago and never heard back. I was hoping I might have been accepted."

"There's a shuttle leaving this afternoon. I'm going to assume by the contents of your box that you need to be on it," he said. "Are you in trouble?"

"Not the legal kind. But I find myself without a home or transportation, and I lost my job. The bride program is my only hope of staying out of the homeless shelter. I knew this was coming, but I seemed to be powerless to stop it. I've been turned down for every job I applied to, and now I don't know what else to do."

"When we reach the Terran Station, I'll take you to Zlyer. He oversees the Terran Station here. If anyone can figure out why you weren't contacted, he would be the one. Even if you'd been denied, you should have received something. It's possible they're just backlogged if there have been a lot of applicants."

She bit her lip. "If I was denied or mine hasn't been processed yet, do you think you could help me get to the homeless shelter? It's on the other side of town and I don't think I can walk that far today."

"I will see to your accommodations if you are unable to take the shuttle this afternoon."

She nodded, feeling a little relieved. At least she wouldn't be stuck at the station with no way to get to a bed for the night. Things could be worse. At least she was healthy. The limo pulled to a stop and she peered through the tinted glass at the Terran Station. Bancheck slid out of the car, then held a hand out to her. Abbie let him pull her from the car, and then he reached inside for her box, cradling it in his arms.

"Follow me," he said as he headed for the main entrance.

A perky receptionist smiled as they entered the station.

"Good morning, Doctor Bancheck."

Doctor? She gave him the side eye as they moved through the station. Toward the back was a corridor that looked like it was filled with offices. He knocked on the door at the end of the hall.

"Enter," a voice called out.

Bancheck pushed open the door and motioned for Abbie to enter. He followed her into the office and shut the door behind them, setting her box aside. Abbie stood nervously, shifting from foot to foot as she glanced around the space. The Terran behind the desk looked imposing.

"Zlyer, I found this young woman on the side of the road. She was on her way here to check on the status of an application she filed weeks ago for the bride program. I thought you could look into it for her," Bancheck said.

Zlyer stared at her. "And what is your name?"

"Abbie Carson," she said softly.

"Miss Carson, we always contact our applicants. Are you certain you didn't receive anything?"

"As of yesterday's mail run, I hadn't received anything, nor do I have any missed calls from here," she said. "I was hoping maybe I'd just slipped through the cracks."

Zlyer's nose flared and his lips thinned, but he turned toward his computer and began tapping on the keys. His expression went from annoyed to perplexed.

"Miss Carson, you were approved for the program a week ago. Are you certain you didn't receive a letter?" he asked.

"I'm certain."

"You'll need to undergo a physical before we can send you off world. Bancheck, how soon could that be taken care of?" Zlyer asked.

"Now," Bancheck said. "Assuming everything is fine with the physical, could she leave on this afternoon's shuttle?"

Zlyer nodded. "Absolutely. Miss Carson, will you have time to gather your belongings and return before the flight leaves at noon today?"

Abbie looked at her box.

"She already has belongings with her," Bancheck said.

Zlyer glanced at the box then at her. "You'll want something cooler to wear on our world, Miss Carson. The weather is quite a bit warmer there. Do you have access to spring or summer type clothes?"

"Not anymore," she said.

Zlyer slid a pad and pen across the desk. "Write down your clothing sizes. I'll see that you have a few outfits to get you started, but you can purchase items on our world when we get there. Anything bought will be debited from your mate's account once you choose one."

"It hardly seems fair he has to pay for me before we're even married," Abbie said. "And what happens if no one wants me?"

Zlyer gave her a kind smile. "Someone will want you. There are countless males on my world who are looking for mates. You're going there with a handful of potential brides. The four of you will be in high demand."

Abbie wasn't convinced, but he knew his world better than she did.

"Does everyone there speak English?" she asked.

"You'll be given a translator behind your ear and a chip in your wrist will allow you to pay for things. We can handle that here if the results of the physical show you're capable of handling the trip and bearing children," Zlyer said.

"Then I guess I'm ready for the physical."

Bancheck picked up her box and motioned for her to follow him. She cast a glance over her shoulder at Zlyer, who had already turned back to his computer. They went through several twists and turns before a medical clinic came into view. He used a key to unlock the door and she followed him back to an exam room.

He set her box on a chair and patted the exam table.

"I don't have to strip down or anything?" Abbie asked.

Bancheck smiled. "Normally I would have you change, but since we're in a bit of a rush, I think we'll skip that part. I'm going to do some bio scans and take some blood samples. I'll listen to your heart and lungs, and if everything checks out, I'll knock you out long enough for the implants. The surgery is done with a laser so there will be some pain, but not as much as if I were to cut you open with a scalpel and stitch you back together."

Abbie followed all of Bancheck's instructions as he moved through each step of the exam. When he was satisfied that she was in perfect health and could easily bear children, he pulled out the implants she would need to survive on his world. Abbie eyed the syringe of blue goo that he held in his hand as he motioned for her arm.

"This will put you to sleep long enough for the procedures. When you wake up, it will be close to time to board the shuttle."

Abbie nodded and held her arm out to him. The needle slid in and a rush of cool liquid made her shiver. Before she could ask if it was normal, her eyes began to slide closed. The next time she woke, there was a slight pain behind her right ear and in her right wrist. A look at her arm showed a pink line where he'd cut her open to insert the implant.

"You have thirty minutes until the shuttle boards," Bancheck said. "The clothes Zlyer ordered are here and I placed the bag with your box. We peeked at your shoes while you were asleep to get your shoe size. He wanted to make sure you had more than one pair."

Their kindness touched her. "Thank you."

"The council is covering the cost of your new things since it's our fault you weren't prepared for this trip. A miscommunication happened somewhere and because of that, you were without your things or a home. We can never apologize enough. You should have known before today that you were approved."

"It's fine," she assured him. "I mean, it's not fine I was stressed over losing my home and belongings, but it's all worked out in the end, right?"

He smiled. "Yes. I wish you luck in finding a mate, Abbie Carson. You will make someone a fine bride."

"Where do I go to wait for the shuttle?"

"There's a coffee shop near the shuttle waiting area. You can get something to drink and a snack while you wait. There will be an announcement before the shuttle boards. I'll make sure your things are delivered if you want to leave them here."

She nodded. "I really appreciate everything you've done for me today."

"Any of the males here would have done the same."

She paused a moment before leaning up to kiss his cheek. He seemed surprised, but smiled at her warmly. When they reached the front of the clinic, two Terrans stood waiting.

"This is Vordro and Krelor. They'll show you the way," Bancheck said.

On impulse, Abbie gave him a hug and then followed the Terrans through the station. They gave her a friendly wave and wandered off once she was safely delivered to the coffee shop. As she stood in line, she wondered if they accepted human money, particularly American currency, since that's all she had. She'd never purchased anything at the Terran Station before, even though she'd come here twice before. Once to ask about the bride program and the second time to apply.

It was her turn to approach the cute Terran behind the counter.

"Um, do you take American money?" Abbie asked.

He smiled. "Of course. Are you here for the bride program?"

She nodded.

"Then it's on the house today. Pick anything you'd like, but I'd caution you to keep the meal light. The flight to my world makes some people sick."

"Maybe a muffin and a small mocha?"

He nodded. "Would you like the muffin warmed?"

"Please."

He flashed her another smile as his gaze skimmed over her. "I'm Jarok. If you need anything before you board the shuttle, don't hesitate to come get me. You're the cutest of the brides I've seen today."

Her cheeks warmed. "Thank you."

He handed her a mocha and used tongs to pull a muffin from the glassed-in cabinet, sticking it in a paper bag, then warming it for her. When he handed her the treat, he winked and she couldn't help but giggle. She wondered if all the Terrans were as good-looking as the ones who had helped her today.

Taking her muffin and drink to a nearby table, she sat and tried not to eat the snack in one bite. It had been dinner the last time she'd eaten and her stomach rumbled its displeasure. She didn't know how long the flight would be, but hopefully it wouldn't be long before she had a chance to eat a full meal. The minutes seemed to fly by and before long an announcement was made that the shuttle was now boarding. Abbie saw three other women not too far away approaching what looked like a regular flight gate. Throwing away her trash, she went to get in line.

A human woman manning the gate held out her hand. "Letter."

"I don't have one. My letter never arrived, but Zlyer said I could leave on this flight."

"Name?"

"Abbie Carson."

The woman unclipped a radio from her belt and pressed the button. "Can I please get confirmation that a bride by the name of Abbie Carson is supposed to leave on this flight?"

There was static and a moment later, Abbie heard Zlyer

respond.

"She's cleared," he said.

The woman smiled at her. "I hope you have a nice flight, and good luck selecting a mate."

Abbie thanked her and walked down the corridor to the waiting shuttle. The front row had one seat open and she claimed it. The other three women were giggling and talking together, but Abbie took the time to inspect her surroundings. She didn't see anyone else on the flight and wondered if the four of them were it.

Another sexy Terran boarded and smiled at them. "My name is Sentir and I'll be your captain today. The trip takes around eight of your Earth hours and you'll be asleep for almost the entire journey. Any questions?"

One of the women giggled. "Are you searching for a bride?"

He winked at her. "I'm one of many. I'm sure there will be a crowd waiting to meet you when you arrive. Enjoy the flight, ladies."

She giggled again, and Abbie fought the urge to roll her eyes. The captain paused in front of Abbie.

"I'm glad you're joining us on this flight. Again, we're really sorry about the miscommunication."

"It worked out in the end," she said.

He nodded and went into the cockpit. Or was it called something else on a shuttle? Abbie braced herself as the shuttle began to move, slowly at first, and then they were rocketing through Earth's atmosphere. A mask dropped down in front of her and she pressed it over her nose, breathing deep. She cast one final glance out of the shuttle window and then her eyes began to close. There was a fleeting worry that she'd made a mistake in coming, but soon her thoughts turned to sweet dreams.

When she next opened her eyes, the other brides were also waking and they were landing on another world. A look out the window brought a smile to her lips. Three suns were rising in the sky, casting the world in pinks and oranges. It was a stunning sight. Sentir made an appearance and opened the shuttle door.

"We're here, ladies. Be careful disembarking," he said.

Abbie followed the others, hanging to the back as she looked at her surroundings. Crowds of men had gathered and it made her a little nervous. When she'd heard that brides were in high demand, she hadn't realized how desperate they were for wives. Were the crowds going to follow her everywhere? No one had explained exactly how the bride program worked, only how to sign up for it. She'd hoped there would be someone on this end to guide her through the process.

A warm hand at her lower back made her jolt. She gave an apologetic glance at Sentir.

"I'm going to take the women to their apartments, but I think someone wishes to speak with you," Sentir said.

"Who?" she asked, scanning the crowd.

A Terran who easily stood over six feet began making his way toward them. His long hair flowed down his back, and the black leather hugging his body showcased an impressive set of muscles. There was a flutter in her stomach and this time it wasn't from nerves. He was handsome, by far the best-looking Terran she'd seen so far, and none of them were ugly.

The alien stopped in front of her. "Miss Abbie Carson?"

She nodded.

"I'm Councilman Larimar. I wanted to meet with you in person to apologize for what happened. Zlyer is looking into the matter. So far, it seems your letter was the only one that didn't go out. Whoever is responsible will be punished."

"Oh, I… I don't think it's necessary to punish anyone. I mean, I made it here, right?" she said.

He smiled at her kindly. "You're not furious?"

"No. I'm just grateful I was able to come now."

Sentir moved away. "I'll have your belongings sent to your apartment. Councilman, will you escort her? I need to get the other ladies settled."

"Of course," Larimar said.

Abbie looked up at him, feeling dainty and delicate in

his presence. "I'm staying in an apartment?"

"A small one, but yes. It's our hope you won't be there long. The sooner each bride finds a mate, the sooner we can bring more to our world. We try not to have more than six here at a time. In the early days, we brought more here, and even had some humans working here. But it didn't work out as planned."

He reached for her, placing his hand gently at her lower back and guiding her along. She fell into step beside him and tried not to gawk at everyone and everything along the way. There was a large pool area that looked promising, except she didn't have a swimsuit. She'd always loved to swim but hadn't had much opportunity for it.

When they approached a large building, easily fifteen stories high, she paused. "I'm staying there?"

"Yes. Is there a problem?"

"No, I just didn't know what to expect. The building is quite large."

"The top two floors are suites that are occupied by Terrans. Some of the apartments on the lower floors are also occupied by Terrans, but none will bother you. If anyone approaches you, it will be to ask you to join them for an outing or a meal. There's no cheating on this world so if anyone asks you out, they're single and looking for a mate."

She bit her lip. "How exactly does everything work? The program wasn't explained to me in detail, except for how to apply and the general idea of what happens afterward."

"I can see we may have to make some more adjustments to the program. Not only was your letter lost, but no one explained anything to you. It was brave of you to come all this way without knowing what to expect."

Abbie shrugged.

"The implant in your wrist will let you in and out of your apartment and the building. We encourage you to share meals with prospective mates, but should you dine alone, your implant will cover the cost of your meal. If there's any shopping you'd like to do or need to do, please do not hesitate to use the implant to pay for them. Your mate would want you to be taken care of."

"What happens if I don't find one?" she asked softly. "What if no one wants me?"

He stopped and reached out to tip her chin up so that she looked him in the eye. "Someone is going to want you, Abbie. I have a feeling you won't be single for long. Our males can be pushy when they find something they want, but don't go into a mating half-heartedly. If you don't think you can grow to love him, then tell him no and keep searching. We aren't just interested in the happiness of our males, but in yours as well."

"Are you one of the single males seeking a mate?" she asked, her cheeks burning.

"I think I'm a little too old for you, but yes, I'm seeking a mate. I have been since the bride program started."

She pulled away from him and stared at the door in front of them. "Is this my apartment?"

"It is."

She waved her wrist across the door lock and the door popped open. She stepped inside and saw her box and bag of clothes had already been delivered. Turning to face the councilman, she felt a twinge. He'd claimed to be too old for her, but she wanted to keep talking to him. Moving closer, she reached out and lightly placed her hand on his chest.

"Thank you for bringing me to my quarters." She licked her lips. "And thank you for explaining things to me. Would it be too presumptuous of me to ask to maybe have dinner or breakfast with you sometime? You're the only one I know here other than our captain."

There was something shimmering in his eyes she couldn't quite define, but gave a regal nod of his head. "Our world is a bit warmer than your Earth is right now. Why don't you shower and change, do whatever women need to do before an outing, and I'll return in an hour to pick you up for breakfast."

She smiled up at him. "I'll be ready."

He backed away and waited for her to close the door.

She leaned her forehead against it, willing her heart to slow its fast pace. If she'd known Terrans were *that* hot, she'd have applied to the program long ago. Now she just needed to convince him that she wasn't too young for him. Because if he thought she was going to back away he was sadly mistaken. Abbie had never backed down from a challenge, and this was the greatest one of all.

## Chapter Two

Larimar sat in the park not far from The Tower, and Abbie. The moment he'd seen her, his heart had raced out of control. He'd never seen a more beautiful woman, but after reviewing her file, he knew she was too young for him. There were twelve years between them. He'd seen the look in her eye and knew his attraction wasn't one-sided, but once she met some of the younger males she'd move on. But for once, he wished someone would look at him and only him like that.

Brides had come and gone over the years the program had been in place, but never once had he been tempted to claim one for himself. Until now. It had been insane to agree to breakfast with her, but he'd never wanted anything more. He'd enjoy a meal with her and then he'd step aside so the younger males could have a chance with her. And if his gut churned at the thought of another male touching her, then that was his problem.

Councilor Borgoz eased onto the bench next to him. "It isn't like you to sit in the park and glare at the grass."

"I'm meeting Abbie Carson for breakfast. She seemed insistent."

Borgoz smiled. "Perhaps you've finally found your mate."

Larimar snorted. "She's twelve years younger than me. The best thing I could do for her is let someone else claim her."

Borgoz raised an eyebrow. "So, you're saying I should have stood aside and let someone else claim Charlotte? Or have you forgotten there's more than twenty years between us?"

Larimar felt his cheeks flush. "The age difference doesn't pose a problem?"

Borgoz smiled. "Does my Charlotte seem to be lacking for anything, or my daughter? They make my life better, Larimar. It's up to you if you wish to claim Abbie, but don't step aside because you're older than she is."

"We haven't even shared a meal together, or really sat

down to talk. I met her for only a few minutes."

"Sometimes you just know," Borgoz said. "Most of our mated males knew within minutes of meeting their brides that they were meant to be together. If that's how you feel, if you truly want her, then don't back down. Go after what you want. But if you aren't certain, if you have doubts, then maybe you need to think long and hard before you pursue her. I doubt she'll be lacking for company."

Larimar nodded. The Chief Councilor had given him much to think about. He'd spend the morning meal with Abbie and see how he felt at the end. Maybe after spending more time with her he'd know if he'd just been struck dumb by her beauty or if what he was feeling was real. Or at least the start of something real. He'd heard the human phrase love at first sight, but he wasn't certain he believed in such a thing, despite what Borgoz said.

The minutes ticked by and when it was almost time to pick up Abbie, he left the park and made his way back to the Tower. His heart rate picked up the closer he got to Abbie and he couldn't deny that he was anxious to see her again. There was a crowd of single males lingering outside of the building when he arrived and one of the brides was out front cooing at them. Something about the woman made him clench his teeth and he tried to hurry past her.

He felt a finger slide down his biceps as he walked by and he paused, turning to face her. "Did you just touch me?"

"Why don't you take me out somewhere?" she said, eyes big and her lower lip protruding in what he assumed was supposed to be a sexy pout.

"Sorry, but I already have plans."

She smiled and rubbed his bicep, making him pull away.

"Better than taking me out?" she asked.

"Yes."

Anger flashed in her eyes as he turned from her. Now that her hands had been on him, Larimar felt like he needed a shower. He went up to Abbie's apartment, a scowl on his face as he knocked on her door. Her eyes went wide when she opened it and saw his fierce expression.

"I hope that isn't because of me," she said.

"No." He tried to soften his expression. "Sorry, I had a bit of trouble downstairs."

Her lips twitched. "Would it have anything to do with a persistent blonde?"

He nodded.

"She started by harassing anyone who had the misfortune of being on this floor and made her way down to the lobby. I think she likes preening in front of the crowd down there."

"She doesn't understand the word no."

"Women like her generally don't. You should have heard her flirting with the captain of the shuttle. Maybe she recognized you as someone important. I doubt she'll settle for anyone considered common."

Larimar shrugged. "Everyone on my world has a job that is important in its own way. She'll soon learn that, or she'll go home without a mate. I almost feel sorry for anyone who ends up with her. I don't know how she slipped through the application process. We try not to bring women here who act like her."

"Sounds like the application might need a bit of tweaking."

"Perhaps. Are you ready to go eat?"

Abbie nodded. She stepped out into the hall, letting the apartment door close and lock behind her. Her hand crept around Larimar's biceps as he led her down to the lobby. The blonde was still out front, playing to the crowd. When she saw Abbie clinging to his arm, her eyes narrowed and her lips thinned, but she quickly smiled and faced her audience once more. He didn't know her name offhand, but he'd have to check the files and let the other council members know they might have a problem.

"Do you want to try Terran food or would you prefer the human café that opened a few years ago?" he asked.

"I think I'd like to try Terran food. If I'm going to live here, it makes sense that I get accustomed to everything. It's not like I could eat all of my meals at the human café."

He was pleased with her answer, but there were few options for the morning meal at Terran restaurants, as most spent the morning meal at home. If he'd been better prepared, he could have taken her to his home and asked his cook to prepare something. Each of the council members had someone to manage their household and a cook. It was one of the perks of his position, giving them more time to devote to their people.

He took her to a restaurant he'd heard was really good, but he hadn't eaten there before. He seldom had meals out, unless someone delivered something to council when their meetings ran over. When they entered the establishment, Abbie looked at everything in wonder. Larimar selected a table near the window, holding her chair out for her.

A screen mounted on the wall showed the menu options, but they were all in his language, and since everything was made with Terran ingredients, he was at a loss as to how to help her order. A frown marred his face as he stared at the screen.

"Larimar, I trust you to select something for me. The only food on Earth I've tried and didn't like was sushi, which is raw fish." Abbie smiled at him. "Anything will be fine, I promise. I'm not a picky eater."

He felt a little more confident as he studied the menu, then pressed the selections for their orders and held his wrist over the screen to pay.

"Did you just pay for the meal?" she asked as he pulled his arm back to his side.

"Yes. Is it not customary on Earth to pay for meals?"

"We pay after we eat."

His brow furrowed. "But the restaurant has to prepare the food beforehand, so they use their ingredients whether you like the meal or not. Should you not pay first?"

"It does make sense to do that, I suppose, but I've eaten at quite a few places on Earth where my order had to be cancelled because after an hour I still hadn't even gotten a drink. Service probably is better here."

He nodded. "Our meal will be out as soon as it's cooked, and I ordered juice for both of us to drink. I think you'll like it. It's sweet but not too sweet."

"You introduced yourself as Councilman Larimar. I'm not certain I understand what a councilman does here on Terran."

"First, if you're going to be a mate, you might as well know we aren't really called Terrans. This world, before the agreement with Earth, was called Zelthrane-3 and my people are called Zelthranites. It was believed negotiations with Earth would go easier if we changed our name. After studying Earth and its history, the council decided calling ourselves Terrans would make things go more smoothly with Earth. We were worried your people might be frightened of us."

"Zelthranites?" she asked. "I think I can remember that. But now that things are established with Earth, why haven't you gone back to being Zelthranites?"

"Our Chief Councilor has been discussing the issue with Earth's leaders, and they will decide how best to handle the situation. If it's believed your people will become frightened or angry, then we will remain Terrans to Earth's people, and Zelthranites here on our world and in dealings with other races."

"Sounds very confusing," Abbie said. "But I can understand why you'd be cautious. Frightened humans can be deadly."

Larimar nodded. "People tend to either react to fear by cowering or by attacking. We weren't certain how humans would react."

"Probably a mixture of both. But the ones who would want to attack are the ones you need to watch closely. I've found a lot of my people don't play fair."

"You asked what a councilman does here. I'm not certain what the position warrants on Earth, but here a council was formed to create laws for our people, to hand out justice, and to govern the people day to day. I suppose we're a lot like your America's president and congress combined."

She shrugged and gave him a small smile. "I hate to admit it, but I've never been very smart when it comes to the government. I do my part every election year, but I sometimes feel like I'm just choosing the lesser of two evils. I don't trust any of the politicians in my country, but then most of them are all a bunch of crooks and liars."

His eyes narrowed a little. "You don't trust politicians?"

"Not the ones where I come from. They accept bribes, get away with crimes, and lie just to get elected. They hardly ever deliver on what they've promised the people."

"I understand. It isn't the position you dislike, but the corrupt people who run for office."

"Exactly." She smiled. "But I can already tell you aren't like them."

"What makes you say that?"

"There's kindness, compassion, and honesty in your eyes."

"All that?" he asked with a smile.

Her cheeks flushed.

"What is it you did on your world?" he asked. The information had been in her application, but he wanted to keep her talking.

"Well, I did work in human resources for a small company, but they let me go a few weeks ago. Just after I applied to the program actually. So, when I came here this morning, I was jobless, and thanks to not having money for rent, I was homeless too. I brought very few possessions with me, and the few clothes I have are courtesy of your council. But then, you already knew that, didn't you?"

"Yes, I received the report this morning. But I like to hear you talk. Your voice is soft."

Her cheeks burned a brighter shade of pink.

Their drinks and food arrived, the server dropping everything off at the table and scurrying off to hand out another order. Abbie stared at the plate and used the utensils to move things around, as she inspected each item.

"Try something," he said.

She lifted a bite and took a nibble, and her eyes widened in surprise. She smiled widely as she began taking bites in earnest. He liked that she seemed to enjoy his world's cuisine and couldn't wait to introduce her to more new things, if she continued to see him. Just because he liked her, and they seemed to get along, didn't mean she would accept him as a mate. It would be foolish to get ahead of himself.

"What is there to do here for fun?" she asked.

"We have downloaded some of your Earth movies and can watch them on the Vid-Comm units that are in every home, including your apartment. There's also a community swimming pool, which was added after we studied Earth, as well as a park. I'm afraid my people are a hardworking lot and what time we don't spend working, we spend at home talking with our families."

"Do you have a family you spend time with?" she asked.

"My father was killed in battle and my mother died a year later of a broken heart. I have a younger brother who is a warrior. He spends most of his time off-world, but he's here right now. When he's home, we meet and have dinner a few times a week, but we both stay busy."

"Is he mated?"

He stopped chewing. Was she asking because she might be interested in his brother? Or was she just being curious?

"He's not mated," Larimar said.

"So, neither of you have children?"

"No, but we both hope to someday. All Zelthranite males wish for families of their own. We're a very family-oriented society."

"I've always wanted a family of my own." She smiled wistfully.

"Did you have a big family when you were growing up?"

"I had an alcoholic father who would just as soon beat us as speak to us, and a mother who cowered around him.

She never lifted a finger to protect us, but I can't blame her. She was just as scared of him as we were."

"But you had siblings?" he asked.

"Three. When I was seventeen, I left home and never looked back. I've been on my own ever since."

"So you had to grow up quickly," he said. "I'm sorry you didn't have a nice childhood. Zelthranite parents are strict, but we know from the beginning how much we're loved. It's sad that you never had that."

"It's why I want a family. I want to make sure my children have the kind of life I didn't have. I want them to know they're loved and wanted, and I will never raise my hand to any of them."

"I'm sure you'll be a wonderful mother," Larimar said, envisioning her with a rounded stomach, pregnant with his child.

"What should we do after breakfast?" she asked.

His eyebrows lifted. "You want to do something else with me?"

Her cheeks flushed again. "I'm sorry. It was presumptuous of me to think you wouldn't be busy today. And I know there are three other brides who arrived with me. I shouldn't monopolize your time."

"Why don't I take you shopping when we leave here?" he suggested softly. "You'll need more clothes than what Zlyer had purchased for you on Earth. You can buy one those swimsuit things and maybe we can go to the pool. Do you like to swim?"

"I never learned," she admitted. "But I like floating around the shallow end. One of the apartments I lived in had a pool and I would do that on my days off."

"You're so fair you'll likely burn under our suns. We have lotions that will protect you, so we'll need some of that too."

"Sunscreen?" she asked.

"It's the Zelthranite version. What you sell on Earth wouldn't protect you from our three suns. Even though the weather remains mild compared to some of the summers on

Earth and other worlds, the rays can burn you quickly."

"Then we definitely need some of that," she said.

They pushed their empty plates aside and Larimar stood, holding his hand out to help her up. He placed a hand at her lower back, guiding her through the restaurant and back outside. The shops weren't far, as everything in the vicinity of the Tower could be reached on foot. Only those living on the outer edges of town, or in other towns, used vitras to get around. Most people in Terran Prime walked.

"This city is known as Terran Prime," he told her. "Once it was called Solaris."

"Why keep the name Terran Prime if you tell the brides your true name?"

"It's better that way. We only inform those who will likely mate with someone. Typically, you wouldn't have been told until after the mating, but I have no doubt you'll find someone. Those who are returned to Earth are better to still believe we are Terrans, until your government decides to say otherwise."

She nodded.

"We have several shops that cater to human females and carry a wide selection of clothes and shoes for you. I'll take you to the most popular one and then we'll head over to the shop that carries swimsuits and those float things you mentioned."

Abbie gripped his biceps again and fell into step beside him as they made their way to the first shop. It felt right having her hand resting there, and even though he towered over her by more than a foot, he had little doubt they would fit together perfectly if he ever had the privilege of holding her. Just the thought of taking her into his arms made his heart skip a beat. Being with Abbie made him feel young and carefree, something he would have to watch. As much as he'd love to spend every second of every day with her, he still had responsibilities to attend to.

Larimar pushed open the shop door and ushered her inside. The place was small from what he'd heard, by Earth standards anyway, but it had a little bit of everything she would need. He watched as she perused the shelves, almost seeming hesitant to pick anything out to try on. When she put back the fifth item in a row, he decided to find out exactly why she wasn't buying anything. The last sundress she'd put back would have looked fetching on her.

He moved in closer and peered over her shoulder, catching her staring at the price tag with a frown on her face. He knew there was no way she could interpret the tag, as everything was set for the money on his world. Was she worried it was too costly? And if so, had he not explained well enough that she wouldn't incur the cost of whatever she purchased?

"Why aren't you buying anything?" he asked.

"I'm sure whatever I have already is sufficient."

"Abbie," he said softly. "Your mate will cover the cost of whatever you wish to purchase. He would gladly accept the burden of a shopping trip or three, if it made you happy to have new things."

"But what if it's too expensive? I can't tell how much anything costs. I don't want to put him in debt before we're even married."

He smiled, smoothing the lip she was worrying with her teeth. "Abbie, buy whatever you want. I will personally pay for anything you purchase today, and I can afford quite a bit. My money is used for little since I don't have a mate or children, and I'm very seldom off-world because of my responsibilities. I work and do little else. Let me spoil you a little today."

"But..."

He placed a finger over her lips. "No buts. Buy anything you want."

She nodded and faced the racks of clothes again. Larimar moved back and watched her shop, but she still was a little hesitant. After she'd picked up a handful of things, she started off to the dressing room, but he drew her to a halt.

"Abbie, you have four outfits in your hand, and I know only three were purchased for you on Earth. You need more clothes. And please don't argue. Let me do this for you."

"Why would you want to buy me clothes when we barely know one another?"

"Because you need them and I like taking care of you."

She bit her lip and faced the racks again. After selecting a few more things, she turned to him and he pointed to the clothes once more. When he was satisfied she had enough items, he gave a nod for her to go try her clothes on. He'd never thought it would be so much trouble to get a female to spend money. But he supposed with her upbringing, she probably hadn't had much growing up, and she'd earned everything she'd had since then. It would probably be hard for her to let someone take care of her, but he was determined to do it.

After paying for the items that fit, and encouraging her to pick out some shoes, he arranged for her items to be delivered to her apartment before steering her further down the string of shops in search of a swimsuit. His blood heated at the thought of her in very little clothing, and he hoped he didn't embarrass himself. His swim trunks were at home, and he planned to take her there after her next purchase. Not only for her to change and him as well, but in hopes she might see his home and decide he would be a good mate.

He had no idea what Earth women sought in a life partner, but he wanted to be whatever it was Abbie needed and wanted.

# Chapter Three

Abbie stared in awe at the house in front of her. They'd passed many along the way, but none were as grand as this one. A much larger one stood by itself up on a hill, and she was thankful they hadn't gone there. It looked imposing and almost cold, but the one in front of her exuded warmth with the splashes of color across the lawn as random flowers clustered here and there.

Larimar led her up to the door, her bags from the swim shop clutched in his hand. He waved a wrist over the door lock and it popped open. She didn't know what type of stone the floor was made of, but she liked the pale blue color. Following him deeper into the house, she took everything in, not wanting to miss anything. He led her up a winding staircase to a second level that had six doors, three on either side of the stairs.

He went to the left and she followed along behind. When he reached the second door, he pushed it open and motioned for her to enter. It was a spacious room with an attached bathroom. The bedding looking to be some sort of silk or satin equivalent, and she itched to run her fingers across it to see if it felt as soft as it looked. The room was done in pale grays and blues, the walls almost a silvery color. It was a soothing room, and one she wouldn't mind spending more time in, if she were here for any reason other than to just change her clothes.

"This is one of my guest rooms," Larimar said. "Make yourself at home. I won't be long and I'll meet you at the top of the stairs."

She nodded, still looking around the room. When the door clicked shut, she opened one of the sacks he'd left behind. She'd never been daring before in her swimwear, but she'd wanted to make a lasting impression on the alien hottie, so she'd chosen a green two-piece that would accent her curves. It didn't take her long to change and apply the sun lotion, but she wasn't ready to leave the room just yet.

Walking over to the bed, she reached out and brushed her fingers over the bedding, sighing at the divine texture.

What would it be like to sleep on something so soft, so decadent? Curiosity got the better of her and she made her way into the attached bathroom and explored for a moment. For a guest room, the space was rather large, and it made her wonder just how big his bedroom and bathroom were. And then she wondered if she'd ever get close enough to him to actually see them. He seemed open and welcoming, but it didn't mean he saw her as mate-worthy.

Abbie grabbed her float and beach towel out of the other bag and made her way to the staircase. Larimar was leaning against the railing, staring out the window that covered most of the wall above his front door. He smiled warmly when he saw her, his gaze caressing her from head to toe.

She did a little perusing herself, taking in the broad expanse of his bare chest and smiling a little when she saw his black and gray swim trunks. The man looked fine, very fine, and she couldn't believe that he was still single. Surely, the other brides had noticed how attractive he was? Abbie found it hard to believe that no one had shown him any attention since the program had started. She'd still been in high school when the program had launched, but she remembered hearing about it on the news.

"You look beautiful," he murmured. "Are you ready to have some fun?"

"Promise you won't let me drown?"

"You have my word that you will be completely safe. We don't have a lifeguard on duty, but perhaps we should create such a position since we're getting so many human mates on our world. I wonder how many others can't swim?"

"I've met several people on my world who can't. If your children play there too, it wouldn't hurt to have an extra set of eyes watching over the water," Abbie said. "What if the parents were busy talking and a child fell in?"

"I'll bring it up at the next council meeting."

"I think I'm as prepared as I can be, but maybe I should have bought a cover-up to wear on the way to the pool. I don't want people staring at me."

"Abbie, if they stare, it's because you're a beautiful woman. Plenty of people go to the pool just in their swimwear."

She nodded and reached up to wrap her hand around his arm. The first time she'd done it had been more of way to touch him in an acceptable manner. Now she just liked how it felt to hold onto him. She felt protected standing by his side. Even though they'd just met, she had no doubt that if anything happened, he would protect her at all costs. There was something about the way he looked at her, almost a longing in his gaze, as if she were everything he'd always wanted.

Abbie knew exactly how he felt because he was certainly what she'd been searching for her entire life. And it didn't have anything to do with his position on this world, or his large home. He made her feel safe, cherished, just by standing in his presence. She valued that far more than riches.

Larimar guided her out of the house and back toward the part of town where the community pool lay. The area was fenced off with something that looked like black wrought iron, but she doubted that's what it was. Not unless they'd brought it here from her world. It was possible they'd done exactly that, especially if they were trying to mimic the pools on Earth. The lounge chairs lining the length of the pool on both sides definitely looked like they came from Earth. She wondered just how many things they'd brought from her world in an effort to make the brides feel more at home.

Larimar removed the towel from his shoulder and tossed it onto a lounger before taking hers and setting it on the chair next to his. He reached out a hand to take the float from her and he motioned for her to have a seat.

"It won't take me long to blow this up."

"Have lots of experience with it, do you?" she asked with a smile.

He shrugged. "A lot of the kids are fond of them and I

try to help out when I'm here. I have more air than the females do, so it makes sense for me to blow the toys up."

Her cheeks warmed. Great. Now he was going to think of her as a child since it seemed only Zelthranite kids used the pool floats. Maybe learning to swim would be a good idea, and she wondered if they taught lessons. Might be another thing to mention to Larimar for him to discuss with his council. Their children had to learn to swim somehow, right? So why not include any adults who didn't know how?

He stopped puffing air into the float. "What's that look for?"

"Do your children take swim lessons?"

"No. We're born with the ability to swim. At least, the fully Terran children have been. The new generation seems to be hit and miss. Some know how, and others cling to their parents in the water, as if they're frightened."

She bit her lip. "What if you offered swim lessons and not just for children but for anyone who can't swim?"

"Do you want to learn how?" he asked softly.

"Yes, but maybe not when the pool is so crowded. It will be embarrassing enough already. I'm sure I'm going to be awkward and uncoordinated."

"If you truly wish to learn, I will be happy to teach you."

"I'd like that, just not today."

He nodded and went back to blowing up her float. When he was finished, he held out a hand, helping her off the lounger. Tingles raced up her arm when he didn't release her right away. Instead, he held onto her as they descended the steps into the shallow end of the pool. He held the float still as she climbed onto it, stretching out on her back.

Larimar gripped the side of the float and began moving toward the deep end. When he was chest deep, he stopped and folded his arms, leaning them on the float next to her. Abbie rolled to her side, not caring if she tanned unevenly. Larimar reached out to run his finger across her cheek and she wanted to lean into that touch.

"Why did you apply to the bride program?" he asked.

"You read my application, right?"

"Honestly, I skimmed over it. The council is supposed to read every application that meets our requirements, but I admit I didn't pay as close attention as I should have."

"Maybe if someone had paid closer attention, the blonde wouldn't have passed and been flown here."

He winced. "You may have a point. Perhaps we've gotten too lax. The last thing we want or need are troublemakers."

"To answer your question, the idea of finding my forever guy was too appealing to pass up. I knew there was a chance I wouldn't meet anyone, but better to try and fail than not try at all."

"Because your acceptance was overlooked, you're owed some money. All accepted brides receive compensation for giving the program a try."

She thought about it a moment. "If I return to my world without a mate, I will accept the money. But if I make my home here, I won't need it. I'd rather have the money donated to a charity on Earth if I remain on Zelthrane-3."

His eyebrows lifted and there was curiosity in his gaze. "What charity would you wish to donate the money to?"

"Maybe an abused women's shelter. My mom was never brave enough to go to one, but I know there was one not too far away. I think funding a place like that would be a worthy cause."

"I'll make a note of it in your file," Larimar said.

"What are you looking for in a mate?" she asked.

"Someone honest with a sweet disposition." He caressed her cheek again. "Someone beautiful on the inside as well as outside. That's an Earth saying, isn't it?"

"It is." She smiled.

"And what do you seek in a mate?"

"Someone who makes me feel protected and safe. Someone who makes me feel like I'm important to them, and maybe someday that I'm loved." Her lips twisted a little. "I've never been loved before, but I've read countless romance novels and it sounds really nice."

"I think you would be easy to love, so once you find your mate, I'm sure that love will follow."

"Do you think you'll ever fall in love with someone?" she asked.

His gaze burned as he stared down at her. "Yes, I do."

She warmed from the inside out, hoping that he meant her. Even though they'd only spent a day together, she felt closer to him than she'd ever felt with anyone before. She knew he couldn't spend all day every day with her, but she hoped they'd have more outings together. Abbie already craved his company, which scared her a little, and thrilled her at the same time. She felt like she might have finally found her match, and hoped he felt the same way.

They spent the next hour lounging in and around the pool, growing closer. When her skin started turning a little too pink, Larimar suggested they head back to his house to shower and change -- separately. Abbie was a little disappointed to end their time at the pool because she was certain it meant an end to their day of fun. She didn't know what tomorrow would bring, or when she'd get to see Larimar again. Was she supposed to date other men when he was the one she really wanted?

The walk back to his house was quiet and when they entered the large home, he drew her to a halt. She figured he was about to ask her to leave and her throat grew tight. They'd missed lunch and she knew dinner wasn't far off. She didn't want to share the meal with another male after having such a great time with Larimar, nor did she want to eat alone.

"After you've showered and changed, come back down here. I'll ask my cook to make an early dinner for us. If you'd like to stay a while longer, we could watch a movie on the Vid-comm." He reached up and tucked her hair behind her ear. "I'm not ready to say goodbye just yet."

Her heart soared and she smiled broadly. "I'd like that."

Larimar took her hand and they walked up the staircase side by side. When they reached the guest room door, he released her and went further down the hall to his room. She tried to steal a peek inside, but he was too quick to shut the door. Abbie sighed and went into the guest room, gathering the clothes she'd taken off earlier and carried them into the adjoining bathroom. With a perplexed look, she opened the door to what she assumed was a shower, except she wasn't certain how to work it. It took a bit of experimenting before the water came on.

Abbie stripped out of her swimsuit and got under the spray. The water was scented, making her wonder if it was a special thing for their showers or if the water out of the sink tap would smell the same. She didn't see any shampoo or shower gel, so she just let the water cleanse her. When she felt clean enough, she got out and located a towel to dry herself, then she got dressed.

Larimar's door was closed when she exited the guest room, her bag with her swimsuit clutched in her hand. Abbie went downstairs in search of her handsome host. She set the bag down at the base of the stairs and wandered the first floor. She found Larimar in the living room, or what she assumed was the living room. There was a large screen on the wall and he was scrolling through a list of titles. He'd changed into another pair of leather pants, but had left his black vest off and was bare from the waist up. It was a sight she could get used to seeing on a regular basis. When Larimar tapped on one of the titles, a movie pulled up that she hadn't seen before.

Instead of a couch, he had what looked like a padded bench pressed against a wall with pillows tossed along the back. It didn't look very comfortable, but she settled on the seat. Larimar joined her a minute later. He sat close enough she could feel the heat of his body, and as the movie played, she found herself getting closer to him. By the time the hero and heroine had shared their first kiss, she was pressed against his side with her head on his shoulder.

Larimar placed his arm around her, holding her close, and she sighed in pleasure. She felt his gaze on her and looked up, finding his pansy-colored eyes focused on her.

Her heart skipped a beat. Larimar reached his hand toward her face, cupping her cheek against his palm. She'd never wanted someone to kiss her so badly before, but she craved it more than anything.

His head lowered slowly and then his lips touched hers softly, gently. Her hand pressed to his chest and she leaned into him even more. She didn't want a single inch between them. His mouth moved against hers, coaxing her to kiss him back. When his tongue touched her bottom lip, she opened to him. Kissing Larimar made her head spin, her heart race, and made her want so much more from him. She'd had lackluster experiences with men in her past, but the touch of his lips against hers was enough to assure her there would be plenty of sparks between them.

He kissed her slowly, as if savoring every minute. The movie played in the background as she straddled his lap, placing her hands on his shoulders. He met her gaze steadily, his hands gripping her hips. She could feel the bulge in his pants and knew he wanted her as much as she wanted him. The question was how far could she push him on their first date, or rather, how far did she want to push him? She'd never slept with anyone just after meeting them before, and part of her shied away from doing so now. But there had never been anyone like Larimar before.

His lips met hers again, the kiss hungrier than before. Her toes curled and she ground against him. Larimar's hands slid around to her ass, squeezing her cheeks as he pulled her tighter against him. She couldn't get enough, didn't know if there was such a thing as enough. She wanted his lips and hands everywhere, wanted to explore his hard body and drive him mad with desire.

"Wait," he said, pulling back. "We should stop."

"Why?"

"I'm the only male you've met since coming here. You deserve a chance to see if there's anyone out there you might be better off with than me. I won't lie. I want you, never mistake that, but I don't want you to feel trapped either."

She smiled softly. "I wouldn't feel trapped. But if it

makes you feel better, even if we sleep together, it doesn't mean you have to marry me."

"It wouldn't be right," he said.

"Larimar, shut up and kiss me."

His gaze dropped to her lips and he groaned before claiming them again. Abbie felt like she was heating from the inside out, her body melting against his. Kissing Larimar felt perfect, like everything was suddenly right in her world. Things had gone so horribly wrong for her the last several weeks, but she'd gladly live through it all over again if brought Larimar into her life.

He groaned and pulled away, panting hard. "Abbie --"

"If the words about to come out of your mouth are that we should stop, then quit talking."

"You tempt me so damn much."

"Then take me," she said softly. "I promise I won't regret it or change my mind later. I've never wanted anyone the way I want you right now."

He flipped her onto her back across the padded bench, his body coming down over hers. He kissed her again, harder, deeper, as his hands explored every curve. Between kisses, their clothes quickly disappeared. She couldn't stop touching him, wanting to run her fingers over every muscular inch of him.

As Larimar sank into her, she wrapped her legs around him, pulling him in closer. His lips trailed kisses down her throat before he lightly nipped her. He set up a steady rhythm -- thrust and retreat -- until she was clinging to him and begging for more. His name was a prayer on her lips as he took her to dizzying heights, every stroke of his cock driving her need higher. Abbie could feel her body tightening, straining for release.

"So tight," he said before kissing her. "So sweet."

"Feel so good," she murmured. "Don't stop."

"I don't think I could if I wanted to."

Her legs tightened around him and he took her harder, faster. Their bodies slapped together, her nails biting into his shoulders. Abbie threw back her head as her world shattered, her climax leaving her breathless as she cried out his name. Larimar groaned against her neck as he came inside of her, his hips thrusting until his body shook.

He kissed her softly as he withdrew from her body, rolling to his feet and lifting her into his arms. Abbie looped her arms around his neck and held on as he carried her upstairs and down the hall to his room. He nudged the door open with his foot and then gently laid her on the bed.

"Don't move," he said, as he pulled out a pair of loose pants and stepped into them.

She looked around the room as he disappeared back down the hall. There wasn't much in the room that told her anything about the man who had just rocked her world. The furnishings were plain, but seemed well made. The bedding under her was just as soft as that in the guest room, feeling like silk under her. Her hand smoothed across the dark blue sheets and blankets. A chill made her shiver and she slipped under the covers, pulling them up to her shoulders.

When Larimar returned, he had her clothes tucked under his arm and carried a tray that was full of delicious-smelling food and two glasses filled with a pink fizzy liquid. He set the tray on the dresser and tossed her clothes onto a nearby chair. Picking up one of the plates, he brought it over to her.

"Dinner was ready and I thought you might be hungry," he said.

"Thank you." She accepted the plate and her mouth watered, even though she didn't recognize anything on the dish. She hesitantly took a bite and was surprised that the fish tasted a lot like salmon. The vegetables were tender and practically melted in her mouth.

Larimar seemed to be deep in thought as he ate, and she hoped he wasn't having second thoughts. She'd meant what she said. Just because they'd slept together she didn't expect him to claim her as his mate. Maybe if they'd known each other longer, but after one day? Things like that just didn't happen. At least, on her world they didn't. She was still trying to figure out this strange, new place and she knew the Zelthranites played by a different set of rules. Obviously the man had had sex before, because he was damn good at it, but she didn't understand where he had gotten his skills. There were so few females on his world, and they all seemed to be mated or part of the bride program. It didn't mean she wanted to spend more time with other males, just more time with him.

"You should stay here tonight," he said.

"You want me to spend the night?"

He nodded. "I'll probably be gone in the morning when you wake. Council business. You're welcome to stay here as long as you'd like. I'll tell the cook to remain here until you leave, in case you'd like to take your meals here."

Well, it wasn't an invitation to move in and be his forever, and she hadn't asked for one, but she did like the idea of spending the night in his arms.

"I'll stay," she said.

Larimar smiled, his eyes twinkling. He put their empty plates back on the tray, slipped out of his pants, and slid under the covers next to her. Pulling her close, he kissed her, taking his time and making her body heat all over again. She sighed against his lips and cuddled closer. Everything she'd always wanted was within reach, and she was ready to hold on tight and never let go.

# Chapter Four

Larimar had extracted himself from bed this morning while attempting not to wake up Abbie. He'd succeeded and then stood beside the bed staring down at her like a lovesick fool. Assuming that funny feeling he got when he looked at her was love. He'd never experienced it before. Maybe Borgoz had been right and sometimes you just knew when you found the right one.

The council had convened as the suns had peeked over the horizon and now it was nearing lunch. His stomach growled as they closed out another matter, and he hoped like hell Borgoz would call a break. When the Chief Councilor opened another file, Larimar stifled a groan. He couldn't complain really. The work they did was important, essential to their world, but sometimes it was rather tedious.

"Larimar has brought it to my attention we may have an unfit bride on our world," Borgoz said. "I inquired with some of our single males and they concur that she shouldn't be here. She's pitting our males against one another and teasing them. I think she's after a… what's that Earth saying? A sugar daddy? She wants someone well-connected and doesn't care about the males one way or another. I think we need to have her escorted back to the shuttle and sent home."

Faltz frowned. "We've never sent a bride home before for being unfit. I thought we had an application process in place that kept this sort of thing from happening."

"Either she's a very good test manipulator, or we were too lax when we reviewed the files," Borgoz said. "Regardless, she doesn't belong here and the sooner we get her off our planet, the better for our males. I'm worried that someone will be so desperate for a mate he won't care that she's a manipulative little schemer."

Faltz nodded. "Then I concur. It will just make more room for those who are serious about the program. If she's not a good fit, then we're wasting time."

Larimar cleared his throat. "Abbie mentioned something to me yesterday that I thought I would bring before the council. I took her to the pool, but she doesn't know how to swim. It seems humans aren't born with the ability. There could be mates here who also can't swim, or future brides, and I thought perhaps we could station a lifeguard at the pool. That's someone who oversees the safety of those in and around the water. Maybe one of our older males who might prefer a different job?"

"I might know of someone," Helio said. "What about Zoralk? He was injured in battle and retired from service, but he's still one of the best swimmers we have. He's only forty and still in his prime. He might welcome a way to feel useful to our society again."

"I think he would make a fine lifeguard," Alrian said. "I'll speak to him personally about the matter and report back tomorrow."

"Anything else?" Borgoz asked.

Everyone at the table remained silent.

"Good. Then there's another matter I wish to discuss. As you know, we've started taking other races into consideration for our bride program. We haven't made anything official yet, but some of the more peaceful races should be contemplated. Our people aren't the only ones who could die out without females. As you know, we've been allowing different races to land at our Terran Stations and mingle with the humans. They've been well received and so far, no one has caused any trouble."

"The Tourmalanes are desperate for mates. Perhaps we should send a handful of them to Earth to find their brides?" Helio asked.

Borgoz nodded. "They're on my list. They attempted to abduct one of our brides in the past, but I don't think they really meant her any harm. They were simply looking for a way to keep their people from dying out."

"Perhaps you should make a list of the races you think we should consider for this first trial run," Larimar said. "Then we can look over it at another council meeting."

Borgoz fought a smile. "In a hurry to take a break? Perhaps head off to find a certain new bride?"

Larimar felt his cheeks warm and he refrained from answering, though that was precisely what he wanted. He was curious as to whether or not Abbie had remained at his house, or if had she left and was now out with another male. What they'd shared had been special to him, but he knew humans treated sex differently. He wasn't a virgin by any means, but he'd only been with the women at the floating brothel nearby, and even then he'd used the bots. They were rather informative of what human females would like and he was anxious to use his knowledge on Abbie, if she gave him another chance. He'd thought things had gone well though. She'd seemed happy.

"Larimar is going to finally take a mate?" Alrian asked with a smile. "I never thought I'd see the day."

"Not all of us were fortunate enough to snag the first woman who stepped foot on our world," Larimar said. "You snapped up our very first potential mate through the bride program. Besides, I've had other things on my mind, like council business."

"Larimar is overdue for a mate," Borgoz said. "All of our unmated males are. It's my hope that in time, everyone will happily be paired off, if not with humans through the bride program, then maybe through other means. Some of our warriors have mated females from other worlds, but they have better access to those places as they travel the galaxies on missions."

"Good thing the humans outnumber us," Helio said. "At least we don't have to worry about running out of bride candidates anytime soon. I don't know about the rest of you, but I'm rather partial to the humans. They come in such a variety."

"Maybe in time we can open the program to other worlds," Borgoz said. "Places where females outnumber the males, as long as we're compatible and can have children. But I don't think we're ready for that just yet. Let's worry about getting our current program running as smoothly as possible. It's been going for years now and so far we've been luck. It's worked well. But I think our unfit bride has shown us that there's room for improvement. Maybe we need to get stricter with the application process."

Larimar nodded. "I've heard Earth has doctors called psychiatrists. I believe they studied the human mind and personality. Perhaps we could use one of those to help us get the process to run a little tighter. We could try it at one Terran Station and see how it works."

Borgoz nodded and made some notes. "I think we've done all that we can for now. I know you're all tired of sitting on those chairs. Let's end the session for today and reconvene tomorrow."

The council members stood and filed out, with Larimar at the back. He paused and turned to Borgoz.

"Would it be possible to take a short break from my council duties while I court Abbie? I think things are going really well between us, but I'd like to spend more time with her."

"And you're worried another male might take her if you're here working?" Borgoz asked.

"It crossed my mind. I know we work long hours, but you've cut back on how long our sessions run now that you have a family. Maybe we could cut back a little more in the future as more of us pair off. Alrian has two children I'm sure he'd love to spend more time with, and Helio and Faltz are still looking for mates."

"I'll take it into consideration. I know Charlotte wouldn't complain if I were home more. Take tomorrow off to spend with your Abbie and we'll meet again day after. In fact, I'll give everyone tomorrow off. A day at home with my mate and daughter sounds wonderful."

"Thank you, Chief Councilor."

Borgoz smiled and motioned for him to leave, following right behind Larimar. As they exited the building, the suns nearly blinded Larimar. He hurried home, hoping Abbie was waiting for him. His cook had been asked to remain at the house all day so if she'd needed help with the Vid-comm or anything else, Shariz would have been able to assist her.

As Larimar entered his home, he listened for any sound

that might tell him where Abbie was, or if she even remained in the house. The place was too large and he began searching the lower level, finally locating her in the living room, asleep in front of the Vid-comm with a movie playing. He knelt beside her, brushing her hair back from her face and smiling at how beautiful she looked even in sleep.

Her eyes slowly opened and she stretched. "You're home," she said softly.

"The session is over for the day, and it seems I have tomorrow off as well. I don't suppose you'd like to spend some time with me, would you?" he asked.

"I can't think of anything I'd like more."

"Did you request lunch from the kitchen yet?" he asked.

She shook her head.

"Then why don't I take you to the human restaurant? It's run by one of the human mates and she has all of the ingredients imported from your world. You might like something that reminds you of home."

"I'd love to go."

"Once you know where it's located, you can walk there anytime you'd like. They serve breakfast, lunch, and dinner. They're open from morning until after the evening meal."

She smoothed a hand down her wrinkled clothes. "I should change. This is all wrinkled from me falling asleep."

"You look beautiful," he murmured. "Don't change unless you really want to. No one is going to care if you have a few wrinkles in your clothes."

Larimar helped her stand and he stopped by the kitchen long enough to let Shariz know they would be dining out. He wasn't certain if Abbie would be with him for the evening meal or not, and didn't want to ask just yet. As much as he wanted to spend the entire day with her, he didn't want her to feel like he was monopolizing her time either.

The human café wasn't very busy when they arrived and Larimar escorted her to a table near the window. He liked being able to watch passersby and feel the warmth of the suns. The café was set up the same as the Zelthranite restaurant he'd taken her to before, with the digital menu and payment system. All restaurants on his world came equipped with them, regardless of what they served.

Aside from that, the café looked very much like something you would find on Earth, with its black and white checkered floor and red leather booths. Everything had been brought over from her world to make the café as authentic as possible. He'd been to Earth a few times on business, and had enjoyed dining out while he was there. If Abbie became his mate, would she want to return home every once in a while? As much as he'd liked his time on Earth, he much preferred being at home.

They placed their order and Larimar paid for their meal. Abbie fiddled with the napkin dispenser, pulling a handful out, placing a few in front of each of them. There were four sets of silverware already on the table, and music played from a jukebox that stood against one wall playing music.

"If you don't have outlets like we have on Earth, how is that thing playing?" Abbie asked.

"I believe the owner of the café asked one of our inventors to find a way to make it play here on my world. If you have one of those smartphones your world is so crazy about, there's a store that just started selling solar chargers for them. I've heard some people download books, movies, and music to their phones."

She nodded. "I don't have any movies on mine, but I do have some music stored on there. Maybe I can pick up one of the chargers and see if it will work with my phone."

"We can stop by there when we leave here."

"How was work?" she asked.

"Busy." He smiled a little. "I don't think I've ever had someone ask me that before."

"Did you talk to them about the lifeguard idea?" she asked.

"I did, and we may have a possible lifeguard lined up. One of the councilmen was going to speak with him soon.

They liked the idea of added safety to the pool area, not having realized your kind don't always know how to swim."

"Is your council only made up of men?"

"Yes. The females of our world have never shown an interest in joining. They seem content to take care of the house. Will you want to work after you're mated?"

Her brow puckered. "I'm not sure. I like the idea of being home whenever my husband gets off work, but if today showed me anything it's that I'll be bored just sitting around the house. I'm used to being gone eight hours a day working a full-time job five days a week. There's only so much time I can spend at the pool or out shopping."

"You worked in human resources, but I'm not certain I understand what that is."

"The company I worked for hired me to oversee job applications, employee benefits, and if anyone was disgruntled I had to defuse the situation."

"I'm afraid we don't have anything like that here. Most shops are family-owned and the council oversees the majority of the jobs here. Any position that benefits our people as a whole, we select the proper person for the job. Like the lifeguard position. Our scientists and inventors are selected based off their innate abilities and their love of discovering new things."

"So your jobs here are aptitude-based and not necessarily something one would apply for just because it sounded interesting."

He smiled. "Exactly."

"Maybe I could take up some hobbies then, because I don't think I'm qualified to do much on your world. For that matter, I wasn't qualified to do much on mine either."

"There is a place here that has opened in recent years called a craft store. The human females seem to like it a lot. Perhaps you will find something there for your new hobbies."

She nodded. "It's something to consider. I don't know how to knit or anything, so if I picked up one of those hobbies, I'd have to have someone teach me."

"A few of the mates offer crafting classes two days a week. What they teach depends on how many people are asking for a particular course. The craft store will have information on what's being offered now if you're interested."

Their food arrived and Abbie asked more questions about his world. He was happy she was showing an interest in the place she would call home. Her words about being bored bothered him though. Were there other mates who felt the same way? There had to be something they could do to keep their human females happy. They were giving up everything they knew to start a new life on a strange world, with males they barely knew. It hardly seemed fair to ask them to give up so much and give them so little in return. They provided a home and meals for their mates, but what else did they really do for them?

Most seemed content to start families with their chosen males, and he hadn't heard any rumblings of discontent, but it didn't mean there wasn't room for improvement. He'd studied Earth extensively before they ever reached out to Earth's government. Females on Earth had a lot of freedom. They didn't require males to take care of them. But what more could they offer? They had installed the pool and set up the park based off things they'd seen on Earth. More shops had opened, carrying human items, and this café catered to humans.

When he really thought about it, a park, pool, one restaurant, and a bit of shopping didn't really seem like much. They had an entire planet of males needing mates and they weren't offering enough to these women in return. Why hadn't anyone brought it to their attention before? Hell, why hadn't they realized it sooner? It wasn't like they were stupid males. Change took time, and any ideas he came up with could take months or years to put into place. So how did he fix the immediate problem?

Once he had some ideas in place, he'd have to take a meeting with Borgoz, or ask the full council to convene to discuss the matter. Normally only a few were present each day. They prided themselves on taking excellent care of their mates, but it seemed they had failed them in a big way. While Abbie didn't have family she wished to associate with, others did. It wasn't right for them to ask their mates to give up their parents or siblings. Yes, they gave them money for being accepted into the program as a way to ease the burden of leaving their world for the unknown, but was money really the solution? He knew some of those families needed the cash, but others, like Abbie, had no use for it.

"You're thinking hard," Abbie said.

"You've just made me realize our system is faulty. I was contemplating how to fix it. Your world is full of ways to keep you entertained, and ours offers nothing. We're a society that revolves around hard work and taking care of our families, and while those things are important, humans are used to so much more. I feel like we've punished our mates by asking them to give up so much and getting so little in return."

"So, now that you know there's a problem, maybe you can come up with a way to fix it."

He frowned. "I'd have to do more research on Earth to come up with ways to improve our society. It isn't a simple fix that will take place immediately, but something that could take a while."

"When mates have children, do the women always take care of the children? Are they with them every hour of the day?" Abbie asked.

"Yes, except for those who are school-aged, then they're gone a few hours learning science, math, and other things that will help them in our society."

"Are the girls taught the same things as the boys?"

"Well, no. The girls are taught how to keep a home and raise a family."

"Barbaric," she muttered.

"I don't understand."

Abbie sighed. "You've studied our world, correct? So you know we have female doctors, lawyers, politicians, scientists... the majority of your offspring are half-human.

Doesn't it stand to reason those female children will be just as adept at those subjects as a male? For that matter, who's to say your Zelthranite females aren't capable of the same?"

Larimar's food settled in his stomach like a weight.

"We are a male-oriented society, but I see that perhaps we need to change. What you're asking isn't an easy thing to accomplish. Many will believe a female's place is at home, and to ask them to accept otherwise will cause great strife on our world. There are a few who have the support of their mates to open businesses, like the human cuisine place. But most will want their mates at home."

"I'm not asking you to change your entire society overnight, but perhaps you can change small things here and there, build on one idea so the changes are subtle and easier for everyone to accept."

He smiled a little. "You're very smart, Abbie. Perhaps there's something that could occupy your time after all."

"What's that?" she asked.

"You could be an ambassador for the females on our world. You could be their voice."

Her mouth opened and shut a few times. "I don't think I'm qualified for something like that. I mean I have some ideas, like letting the girls take the same classes as the boys in school. But I don't know anything about your world and how it works. I'm likely to piss off a bunch of males and that's the last thing I want."

"Would you at least consider meeting with some of the mates and find out if they're happy with the way things are now? We've always assumed they were content to adapt to our way of life. But if they want something more, then we're obligated to see that they get it. You're giving us so much by giving us the families we sorely want and need. It only stands to reason that we give something back."

Her fingers tapped on the table. "I don't think your world needs to become the new Earth. Things are far from perfect on my world, and at least you don't have crime here, right? There's a balance here that seems to work for your people, but you're right. You're asking a lot of us and there are some small concessions that might make life on a strange planet happier for the humans, and possibly even for the non-human females."

"So you'll consider it?"

She nodded. "I don't have the first clue how to call a meeting with the female population, or where we'd even meet. Maybe the fastest way to get the knowledge we seek is to ask them to complete an anonymous survey. If they aren't happy, they won't want their mates to know. There would have to be a way to collect the data without it giving away anyone's identity."

"I think there's a way to do it through the Vid-comm units. I'll consult with our communications expert on the matter, but I'll need you to create the survey questions. It will take time to build it in the system, as we would have to offer it in different languages to make sure all of the females could take part."

"I think giving them a voice is the right thing to do," Abbie said. "I haven't seen anyone who looks unhappy, and they may be perfectly content with the way things are run now, but if they aren't this is the perfect opportunity to find out."

They finished their meal and Abbie easily fell into step beside him as they walked back to his home. He knew he should return her to the small apartment in the Tower, but he liked having her around. As they entered his home, he stopped in the front entry and took a good look at his house. He'd thought he had everything he needed, except a mate, but her words at the café were making him question what he really had to offer her.

She'd fallen asleep watching a movie, and she'd probably watched more than one. He had nothing here to keep her entertained except the Vid-comm unit. If he wanted to claim her as his mate, he needed to start the changes to his world by changing his home. They were still learning about one another, and he didn't know her likes and dislikes. What had she done on Earth when she wasn't working? Was there something he could add to his home that would make her feel more welcome here?

As much as he loved having her here, it was time to send her back to the apartment until he could figure out exactly what he had to offer her. If he'd been worried about their age difference before, that paled in comparison to his worry over making her unhappy if he claimed her. She watched him with a furrowed brow, and he tried to smile at her reassuringly.

"Larimar, what is it?"

"You should return to your apartment this evening. I'll come get you for the morning meal and we can discuss what you'd like to do for the day."

"You're throwing me out?"

He winced. "No, I'm not throwing you out. I want you here, more than anything, but…"

"But what?"

"This house isn't ready. Maybe I'm not ready to claim a mate just yet. There are changes that need to be made."

"Is this because I said I'd be bored?" Abbie asked.

"In part." Well, it was mostly that.

"Larimar, I enjoy spending time with you regardless of what we do together. Why waste a single minute apart if we don't have to?"

"My people have felt entitled to have mates and children. I've felt that way. Until I'm certain that I can give you what you need, I won't claim you as mine. It isn't fair of me to ask you to remain here while I figure things out."

She sighed and he could have sworn she rolled her eyes.

"Are all of the males on your world the same? Will they all be able to offer me the same things you can right now?" she asked.

"Well, yes."

"Then what's the difference in me sitting in an apartment by myself instead of staying here with you? Is everything going to magically change overnight?" she asked.

"No."

"Do you expect me to wait months or years for you to

feel like you're better prepared to have a mate?" she asked.

He hesitated a moment. "No?" he asked uncertainly, not quite sure what the proper response was.

"Damn right the answer is no. I want you, Larimar. We're good together. I don't give a crap if there's an age difference between us. I don't care that you're a workaholic. And I damn sure don't care that you don't feel 'prepared' for a mate. You have the same thing to offer me as every other male on this planet, so unless you're going to suspend the bride program and send everyone home, there's no reason for me to return to my apartment."

He stared at her a moment.

"Are you always this feisty?" he asked.

"Only when you piss me off."

He smiled a little. "If you truly wish to stay, I won't make you go. But if you don't plan to return to your apartment, we should probably have your things delivered here."

She moved closer, placing her hand on his chest. "Does this mean you're going to claim me as your mate?"

"Before we take that step, we should probably talk to the council about your ideas. It would be good to know ahead of time if we're both going to be kicked off the planet. A Zelthranite mating won't be recognized on some of the possible worlds we could call home. Best to do it right the first time."

"Are you really concerned they will be angry with the suggestion of a survey?" she asked.

He hesitated a moment. "Those who are mated will feel ashamed that they just assumed their mates were happy. Knowing they may have failed them will hurt. Those who have never had a mate may put up a fight at changing the way things work on this world. They will be resistant to change, but I think in time, once they find their mates, they will better understand what we're trying to do."

Abbie sighed. "I didn't intend to turn your planet upside down when I came here. I just wanted a chance at a better life."

"And I intend to make sure you get it."

Abbie pressed her lips to his and Larimar felt the stirrings of desire. Would he always want her with the same hunger he felt now? It went beyond her physical looks, even though she was beautiful. He loved her fire, her heart. But mostly he loved the way she made him feel. Like he could do anything. And he *would* do anything to ensure her happiness and prove himself a worthy mate.

He just hoped the council would be receptive to making some changes.

# Chapter Five

"You agreed to live your life according to our laws when you accepted the money to come here," Faltz said.

Abbie's chin jutted out. "I didn't accept any money. And I have no problem with your laws. I merely suggested that there might be a better way of handling the female population. We aren't meek little women to be patted on the head and told what to do. We have thoughts and feelings, needs and desires, and your archaic male-oriented society is stifling your mates."

Faltz's face turned red, but he sat back down.

Borgoz observed her and seemed to be listening intently. "What precisely is it that you want us to do?"

"Like I said, I want to send out a survey for all of the females on this world to take. But it needs to be done in way that allows them to be anonymous. We want their honest feedback on their feelings and suggestions for how to improve things on Zelthrane-3. Human woman are used to having jobs, having countless forms of entertainment available for them, and we're used to using our brains for more than running a house and raising kids. Even the stay-at-home moms on my world help out with paying bills, help their kids with homework, and they usually spend time with other females without children or mates present."

"And you honestly believe our mates are unhappy?" Borgoz asked, looking unsettled by the thought.

"I think they love you and want to be here with you. But yes, I think deep down, there are things they miss from our world. Larimar said there's a crafting store and some of the women offer classes. I think that's a great idea, but not all females want to take up knitting. You're doing them a disservice by squeezing them all into the same box instead of giving them options to express themselves." Abbie blew out a breath. "I'm not saying change everything about your world. From what I can see, it's a pretty great place to live. I'm only asking that you adapt a little to your growing female population by seeing that *all* of their needs are met."

"I have a mate," Borgoz said. "She's never once said

anything about being unhappy. Wouldn't she have told me if she were?"

"Not all women will speak up for what they want. Some just go with the status quo and they're content. But it doesn't mean there aren't things they long for. She may just not know how to ask for it. Or maybe she doesn't think what she wants is even possible," Abbie said.

"A survey." Alrian crossed his arms over his chest. "It would take some work to send out something everyone would be able to take, which means it would take some time to implement your idea. But I think it's a sound suggestion. If my mate needs something I'm not providing, I want to know."

Borgoz nodded. "I feel the same."

"You want to change our society just to cater to some females?" Faltz asked.

"No," Borgoz said. "We want to better our society by making sure everyone has what they need to be happy here. The bride program is still growing, and in the grand scheme of things, it's still fairly new. What if ten years from now my mate decides she can't handle life here anymore? What if she gets tired of not having enough to do, or not getting enough quality time with other females? I don't want that. If making a few changes means she'll never want to leave, then I'm all for it."

"What's that human phrase?" Faltz asked. "Pussy-whipped?"

Borgoz growled at him and the councilman quickly shut up.

"I'll take your suggestion to our communications team," Borgoz said. "If you will kindly come up with some questions for the survey, I'll get them to start working on it immediately."

Abbie smiled, liking the Chief Councilor. "I'll have them to you by tomorrow."

"I think we can dismiss for the rest of the day," Borgoz said. "Some of us have a lot of thinking to do."

He gave Faltz a pointed look.

As Larimar began escorting her out of the room, Borgoz drew them to a halt.

"I'd like to invite the two of you over for dinner tonight. I think Charlotte would like you, Abbie, and she can always use a new friend. My mate is deaf. She reads lips and she can speak, but her voice is unusual. I didn't want it to come as a surprise when you meet her," Borgoz said.

"I'd love to meet her," Abbie said.

"Then I'll see you both tonight." Borgoz smiled.

When they exited the council headquarters and stepped into the sunshine, Abbie smiled up at Larimar. He seemed more relaxed now that the meeting was over and he hadn't been asked to leave his world. She'd never doubted the outcome. If Larimar was receptive to new ideas, it stood to reason that others on this world would be too.

"I know you had more suggestions," Larimar said. "Maybe we can discuss the matter more with Borgoz at a later date."

"Just knowing the council was receptive to the idea of a survey is a great start," Abbie said with a smile.

"If there was anything you could bring here from your world, what would it be?" he asked.

"That's a hard one. I love books, movies, and music. But I think, as far as things you do with more than one person, I would miss dancing. I never got a chance to go very often, but I had fun when I did."

"Dancing." His brow furrowed. "I've seen people dance on the movies we've procured, but I've never done it before. Is it hard?"

"I guess it depends on whether or not you have any rhythm." Abbie shrugged. "Some people can dance because it's natural to them, and others never quite get the hang of it. It's hard to say where you'd fall until you gave it a try."

"You have the solar charger for your phone at my place, don't you?" he asked.

"Yes. Why?"

Larimar tugged on her hand, guiding her back toward his place. "Because I think I want to try dancing and you said you have music on your phone."

Abbie laughed and went with him willingly. She was glad they'd settled the issue of her returning to her apartment. The last thing she wanted to do was be apart from him. So far, she'd pretty much been living with Larimar, but he hadn't said a word about claiming her. She wondered if he was hung up on their age difference, or if it was something else. On Earth, there were rumors that plenty of brides found mates their first day on this world, and Abbie was certain she'd found hers. But how could she convince him she didn't want anyone else?

At his house, she retrieved her phone from the bedroom, along with the solar charger. She plugged in the phone, since it had a low battery, and scrolled through her music, trying to decide what the best dancing song would be for the alien's first time. She wanted something with a good beat and finally settled on Flo Rida's latest hit. Abbie cranked the volume on her phone and when the song started, Larimar looked at it, perplexed.

"How do you dance to that?" he asked.

Abbie began moving and drew him closer. He seemed to study her for the first few songs, but by the fourth one, he was attempting to move to the beat. She couldn't help but laugh at how rigid he appeared.

"You have to loosen up," she said. "You're too stiff."

He muttered something as he eyed her that sounded suspiciously like *that's not all that's stiff*. She fought not to smile as she glanced down and saw the sexy alien was definitely aroused. Abbie decided that Zelthrane-3 definitely needed a place where people could dance. If the other males were half as stubborn as Larimar, they needed all the help they could get.

Abbie switched to a slower song and curled her body against Larimar's, pulling his arms around her waist. She swayed against him and after a moment he mimicked her movements. He held her close, his body relaxed.

"I like this song," he said. "We should do more of this type of dancing."

She felt his hard cock pressing against her and smiled. If Larimar wanted more slow dances, she'd give him as many as he'd like. Especially if it meant he'd hold her like this every time. And maybe, there would be a little fun at the end of the dance, of a different variety.

"I'm all sweaty from dancing," she said. Peering up at him through her lashes, she pulled away a little. "Maybe I should take a shower, and you could wash my back?"

He stiffened and gave her a heated look. "Our cleansing units having a cleaning agent built in. There's no need for someone to clean your back."

She leaned in close again. "Then maybe we should switch to plain water and use my shower gel. Then you could help me wash… everywhere."

He visibly swallowed then gave her a nod. Abbie took him by the hand and led him upstairs. She paused outside of the guest room, but he tugged her toward his room. When they stepped inside, she saw that her things had been brought to his room at some point while they were gone. She didn't question why he'd asked for her things to be moved, but secretly, she hoped it meant he was closer to claiming her as his mate.

Abbie retrieved the shower gel and shampoo from her bags and followed Larimar into the bathroom. He did something to the panel on the wall beside the shower and when the water started, it didn't smell like the cleansing agent was in it. She placed the gel and shampoo in the shower and then began removing her clothes. Larimar leaned against the bathroom counter, arms folded, and watched her as each piece was removed. When her clothes lay at a pile at her feet, he began removing his leather vest and pants.

Abbie stepped under the spray and wet her hair and body. When Larimar joined her, he pulled the glass door shut behind him. She couldn't help but admire him. No matter how many times she got to see him without his clothes, the sight of him would always leave her in awe. She poured a generous amount of shower gel in her palm and rubbed her hands together before reaching for him.

A soft growl escaped Larimar as her hands caressed his chest and worked her way to his shoulders and down his arms. His cock seemed to pulse in time with his heartbeat and she couldn't wait to get her hands on it. He held still, watching her with enough heat to scorch her from the inside out. When she reached for the hard length of him, wrapping her hand around his shaft, he hissed in a breath and his eyes darkened to an intense purple. She stroked him, feeling him harden even further. He was an impressive size, and she felt a flutter in her belly as she thought about how he'd felt inside of her.

"What's that Earth saying?" Larimar asked. "You're playing with fire."

She smiled a little. "And just what are you going to do to me?"

He moved closer, crowding her against the wall. "Anything I want."

Her legs nearly buckled and a whimper slipped past her lips. Yes, she wanted that, so very much. She wanted him to take what he wanted from her, and give her an orgasm so intense she wouldn't be able to stand. And she knew he could because he'd done it before. The water rinsed away the soap she'd lathered on his skin as he stood under the spray.

"Make me yours," she said softly.

Larimar growled, and then his lips came down on hers. The kiss was deep and full of promises that she wished he'd make and keep. His arms came around her, lifting her off her feet. Abbie wrapped her legs around his waist. With one thrust, he filled her completely. Abbie groaned and dug her nails into his shoulders.

Larimar moved with easy, shallow thrusts. He felt incredible and she wanted the sensations to last forever, but she also wanted more.

"Harder. Faster," she urged.

Larimar's self-control seemed to snap as his grip tightened on her hips. Every stroke was deeper, harder, until she was crying out in pleasure. Her pussy gripped him tight as she came, calling his name. Larimar pounded into her until she felt him coming, every spurt of his cum splashing the inside of her. She squeezed him tight and he thrust deep and hard one last time, burying himself inside of her. Abbie clung to him, shaken and spent.

"I'm sorry I didn't make that last longer," he said. "I should have had better control."

"Do you hear me complaining?"

"No."

"Then shut up and kiss me. I thought it was perfect."

He kissed her softly, his hand coming up to cup her cheek. She leaned into his touch and wished they could stay like this forever. But even on an alien world she figured the water would eventually turn cold or run out completely. They might have advanced science, but they weren't magicians.

"We should get cleaned up and dressed," Abbie said. Her stomach rumbled.

"And it seems I should feed you," Larimar said with some humor.

"Food would be good. But maybe we can do this again? In the bedroom instead?"

"I'd like that."

He withdrew from her and eased her down his body. As they washed one another, Abbie thought about how great life would be with Larimar, if he ever decided to commit to her. The sex between them was incredible, and she thought they had a good time together outside of the bedroom too. For whatever reason, Larimar was dragging his feet. Most brides seemed to find their mates within a few days. Unless you went unmatched, and then you were returned to Earth. He wasn't going to send her back, was he?

When they were finished and dressed, Larimar took her by the hand and led her down to the kitchen. Another alien was leaning against the counter, staring at what looked like a tablet. He glanced up when he saw them enter and smiled broadly.

"You finally bring your chosen mate to the kitchen," he said.

"Oh, I'm not his mate," Abbie said. *Yet.*

The alien cocked his head and some unspoken communication seemed to pass between Larimar and him.

"I'm Shariz," he said with a slight bow. "And you must be Abbie."

"Abbie is hungry," Larimar said. "We missed the noon meal. Do you have anything prepared we could have until the evening meal?"

"Of course," Shariz said. He rubbed his hands together and began pulling things out of what looked like a pantry and refrigerator. Taking down two plates from a cabinet overhead, he began arranging the food, heated it, and then presented it to them. "Nothing fancy. I believe this is similar to the fish tacos on your Earth. I had the avocado brought in on the shuttle that landed this morning so it's fresh from your home, along with some other fruits and vegetables I've put aside for later meals."

Larimar accepted the plates. "Thank you, Shariz. Your attention to detail is appreciated as always."

The alien smiled and gave Abbie a little wave before going back to his tablet.

Larimar led her out of the kitchen and to the dining room. He set their plates down beside one another, then held her chair for her. She had to admit that whatever the concoction was it smelled delicious. Just as they sat, Shariz appeared with two glasses of something fizzy and orange.

"You forgot drinks," Shariz said. "I'll be in the kitchen if you need anything else."

Larimar thanked him again before digging into his meal. Abbie took a bite, curious what a combination of Terran and human food would taste like. It was rather good, and she quickly finished both tacos and ate the raw avocado slices. She probably should have put them on the tacos, but it was just as good this way. She finished her meal and drank the fizzy stuff, surprised to find it tasted almost like orange soda, but a little sweeter.

"Now that I've fed you," Larimar said, "let's watch a movie and relax for a little while."

"Maybe a romantic comedy?" Abbie asked. "They're my favorites."

"Then I'll endeavor to find one." Larimar smiled at her. "And if there aren't any in the library already, I'll put in a request for a few in the next batch of movies that are transferred to our Vid-comm units."

Abbie held his hand as they walked to the living room, then cuddled against him as they watched one of her favorite movies. All in all, it had turned out to be a great day. Now she just had to figure out how to get him to claim her. There had to be something she could do that would speed up the process. He obviously wanted her in his home, but as what? She didn't think Zelthranites did the casual dating thing, or lived together without being mates, but that seemed to be the path they were on. It left Abbie confused and out of sorts.

Larimar was going to be hers. She just had to figure out how to make it happen.

## Chapter Six

Larimar woke the next morning with Abbie curled against his side. He watched the light from the suns play across her face as it streamed through the window, and marveled at how beautiful she was. Every time he really took the time to look at her, it left him speechless that someone like her could want an older man like him. She could have anyone she wanted, and yet she seemed to have chosen him. With everything that had been going on, he hadn't had time to ask if she would be his mate, but he wanted to do it soon. Now that her ideas for improving their society would be put into place, he didn't have to worry about her tiring of this place. He did still worry a little that she would regret being mated to someone older, but as Borgoz had pointed out, age didn't seem to matter.

Larimar eased out of bed so he wouldn't disturb Abbie and pulled on a pair of loose pants before going to his office. He had a smaller Vid-comm in there, along with a unit similar to Earth's computers, where he stored all of his notes from the council meetings. The council calendar was kept there as well. He reviewed his schedule, surprised to see that his presence wasn't required at the next few council meetings. Borgoz had mentioned giving him some extra time, but he hadn't realized how much. Had it been a mistake?

Pulling up Borgoz's number on the Vid-comm, he dialed the Chief Councilor and hoped he wouldn't wake everyone else in the household. When Borgoz answered, he was shirtless and looked rumpled from sleep.

"I apologize for disturbing you at such an early hour," Larimar said.

"I was awake. Arabella isn't feeling well and she was up and down all night. I've already notified the council to either convene without me or postpone everything for a day or two."

"I noticed I was taken off the meetings," Larimar said. "Is there a reason?"

"I have a job for you. Well, for you and Abbie. I want

you to take her to Earth. Using the portable Vid-comm, record some of the things she'd like to bring to our world so that when she submits her survey, we can include some clips for those females not from Earth so they will better understand what she hopes to bring here."

"When should we leave?" Larimar asked.

"Today would be good, but she'll need a physical to make sure she's still in good health. Arabella seemed fine yesterday, but whatever this is hit her fast and hard. I'm waiting on Vyrex to get here. I didn't want to carry her to the clinic with as poorly as she feels."

"Understood. I'll take Abbie to get checked out today. And I hope Arabella is feeling better soon."

Borgoz nodded. "Me too. I'm not sure what's worse. Being jolted awake by her screaming, or being unable to help her. I called Vyrex hours ago, but both he and Bancheck went to the outer provinces to help those communities. I'll have to speak to them about leaving our main city without healthcare in the future."

"I'm sure it was an oversight."

"Get Abbie to the clinic as soon as you can this morning, and then you can take the evening shuttle. You should land at the Terran Station in Virginia in time for dinner. Accommodations will be made for the two of you. I'm assuming you'll be sharing a suite? Are you prepared to claim her yet?" Borgoz asked.

"I want to claim her, but I want the timing to be right. Maybe I can study the human customs of marriage and see how they handle it."

"I believe it's called a proposal," Borgoz said, "and involves a flashy ring and making a fool of yourself."

Larimar laughed. "That sounds easy enough."

"Good luck, Larimar. I've already discussed your possible mating with the other council members. Whenever she accepts, just get word to me and I'll file the papers. You're as good as mated as far as I'm concerned."

"Thank you."

Larimar signed off and did a little research on Virginia

before going to wake up Abbie. She was already in the shower when he went back to the bedroom, a pretty dress laid across the bed with some silky underthings. He couldn't wait to see her in it, but worried if they were going to Earth that she might not be warm enough. From what he'd just read, it was cold there this time of year and he didn't want her to get chilled and become ill. A bit of shopping might be in order when they reached the Terran Station.

"Abbie," he said, stepping into the bathroom. "When you're done, we need to discuss something."

The water shut off and she peeked around the shower door. "What kind of something?"

"Borgoz would like for us to take a trip. To your home in Virginia."

She stepped out and dried off. "Why?"

"He wants me to record images on my portable Vid-comm of the things you'd like to have here on my world. Like dancing, I would imagine." Although, he had a feeling there was more to their trip than that. They had plenty of images of Earth already.

Her brow furrowed. "Larimar, most of my ideas can't really be recorded. The dancing is one thing, but maybe just pictures of some of the rest? We could get a disposable camera and have the pictures developed before we came home."

"There's one more thing. You have to go to the clinic before they'll clear you to leave. There's apparently a virus or something going around and Borgoz wants to make sure you're healthy before getting on the shuttle."

"I have no problem going to the clinic."

"Then we should dress and I'll take you straight there. A shuttle leaves tonight and I'd like to make sure you're cleared in plenty of time for us to pack. I would imagine we'll be on Earth a few days."

While Abbie dressed, he showered quickly and pulled on his black leather pants and vest. He eyed the contents of his closet and wondered if Abbie would like for him to dress more "human" on occasion. A lot of the males, like Dryden, who had spent a good portion of their time on Earth, had a tendency to wear the denim pants humans seemed to like so much. Larimar had to admit they looked more comfortable than his leather.

Once they were dressed and had eaten breakfast, he took Abbie by the hand and led her to the clinic. A few people were waiting ahead of them, but a Vid-comm unit on the wall played a movie to keep everyone occupied. The time passed quickly and soon Bancheck was calling her back.

The doctor stopped him at the hall doorway. "Are you mated?"

"No," Abbie said before he could respond. She was always so quick to say they weren't mated. A lesser male might have worried over it.

"You'll need to wait out here. New policy," Bancheck said.

"I'm aware of the policy and why it was created. I'm not stalking Abbie and didn't bring her here against her will. She's been staying with me."

Bancheck frowned. "She's living with you, but you aren't mated? Are you her guardian like Borgoz was for Charlotte?"

Larimar growled. "Because I'm older I'm her guardian?"

The doctor paled and took a step back. "My mistake."

"I don't mind if he comes back," Abbie said. "It's not like I have anything to hide. I passed the physical on Earth just a few days ago. I doubt anything has changed since then."

"Very well," Bancheck said. "Since you give your consent, he may come back."

Larimar didn't care much for the revised policy if it kept him away from Abbie. When they stepped into the exam room, he helped Abbie onto the table, then stood back out of the way. Bancheck did some bloodwork then ran some scans. The doctor frowned and did another scan before looking at Larimar with a hard stare.

"What?" he asked.

"In the hall, please," Bancheck said, looking furious.

Larimar went into the hall and Bancheck closed the door behind them.

"She's good enough to take to your bed, but not good enough to mate?" the doctor asked harshly.

"What are you talking about? A bio scan can show we're having sex?"

"She's pregnant, Larimar! I don't know what game you're playing with her, but you either mate her, or I'm taking the matter to the council. The council is supposed to be above reproach and you've done the one thing we always caution our males against. Casual sex."

"It wasn't casual," Larimar muttered, reeling a bit from the news that his Abbie was pregnant. Pride and joy filled him, and then a hint of worry. Having agreed to join the bride program, she'd have known that children were required, but she might not have wanted one so soon.

"I have to tell her," Bancheck said. "You should wait here."

Larimar leaned against the wall, wanting to go to Abbie and hold her. He wanted to confess everything he was feeling and beg her to be his mate, but maybe Bancheck was right. Maybe it was best if the doctor gave her the news and gave her a moment to accept the fact she was going to have a child. He'd heard it could be an emotional moment for a female. Hell, he was a strong male and it had nearly taken him to his knees.

The door opened and a pale Abbie came closer, her lower lip trembling. As she looked up at him, a tear slipped down her cheek. His heart clenched, thinking she was upset about the baby.

"I'm sorry," she said softly.

"Sorry for what?"

"I didn't get pregnant on purpose."

He gathered her close and kissed the top of her head. "I never thought you did. Does the idea of having a baby make you sad? I'd always thought babies were supposed to make people smile."

"But now you're going to feel obligated to ask me to be your mate." She blinked up at him, wiping the moisture from her eyes. "I never wanted that. I wanted you to be with me because it's what you wanted, not because you felt like you had to."

Bancheck was glaring at him over the top of her head and Larimar decided the clinic wasn't the best place for their much-needed conversation. With his arm around Abbie, he ushered her out of the clinic. As much as Borgoz had wanted them on the shuttle tonight, Larimar was thinking it might be best to postpone the trip. He paused outside the clinic door.

"Abbie, can you wait here for just a moment? I need to ask the doctor something."

She nodded, looking miserable.

Larimar hurried back inside and found Bancheck. The doctor still looked pissed at him, but there wasn't much he could do about it. Besides, it wasn't Bancheck's business whether or not he asked Abbie to be his mate.

"Is it safe for her to travel back to Earth tonight?" Larimar asked.

"You're kicking her off our world knowing she's carrying your child?" Bancheck asked with ice in his voice.

"No! Of course not. But Borgoz wanted me to take her to Earth tonight for a special assignment. I need to know if she's able to go or if she should remain here."

"What she should have done was found a male who would honor her and do right by her. Instead, she ended up with you. How could you move her into your home and not claim her? She was so damn scared that you would be angry about the baby."

Larimar winced. "It wasn't my intention to make her think I didn't want her. I was just waiting for the right time."

"I think the right time came and went. As for travel, she's perfectly healthy. Just pregnant."

"I think we've established she's carrying my child," Larimar said. "You don't have to keep saying it."

"You need to fix this and you need to do it quickly. Stress isn't good for her. Abbie may be perfectly healthy, but it's her first pregnancy. I don't know if she'll carry the baby easily or if she'll have a rough time. If being around you upsets her, then she'll need to go back to the apartment or stay with another male," Bancheck said.

Larimar snarled at him. "And I'm guessing you'd be happy to be that male."

"I would offer the comfort of my home to any female in need. But if you want her, and not just because she's pregnant, you need to tell her. Abbie thinks you just want something casual with her. I don't know how you could have screwed up this much in such a short amount of time."

Bancheck threw his hands in the air and stormed off down the hall. The doctor should have never spoken to a councilman that way, but Larimar had to admit that he deserved a bit of fury. He just hadn't expected the doctor to side with Abbie so fiercely. Larimar wasn't certain if that made Bancheck a more than competent doctor, worried for his patient, or if it made him competition. Bancheck had yet to take a mate.

Larimar went back outside to find Abbie standing just outside the door where he'd left her. She looked so small and uncertain as she watched people pass by. He took her hand, giving it a comforting squeeze, before leading her back to his place. They needed to talk and get a few things straight. He'd wanted to wait for the perfect opportunity to ask her to be his, but now his time had run out. He needed to make sure she knew that she meant something to him, that she wasn't a casual affair. It sickened him that she felt that way about what they'd shared, but he knew he only had himself to blame.

When they reached his home, he lifted Abbie into his arms and carried her upstairs. He eased her onto the bed and removed her shoes before lying down next to her. Her eyes were red-rimmed and she was still sniffling as she fought back more tears. His fingers lightly caressed her cheek as he tried to soothe her.

"I don't have experience with finding a mate," Larimar said. "I've never really tried. But when I saw you, I knew that you were special. I brought you here, and kept you in my home, because it's where I wanted you. Where I needed you."

"If you wanted me as a mate, you'd have said something by now. The only reason you're going to ask me today is because of the baby. If the doctor hadn't told you I was pregnant, you wouldn't be lying here trying to make me feel like you want me."

He tipped her chin up. "Have you ever doubted that I want you?"

"No, but wanting me in your bed and wanting me in your life are two different things, Larimar. We're good in bed together, but I thought we were good together outside of the bedroom too. I kept waiting for you to see it."

"Abbie," he said softly. "I did see it. I was waiting for the right time to ask you to be mine. I didn't want to ask when we were in bed together because I didn't want you to believe I only wanted you for sex. And I didn't want to blurt it out over a meal."

"How can I believe you were ever going to ask?" Abbie said.

"You're going to have to trust me, Abbie. If you feel anything for me, you'll give me a chance to make things right."

She snorted. "See. You just want to make it all better because I'm pregnant."

"No, I want to make things right because I gave you cause to doubt the way I feel about you. I want to make things right because you should have known from the beginning that I wanted to keep you, even if I did try to convince myself you'd be better off with someone else."

"I want to believe you. I want so much to believe that you truly want me and not just the baby. Do you know what I thought when I first saw you?" she asked.

"What?"

"I thought I'd found the guy I wanted to spend the rest

of my life with. You were handsome and obviously took your job seriously if you sought me out to make yet another apology. And then we talked the rest of the day and I saw how kind you were, how sincere."

"Abbie." He softly brushed his lips against hers. "I'm sorry I gave you cause to doubt me. But if you'll agree to be my mate, I'll spend the rest of my life making it up to you."

"I need to think, Larimar. You're saying all the right things, but I don't know if they're just words or if you really mean them."

He sighed and leaned back. "We'll go to Earth tonight as planned, and while we're there, I'm going to do everything I can to prove to you that you're who I want by my side."

She blinked away more tears as she snuggled against his chest. She might not know if she could believe what he was telling her, but she obviously still wanted him to hold her. He'd take whatever he could get at the moment. And hopefully by the time they returned from Earth, she'd be his in every way.

# Chapter Seven

Abbie looked around the spacious hotel suite, then stared at the shopping bags near the sofa. "What are those?"

"Your new clothes. I called ahead to request they pick up a few things for you. I knew it would be cold here and everything you bought on my world is for warmer weather." He pointed at two sacks set off to the side. "Except those. Those are mine."

She chewed on her bottom lip. Hesitantly, she opened the sacks and looked at the contents. He must have told them her preferences for either soft dresses or denim because the bags were filled with both. A purple angora sweater caught her attention and she lifted it from the bag. It was the same color as Larimar's eyes and it made her love the stupid thing even more. She should be upset with him, but all she could feel was worry.

He claimed to want her in his life permanently, but he hadn't seemed determined to make her his until they'd found out she was pregnant. If her past had taught her anything, it was that men couldn't necessarily be trusted. She'd been burned one too many times. Abbie had thought Larimar was different, would have even bet on him being the one to prove her wrong, but now... How could she believe that he truly wanted her for her and not because of the baby?

"You're probably hungry," Larimar said. "Why don't we shower and change and then head out for dinner?"

Her stomach chose that moment to rumble, making her cheeks warm. They'd left before the evening meal on Zelthrane-3 and then taken an eight-hour shuttle ride to Earth, but because of the time difference, it was still dinnertime. She gathered her sacks and then stood, uncertain. Did he still intend for them to share the same bedroom, or had he requested two rooms so she'd have her own?

Larimar picked up his sacks, then pushed open the bedroom door on the left. He paused in the doorway, watching her.

"Abbie, I still want you with me, but only if you want to be in my bed. There are two bedrooms if you'd prefer to sleep alone. I won't like it, but I'll understand."

She saw the sincerity in his eyes, and knew she'd sleep better with his arms around her. Making a decision she hoped she wouldn't regret, she followed him into the bedroom and set her bags down. Larimar pulled out a few soft-looking sweaters and some jeans out of one of his sacks, surprising her. She'd never seen him in anything but leather or the loose pants he wore around his home. She smiled a little as she realized all of the sweaters were either black or some shade of gray. It seemed even if he was going to wear human clothes, it didn't extend to bright colors.

"I won't presume to share the shower with you," Larimar said. "I'll let you go first."

It looked like it pained him to say the words, and she wondered if maybe he did care for her, at least a little. Abbie didn't want things to change between them. Even if she wasn't ready to believe he truly wanted her as his mate, she enjoyed their time together, liked living in his home. And she enjoyed their intimate moments. But would it be enough long-term? She wanted love. She *needed* love. Abbie couldn't remember a time anyone had ever loved her, and it was the one thing she longed for the most.

Regardless of what happened with Larimar, she vowed to be the best mother to her baby, to never let her son or daughter go a day without knowing they were loved and cherished. That they were wanted. The baby might have been a surprise, and might have been created a little sooner than she'd anticipated, but it didn't change how she felt about the little being growing inside of her.

"We can share the shower," she said, coming to a decision.

As much as she wanted love, she had to put her child first. It was obvious that Larimar wanted to be a dad, all the males on his world did, and it would be selfish to keep his baby from him. Whether love ever grew between them or not, she owed it to her child to give things between her and

Larimar a chance.

He looked relieved as he stood and followed her into the bathroom. It wasn't as luxurious as the one in his home, but it was nicer than anything she'd seen on Earth before. She'd lived most of her life in the poor part of town and crawled very far up the ladder to get away from that place before she'd been evicted. The way Larimar spent money was foreign to her, having to watch every penny out of every check to make sure she had food to eat and a place to sleep. He seemed to purchase whatever he wanted whenever he wanted, and never seemed to worry about the consequences. She'd imagine a nice hotel suite like this one was costing quite a bit. She didn't know if Larimar was paying or the council.

The water warmed quickly and they stripped out of their clothes. The hotel had provided shower gel and shampoo. She missed her floral body wash and wished she'd thought to bring it with her. Abbie started to reach for the shower gel when Larimar got to it first. He poured a generous amount onto his palm, then lathered his hands before reaching for her. Her heart skipped a beat as his hands smoothed the gel down her neck, across her shoulders, and down her arms. He worked the soap into her skin, massaging her achy muscles as he explored every inch of her body.

Abbie brought her hands up to rest on his chest, feeling the muscles flex under her fingertips. Her eyes misted as she realized he wasn't trying to turn her on, just take care of her. When he was finished, he washed her hair then helped her rinse. Pulling her closer, he pressed his lips to hers in the gentlest of kisses.

"Go get ready and I'll finish up in here," he said, giving her a nudge toward the shower door.

Abbie reluctantly got out, dried off, and went into the bedroom to pick out her clothes for the night. She picked up the purple sweater again, loving the color and the feel of it. Pairing it with some black jeans, she quickly dressed then dug through the bag of shoes and selected a pair of black ballet flats to go with it. Larimar hadn't allowed her to pack anything, telling her everything would be provided for them when they arrived, and he hadn't been wrong. There was a hairbrush, two toothbrushes, toothpaste, and both a bottle of perfume and a bottle of cologne on the bathroom counter.

Abbie used the hairdryer attached to the wall to dry her hair, then brushed the tangles from it. She wished she had a little make-up, especially as pale as she looked. Even though she'd come to terms with the fact she was pregnant, and was even starting to look forward to having a baby, the color hadn't returned to her cheeks yet. The water in the shower shut off and Larimar stepped out. She handed him a towel, feeling a little envious of the water droplets clinging to his broad chest, then went into the living room to wait for him.

When he stepped out of the bathroom, her jaw dropped a little. The jeans molded to his thighs and the sweater stretched across his chest and shoulders. Abbie stood and moved closer, her fingers itching to touch him. Hell, she might be conflicted over whether or not they could have a happily-ever-after, but there was no denying she still wanted him. The man was too sexy for his own good, or hers.

He looked down at himself. "Do human clothes look all right on me?"

"You look very nice." More than nice.

"The hotel has a restaurant downstairs, or we could go somewhere else if you have a favorite place to eat."

"I never really got to eat out much," Abbie said. "Anywhere is fine with me."

"You mentioned a need for a camera of some sort. Is there a place open this late that would sell one?" he asked.

"Yes. I can give you directions to the store. They're open twenty-four hours."

He nodded. "Then we'll go there after we've eaten."

Larimar placed a hand at her waist and guided her to the door. As they made their way down to the restaurant, he stayed close to her, even if his touches were innocent enough. She hadn't noticed it before, but he seemed to always be touching her. Even if it was just holding her hand.

The restaurant wasn't very busy and looked like it might be closing at any moment. When the hostess saw Larimar, she smiled broadly and wiggled her shoulders in a way that made her breasts bounce. Abbie narrowed her eyes at the blonde and wondered how much trouble she'd get into if she ripped out some of her hair. Larimar didn't seem to notice the attention the blonde was giving him and it helped soothe Abbie's ruffled feathers. When the woman placed her hand on Larimar's arm, batting her lashes at him, Abbie reached over to remove the woman's arm and made sure to squeeze as hard as she could.

"That was uncalled for," the blonde said.

"You were flirting with me," Larimar said, "even though I showed no interest in you. It's obvious I'm here with Abbie. Your behavior was rude and reeks of desperation."

The blonde's cheeks flushed and she hurried away. A man dressed in a sharp suit noticed the commotion and came over.

"Is there a problem, sir?" the man asked Larimar.

"The woman offended my female by flirting with me. Then she touched me."

The man's back straightened. "I assure you we don't tolerate that kind of behavior from our staff. My apologies. Your meals tonight will be complimentary and I hope you'll dine with us again during your stay. My name is Peterson and I'm the manager. Please don't hesitate to ask for anything."

"Thank you," Larimar said.

He pulled out Abbie's chair before taking his own seat. Menus were already on the table, along with silverware rolled in cloth napkins. Abbie warmed a little at Larimar's defense of her, and she was glad he hadn't been interested in the other woman. The words on her menu blurred as she realized she'd come to a decision, one she might regret in later years, but the surge of jealousy she'd just felt proved one thing for certain. She already had feelings for the sexy alien. Never before had she been jealous when a woman came onto her man, but she'd have gladly beaten the blonde bloody tonight.

She set her menu down.

"Already know what you want?" Larimar asked.

"Yes. No. I mean I don't know what I want to eat, but I need to tell you something."

Larimar pointed to her menu. "Food first. You need to eat, Abbie. Find something you really want on there and after we order you can tell me whatever you want."

She nodded and picked up the menu again. There weren't prices, which told her the place was probably expensive, even if they had comped their meal. She decided to try something she'd never had before and when the waiter arrived, she ordered the seafood platter with lobster, shrimp scampi, and calamari, with a loaded baked potato on the side.

When the waiter hurried off with their order, promising to return momentarily with their drinks, Larimar smiled at her.

"Now, what did you want to talk about?" he asked.

"Were you serious about claiming me as your mate?" she asked.

"Of course. It's what I want more than anything, Abbie."

"I don't know that I'll ever believe you meant to claim me before finding out I'm pregnant, but I do know I want my baby to have a loving home with two parents. You're an honorable man, Larimar, and I think you'll make a good father. It would be wrong of me to walk away and deny my baby the home he or she could have had if we're together."

He frowned. "Wait. You don't believe that I want you, regardless of whether or not you're pregnant, but you'll accept because of the baby?"

"I... I care about you, Larimar, and maybe that's enough for now. It's not what I dreamed of when I imagined getting married, but plenty of relationships are built on less. And I think it's undeniable that we have chemistry."

"So, you want to be my mate because we're having a child together and the sex is good between us? And you care about me?" he asked, not looking thrilled with the idea.

Had she read him wrong? She'd thought he would be happy she was accepting his offer, but he looked like he'd bitten into something sour. Abbie dropped her gaze to the table and wondered if the situation could be salvaged. She hadn't meant to offend him, even though it appeared she'd done just that.

"I thought you'd be happy," she said softly. "I didn't mean to upset you."

"Happy? You thought I would be happy that you're settling for a relationship with me? I want what my friends have, Abbie. I want a relationship built on more than fondness and sex."

Could he want the same things as her? Was it possible she'd read him completely wrong and misunderstood? He'd said he didn't want her just because of the baby, but she hadn't believed him. But what if he really did want her because he cared for her? And now she'd gone and screwed it all up.

Larimar stood, tossing his napkin on the table. "I think I need some air."

She wanted to cry as she watched him walk away, torn between going after him, or giving him the time he seemed to need to cool off. She'd offended him, even though it hadn't been her intention. Their food arrived and she stared at the empty place across from her. When it became apparent Larimar wasn't returning, she picked at her food, not really tasting it. She requested that both their meals be boxed and sent up to their room, and then she left the restaurant.

Abbie didn't know where Larimar had gone or when he'd return. She set off down the sidewalk on foot, the winter air biting into her skin. She shivered against the cold and wandered aimlessly around the city. By the time the pain in her feet registered, she had no idea where she was. She looked around, trying to find something familiar, and with a jolt, she realized she was in her old neighborhood.

The homes and apartments looked shabbier than she remembered. Some of the stores had been boarded up. She hadn't been to her childhood home since she left at the age of seventeen. Curious, she wandered further down the street and stopped in front of her old home. The shutters hung crooked and some windows were broken. Tattered curtains hung in the windows and the front door stood ajar, lightly blowing back and forth in the breeze.

Abbie found herself walking up the broken path and stopping on the sagging porch. The boards creaked and groaned under her weight as she pushed the door open wide. The same furniture she'd sat on as a kid and teen still stood in the living room, now stained and covered in cobwebs and grime. She didn't know what had happened to her parents or to their home. She stepped across the threshold. The scent of mildew and mold hit her, and she covered her nose.

The house felt eerie, as if ghosts haunted the halls. She didn't dare go upstairs, not certain they would hold her weight, but she moved room by room through the downstairs, assaulted by memories best left forgotten.

"You shouldn't be in here," a male voice said behind her.

She gasped and spun, nearly losing her balance.

"Jesus. Abbie?" he asked.

He stepped into a shaft of moonlight, and even though he was much older now, she knew him instantly.

"Parker."

"What are you doing here? You don't belong here anymore."

"I -- I don't know. I was walking and then I found myself here. What happened?"

"You really don't know?" he asked.

She shook her head.

"You should leave the ghosts of the past where they belong. This place... walk away, Abbie. Leave and don't look back this time."

"You still live here?"

"My parents left the house to me. I've lived across the street my entire life, and this is where I'll die, if I don't rot in prison first."

"You had plans to get out," Abbie said.

"Sometimes you can't escape the hand life deals you. I'm no better than my old man. I boost cars, Abbie. It pays the bills, and for other things."

"Drugs?" she asked. "You swore you'd never touch that crap."

He shrugged. "Things change. Get out of here, Abbie. I mean it. Don't come back again. You're lucky I'm the one who found you."

She nodded and left her childhood home for the last time, not stopping until she was in a better part of town. Her heart raced and she couldn't help but wonder what had happened to her parents. They'd been horrible to her, but still... they'd given birth to her and raised her as best they could. Neither had graduated high school and both were heavy into drugs and alcohol. Maybe if her mom hadn't gotten pregnant in high school, things might have been different, but she'd never know.

By the time she realized she was more than lost, she was shaking so hard her teeth had nearly rattled out of her head. She hadn't paid attention to the name of the hotel and had no idea how to get back to it. She fought not to give up and have a good cry, but her hope was dwindling. If she caught a cab to the Terran Station, would someone there pay for it? She didn't have any money, but she didn't want to walk another five or six miles to the station.

Up ahead she saw a tall Terran step out of a club, a woman on either side of him. A crowd gathered around him as he moved down the sidewalk and she rushed to catch up. She recognized him from an interview he'd done a few months ago.

"Brexton," she called out, trying to be heard over the crowd.

He paused and looked around. She waved at him and

moved a little closer. He whispered something to each of the women at his side and met her halfway.

"Do you want an autograph?" he asked.

"I need your help."

"Help?" he asked, an eyebrow raised.

"I'm here with Councilman Larimar and we're staying at a hotel, but I don't remember the name and I don't know how to get there." She shivered again, clenching her teeth so they wouldn't clack together.

"You're freezing," he murmured. "There's a limo down the street. I was going to use it to take my party elsewhere, but I think you need it more than me. Come on."

She followed him back to his adoring fans and then down the sidewalk where a large white limo waited. Brexton said something to the driver then opened the rear door for her.

"He'll take you to the hotel. Next time you go for a walk, you should dress warmer."

"Thank you," she said through chattering teeth.

He shut the door and tapped on the roof. The limo pulled away from the curb and before long she was at the hotel. Shivering and shaking, she made her way to the front desk, not even remembering what room they were staying in. Since she had so little information, and she wasn't listed as a guest, they refused to help her into the councilman's suite.

Fighting tears and still frozen through, she curled on a sofa in the corner of the lobby and tried to get warm. Pressing her head to her bent knees, she wondered how things could have gone so wrong so fast, and hoped that Larimar would find her soon.

# Chapter Eight

Larimar had walked for a bit to clear his head and then returned to the restaurant, to find that Abbie had left. She'd requested their food be sent to their suite, but hadn't given the waiter the room number, so they'd kept it warm downstairs. He carried the containers up to the suite and pushed the door open, expecting to find Abbie. The suite was dark when he entered and he placed the containers on the counter.

"Abbie?" he called out.

He checked the bedrooms and bathrooms, he didn't see her anywhere. Larimar even stepped out onto the balcony, even though she'd have to be crazy to be out there in this weather. He frowned, wondering where she would have gone. Not knowing what else to do, he checked with the doorman downstairs to see if he remembered Abbie leaving, but the man couldn't recall.

He scoured the hotel and even called the Terran Station, wondering if perhaps she'd gone looking for him. When he exhausted his resources, he went back up to the room to wait. As the hours passed, his worry for her grew. He'd been harsh with her, but she wouldn't have run away, would she? Had he hurt her feelings enough she would leave him? There was much he still didn't understand about human females, particularly his Abbie.

The food lay forgotten as he paced the confines of the suite. The longer she was gone, the more he worried. When he couldn't take another moment of it, he went back downstairs, determined to find her even if he had to drive the streets all night. A commotion in the corner of the lobby drew his attention and his heart nearly stalled in his chest when he saw Abbie sprawled on a sofa.

"Abbie!" He rushed forward and the crowd of hotel employees parted.

"She claimed to be here with a Terran," one of the front desk employees said. "A councilman."

"She is. She's with me," he told her. "Why wasn't she brought up to my suite?"

"She wasn't listed as a guest and it's our policy not to allow strangers entry into hotel rooms. Just because she claimed to be here with someone didn't mean she really was," the woman said defensively.

He touched her pale cheek and winced at how cold she felt.

"Move," Larimar said, shoving everyone out of his way.

He lifted Abbie into his arms and carried her out to where a line of limos stood waiting for any of his kind who needed a ride. He stopped at the first one.

"Can you take us to the Terran Station?" he asked the driver. "She needs the clinic."

"I'll get you there as quickly as I can," the driver said, holding the door open for him.

Once he was settled on the seat with Abbie in his lap, the door shut and a moment later they were pulling away from the curb. She whimpered and burrowed closer to him, her teeth chattering slightly, but she didn't open her eyes. Her entire body felt like it was a block of ice, she was so cold, and he cursed himself for a fool to leave her alone like he had. If he'd stayed with her, if he'd kept his temper and shoved his wounded pride aside, then she'd be fine and probably sleeping in their bed.

The limo pulled to a stop outside the Terran Station and the driver opened the door for them. Larimar stood, still holding Abbie, and carried her inside. He walked past reception and toward the back where the clinic took up part of a long hallway. The lights were still on even though it was nearly three in the morning. The doors slid open as he approached and he pressed the bell on the counter. A very tired Prylo appeared moments later.

"I didn't realize you were on Earth, Councilman Larimar. It's good to see you."

"Abbie is sick."

"You know we're only allowed to treat mates."

"She's mine. We just haven't made it official yet. Borgoz said it was as good as done once I got word to him," Larimar said. "Please. She's freezing to the touch and won't stop shivering."

Prylo motioned for Larimar to follow him down the hall and they entered an exam room. Larimar laid her on the table but stayed by her side. Prylo pulled out a bioscanner and checked her vital signs.

"We're going to slowly warm her back up," Prylo said. "It looks like she was out in the elements for a while. Did you let her leave the hotel without a coat? The temperatures are below freezing and the wind makes it even colder."

"I didn't know she'd left. I went for a walk and when I came back, she was gone. I've been worried about her and found her on a sofa in the hotel lobby."

"So she's been in a warm environment for at least a little while. I'm going to heat some blankets and bring them in to wrap around her and then I'm going to give her some warm oxygen just as a precaution. Her heartbeat is slow, but I think she'll pull through just fine."

"She's pregnant," Larimar said. "With my child."

Prylo smiled a little. "I'm aware that she's carrying a baby. And I assumed it was yours. We'll take care of her, Councilman. She'll be warm in your bed by morning."

"Is there nothing else we can do for her?"

"I'm going to inject her with a serum that will help warm her and should help her awaken shortly. She's showing signs of hypothermia, but I think we caught it in time. The fact she went into someplace warm probably helped. If she'd stayed outside..."

Larimar's heart clenched at the thought of losing Abbie. He held her hand while Prylo got the things he needed, then helped wrap Abbie in the warm blankets. Within an hour of Prylo giving her the serum, her eyes fluttered open and she reached for the oxygen mask that was over her mouth and nose.

Larimar took her hand. "Leave that there."

"It's fine now," Prylo said. "She can remove it."

Abbie pulled the mask loose and looked up at Larimar. "What happened?"

"I found you in the hotel lobby, freezing cold and unresponsive. Where did you go, Abbie? I looked for you."

"I went for a walk," she said. "And then I got lost. Brexton sent me back to the hotel in a limo, but they wouldn't tell me what room number we were in. So I sat on the sofa downstairs and thought maybe you'd find me."

He held her close, stroking her hair. "I'm so sorry," he said. "I never should have left you like that."

"I made you angry," she said softly.

"You hurt my pride, but I should have stayed with you. If I hadn't run off, then you wouldn't have gotten sick."

"I don't know what I said that upset you so much. I thought I was giving you what you wanted," she said. "I never meant to offend you."

"We can talk about it later. Right now, I think you need a hot bath, maybe something to eat, and sleep."

Prylo did another bioscan of her. "Your heart rate is back to normal and everything looks good. The serum I gave you may give you an energy boost, but don't overdo it or you'll regret it later. Listen to Larimar and let him take care of you for at least another twenty-four hours. After that, you should be in the clear."

Her hand went to her stomach. "The baby?"

"The baby is fine," Prylo said.

"I can take her back to the hotel now?" Larimar asked.

"Yes, just keep an eye on her for another day. If it looks like she's relapsing, bring her back, but I don't expect any problems."

Larimar lifted Abbie into his arms and carried her back to the line of limos outside of the Terran Station. It was still dark out, and extremely cold. When they got into one of the cars, he asked the driver to turn the heat up, worried his Abbie could catch another chill. She'd finally stopped shivering and he didn't want it to start back again.

At the hotel, he took her straight to their suite and prepared a hot bath for her. He helped her undress and get into the tub, then he sat on the floor nearby to keep an eye on her. Abbie sank into the water up to her neck and closed her eyes, but he could see the steady rise and fall of her chest, assuring him that she was fine.

"Our food is probably cold again," he said. "I can warm it up after you're dressed for bed."

"They didn't purchase pajamas for me," she said, sounding tired.

"Then you can put on one of the complimentary robes while we eat and I'll keep you warm tonight while we sleep."

"Larimar?"

He inched closer. "What is it, Abbie?"

"I'm sorry. I shouldn't have run out into the cold. You left me and I was scared you weren't coming back. I didn't mean to go so far."

"Where did you go?" he asked.

"My old house. The one I grew up in. It's falling apart now. I don't know what happened to my parents, but they weren't there. The windows were broken and the curtains were torn. Everything was covered in filth and cobwebs."

"Would you like for me to find out what happened to your parents?" he asked. "Even if it's not pleasant?"

"I need to know." She opened her eyes and looked at him. "I left and never looked back. Did they ever search for me? Did they even care that I was gone?"

"I'll see what I can find out for you."

She pushed herself up and tried to stand. Larimar helped her, then dried her off and tied the fluffy robe around her. Keeping an arm around her waist in case she was unsteady, he helped her to the small dining table in the living area, then went to heat their food.

"I'm not sure how this will taste reheated," he said. "If it's not good, don't eat it. I'll order something else for us."

"I'm sure it's fine." She smiled wistfully. "It was my first time having seafood."

"And I ruined the moment by being a coward and running away," he muttered.

"Are we okay?" she asked.

He kissed her brow and smoothed her hair back.

"We're more than okay. I'll contact my council and ask that our mating papers be filed. I should have done it days ago."

"You said you were going to prove to me that you would be a good mate. What had you planned to do?" she asked.

"I was going to take you dancing, take you to a nice place to eat, and I had planned to buy you a ring. I've heard it's customary for human females to wear a ring when they are mated. I wanted you to have that."

"And you planned to do those things before you found out about the baby?" she asked.

"Yes. I wanted to show you how much I value you, and that you mean something to me. I know you think what we've shared was casual, but it wasn't. It's very rare for my people to have casual relationships with females. I've heard some have since coming to Earth, but most of us want mates. When I brought you to my home and kept you there, it's because I wanted you there always."

"Maybe we need to work some more on our communication skills."

He smiled a little. "That might be a good idea. I obviously have a lot to learn about human females, and I think there's still much for you to learn about my people. Perhaps we just haven't known one another long enough and in time the matter will resolve itself."

Abbie finished eating and Larimar tossed the food containers away. She yawned widely and he helped her out of the robe and into bed, where he curled his body around hers to keep her warm. They were sent to Earth for a specific purpose, but Larimar had already decided it would have to wait. As soon as Abbie was rested enough, they would return to Zelthrane-3, where he'd keep her until their child was old enough to travel. If something as simple as the weather could nearly take her from him, he didn't want to know what else on Earth might be lurking to claim her life, and he wasn't staying around to find out.

"Your world is dangerous," he said.

"Compared to yours I suppose it can be a violent place.

We have thieves, liars, murderers, rapists. But there are good people here too. Sometimes it's just hard to tell which kind you've met until it's too late."

"I'll make arrangements soon for our return trip to Zelthrane-3. I want you home where I know you're safe," he said.

"I like your world, even if there are things I'll miss here."

"Whatever you want to take with us, I'll make it happen."

She mumbled something he couldn't understand and then her breathing evened out, letting him know she'd fallen asleep.

Larimar stayed up a while longer, well after the sun rose. How strange that there was only one. He eased out of bed long enough to contact Borgoz. The Chief Council was already at the large table in the council chambers, and appeared to be going over paperwork alone.

"You look worried," Borgoz said.

"Abbie was really sick last night. I think I could have lost her if I hadn't gotten to her in time. We haven't accomplished our mission, but I'd like to bring her home. I don't think this place is safe for her and our child."

"Am I filing mating papers?"

"Yes," Larimar said. "And I need another favor. Abbie would like to know what happened to her parents. She found their home abandoned and in a state of decay. She said even if the news is bad, she wants to know."

"I'll have a report to you in a few hours. We have her parents' names on her application form, as well as their last known address. It should be simple enough to track them down."

"Thank you," Larimar said. "Once the clinic clears her for travel, I would like to return home."

"We have a shuttle coming here tomorrow and another the day after. One is bringing more brides and the other is bringing supplies, so you'd be the only passengers on board. Let the Terran Station know which shuttle you'll be on. I'll make them aware of the situation."

Borgoz signed off and Larimar crawled back into bed with his Abbie. When his portable Vid-comm dinged a few hours later, he opened the report with trepidation, not knowing what he'd find. The last thing he wanted was to give his mate bad news, but he understood her need for closure. As he scanned the document, he bolted upright in bed.

"What is it?" Abbie mumbled, half asleep.

"Abbie, your mother has been looking for you."

Her eyes widened and she sat up. "When?"

"After you left, your father tried to kill her then committed suicide. Your mother was put into a rehab facility then went into a halfway house, where she remained for two years."

"Are you telling me my mother is no longer an addict?" Abbie asked.

"Your mother…"

"Larimar, what is it?"

"This isn't easy to say. Your mother is damaged from the incident with your father. There was permanent brain damage. According to the medical notes the council was able to obtain, she's more like a teenager than an adult. She can carry on conversations and can hold a simple job, but she's not the woman you once knew."

Abbie seemed to mull over his words. "I want to see her."

"Borgoz provided an address where we can find her. I'll find out from Prylo if you're allowed out of the hotel suite today. He may want you to rest one more day."

Tears gathered in Abbie's eyes. "You don't understand. All this time I thought they forgot about me, that I was unwanted. You said she's been looking for me."

"She remembers you, and seems to retain all knowledge of her past, but she has mood swings like a teenager and her impulse control has been impaired. She can't live on her own. She's in a state facility."

"All of that was in your report?" she asked.

"That and more, but you don't want the other details. Let me check with Prylo about when you're allowed to go back out into the cold. You could have died last night, Abbie. I won't take the chance that could happen again."

She nodded her acceptance and got up and went into the bathroom.

While she was gone, Larimar checked with Prylo and was given clearance for Abbie to go outside, as long as she didn't stay in the cold for long, and assurance she could be on tomorrow's shuttle home. Assuming he could pry her away from her mother. He couldn't imagine what he would do if he were in her position. She'd thought her family was lost to her, and now she had her mother back. He would give anything to have more time with his parents.

Knowing that he wouldn't be able to hold Abbie back for long, he placed a call to the facility where her mother lived and explained the situation, getting permission for a visit. As it happened, her mother didn't work today and would be home. He only hoped that Abbie was prepared for what she would find. There were no pictures of her mother and he didn't know what other damage may have been done. If her mother didn't physically look the same, it might be hard on Abbie.

He leaned against the bathroom doorway, admiring her curves through the glass shower wall. "We can visit your mother any time today."

"After we eat?" she asked.

"Yes. After we eat. It's after lunch, but we can grab a bite downstairs. The restaurant should be open. Maybe you can try something else you haven't had before, and this time you'll get to eat it while it's hot."

"I won't be long. Do you need to shower too?" she asked.

"I probably should."

She opened the shower door and peeked out. "Then come join me."

Now that was an invitation he couldn't refuse. It didn't take him long to strip and step under the spray, pulling her tight against his body. His cock, always at least semi-hard when in her presence, was fully erect and wanting to play. His body didn't understand that she'd been seriously ill the night before.

And judging by the mischievous look in her eyes, she didn't either.

"Abbie, whatever you're thinking, we shouldn't."

"Oh, but we should," she said, falling to her knees.

His eyes nearly rolled back in his head as her lips closed around the tip of his cock and then slid down to the base. Her tongue lashed the underside and her cheeks hollowed out as she sucked him hard as she drew away. He sank his fingers into her hair and fought to stay upright. Her lips and tongue drove him to distraction, but when she reached up to cup his balls, he nearly came down her throat. She rolled them gently, then gave them a bit of a squeeze and he couldn't hold back another moment.

Without time to give her warning, he cried out and shot spurt after spurt of hot cum down her throat. Abbie didn't seem to mind and swallowed every drop before giving him soft licks and kisses. Even his fast release hadn't deflated his poor cock and with a growl, he gripped her around the waist, spun her to face the shower wall, and bent her over.

"You're playing with fire. Isn't that the Earth saying?" he asked.

"Maybe I was hoping to get burned."

He lined up his cock with her slit and sank into her, holding tight to her hips as her luscious ass cushioned his pelvis. She felt like heaven wrapped around him. He wanted the moment to last forever, but he knew it wouldn't. The minute she started coming, started squeezing him, it would all be over. With the sex bots he'd used at the floating brothel, he could go for hours. But with how incredible Abbie's pussy felt, it was a miracle he didn't come the second he slid inside of her.

He took her slow and easy, his hand sliding around her belly to delve into her curls and stroke her little clit. Her fingers fisted against the shower wall as her head dropped and she pushed back against him. He stroked her faster as he powered into her, every thrust taking her up onto her toes. Larimar pinched her clit and she came, screaming his name, her pussy milking every drop of cum from his balls.

He slowly withdrew from her body and trailed kisses up her back to her neck, giving her a gentle nip. When she turned to face him, he couldn't help but kiss her.

"We should dress and eat so we can go visit your mother," he said.

"I'm both excited and scared. What if you're wrong? What if she wasn't searching for me? What if she doesn't want to see me at all?"

"Is that what you're most afraid of, or are you worried that seeing her in her present condition might change things? Maybe you aren't ready to let go of your anger from the past and you're worried you won't be able to hold onto it once you see what's become of her."

She sighed. "You might be right. I want to see her and I don't. All these years I longed for someone to miss me, to prove they loved me, and I thought they'd failed me. If I'd gone looking for her sooner, things could have been different."

He cupped her cheek. "If you'd sought her out sooner, you might have never applied for the bride program, and then we would have never met."

"You're right. Everything always happens for a reason. I know that, but… I'm just having a hard time wrapping my head around this sudden flood of information. I'll adjust."

"I know you will, because you're a fighter. You're strong, Abbie. I've always known it, and deep down you know it too. What are those fairy tales where the knight rescues the princess? You're the one swinging the sword and slaying monsters. I only want to give you the support you need along the way, and if the burden should get too heavy, I'll be more than happy to help you carry the load."

Her eyes softened and something in her expression shifted. Her lips parted, but whatever she was going to say, she decided against it. He kissed her once more, then shut off the water. The sooner they dressed and got the day started, the sooner he could determine what would be done with Abbie's mother. If the reunion went well, he knew she'd have a hard time leaving the woman behind, and he was *not* home without his mate.

# Chapter Nine

Abbie smoothed her winter dress and shifted from foot to foot. The facility where her mother was staying looked more like a prison. There were even bars on the windows, and a secured door with a video camera pointed at anyone wanting entry. An intercom was attached to the concrete wall and Larimar pressed the button.

"Name," a voice asked.

"Larimar and my mate, Abbie. We're here to see her mother, Winona Carson."

After a moment, there was a click and a buzzing sound as the door was released. Larimar pulled it open and motioned for her to enter first. She looked around the lobby, trying to picture her mother living in such a place. The walls and floors were solid white and very sterile looking. No artwork adorned the walls. The reception desk straight ahead was a plain brown with no decoration.

A woman in scrubs stood behind the desk, a tablet in her hand.

"Is Winona expecting you?" the nurse asked.

"No, it's a surprise visit from her daughter," Larimar said. "I cleared it with a Mr. Williams. He knew we were stopping by."

The nurse tapped on the screen of her tablet.

"Winona is in the day room right now."

Abbie's brow furrowed. "She has a schedule?"

The nurse gave her a humorless smile. "No, honey. She has a tracker. All of our patients have them so we can find them at any time, in the event they get lost or confused."

They'd chipped her mother like a wayward pet? Abbie was disliking this place more and more. The nurse called a guard, who escorted them to the day room. Abbie scanned the space trying to find her mother, but no one looked familiar. A badly scarred woman with a misshapen jaw approached them, her dishwater blonde hair hanging limp and looking as if it hadn't been cared for in a while. Abbie's gaze scanned away from her, in hopes of finding her mother.

"Abbie?" the woman asked, her words slurring slightly.

She froze.

"You're my Abbie," the woman said again, a smile sliding across her lips and making her jaw look even more deformed.

"Momma?" Abbie asked.

The woman nodded. Larimar placed a hand on Abbie's lower back, reassuring her as she took a step closer to her mother. The Winona Carson in front of her looked nothing like the strung out junkie she'd known as a child. Her skin wasn't as sallow and her eyes were brighter. The longer she looked at her, the more she recognized the woman, despite the jaw and rough-looking hair.

Her mother wrapped her arms around Abbie and hugged her. "My Abbie found me," her mother said.

"Yes, Momma. I found you."

Her mother drew away and looked up at Larimar, fear entering her eyes upon seeing the imposing councilman.

"It's okay, Momma," Abbie assured her. "He's my husband. He would never do anything to hurt you."

"Husbands are bad," her mother said, inching further back.

"Mrs. Carson, my name is Larimar. I'm a Terran. Do you know what that is?" he asked in a soothing voice.

"Alien," her mother answered.

"Yes, I'm an alien, and your daughter lives on another planet with me. Have you met others like me before?" Larimar asked.

Her mother slowly shook her head, but some of the fear had eased from her eyes.

"I'm very pleased to meet you, Mrs. Carson."

"Momma, Larimar is your son-in-law. I promise you're perfectly safe with him. They keep bad people out of this place, right? But they let him come in to visit with you."

Her mother moved a little closer again. Hesitantly, she reached toward Larimar and ran her finger down the top of his hand. Larimar turned his hand over and gently grasped her mother's. He went down on one knee in front of her, making himself smaller, and it seemed to ease her mother's fear even more.

Abbie had thought her old feelings of hate and resentment would consume her when she met her mother, but she wanted to cry. The pitiful woman in front of her was nothing like the spiteful creature she'd grown up with. There was almost a childlike innocence about her. Despite the cruelty Abbie had suffered at her parents' hands, she felt sorry for her mother and wished there was something she could do. No one deserved to live in a place like this.

"Mrs. Carson, would you like to go sit somewhere and visit with Abbie for a little while? Maybe we can find an empty table," Larimar suggested as he scanned the room.

Abbie's mom pulled away from Larimar and shuffled toward a table in the corner of the room, sitting down in one of the empty chairs. Abbie and Larimar followed, sitting across from her. Her mother smiled at her again, happiness shining in her eyes. It seemed as if the report was correct and her mother had been searching for her, or at the very least had inquired about her. In her mother's present state, Abbie doubted she had the mental capability of actively searching for someone.

"Momma, I heard you have a job."

Her mother frowned a little. "I did."

"What happened?" Abbie asked.

"They don't like it when I work."

Abbie leaned a little closer. "Who doesn't like it when you work?"

Her mother waved a hand. "This place. If I work, I can afford to leave."

"Momma, they want to take care of you here," Abbie said, hoping she was right. By the looks of the place, it felt more like a prison. "Aren't you safe here?"

Her mother looked frightened of something and Abbie looked around the room. A guard stood in the doorway. Larimar noticed the direction of her gaze and focused on her mother again.

"Mrs. Carson, do they hurt you here? Is there someone who causes you harm?" he asked.

"I'm not allowed to talk about it," her mother said and Abbie's stomach pitched.

"Would you like us to move you to another place?" Larimar asked. "I have the funds to place you in a private facility where you won't be harmed."

Her mother's eyes glassed over with tears. "I thought you were here to take me home."

"You want to come home with us?" Abbie asked. "We don't live on Earth anymore, Momma. Home is really far away."

A tear slipped down her mother's cheek.

"Mrs. Carson," Larimar said softly. "We're going to take you back to the hotel with us tonight. You'll have your own bedroom. If you want to go to my world with us, you will have to be examined by a doctor first."

"I can go home with you?" her mother asked pitifully.

"Yes, Mrs. Carson," Larimar said. "You may come home with us."

He leaned closer to Abbie and whispered in her ear, "Get your mother to take you to her quarters and pack her things. I'm going to make the arrangements to get her out of here right now."

Abbie kissed him softly. "Thank you."

He nodded and rose, leaving them alone. Abbie stood and held her hand out to her mother. "Can you show me where you live here? I want to see your room."

Her mother smiled and took her hand. A guard stopped them on their way out of the room.

"She can't leave," he said.

"She wants to show me her room," Abbie said.

He hesitated a moment then nodded for them to go.

Abbie's mother led her to the elevator and pressed the button for the third floor. When the doors opened, the antiseptic smell assaulted Abbie's nose. It smelled more like a hospital than a place where her mother should be living. She followed her mother down the hall and stopped at one of the metal doors. There were rectangular windows in all of the doors and she didn't like the fact you could see into her mother's room. Did she not have any privacy?

They entered the room and Abbie looked around the small space. There was a metal frame twin bed bolted to the floor and a small four-drawer chest. Two pairs of shoes were neatly placed beside it. Another door led to a bathroom that was so small Abbie didn't know how her mother managed to shower and change in the space.

"Do you have a bag for your things?" Abbie asked.

Her mother nodded and opened the bottom drawer, pulling out two canvas totes. They quickly filled them with her mother's meager possessions and then walked down to the lobby. Larimar waited for them by the reception desk, a fierce expression on his face.

"Is something wrong?" Abbie asked.

"They weren't going to release her until I threatened to report them. We're getting her out of here now," Larimar said.

Larimar took the tote bags from them and they stepped out and went to the limo waiting at the curb. Abbie's mother clutched her hand tight, looking worried and a little scared. Once they were safely in the limo and it didn't seem like anyone would come after them, her mother relaxed a little.

"You're safe now, Momma," Abbie said.

"Go home?" her mother asked.

"We're going to the hotel, but we'll go home tomorrow. Right, Larimar?" Abbie asked.

"Let's go to the Terran Station first and get your mother checked out. She needs to be cleared to ride on the shuttle tomorrow. If there's something medically wrong that will prevent her from taking the trip, we'll have to make arrangements for her here," Larimar said.

"Or we could stay until she's well enough to travel," Abbie said. "Are we really going to place her in another institution?"

"It wouldn't be anything like that last place, I can assure you of that," Larimar said.

Her mother looked at them tearfully. "Home," she repeated.

"Doctor first," Abbie said.

Her mother violently shook her head and crammed herself into the corner of the limo. Abbie frowned and wondered just what the hell that horrible place had done to her mother. She looked at Larimar, not knowing what to do. If her mother didn't see a doctor, she couldn't go on the shuttle.

Larimar leaned forward and slowly reached for her mother, taking Winona's hand. "Mrs. Carson, we will be by your side the entire time. No one is going to hurt you ever again. Abbie can hold your hand while the doctor examines you. He'll be an alien like me, and I can promise he would never do you harm."

Her mother seemed to relax a little. "Alien?"

Larimar nodded.

"Okay," her mother agreed.

Larimar released her hand and leaned back again. When the limo stopped at the Terran Station, they got out and Abbie took her mother's hand again. Larimar led the way to the clinic and she was thankful to see it was empty. The last thing she wanted was a lengthy wait. It would have only given her mother time to worry again.

Prylo came from the back and smiled at them. "I see you're here with a guest."

"This is Abbie's mother, Winona Carson," Larimar said. "We'd like for her to be examined. My mate would like her mother to come home with us."

Prylo studied her mother a moment then held out his hand. "Mrs. Carson, if you'll come with me, we'll get started. My name is Prylo and I'm one of the doctors here at the Terran Station."

Abbie's mother clutched her hand tighter and Abbie began walking, pulling her mother along. "We'll all go."

Prylo nodded and led the way. In the exam room, he pulled out the same instruments that had been used when Abbie was examined prior to her trip to Zelthrane-3. The exam didn't take long and they waited patiently as Prylo looked over everything. When he was finished, he tipped his head toward the hallway.

"Momma, I need to step out for just a minute, but I'll be right back," Abbie said.

She followed Larimar and Prylo out of the room.

"What do you know of your mother's condition?" Prylo asked.

"I know she suffered injuries from an attack by my father," Abbie said.

"There's the obvious damage to her jaw, but I don't believe it can be repaired even with our technology. Perhaps if she'd been brought to us before the hospital tried to put her back together... and then there's the brain trauma," Prylo said.

"I was aware of both of those things," Abbie said. "Can she make a trip to Zelthrane-3?"

Prylo hesitated.

"What?" Abbie asked.

"Your mother's liver and kidneys aren't functioning one hundred percent. A transplant is out of the question because I don't believe it would work, should she survive the surgery. At best, I think your mother has another two or three years to live. I would suggest finding her a place here where she can receive the care she needs," Prylo said.

Abbie's eyes misted with tears. "If she has such little time left, I want her to go with us. We'll do whatever it takes to make her comfortable."

"You'll need a trained nurse to live with you until she passes. It would be best if they could live with you, but if one of the mates already on our world was a nurse here on Earth, just having someone around during the day might be enough," Prylo said.

"What about one of our doctors in training?" Larimar asked.

"Or you could request Zaylon. He was punished after his treatment of Xonos' mate, but I believe he's learned his lesson. He is not actively practicing right now, but he has the skills necessary. Your home is large and you could place Winona and Zaylon in another wing. He'll need to be close to her in case she wakes in the middle of the night." Prylo shrugged. "It's up to you, but I would worry a human female nurse might try to lure you from your mate if she wasn't already mated."

"Can you send Winona's files to Zaylon and the council?" Larimar asked. "We'll be arriving on tomorrow's shuttle and I'd like everything to be in place when we arrive."

"If this Zaylon was mean to someone's mate, what makes you think he would treat my mother differently?" Abbie asked.

"He thought he was looking out for Xonos by trying to chase Victoria away. He has since understood that he was wrong and has been allowed to treat human females again," Prylo said. "He is unmated so he doesn't have to be home every night. Although, I would imagine he would like some days off occasionally."

"I know Zaylon," Larimar said. "If he will accept the job, I believe he will treat your mother fairly. I also like the idea of having a trained physician in the house in case anything happens to you or the baby."

"Fine." Abbie said. "I'll go tell Momma that she can go home with us tomorrow."

She re-entered the exam room and found her mother crying.

"Home?" her mother asked again.

"Yes, Momma. We're going to the hotel tonight, but tomorrow we'll go home. To your new home. Do you understand it's not the one you shared with Daddy?"

Her mother nodded and slipped off the exam table, reaching for her hand again. Abbie led her out of the room and they left the Terran Station to return to the hotel. After Abbie had her mother settled for the night, she curled against Larimar's side on the couch and stared at the TV. Today hadn't gone as she'd planned, but at least she had her mother back in her life. For however long the woman would live.

# Chapter Ten

It had been a week since they'd returned to his world and Larimar thought things were going well. Zaylon had agreed to be Winona's caretaker and the doctor had moved in almost immediately. Larimar had made it clear that as long as Zaylon was looking after Winona, he couldn't seek a mate, and the doctor seemed fine with that. They'd taken over the wing opposite Larimar's. It gave everyone some privacy and yet kept Winona close enough for Abbie to spend as much time with her as she pleased.

Abbie's hands crept around his waist as he stood at the balcony railing off their bedroom. A breeze blew, teasing his nose with the scents from the garden below. The three suns rose slowly over the hills in the distance and Larimar felt at peace. He had a family now, something he'd always wanted. A mate with a baby on the way, and with Abbie had come her mother. Even though Winona wasn't like most mothers, it was nice having her around.

"You're up early," Abbie said, kissing his back.

"I'm sorry if I woke you."

She pressed her cheek against him. "I only woke because the bed felt empty. I've gotten used to you sleeping by my side."

He smiled a little. "More like you've gotten used to sleeping sprawled across me."

He felt her lips curve against his back. "That too."

"How do you feel this morning?" he asked. "Any morning sickness?"

"No. Bancheck told you I may never experience any. Each pregnancy is different. Maybe I'll be one of the lucky ones."

Larimar turned and wrapped his arms around his mate. Her belly was still flat, but he placed a hand there, knowing his child was inside. His heart skipped a beat every time he thought about the incredible gift Abbie was giving him. Not just a baby, but herself as well. The emotion he felt when he thought about getting to wake up next to her every morning made his throat tight. As the years had passed and brides had come and gone, he'd worried that he would never have a mate. And then the incredible woman in his arms had arrived, and everything had changed.

"You have that look again," she said.

"What look?"

"Almost a look of awe and I can't figure out what puts it there. I've seen it at random times throughout the day and it makes me wonder what you're thinking about," she said.

"You," he answered honestly. "You and the family you've helped me create. I'm so blessed to have you in my life, Abbie. I don't know what you saw in me that day that made you want to get to know me better, that made you want to stay with me, but I'll be eternally grateful for the rest of my life that you chose me."

"It wasn't really a matter of choice," Abbie said. "When I looked at you, I just somehow knew that we were meant to be together. I saw you and I knew I wanted you to be mine, that I wanted to be yours."

"I'm not always good at expressing my emotions," Larimar said. "But I want you to know how important you are to me, and not just because you're carrying my child. That's just a bonus. I think I fell under your spell the moment you stepped off the shuttle and I saw you across the crowd."

Abbie bit her lip, looking like there was more she wanted to say, but there was a knock on their bedroom door. Larimar growled softly at the interruption and went to see what was wrong. It was too damn early for an emergency to have popped up, but he couldn't think of any other reason for someone to disturb their private time at this hour.

He jerked open the door and a distressed Zaylon stood on the other side.

"Is something wrong with Winona?" Larimar asked, his heart stuttering at the thought of Abbie losing her mother so soon.

"In a matter of speaking," Zaylon said. "Other than bodily throwing her over my shoulder, I couldn't think of a way to wrestle her back into her bedroom, so instead I just followed her to keep her safe."

"Followed her where?" Larimar asked, sensing his mate's approach and not wanting the other male to see her in her pajamas.

"Lortok's house."

Larimar's eyebrows rose. "Why is she at Lortok's house?"

"She met Lortok when we went on our outing yesterday and for some reason she formed an attachment to him," Zaylon said. "She insisted on staying with him and he allowed her to go to his home, even invited us in for a drink and talked to her. And then I brought her home. I thought the matter was finished."

"But she left at dawn to go to Lortok's house?" Larimar asked.

"He let her in and said he'd watch her while I came to tell you. I don't know how to remove her without upsetting her. I don't know if she fancies herself in love with him, or if he makes her feel safe, or what she's thinking."

"Go back to Lortok's and wait there with her. We'll dress and be there shortly. I'm sure my mate will want to go."

Zaylon nodded and hurried away.

Larimar sighed and shut the bedroom door, facing his mate, who was standing an arm's length away. She looked troubled and he wanted to ease her worries, but he honestly had no idea what it meant that Winona had fixated on Lortok.

"Who is Lortok?" Abbie asked. "He won't harm her, will he?"

"She's perfectly safe with him. He's about ten years older than I am and heads up the communications team for our world. Lortok would never do anything to harm her. We'd better shower and dress so we can go find out what's going through your mother's head and see if we can convince her to come home."

Abbie nodded and rushed into the bathroom, pulling off her pajamas as she went. Larimar joined her in the shower and wished they had more time. They finished and dressed as quickly as possible and went straight to Lortok's home to hopefully retrieve her mother. The large Zelthranite answered the door when they arrived and motioned for them to enter.

"I gave her breakfast," Lortok said. "She's watching a movie on the Vid-comm right now."

They followed him through the house and saw Winona staring at the Vid-comm in rapt fascination. Abbie moved across the room and sat beside her mother, taking her hand. Larimar moved closer but gave them space, with Zaylon and Lortok nearby as well.

"Momma," Abbie said. "Why aren't you at home?"

Her mother dragged her gaze from the Vid-comm and then smiled broadly at Abbie.

"Good morning, Abbie," Winona said. "Lortok gave me breakfast."

"So I heard," Abbie said. "Why did you leave the house this morning, Momma? It's really early. I'm sure Lortok was still sleeping when you decided to visit."

Her mother frowned and her brow furrowed as she cast a worried glance toward Lortok. The alien came closer and knelt by her mother, and Larimar realized their head of communications was close to the same age as Abbie's mother. Did Winona have a crush on Lortok? He was an unmated male, but there was no way they could have a true relationship. Abbie's mother was too damaged for that.

"Winona," Lortok said, reaching for her hand. "You're welcome here anytime, but you have to remember that you live with Abbie and Larimar. You can't run off in the mornings to come here before everyone is awake."

"Home," her mother said.

"This isn't your home, Momma," Abbie told her. "My house is your home."

Larimar's heart swelled at hearing Abbie call his home hers. Even though they were officially mated now, it still surprised him when she claimed ownership of anything that had belonged to only him before she entered his life. He was glad that she'd settled into her life on Zelthrane-3 and hoped she was happy here. Now they just needed to make sure Winona was happy and understood that her place was with Abbie. Larimar didn't have a clue how to accomplish that.

Winona frowned harder. "Home," she said again.

Lortok squeezed her hand. "Winona, you are welcome to come visit me anytime, but this isn't your home."

Winona became agitated and bolted to her feet. She looked around frantically and then ran out the back door and into the walled-in garden. Abbie sighed and stood, as if she were going after Winona. Larimar placed a hand on her shoulder.

"Give her a minute out there," Larimar said.

"Why does she think this is her home?" Abbie asked. "I don't understand."

They went into the garden, where Winona sat on a stone bench. She seemed calmer, but Larimar held Abbie back, not letting her get too close. The last thing they wanted to do was upset Winona further. He worried that if she became too agitated they would have to sedate her.

Zaylon went to Winona and sat beside her. "Winona, why do you think this is your home?"

"My husband lives here," Winona said.

Lortok's eyebrows nearly rose into his hairline at the declaration.

Zaylon took Winona's hand. "Lortok isn't your husband, Winona. Your husband lived on Earth and died, remember? But you have a daughter here. Abbie. Do you remember coming to live with Abbie?"

Winona looked at Abbie then at Lortok. "Not my husband?"

"No," Lortok said. "I'm not your husband, Winona. But I would like to be your friend. You're welcome to come visit me anytime I'm home. Maybe Zaylon could bring you for dinner a few times a week?"

Winona looked at Larimar. "I live with you and Abbie."

Larimar nodded. "And Zaylon lives there too, remember? He's your friend too."

She nodded.

"Are you ready to go home, Momma?" Abbie asked.

Winona looked uncertain.

"Why don't you leave her here with Zaylon for a few hours?" Lortok suggested. "I'll take the morning off until she's ready to go home. It will give you some alone time. I'm sure that's been in short supply lately."

"Are you certain she's not any trouble?" Larimar asked.

"She'll be fine here," Lortok assured him. "I'll walk home with him to make sure she's okay returning to you. Maybe we can come up with a rotation where on certain days she and Zaylon come eat at my house and stay to watch a movie. It will give your mate and you some time to yourselves."

"Thank you," Larimar said. "Bring her home whenever you're ready."

Abbie went over to her mother and hugged her. "I'll see you in a little while, Momma."

Winona beamed and seemed content to remain in the garden. Larimar took Abbie by the hand and took her back home. The house was quiet when they arrived even though Shariz, and his house manager, Kwirel, would be moving about. Larimar lifted Abbie into his arms and carried her to his office on the lower level, not wanting to wait long enough to reach their bedroom before he claimed his mate again.

He kicked the office door shut and made sure it locked before carrying Abbie to his desk. He shoved everything onto the floor, clearing the top, before easing her down on the cool surface. She gave him a bemused smile as he began removing his clothes.

"What are you doing?" she asked with laughter in her voice.

"I'm going to ravish my mate. The bedroom was too far away."

"Did you really just dump all of your important papers in the floor?" she asked. "You're going to regret that later."

"I will never regret any time that we have alone

together. Strip, mate. You have on too many clothes."

Abbie eased off the desk and began removing her clothes, a smile on her lips. When they were both naked, Larimar kissed her until they were breathless. His hands caressed every inch of her, loving the feel of her curves and silky skin. He lifted her onto the desk and spread her thighs wide, falling to his knees in front of her. Her eyes went wide as he leaned forward and breathed in her sweet scent.

"Larimar, you shouldn't…"

"Shouldn't take my mate?" he asked. "Why not?"

Her cheeks turned pink. "No one's ever done that before."

"Then it seems only fitting that I will be the first and the last."

She leaned back on her hands and didn't argue further. He parted the lips of her pussy and slowly licked her. She was so hot and wet, and tasted so damn good. He sealed his lips around her clit and sucked on it long and hard, making Abbie moan and push her hips closer to him. He dipped his tongue into her core, flicking it in and out several times, before paying attention to the hard little bundle of nerves again.

Larimar's hands tightened on her hips as his lips devoured her tender flesh. Her cries of pleasure filled the air as she came, her release coating his lips and tongue. When she collapsed on the desk, he kissed the inside of her thighs and worked his way up her body, stopping long enough to suck on her pretty nipples. Abbie trembled and shivered and Larimar knew he had to have her right then.

He slid her closer as he lined his cock up with her slit, and then he thrust home, all the way until nothing separated them. Abbie locked her legs around his waist as he drove into her again and again, taking her with a passion that burned inside of him until he thought he might go up in flames. Her sweet little pussy gripped him tight, and as she came a second time, she pulled every drop of cum from his balls as he pounded into her. He'd never taken her so roughly before and he worried he might have hurt her.

As his heart raced and his breath came out in labored pants, he stared down at Abbie. She was flushed from her orgasms and her skin was dewy with sweat. He'd never seen a more beautiful sight, and knew that once he was rested, he'd want her again. She smiled up at him and reached out to run her fingers through his hair.

"I love you," she murmured.

His breath froze in his lungs as he looked down at her in wonder. "You love me?"

She nodded. "Do you think maybe one day you'll love me too?"

"Oh, Abbie." He pulled her up and held her close, stroking her back. "I already do. I love you so much."

"You're not just saying that?" she asked.

"I promise I'm not just saying the words. I've known for a while how I felt about you. I think I fell in love with you the moment our eyes met, and those feelings have just grown deeper as the days have passed. You're my everything, Abbie."

She kissed him, her arms going around his neck.

"What are we going to do about Momma?" she asked as she pulled back.

"We'll take it one day at a time. Let's try Lortok's idea and see if just having a friend will help her. Maybe she can meet some of the other mates or older Zelthranite females and make more friends."

Abbie nodded. "I think we could both use some friends."

"We're scheduled to have lunch with Borgoz and Charlotte since they had to cancel last time. Maybe your mother will be home and we could take her."

Abbie bit her lip. "I'm not sure how Momma would react to Charlotte, since Borgoz said she's deaf and talks differently from us. I'd rather meet her first and prepare Charlotte before she meets Momma, in case anything offensive is said."

"If that's what you want."

"I think it's best," Abbie said.

Larimar lifted her into his arms, leaving their clothing behind, and carried her up to their room. If they had a few hours of time to themselves, he was going to make the most of it.

## Chapter Eleven

Abbie felt a little intimidated by the Chief Councilor's home, but the woman who greeted them smiled warmly and even hugged Abbie. She was petite with shoulder-length brown hair, and eyes that seemed to shine. It was obvious the woman was completely happy with her life here on Zelthrane-3 and Abbie hoped she felt the same way after she'd been here as long as Charlotte had. She'd heard the couple had been mated for years.

"I'm so glad you're here," Charlotte said in her sing-song voice. "I'm sorry we had to cancel before. Arabella was sick again. She just can't seem to get well."

"I hope she's feeling better now," Abbie said.

Charlotte looked sad. "Her fever broke, but she's still in bed today. Bancheck assures us that the serum he gave her yesterday will make her better in a few days. We aren't sure where the virus came from, but it seems to linger."

"Bancheck said Arabella is no longer contagious, but she'll remain upstairs just to be safe," Borgoz said. "We didn't want to alarm either of you, knowing that Abbie is pregnant."

"Not to rush you straight to the table, but dinner is ready," Charlotte said. "I asked the chef to prepare some Earth dishes for us. He's gotten really good at some of my favorite meals."

They followed Charlotte and Borgoz to a large dining room with a table that could have seated twenty, and then they carried on into a sunroom where a table had been set up at the far end of the room. There were four place settings at the rectangular table that could seat six. The light from the three suns brightened the room without making the space too hot.

"This is beautiful," Abbie said, looking out into the garden.

"Thank you," Borgoz said. "Charlotte hates eating in the dining room so I had this table placed in here for our family meals. I hope you don't mind dining in here."

"Not at all," Larimar said.

As they sat, the chef and a staff of two others brought out covered dishes. Abbie couldn't hide her delight as chicken fried steak, mashed potatoes, green beans, meatloaf, and glazed carrots were revealed. Three baskets of rolls were brought with their drinks. She hadn't realized how much she'd missed eating like this until just now. Perhaps Larimar's cook would be able to learn some human recipes as well. He'd already made an effort by bringing in a few human things. It would be nice to get a taste of home without having to go to the human café in town.

"I was telling Charlotte about your idea of a survey," Borgoz said to Abbie. "I've got the communications team working on it and they think they will have something ready in a few weeks. Once we have the data compiled, we can start adding some new places and activities to our world that might bring even more potential brides here and keep our current mates happy."

"It can be a little boring here," Charlotte said, "but I love Borgoz so it's worth it."

Borgoz reached over and squeezed her hand. "I wish you'd told me before you were bored. We could have done something like this years ago. You know I want you to be happy."

Charlotte leaned over and kissed his cheek. "I'm happy. I have you and Arabella."

"What did you do on Earth?" Abbie asked Charlotte.

"I volunteered a lot. My father was a politician and money was always available to me, so I didn't need a job. I would help out where I was needed. I stayed busy and I had some friends, but they were with me mostly for my father's connections. I'm always worried the same will happen here, that someone will befriend me because I'm married to Borgoz," Charlotte said.

"I never thought of that happening in a place like this," Abbie said. "Has it been difficult making friends?"

Charlotte shrugged. "I'm different so some of the human mates aren't certain how to act around me. Everyone has welcomed Arabella, though. She's completely deaf and we use sign language to communicate with her. Our society has learned it over the years so she doesn't feel alone when we go out places."

"I'll have to learn too," Abbie said. "Maybe you could teach me?"

Charlotte smiled widely. "I'd like that. We can have a lunch date a few times a week, if you'd like."

Abbie nodded and smiled. "That sounds great. I can't wait to meet your daughter."

"She can be a handful," Borgoz said.

"Do you only have one child?" Abbie asked.

Charlotte gave her a sad smile. "I had a difficult pregnancy. Arabella was supposed to have siblings, but they died before they were born. It was advised that we not have any more children because the doctors weren't sure I would survive."

"I'm so sorry," Abbie said, wishing she hadn't brought up something so painful.

"Since I don't have siblings," Borgoz said, "Arabella doesn't have cousins to play with. The children on our world have been accepting of her, but she doesn't get invited very many places. And I feel that the invitations she does receive have more to do with my rank or their parents' urging."

"Maybe when our son or daughter is old enough to play, they'll become friends," Abbie said.

Larimar reached over and squeezed her hand. "The council is much like a family, so your Arabella will have cousins even if they aren't by blood."

Borgoz nodded. "Alrian does bring his children over on occasion for a visit, but I wish Arabella had someone to spend time with on a regular basis. I fear that she gets lonely sometimes, even though she has us."

"Is she alone up there right now?" Abbie asked, hating to think of the sick child by herself.

"No, we have someone sitting with her for a little while. We wanted time for lunch today and didn't want to rush you out the door the minute the meal was finished." Borgoz smiled. "Arabella will be well taken care of until then."

"Borgoz ordered some games from Earth that I played as a child," Charlotte said. "We have a handful of board games and some card games. She'll be entertained for a while. She also loves books."

"I love to read too," Abbie said. "I noticed there's a library in town. I should check it out one day soon. Maybe my mother would like to go too."

"How is your mother?" Borgoz asked.

"She's doing well, but a little confused. She spent time with Lortok this morning. She had it in her head they were married for some reason, but he set her straight and promised he would be her friend. She stayed there for a little while and when she returned home she went to her room and took a nap," Abbie said.

"Zaylon has been good with her," Larimar said. "I know we had some concerns after the way he treated Victoria, but I think it's safe to say he's learned his lesson. He did agree, however, not to seek a bride for as long as Winona is with us. I wanted stability in her life and I wasn't certain how she'd adjust to constant changes."

Abbie took another bite of her food, her stomach feeling so full she thought she might burst. "This is really good."

Charlotte smiled. "We can have human food anytime you're here, if you'd like. I ask the chef to make it a few times a week, so that Arabella can experience both sides of her heritage. I don't miss much from home, but I was starting to miss the food when I first came here. Once I was more comfortable with the staff here, I asked if some Earth cuisine could be made. They were very accommodating."

They finished their meal and retired to the living room. Classical music played softly from somewhere and Abbie looked around the room, trying to figure out where it came from. Charlotte noticed and smiled.

"You noticed the music, didn't you? Borgoz found a way for an MP3 player to pipe music through the house and plays it several times a day. It doesn't last long because the device has to be charged every few hours. We have solar chargers here now for phones and other electronics. It's made things so much better," Charlotte said. "Borgoz had someone purchase a tablet for me and had it loaded with books and games. It's helped pass the time."

Larimar leaned back in his chair and looked at Abbie. "Would you like one too? You could tell me what types of books and games you like and I could have a device loaded and brought here for you."

"Would you?" Abbie asked. "That would be so much better than watching movies all the time. Maybe you could get one for Momma and have it loaded with games she might be able to play?"

He nodded. "I'll see to it when we return home."

"I tried knitting," Charlotte said. "But I'm a dismal failure at it. I couldn't even knit a scarf. My stitches kept unraveling."

"I don't think I'd be very good at it either," Abbie admitted. "I've never been able to do crafts with much success."

Charlotte shrugged. "I'd never tried before and thought it looked easy enough, but I was wrong."

Larimar and Borgoz stood.

"We're going to leave the two of you to talk about whatever women discuss," Borgoz said. "I have some files to show Larimar before the next council session convenes."

Charlotte snorted. "Only you would turn a fun afternoon into a work session."

"I don't think Larimar minds," Abbie said. "He's a workaholic."

Charlotte pointed at Borgoz. "That one is too."

The men shared a pained expression and left with the women's laughter following them. Charlotte moved a little closer, her eyes bright.

"Isn't being married to one of them way better than a human guy?" Charlotte asked.

"Definitely. No one has ever made me feel the way Larimar does."

Charlotte nodded. "Borgoz was my first, but no one had interested me until him. I knew almost immediately that

I wanted him, and every time he pushed me away, it broke my heart a little more."

"Why did he push you away?" Abbie asked.

"Silly man thought he was too old for me. There's about twenty years between us."

Abbie nodded. "Larimar tried to do the same thing. There's twelve years between us, but it doesn't bother me at all."

The doorbell chimed and a moment later Abbie's mother and Zaylon were escorted into the room. Abbie shot to her feet, worried.

"Momma? Is something wrong?"

Zaylon shrugged. "She was bored and insisted on coming to you. I'm sorry for the intrusion."

Another commotion drew their attention to the stairs. A little girl was coming down the steps dressed in pajamas with a Zelthranite woman chasing after her. The woman was winded when they entered the room, the little girl looking at all of the strangers with wide eyes.

Charlotte began signing something that Abbie didn't understand and the little girl answered back.

"I'm sorry," Charlotte said. "It seems Arabella was bored too."

"You said she's not contagious. What if she brought a game down to play? I bet my momma would like that too," Abbie said.

Winona nodded and looked at the little girl in curiosity.

"Momma, this is Arabella. She can't hear and uses sign language. Maybe you'd like to learn it with me?" Abbie asked.

Her mother nodded and reached out to take the little girl's hand. Arabella smiled up at Winona and Charlotte signed something else.

"I explained that your mother had an injury," Charlotte said. "I wanted her to know that Winona is different like her."

Someone brought a game into the room and Winona and Arabella sat in the middle of the floor to start playing, while Charlotte and Abbie talked some more. They visited for another hour and then Larimar suggested they head home so the Chief Councilor could spend some time with his family. She held Larimar's hand as they walked back to their home, her mother and Zaylon trailing behind them.

"I take it you liked Charlotte," Larimar said.

"Very much. I think I may have a new friend."

He smiled.

"Thank you for taking me over there today," Abbie said.

"I'm sorry we interrupted," Zaylon said behind them.

"It worked out," Abbie said. "I think Momma and Arabella may become friends."

"Zaylon, would you take Winona upstairs for a little while?" Larimar asked as they entered their home. "There's something I need to discuss with Abbie for a moment."

"Of course," Zaylon said, leading Winona upstairs.

"Follow me," Larimar said, leading her upstairs to their bedroom.

She giggled when he shut the door. "You said you wanted to talk, but I have a feeling there's something else on your mind."

His gaze heated. "That too. Step out onto the balcony. I'll be right there."

She gave him a curious glance before obeying.

When he stepped out into the sunlight a few minutes later, he fell to his knees in front of her. "I had wanted to do something human for you before we were mated, but there wasn't time."

"Larimar, what are you doing?"

He pulled out a small, velvet box and popped the lid open. A wedding set was nestled in satin inside, the platinum bands shining and the diamonds sparkling. She gasped and hesitantly reached for them, only to draw her hand back.

"Those are for me?"

"I made you my wife and by Zelthranite standards that's sufficient. But you're human, and I want you to have the rings a married woman would wear on your world." He took the rings from the box and slid them onto her finger then withdrew another box. "You belong to me, and I belong to you."

Her jaw dropped a little as he removed a plain band from the second box and slid it onto his finger.

"You're going to wear a wedding ring?" she asked.

"You mean the world to me, Abbie. Wearing a piece of metal on my finger is the least I can do for you. I want everyone on my world and yours to know that we belong to each other. And I will spend every day for the rest of my life showing you how much I love you."

She pressed her lips to his. "You could start by showing me now."

He smiled and lifted her into his arms, carrying her into the bedroom and easing her down his body. They slowly undressed one another, unable to keep their hands off each other. As their mouths met again in a hungry kiss, Larimar tumbled them to the bed and Abbie welcomed his weight over her.

He worshiped her body with his lips and tongue, his hands caressing every inch of her. Abbie felt like she was on fire. When his cock brushed against her, she wrapped her legs around his waist, wanting him to claim her. He entered her with one long, hard thrust and she cried out from the pleasure of it. Larimar took her hard and fast, their bodies coming together in a frenzy that left her breathless. Her heart raced and her hands gripped his shoulders, her nails biting into his skin.

As her release hit her, she cried out his name and clung tight to him. Larimar thrust harder until he came, filling her and making her feel complete. As they panted for breath and looked into one another's eyes, she knew that he was the only one for her. He was her other half, the one person created just for her.

"I love you," she said before kissing him softly.

"I love you too. For now and always," he said.

She felt him growing hard again inside of her and knew

it would be a while before they went in search of her mother and Zaylon. It seemed her sexy alien councilman had other matters on his mind. Giving herself to him completely, Abbie basked in his love and affection, until both were too exhausted to do much but sleep.

When she'd lost everything on Earth, she'd have never guessed that her life would turn out so perfectly. She had the love of an amazing man, her mother was back in her life, and she had new friends. Life couldn't have been sweeter in that moment, and she looked forward to what every day in the future would bring.

Jennifer and the Alien Badass
(Intergalactic Brides 15)
Jessica Coulter Smith


Jennifer Montgomery has never needed anyone in her life except her daughter. A single mom of a now eighteen year old, her entire life has revolved around Lila. But when Lila goes missing, Jennifer is devastated and determines to do whatever it takes to find her. She just never expected her search to lead her to the Terran Station and their bride program. Or to learn that her daughter isn't who Jennifer thought she was.

Siril, Captain of the *Herack,* is revered on his world for his tireless pursuit of the space pirates infesting the galaxy. The best of the best, as they say. If killing people were an art, he'd be da Vinci. But all the blood is starting to wear on him. There are only so many heads you can lop off before it grows old. At fifty, he's ready for a break, but when he agreed to a vacation on Earth, he never expected to meet his perfect match, someone he'd decided didn't exist. Who would ever want a battered and broken old warrior like him? But Jennifer is fierce, sexy as hell, and he wants to make her his.

As the two come together, and sparks become a blazing inferno, Jennifer realizes that maybe it's okay to live her life and do something completely selfish -- like fall in love.

# Chapter One

Siril narrowed his good eye and his hands tightened on his weapons, a one of a kind set of perfectly matched Corian steel blades that'd been passed down from father to son for the last four generations. They had been blessed by a priestess and were irreplaceable.

The disease-ridden pirates had been allowed to board this ship, giving them a false sense of security, but now they were putting up a decent fight. No matter how skilled they were though, no one was a match for Siril, especially not as pissed as he was. He should be home right now, training new warriors. But no, he was stuck on board the *Herack* dealing with the lowlifes in front of him.

"You're not welcome in this galaxy," Siril said. "I'll spare your life if you leave immediately and never return."

The pirate spat on the floor at Siril's feet, the green ooze narrowly missing his custom-made boots -- a gift from a Kaspian princess. Siril grinned, remembering the fun he'd had before leaving her world. But now wasn't the time for fun. Now he had to take out the trash, by any means necessary. He really didn't want the pirate's blood on his ship. The dripping sores on his face could be from any number of maladies, none of them good. The ship would have to be scrubbed for days to get it clean again -- the hands and knees kind of scrubbing, because the auto cleaners weren't going to get the job done this time. And then there was the arterial spray that almost always got on his clothes. Killing someone was just more trouble than he liked to deal with, even if he was really good at it.

The pirate lunged at him, his subpar weapon missing Siril by a mile. It was going to be too easy to take this guy out. He resigned himself to having the ship scrubbed top to bottom. The pirate swayed on his feet and Siril took the moment to attack. His blades sliced through the pirate's arms, separating them at the shoulders. Blood sprayed the walls and deck as the pirate's screams echoed down the halls. Being merciful, he crossed his blades at the pirate's neck and lopped off his head, creating blessed silence. The head bounced and rolled across the floor as a spray of blood arced across Siril's shirt.

"You just wouldn't listen to reason, would you?" Siril griped. "No, you made me contaminate my ship with your vile blood. And my damn shirt is ruined."

He grimaced at the mess and wiped his blades on his shirt, since it would likely need to be thrown out anyway, before sliding them back into their sheaths. The blood seeped through the garment and touched his skin. Siril ripped the fabric from his body and threw it on the floor. A shower. He needed a damn shower. But first he went to check on the rest of the crew. He stepped over dismembered bodies as he made his way through his ship, wondering if his council would be overly pissed if he just torched the vessel and requested a new one. The pirates probably carried space-pox and a dozen other contagions. No amount of scrubbing was going to get rid of that.

Maybe he was getting too old for this damn job. Despite the fact he'd recently turned fifty, Siril was still considered the best on Zelthrane-3 at what he did. His hair was still black as pitch, but he bore too many scars to be considered youthful looking. And if his scars didn't scare people away, his missing body parts did the trick. His left eye had been lost in a battle with a Marowak warrior when he was twenty. The pinky on his right hand had been lost a few years after that. His left leg from just below his knee down was made of Corian steel like his blades, and looked enough like a leg and foot, bar the fact it was a shiny silver. It was permanently attached and worked as well as his own had, perhaps even better. But while females didn't mind those things for a quick romp, he wasn't someone they would want to wake up next to every morning. He didn't even care for his own reflection most days, so he couldn't blame them.

His crew was at the docking port, tossing pirate bodies out the airlock. Covered in blood, they made him cringe. He hoped none of them came down with some disease their physicians couldn't heal. It was his only fear when he went into battle. Dying in combat was one thing, but having your body rot from the inside out didn't sound all that pleasant. He was getting checked the moment he stepped foot back on Zelthrane-3. While he thoroughly enjoyed fluid transfers when it came to females, the blood of a pirate was enough to make him scrub his skin until it peeled.

His crew didn't seem to have an issue with it as they laughed and joked, tossing one body after another out into space. "Ship needs to be cleaned," he told them. "Scrub it twice." Yellow sludge seeped out of one of the bodies at his feet and he winced. "Make that three times."

"Should we set a course for home?" Haptir asked.

"Yes. Once you've finished disposing of the pirates. I don't want their remains anywhere near Zelthrane-3." Siril left them to their work and went to his quarters. The door had barely closed before he started removing his boots and pants. He turned on the cleansing unit and stepped under the spray. Scrubbing his body and hair twice, he leaned his head against the wall and wondered what life would be like without constant bloodshed. Not that a good battle wasn't fun -- preferably on someone else's ship so they had to deal with the cleanup.

Such things didn't used to bother him, but the older he got, the less he liked the messy side of his work. Why couldn't they die neatly? Was it really necessary for a decapitation to douse everything in blood? But what else was he to do? If he wasn't beheading people, was he supposed to sit at home and die of boredom? He'd been asked to train their warriors full time, and it was an honorable position, but Siril wasn't certain he was ready to hang up his blades just yet. There were many good fights left in him.

He shut off the unit and dried himself. He looked at his bed longingly, but there would be plenty of time to sleep once they reached home. They'd been after the pirates for days and he'd slept little. In his youth, he could have stayed awake for days on end without feeling the least bit tired. But now, as the oldest active warrior for their world, he was feeling every one of his fifty years. Donning clean clothes, he checked his boots before putting them back on, and went to the galley. He grabbed a Melranian star fruit and leaned against the counter. His crew could handle the cleanup and navigation necessary to get them back home. There was little for him to do.

Except think.

The council had often offered Siril time off over the last few years, encouraging him to take a trip to Earth and get off world without having to engage in battle. He'd always waved them off and gone right back to work, but maybe it was time to take a break. Even a week off might be nice. While Zelthrane-3 was more advanced than the humans' Earth in many ways, the blue planet had a lot of marvels that interested him. Like music and movies. And while he'd heard there would be a place to dance opening soon in Terran Prime, it might be entertaining to see all of those things on Earth and explore the human world a bit. Providing he didn't scare the puny humans.

When the bride program had first opened, they'd welcomed all humans to their world, including males who took temporary jobs on their planet to make the human females feel more at ease. But over time, only brides were allowed on Zelthrane-3, and the screening process had gotten stricter. The first few months of the program, there had been too many fights, as well as human females falling for the human males. Things were streamlined now, and from what he could tell the program was a huge success. He'd often thought of checking out the brides to find a mate of his own, but they all seemed so young. He wondered if the council only approved the young ones to guarantee children for the mated pairs. He didn't know much about humans and wondered if the older females either couldn't have children or if it would be too hard on their bodies. More than likely, he would spend his years alone.

"Captain," Velic said over the system. "We're about to enter warp drive and will be home shortly. It might get a little bumpy."

Siril braced his feet and continued to eat his fruit as the

ship vibrated around him. He wondered what sort of female would ever settle for someone like him. He'd been handsome once, but wars had ravaged his face and body. There were females out there who thrilled over being with a warrior such as he, but they were few and far between. And once the thrill was over, they left and he was alone once more. No one wanted to wake up next to him every day for the rest of their lives.

If he ever did claim a mate, he had a wonderful home for her. The council had provided him one of the best houses on his world. It was large, easily big enough for many children, and had a lush garden out back. He seldom saw it, spending most of his time on this ship trying to keep the galaxy safe. If he did take a mate, he supposed he'd have to spend more time at home. Was he ready to give up this way of life if it meant having a warm female to bed every night?

He wanted to say yes, but he wondered if he'd miss wreaking havoc and striking fear into the hearts of those around him. Just his name was enough to send most running in fear. He'd earned his reputation and was proud of it. Human females seemed fragile, though, and he doubted they would thrill over his many kills. He wanted a female every bit as fierce as he was, but he had yet to meet one. Someone who could take care of themselves if he had to leave on a mission. Worrying about a helpless, fragile mate would only get him killed. No, he needed a warrior. But in all his travels, he'd never met a female warrior. There were stories of some on far off worlds, but it was doubtful he'd ever meet one.

Who was he kidding? No one would ever want a mate like him. He was too damaged for someone to ever love him. But if he did have a mate, if a female ever took a chance on him, he'd shower her with love and affection and make sure she never wanted to leave.

When he was home, he watched the mated couples. Their females smiled at them with such affection, and grew round with their children. Not that he had the slightest idea of what to do with a child. He'd never held one for fear he might hurt them. They seemed so small and breakable. Part of him wanted children to experience the pleasure of having a family, but the thought of bringing a tiny baby into the world was frightening. And at his age, by the time he had grandchildren he might be too old to enjoy them. Gods! Grandchildren?

He shook his head at his folly. He wasn't getting a mate and wasn't having children, so it was a moot point. He'd do better to hone his battle strategies and mold the young warriors who needed a guiding hand. Leave populating the planet to the younger males. The greatest gift he could give his people was keeping them safe, either by his own hand or those he trained. With some luck, he'd die in battle and never have to live a lonely life once the council retired him.

The ship shuddered under his feet and groaned, telling him they'd touched down. Siril tossed the core of the star fruit and made his way through the ship to the docking port. His crew was already exiting as he made his way down to the ground below. There was no one to greet them, but there never was. All of his crew were single, and while some of them still had parents, they were very much on their own.

The suns shone brightly overhead, their warmth caressing his face. It was good to be home, another crisis averted. His people were safe and were none the wiser to the threat that had been hanging over their heads. If the pirates had managed to land, many lives would have been lost. He walked the streets, smiling at the children playing he passed along the way. This was why he spent so much time in space. So families could stay together, could live in peace, and those precious children would have a chance to grow up and maybe become warriors themselves one day.

The clinic loomed ahead and he hoped no one was waiting. He didn't mind the wait, but the fewer people he had contact with the better, until he knew he hadn't been contaminated. He stepped into the cool interior and breathed a sigh of relief when he saw the waiting room was empty. Easing down onto a chair, he extended his bad leg to give his knee a break. Sometimes the metal of his prosthetic made the joints in his knee ache. Getting old was a bitch.

He looked around the interior of the clinic, noting the changes since he'd last been in. Some blocks were stacked in a corner for the children who had to visit. A few books with human females on the cover graced a few tables. What were those called? Magazines? He picked one up, curious as to the contents. As part of his extensive training, he'd learned to speak and read all of the languages of Earth and all of the surrounding planets in his galaxy. The magazine in his hand was in Earth English and had articles on losing weight, the best summer diets, and "the top ten reasons he doesn't love you".

Siril smiled and shook his head, amused by the things human females found entertaining. He'd much rather read a book on the latest weaponry. He flipped through a few more of the books, wondering why all of the females in them were so skinny. The females in the bride program came in all shapes and sizes. Why didn't their magazines have fuller-figured women in them as well?

He tossed the book aside and stood, moving across to the door that led to the offices and exam rooms. He cracked it open and peered down the long hall. Light shone under one of the office doors and Siril decided to make his presence known. His boots were loud against the polished floor and must have alerted the doctor someone was in the building. The office door opened and Vyrex stepped out.

"Siril, it's good to see you. Another successful mission?" Vyrex asked.

"The mission went well, but my ship was covered in the blood of pirates. Some got on me as well. I wanted to make sure I hadn't contracted anything."

Vyrex motioned for him to follow and led Siril to an exam room. He scanned Siril head to toe, ran some blood tests, and gave him a few injections. As the doctor studied the results of the tests, Siril waited to find out if it was bad news or if he'd managed to come out unscathed once more. He figured that eventually his luck would run out. Yes, he'd lost some body parts along the way in his missions, but otherwise he was still very healthy.

"Everything looks fine," Vyrex said. "The injections I gave you will help boost your immune system and should fight off any viruses if any present over the next few days. I wouldn't worry unless you start feeling ill, then come back and see me. We'll run more tests then."

"I think I may go off world for a bit."

"Earth?" Vyrex asked.

Siril nodded. "The council has offered to send me many times for a vacation. I think it's time I took them up on their offer."

"I sometimes take a rotation at the Terran station in Kentucky, if they give you a choice of where to go. I think you'll enjoy the town. There are of course other places across their vast planet. You could see the Eiffel Tower, the castles in Ireland, and I've heard London has a lot of interesting sights. It's amazing how different each place is there, and how different the humans are depending on where they live."

"If you think I'll enjoy Kentucky, I'll request to be sent there."

"Take care of yourself, Siril. And who knows, maybe you'll come home with a bride."

Siril shook his head. "It's doubtful. I'll enjoy my time off and return ready to get back to work. In all the years I've been a warrior, I've never taken a vacation. I think it's time."

"Just remember to visit the clinic at the Terran Station, or wherever you end up, if you start to feel sick."

"I will," Siril vowed.

They shook hands and Siril left to inform the council he was ready for a break. He went to his home and tried to reach the council on the Vid-comm, but no one answered at the council headquarters. He'd heard that Larimar was recently mated, so he didn't want to bother him. Instead, he contacted Borgoz, the chief councilor. The chief councilor's mate answered the call, a smile on her face.

"Good morning, Siril," she said in her sing-song voice.

"Good morning, Charlotte. Is Borgoz available?"

She nodded. "I'll get him. He's in the garden with Arabella."

She vanished from view and several minutes went by before Borgoz filled the screen. He looked like he was in a good mood and didn't seem to mind being disturbed at home.

"The mission was a success?" Borgoz asked.

"The pirates won't be bothering anyone ever again," Siril said.

"Good. Were you wanting to file a report?"

"Not exactly. I can upload something today, but I was hoping to take the council up on their offer of a vacation. Am I still permitted to travel to Earth for a week?" Siril asked.

"Of course," Borgoz said. "Do you know where you want to go? We have two shuttles leaving today and one tomorrow."

"Vyrex suggested I might like Kentucky, wherever that is."

"There's a shuttle leaving for Kentucky in about two hours, if that gives you enough time to prepare. If not, another will depart later in the week. We have a shipment of brides coming from there. Some arrived two days ago, but most have already paired with someone."

"I'll be ready to leave on the shuttle today. I'll file my report and pack my belongings."

"Our reports show that it's a season called spring in Kentucky which means warm mornings and cooler evenings. Whatever clothing you own should be sufficient, but there are plenty of local stores there where you could purchase more things."

"Thank you, Chief Councilor. I look forward to the break and will return refreshed and ready to get back to work."

Borgoz smiled. "Take as long as you want. We'll be fine while you're taking a break. Just enjoy your time on Earth."

Borgoz disconnected the call and Siril began filling in a report on what happened with the pirates. When he was finished, he packed a bag with several changes of clothes and waited for the shuttle departure. He was a little sad about leaving his position if only for a short time, but he knew he needed a break. It was beyond time. He only hoped nothing bad happened while he was gone.

# Chapter Two

Jennifer Montgomery was beyond worried. Her eighteen-year-old daughter had claimed to be staying with friends for a few days, but more than a week had gone by and Lila still wasn't answering her phone. Jennifer had called all her daughter's friends, and they had all seemed nervous about talking to her, but each had assured her that Lila was fine. Had Lila run away? She'd packed a week's worth of clothes, but most of her things remained. Surely, she wouldn't have taken off and left so much behind? But if she wasn't staying with her friends, then where the hell was she?

She'd been loath to toss her daughter's room, looking for something that would tell her where Lila was, but as the days dragged by, she knew she had to do something. If she didn't find any clues or reach her daughter today, she was calling the police and filing a missing persons report. Truthfully, she should have done it sooner, but Lila's best friend assured her that Lila was safe and being taken care of. That was the only thing that had kept her from completely losing her mind.

She rummaged through Lila's drawers, under her bed, all through her closet. With her hands braced on her hips, she surveyed the room, hoping for something to pop out and scream "look here" but everything looked in order. Except... Did the mattress look a little crooked? It wasn't off by much, but it definitely looked like it had been moved at some point, and she didn't think she'd done that when she tossed the bedding off it in her mad search.

Jennifer moved toward the bed and picked up the edge of the mattress, feeling underneath it. Her fingers brushed what felt like an envelope and she grasped it, dragging it out of its hiding place. It was plain white and was no longer sealed, looking as if it had been ripped open in haste. It was addressed to Lila and had come from the Terran Station nearby. What the hell? *Oh, please no!*

The letter inside was missing, but Jennifer had the sinking feeling her baby wasn't on Earth anymore. At eighteen, Lila was considered an adult, and would have been permitted to sign up for the bride program. But why had she done it? She was still a baby, barely out of high school. They'd been talking about college, even though Jennifer had no idea how they would afford it. Had Lila thought this was her only option? Things would have worked out somehow. Yes, they struggled, but she'd always taken care of her daughter to the best of her ability, and she'd thought she was doing a pretty damn good job. Until now.

She had to get to the station and sort out this mess. A glance in the mirror over the dresser made her pause. It was one thing to march down there and get irate with them for letting her baby leave this planet, and it was another to look like an escaped lunatic while doing it. Her hair stood out in disarray, the knots and snarls from a restless sleep giving new meaning to the term "bed head." Her sweats were faded and sagged on her, making her look more like a blue blob than a human. No one would take her seriously if she showed up like this. She smoothed a hand through her hair, wincing when it pulled the strands. Her nose wrinkled. All right, shower, decent clothes, maybe a little make-up to hide the dark circles, and *then* she would give the aliens a piece of her mind.

She placed the envelope on Lila's dresser and went back to the bathroom in the hall. Turning the hot water on all the way and the cold just a tiny bit, she waited until steam was billowing around the curtain and then stripped and got into the shower. Using the comb she kept on the built-in shelf, she worked the tangles from her hair before soaking it. The rosemary and mint scent of her shampoo calmed her a little as she lathered her hair, rinsed it, then drenched it with conditioner.

Jennifer soaped her loofa before scrubbing herself head to toe, pausing to shave her legs and under her arms. *Good lord*! When was the last time she'd shaved? Maybe she'd fallen apart more than she'd realized when Lila had vanished. For so long, it had just been the two of them. And now that Lila was gone, Jennifer wasn't certain what to do with herself. She'd been a mom for eighteen years, a single mom at that, and without her daughter she felt adrift. She'd known that one day Lila would spread her wings and move out, but she hadn't thought she'd sneak away. She'd always imagined a tearful goodbye and a lingering hug as her daughter started the next phase of her life. But no, her daughter had crept away, lied about where she was going, and just vanished without a trace. Why?

Jennifer rinsed her hair and body, then shut off the water and towel dried. The mirror had steamed and she ran a hand towel across it. The woman looking back at her seemed tired and worn out. And was it any wonder? She'd not only been concerned about her daughter, but she'd been working double shifts at the dollar store, trying to put money aside for the summer vacation they'd been planning for two years. She was both angry with Lila and concerned about her. The girl she'd raised wouldn't have been so thoughtless as to have done something like this. Had she gone wrong somewhere along the way, sent her daughter mixed signals, or said something that would make Lila think this was okay?

Jennifer put detangler in her hair, sprayed it with a heat protector, then blew it dry. She was already looking a little more human. She dabbed concealer under her eyes, smoothed it out to hide the shadows, then dusted her face with a light powder foundation. A tinge of blush and a tinted lip moisturizer and she was done. Looking down at herself, she amended that to "done as soon as she got dressed". Although, showing up in nothing but a towel might get her some attention.

She shivered as she opened the bathroom door and marched down the hall to her bedroom. Pulling out her rather plain-looking bra and panties, she grabbed a pair of skinny jeans from another drawer, then rummaged in her closet for a shirt that looked decent. She chose an off-the-shoulder, three-quarter-sleeve navy top with pink flowers across it, and snagged her sexy brown cowgirl boots with the cutout floral pattern from the bottom of the closet.

When she was finished dressing, she looped her locket around her neck. It was a silver oval with *Mom* engraved across the front. One half of the frame had Lila's baby picture and the other half had her high school graduation picture. She wore it every time she left the house, so her baby was always with her. Raising Lila hadn't been easy, especially without a college degree or a stable job. Going it alone had been scary, but there had been no way to track down Lila's father. He'd been a one-night stand and they'd only exchanged first names. While their town was small, no one at the bar where they'd met had remembered him.

Jennifer grabbed her keys and her purse, then locked up the house and climbed into her ancient Honda and drove to the Terran Station. The wind kicked up as she pulled into the parking lot, making her poorly sealed windshield whistle. She seriously needed a new car, but it wasn't in the budget. Parking as close to the door as she could get, which still felt like it was a mile away, she locked her car -- not that anyone would want it -- and trudged across the parking lot to the front entrance.

A perky blonde behind the reception counter smiled brightly at her. "May I help you with something?"

*Penny,* her tag read. "Penny, I need to speak to someone about someone who recently entered the bride program."

The receptionist's eyes went wide. "Oh, we can't discuss our candidates. Not unless they left permission during the application process. You could check with records and see if your name is on the approved list."

Jennifer ground her teeth. "And where is Records?"

Penny pulled out a map and highlighted the way, then handed it over. Following the neon line, Jennifer made her way through the station, trying not to scowl at every alien she passed. It wasn't their fault her daughter had run off to get married to some stranger on another world. When she reached Records, the alien behind the counter smiled at her.

"My name is Zwyk," he said. "Is there something I can help you with?"

"I think my daughter joined your bride program and I'm trying to find out if she's already been sent to your world."

His eyebrows rose. "I see. And your daughter's name?"

"Lila Montgomery."

He tapped away at his computer, a frown marring his face before he looked up at her again. "Mrs. Montgomery, I'm sorry, but I can't tell you where your daughter is right now."

"It's Miss," she bit out. "So, either you really don't know, or she did join your program and said you couldn't tell me where she was."

He looked pained, which was all the answer she needed. It felt like steam was going to billow out of her ears at any moment. They'd allowed her baby to sign up, and now they wouldn't even tell her if she'd made it to their planet safely. *Assholes*. No, that wasn't completely fair. It wasn't entirely their fault. Lila was just as much to blame for this mess, if not more so.

"Who is in charge?" Jennifer asked.

"Tyril. He's..." Zwyk looked over her shoulder and pointed. "Over there."

She turned and looked, seeing two aliens having a discussion in the middle of the station. One was taller and broader than the other, his hair was long and thick; a rather sexy eye patch covered one eye. The smaller one was dressed nicer and looked more... tame. She glanced from one to the other again, and hoped it was the tamer looking one that was Tyril. The taller one looked like he could break her in half without breaking a sweat.

Jennifer approached them and the taller one stopped mid-sentence to look her way. Though he only had one eye, his gaze was appreciative as he took her in from the top of her head to the tips of her toes. A sexy smirk graced his lips when he met her gaze. *Oh lordy*. Now that was a man who was sexy as fuck and knew it. She forced herself to look away and focus on the smaller of the two.

"Are you Tyril?" she asked.

He nodded and gave her a pleasant smile. "If you want to apply for the bride program, the application center is at the front of the station."

"I'm actually here about someone who already signed up."

"I'm afraid we can't divulge information about our potential brides without their permission. You'll have to speak with Zwyk and see if you're on the approved list."

Jennifer folded her arms under her breasts, pushing them up, and stared at Tyril. His gaze momentarily dropped to her chest before he looked up again. Good. She had his attention, or at least part of him did.

"My daughter received something in the mail from this station, and she's been missing for over a week. Your precious Records person won't tell me a damn thing and I demand to know if my daughter is safe. Do I need to go to the police to file a missing persons report, or is she not on Earth anymore?"

Tyril's eyes widened a little. "Your daughter? We would never allow someone underage to…"

She held up a hand. "Lila is eighteen and grown enough I suppose, but sometimes she still acts like a child. Much like now. She disappeared only saying she was going to a friend's house, packed enough clothes for a week, then made sure her friends wouldn't tell me where she was, and she wouldn't answer her phone. I found the opened envelope under her mattress and the letter inside was missing. I guess if she's off-world that would explain why she's not answering her phone."

Tyril looked sympathetic. "I want to help you, but I can't. We have rules in place for a reason. If she did sign up for the program and didn't put you on the approved list of contacts, then there's nothing I can do."

Tears of frustration welled in her eyes and her hands clenched into fists. "So I'm just supposed to wonder for the rest of my life what happened to my only child?"

The taller of the two moved closer. "You have a daughter old enough for the bride program?"

"Yes." Jennifer bit her lip. "I know she's technically an adult, but she's my baby. She's all I have. Isn't there something you can do?"

"The only way any human is going to our world is as a potential bride, or part of an already mated pair," Tyril said, his gaze sliding over her. "And as you're old enough to already have an adult child, I doubt either is a possibility for you."

Jennifer's cheeks flushed with anger, and without thought, she hauled back her hand, made a fist, and punched him right across his jaw. Tyril stumbled back a step, his eyes wide and incredulous, as his hand cupped the injured area.

"You hit me!" he said in outrage.

"And I'm going to kick you in the balls next if you don't help me," Jennifer said. "And I'm not old, dammit. I'm only thirty-eight."

Tyril cupped said balls and took another step back.

The one-eyed alien smiled broadly. "I like her."

"Call security," Tyril said. "Someone needs to escort her from the premises."

"I'm not leaving until you tell me where my daughter is," she shouted at him.

"You're a menace," Tyril said.

Jennifer growled and advanced on him, whacking his biceps with her open palm before cracking her other hand against his cheek. They were *not* going to keep her child from her.

The sexy alien behind her gave a full-belly laugh and wrapped an arm around her waist, hauling her back against his rather impressive chest. His body shook with merriment as Tyril glared at them, looking more than a little irate at her attack. She supposed she should be thankful he hadn't tried to hit her back. While he might not be as built as the alien holding her, he wasn't exactly weak looking either. One punch probably would have knocked her out.

"I believe you've met your match, Tyril. Why not tell her what she wants to know? She's fierce and doesn't seem to be taking no for an answer," the sexy alien said.

"Stay out of this, Siril. We have rules. Policies. I can't go breaking them just because she wants to know where her daughter is. If she's not on the approved list, I can't even confirm whether her daughter was here or not."

Some of her anger deflated and she felt utterly helpless. "You can't even tell me if she was accepted into the program? I just want to know that she's safe. Do you have children? Wouldn't you want to know if they were okay?"

"I do not," Tyril said, but some of the anger seemed to drain from him. "I'm truly sorry, but I can't help you."

"I'll help you," the alien behind her said.

"Siril, you don't have access to the information she wants," Tyril said.

"No, but she can travel with me back to our world. I was leaving on the morning shuttle."

"She's not a potential bride or a mate," Tyril said. "She's not allowed on our world."

"There are humans on our world who aren't part of a mated pair or in the program."

"Yes, but they're related to a mated pair."

Siril's arms tightened around her a moment. "And she's not?"

Tyril looked away then back again. "Her daughter obviously ran from her. How do you know this isn't all an act? Maybe she was a horrible mother and her daughter wanted to escape. I'm sorry, but I believe the council will side with me on this and not permit her on our world. As it is, I've said too much."

Siril's lips brushed her ear, sending a shiver down her spine. "How far are you willing to go to see your daughter again?"

"I'll do anything," she vowed.

"Anything?" he asked. "You're certain?"

Jennifer nodded.

"Then congratulations. You just became a potential mate." She could feel Siril's lips curve into a smile against her ear. "It's only a matter of calling the council."

"Siril, what are you doing?" Tyril asked.

"I'm going to go introduce my potential mate to the council," he said, leading her away.

Her head was spinning and she didn't know whether she should laugh or cry. She'd spent eighteen years alone, except for her daughter, and now there was a hunky alien saying she was his potential mate? Was that like mated, as in married? She'd been willing to do anything to find her daughter, but marry a complete stranger? What if he left wet towels on the floor, or left the seat up? What if he beat her into submission when her smart mouth got the better of her?

They entered a conference room with a large screen on one wall. He pushed in some buttons and a moment later, another purple alien appeared on the screen. He was dressed in white from head to toe and appeared a little surprised by the call. Was this their equivalent of using the phone?

"Siril, I heard you were returning tomorrow."

"Yes, Chief Councilor, but I have a favor to ask first."

The chief councilor looked from Siril to her and back again. "Does this have something to do with the woman at your side? I wasn't aware you'd been dating anyone while on Earth."

Siril looked confused by the word "dating" and she wondered if they didn't date on his world. And if they didn't, how exactly did the brides choose a mate? Had her baby been shipped off just to get attached to the first alien who spoke to her?

"I'm Jennifer Montgomery," she said.

"Montgomery," the chief councilor muttered. "Any relation to the Lila Montgomery who arrived here from that Terran Station over a week ago?"

Relief nearly made her legs buckle. "So she is there. I've been so worried."

"It seems Lila left without telling her mother where she was going," Siril said. "Jennifer was rather fierce in trying to obtain the information she wanted, but Tyril refused."

The chief councilor winced. "I shouldn't have said anything either. Is there a reason your daughter wouldn't want you to know where she is?"

"I don't know," Jennifer admitted. "I thought I'd brought her up to be responsible and thoughtful. She's never done anything like this before. She's always told me where she's going and when she'll be home. I'm really worried about her. I don't know why she signed up for the program and I'm afraid she'll do something impulsive."

The chief councilor nodded. "I understand your concern, and as a parent, I can empathize. I cannot, however, let you come here just to check on her."

"What if she came as my potential mate?" Siril asked.

The chief councilor studied them. "And is it true? Are you considering a mating with Siril? He's our fiercest warrior, the best of the best, if you will. There's nothing I could ever deny him. If he wants to mate with you, then I won't stand in his way. But I need to know if you're serious or just wanting a way to check on your daughter. I won't have him taken advantage of."

Siril snorted. "If anything, you should worry I'll take advantage of her."

The chief councilor didn't smile.

Siril sighed. "What would make you accept her, without question?"

"If the two of you agreed to be mated here and now," the chief councilor said.

Jennifer trembled as she thought about it. She knew her daughter was safe on their world, but was it enough? She wanted to see Lila, to understand why she'd run away. But was tying her life to an alien's worth having peace of mind? She could always leave a message for her daughter and hope she sent one back.

Glancing up at Siril, she noticed that he was watching her, an intense expression on his face. For whatever reason, he wanted this mating, and she didn't understand why. They didn't know anything about one another. She was a complete stranger, and while she knew she was pretty, she didn't think she was beautiful enough to make a warrior like him fall to his knees and beg her to be his. Although, he wasn't exactly begging. Just watching and waiting.

"There's another shuttle leaving for that station in two days to return some potentials who didn't find matches. Take that time to get to know one another and make a decision," the chief councilor said. "I suggest you use the time wisely."

The screen blacked out and she gulped down a lungful of air. What on earth had she gotten herself into?

## Chapter Three

Siril wasn't certain what to make of the female. She was prettier than the other human females he'd seen, and he loved the way she'd gone after Tyril when he wouldn't help her. It was obvious she loved her daughter and worried about her, which made him believe she was a caring mother. Since she already had a grown daughter, and only seemed to have the one, he assumed she couldn't have more. But despite the fact she wouldn't be bearing his children, he still wanted her. She was everything he'd been looking for in a mate.

She, on the other hand, didn't seem as certain about him.

"I'm unfamiliar with the term 'dating,'" he said. "But whatever it is, I'm willing to try it with you."

She smiled a little. "What if it's painful? What if it's a form of torture?"

"Is it?" he asked in curiosity.

"I guess that depends on who you're dating. I've been out with plenty of guys who definitely made the night complete torture." She glanced at him. "A date is when two people go out and have fun, or just sit and talk over coffee, while they get to know one another, and see if maybe there's something more there."

He nodded, as that made sense. He might know that he wanted her, but she needed more time to figure things out. He could respect that. If she wanted to go on one of those dates, he would be happy to oblige. Besides, it would give more opportunities to experience more human things. He'd spent most of his vacation hanging out with males he hadn't seen in many years, and while he'd had a nice time, he hadn't gotten a chance to do many things besides visit their homes, have meals with them, or go to a bar for drinks. The human version of drinking was humorous. He'd finished off three bottles before the bartender had cut him off, even though he wasn't the slightest bit inebriated.

"So, where would you like to go on this date?" he asked.

She pulled a device from her pocket and looked at the screen. His friends had those. A cell phone.

"It's almost dinner time," she said. "Would you like to join me for a meal, and we can figure out where we go from there?"

Would it be too presumptuous to ask that they retire to either his bed or hers when they were finished? His gaze skimmed over her curves and slender legs. He'd love to see more of her, preferably without clothing. The boots she wore had to be the sexiest things he'd ever seen a female wear. He wondered if he could talk her into wearing them all the time, or if she had others like them.

"Dinner would be good," he said. "Do you have a favorite place to eat?"

She snorted. "Yeah, cheap and cheaper. You don't look like the type to enjoy fast food though."

He didn't have any idea what fast food was. "You pick wherever you want to eat and that's where we'll go. My treat. I'll even have a limo take us so you won't have to worry about driving."

Her eyebrows lifted into her hairline. "A limo? Never been in one of those before."

Good, then he could show her that he could provide her with things she didn't have already. If she was used to eating cheap meals, it sounded like maybe she was hurting for money, something he had plenty of. He'd transferred some of his credits into the Earth dollars used here, and hadn't spent even a fourth of what he'd transferred. Things didn't seem to cost very much on her world. He'd transferred two weeks of wages, thinking he would spend more here, but it was laughable how little he'd spent.

"Pick anywhere I want?" she asked.

He nodded.

"There's a steak and lobster place not far from here. If the sky is the limit, that's where I want to eat. Never been, but I've heard it's amazing."

"When we get to the limo, give the driver the location and he'll take us there."

"You're sure about this? From what I've seen on the news, a mating for your kind is serious. It's not like here, where we can get a divorce a week later if things don't work out." She moved a little closer and looked up at him. "I appreciate what you're doing, helping me with my daughter and all, but you're going above and beyond and I don't understand why. That guy said you're the best warrior on your planet. I'd imagine you have your pick of women, so what's so special about me?"

He reached out to lightly caress her jaw, not the least bit surprised that she was as soft as she looked. She didn't flinch when he touched her. If anything, she seemed to like it. She leaned into him, pressing her cheek against his palm, her eyes closing briefly and a look of longing crossing her delicate features. Then she pulled away.

"We'll talk more over dinner," he said.

"All right," she said softly. Her voice was husky, an undercurrent of need there that he hadn't anticipated. Was she as lonely as he was?

He reached down and took her hand, leading her through the Terran Station and out to the waiting limos. He waited while she gave the name of the restaurant to the driver, then he helped her into the backseat before sliding in as well. It didn't seem to take long to reach their destination, but he used the time to study her. Her hair was long and straight, but it wasn't what he'd heard referred to as dishwater blonde. There were streaks of gold and honey in there. It wasn't her best feature though. That would be her incredible legs.

"If you took a picture, it would last longer," she said with a smile, glancing his way.

His lips twitched with humor at having been caught staring at her. He looked away and was thankful when the limo pulled to a stop outside of a place called Rock Lobster. He slid out of the limo and helped her out. With her hand clasped in his, they went through the entrance and waited to be seated. Even though it was the dinner hour, and the place seemed busy, they were taken to a table immediately.

The hostess left them with menus and asked for their drink order, then left them to peruse the choices. Siril had experienced enough Earth food over the last week to figure out what most of the things on the menu were, but he hadn't had lobster yet and wasn't sure how it would taste. Jennifer seemed to be studying the menu hard enough that he wondered if she were preparing for an exam instead of dinner.

A waiter appeared at their table, a smile on his face, and their drinks in his hands.

"My name is Tim and I'll be your server this evening. Who had the sweet tea?" he asked.

Jennifer lifted a hand and the server placed the drink in front of her, then gave Siril his water with lemon. The server pulled a pad from the apron tied around his waist, a pen poised over it.

"Have you had time to decide what you'd like to eat this evening?" Tim asked.

"I'm ready if you are," Jennifer said, looking at Siril.

He nodded and motioned for her to order first.

She smiled warmly, then turned to face the server. "I'll have the steak and lobster with rice pilaf on the side, and a house salad with ranch."

Siril wasn't certain where she was going to put that amount of food, but it pleased him that she had a healthy appetite for someone so small. She didn't even reach his shoulder, and while she had curves, she was far from fat. When the server turned his way, he ordered the seafood platter with two types of shrimp and lobster, and decided to ask for the same rice and salad as Jennifer.

When the server was gone, he focused his attention on Jennifer.

"You only have the one daughter, correct? At least, that's how it seemed at the station," he said.

"Yes, it's just been the two of us."

"Her father isn't around anymore?" he asked.

"I was a little bit wilder in my younger days. Her dad was a one-night stand I met at a bar. We never exchanged more than first names and no one at the bar remembered him after I found out I was pregnant. So it's just been us."

"I find it hard to believe no one wanted to marry you over the years. That's the human term for a mating, correct? Married?"

She nodded. "I had a few boyfriends at first, but it became apparent they weren't that fond of Lila. So I ditched them, and after a few duds, I decided to give up on dating and just focus on my daughter."

"That sounds rather lonely."

"Sometimes it was. But I just focused my attention on her and working hard to pay the bills. She may not have had everything she wanted, but I made sure she had everything she needed. Her clothes and shoes weren't name brand from a high priced store, but they were clean and I did my best to keep them trendy. I didn't want kids to make fun of her because we had so little."

Siril took a sip of his water. "It sounds like you're a good mom and you were doing the best you could. I'm sure she appreciates everything you've done for her."

Jennifer shrugged. "I'd thought she did, until this stunt. How could she sign up for the bride program, take off to another planet, and then make sure no one could tell me where she was or if she was okay? Why would she do that? Was I so horrible to her growing up, just because she didn't have the latest cell phone or gadget?"

"If you agree to be my mate, I will take you to my world and we can find her together and ask why she did it. If she's mated to one of my kind, her home will be there now. Even if she did agree to communicate with you, it's doubtful you would ever see her again, if you remained here."

"That's quite the selling point you have there."

"I'm hoping that you'll spend time with me and see that I'm not so terrible. Maybe we'll get along well and feelings will grow over time. You've been alone a long time, and so have I. Even though I'm quite a bit older than you, I think we could make things work between us."

Her brow furrowed. "You don't look a day over forty. How old are you?"

"Fifty."

Her eyes widened and her jaw slackened. "Fifty? But you don't have wrinkles or gray hair. And… Well, I've never met a fifty-year-old as fit as you. I bet you even have an eight-pack."

Her assessment was a little amusing. And if he understood the human definition of an eight-pack correctly, his was more like ten. Being the top warrior on his world, he'd stayed in shape. Even better shape than a lot of the younger warriors he trained. He was well aware that had it not been for his missing body parts he probably could have crooked his finger and had any female he wanted. But right now, he was glad that hadn't happened, because the more he learned about Jennifer, the more he liked her. He was very willing to be mated to someone like her.

"Fifty," she muttered again before taking a sip of her tea. "And in all that time you've never been mated?"

He shook his head. "I stay busy with my work." *And no one wanted me.*

"What would it be like to be mated to you? What's a typical day for you?" she asked.

"I wake early, work out in my back garden, then report for work. When I'm on my world, I train our current and new warriors. The council sends me out on missions that sometimes last a week or two, and then I return for more training. My mate would have a lot of time to herself, except for the evenings, unless she chose to train alongside me. Obviously, I wouldn't expect a female to do everything our warriors do, but if you wanted a good workout, you could join me sometimes."

Her eyebrows lifted. "Are you trying to say I need to lose weight? I know I'm carrying a few extra pounds, but it's just rude to point it out."

His jaw dropped a little. "What?"

"It's not polite to tell someone they're fat."

He blinked at her in confusion. "I never said you were

fat."

"But you think I need a good workout?"

"It was merely a suggestion of how we could spend more time together, but not a requirement. I'm rather fond of your curves." His gaze caressed what he could see of her. "And I'm most intrigued about what they look like minus the clothing."

Her cheeks pinked.

"I find you to be rather delectable. Between your ferocity when protecting your young and the sexy way you fill out those clothes, I was hard-pressed not to toss you over my shoulder and find the nearest bedroom." He leaned his elbows on the table. "Or is that too forward speaking?"

"You want to have sex with me?" she asked, her face flushing more.

He leaned forward a little more and lowered his voice so no one else would hear. "What I'd like is to take you back to my hotel suite, rip every stitch of clothing from your body, except possibly for those sexy as fuck boots, and take you so hard and fast your legs shake and you scream my name over and over. I want to worship every inch of your body, take you so many times you can't walk tomorrow, and then I want to do it all over again. I want to erase every memory of every other male you've known, eradicate them one orgasm at a time, until you're begging me to never stop."

She was breathing hard and her pulse raced in her throat. Good. She was every bit as affected as he was. And Siril had meant every damn word. He'd never wanted a female the way he wanted her. It wasn't just the mesmerizing tilt of her lips when she smiled, or the way her eyes flashed with sass and amusement. It was the way she'd gone after Tyril, determined to find out what had happened to her daughter. It was the fire he saw in her whenever she talked about being a mom. And all right, a big dose of it was just wanting to feel those incredible legs wrapped around him. He'd always admired the female form, and hers was exceptional.

She lifted her glass and took several gulps of her tea before setting it back down. Her hand trembled as she dropped it to her lap. The look in her eyes said she clearly hadn't expected him to be so open with her, but he had never been one to stand by and wait for things to happen. If he wanted something, he went after it. For the most part. A mate had been the one thing he'd stopped looking for, after being rejected a few times too many.

"When you offered to take me as your mate, it wasn't just you being altruistic, was it?" she asked. "You really do want me."

"Yes, I do."

"No one's ever…" she trailed off.

"No one's ever what?" he asked.

"No one's ever wanted me like that before. I mean, I've slept with guys, obviously, but it's always just been two drunk people trying to feel good for a minute. It's never really been all that passionate or…" She bit her lip. "Intense. I think being with you would be intense, and that scares me a little."

"I don't mean to frighten you."

"I didn't mean it quite like that. It's very tempting to say screw dinner and tell you to take me to your hotel room. But then we wouldn't know anything about one another except whether or not we're good in bed. And while that would definitely be something I'd want to know before agreeing to a mating, I think a relationship should be built on more than that. Sex isn't everything."

"When's the last time you were with a male?" he asked.

Her cheeks flushed. "That's rather personal."

"Perhaps sex doesn't seem as important to you as other things because it's been missing in your life for a while. I'm not saying we should forget dinner and find the nearest bed, but I think you're not putting enough importance on the act of intimacy."

She nodded. "You may be right. So, why don't we spend dinner getting to know one another, and then see where things go from there."

"I can agree to that."

"Are you an only child or do you come from a big family?" she asked.

"I had a sister, one of the last females born to my people, but she took sick and never recovered. Our doctors did everything they could for her, but in the end, the disease was too strong for her body to overcome it."

"I'm sorry. What was her name?"

"Leandara. She was younger than me by two years and would have had a family of her own by now. She died when she was still quite young. My parents were never blessed with more children after the two of us."

"How do your people control the population? Do you have birth control?" she asked.

"I'm familiar with the human ways of not having children, but no, we don't use birth control on my planet. All children are welcome. If it becomes too dangerous for a mate to have more children, either the male or female is sterilized. For those who go off-world and enjoy females while they're away, it is usually the female's job to make sure no children come of it. Brothels in space are required to sterilize their females, or provide some other methods to avoid pregnancies."

"Well that hardly seems fair, putting it all on the woman," she said.

"Not all males think that way and may take precautions, but most assume the female has it covered." He shrugged. "Things are different in other places than here on your Earth. In some ways, I feel humans can be more advanced than other races, but in a lot of ways you're still growing and learning. Your space program is laughable."

"Agreed. You'd think with aliens living on Earth now, they would make improvements, but they seem content to let your people take care of things. I'm assuming the presence of your people on my world is why no one has brought an intergalactic war to Earth. And now more races are coming here. Just the other day, I saw a blue alien walking down the sidewalk."

"We are inviting the possibility of more races joining the bride program. My people aren't the only ones hurting for females. While I don't believe brides will be sent to any other planets, we have agreed on a case by case basis for other races to come here to seek a mate. It hardly seems fair that we have a monopoly on the females of your world."

"It amazes me that when I was little, no one even knew there were other people out there. We just assumed we were the only ones. And now, aliens of all shapes and sizes are parading around town and it's possible for us to travel to other worlds." She smiled. "It's all rather remarkable."

"I know it's common for human females to have jobs. Since you are the sole provider for your daughter, I'm assuming you work?"

She nodded. "I'm a clerk at the dollar store. It's not a glamorous job, but it pays the bills and the work is steady. I've been there a few years now. Before that, I was a barista at a coffee shop. I didn't finish high school, but I did get my G.E.D. later, after I found out I was pregnant with Lila. I wanted to be able to offer her a better life, although I think I failed at that."

"Why do you feel like you failed?" he asked.

"We have a cramped two bedroom, one bath house that I rent, in a questionable part of town. My car is falling apart, and doesn't always run. We struggle, and there's never been money for big Christmas gifts or extravagant trips. I saved up once a year to take her to the amusement park, and the last two years I've been saving so we could have a real vacation. But I guess it wasn't enough for Lila, since she's run off to another planet."

"Sometimes we don't realize what we have until it's gone. She's in a strange place, surrounded by people she doesn't know. I'm going to assume this is her first time away from you for any length of time and she's lost her only support system. There are hundreds if not thousands of males begging her to choose them, and doing their utmost to earn the right to take her out and get to know her. They'll pressure her to choose them and settle down, even if they've only known her for hours, and I have a feeling that about now, she's feeling a little overwhelmed."

"I don't fool myself into thinking she's a virgin, but they won't force her to have sex with them, will they?"

Siril shook his head. "A male would never do something so dishonorable, but I wouldn't put it past them to try tempting her. Some males would wait until after an official mating to try to claim her that way. Not all, but some. Rest assured that whoever she mates with will treat her well."

"I guess I should be thankful for that at least. I'd always thought she'd go to college, get a job, and settle down when she was older. I didn't want her to struggle the way I have. I hadn't figured out the college part yet, but I hadn't given up. There are scholarships and grants out there, and she could always get student loans if she needed to."

"I understand your worry, but on my world, she won't need a job. She will never struggle as you have. Food will be plentiful, she'll have a mate who adores her, and there are a lot of human females on my world now so making friends shouldn't be too hard for her." Siril sighed. "I suppose I'm not doing myself any favors by soothing your fears. Now that you know she'll be all right, there's no reason for you to mate with me."

"I want to see her," Jennifer said. "I want her to know that what she did hurt me, that I would have supported her decision if she'd only talked to me. But despite how much I want that, I promise that I won't agree to be your mate just for that purpose. It wouldn't be fair to you. If by the time you return to your world, I decide to mate with you, then know it's because I think we have a real shot at a relationship."

"You would still consider a mating with me?"

Jennifer tucked a wayward strand of hair behind her ear. "You're obviously a nice guy, trying to help me. And yes, I know you want a mate so it wasn't completely altruistic, but you saw my temper and for some reason seem to like it. Most guys run away. If you're willing to accept me, flaws and all, then I'm open to the possibility of a relationship with you. Just understand that if we do this, if you take me to your world as your mate, you aren't getting just me. You'll be gaining a daughter too. Lila is the most important part of my life and I'll expect her and her mate to come over for family meals. Are you sure that's something you want?"

Siril smiled. "I like the idea of having a daughter, even if she is fully grown already."

There was warmth in Jennifer's eyes and he knew he'd said the right thing, and he'd meant it. He wouldn't have cared if she came with ten kids. The thought of finally having a family made his chest ache. He'd been alone for so long, losing himself in his work, but it was time for a change. He was getting older, and the thought of spending all those years without a mate, without children, made him lonely.

If she would give him a chance, agree to become his mate, he would make sure she knew every day how very much she was wanted and cherished. She could have anything she wanted because in giving herself to him, she would be granting his fondest wish.

# Chapter Four

Jennifer was getting nervous as the night wore on. Not because Siril himself made her nervous, but the way he made her *feel* made her nervous. She'd seen plenty of attractive guys, but it had been a really long time since one had paid any attention to her. After she'd given up on dating, she'd avoided bars and clubs. The few times she'd had a sitter, she'd used the time to just grab a burger and eat in peace, or stop by the coffee shop and linger over a cup of hot coffee.

That wasn't to say no one ever noticed her. But the last guy who'd paid her a compliment had stopped her at the grocery store to tell her she looked amazing. He was probably a perfectly nice guy, even if it had creeped her out a little, but he'd been short, balding, and had a pot belly. Of course, going after the model-like guys was what had gotten her into trouble in the first place.

Siril wasn't perfect, if his eye patch was any indication. She'd also noticed he had a finger missing, probably lost while defending his planet. It made her curious about what the rest of him looked like, the parts hidden by clothes. She wanted him, more than she'd ever wanted anyone before. He was mysterious, even though he was answering all of her questions. His one eye stayed trained on her, his gaze intense and scorching, as if he were mentally undressing her between bites of dinner. He'd admitted he wanted to see her without her clothes.

The shirt he wore was stretched across his broad chest and shoulders, and did little to hide how muscular he was. She'd been with fit guys before, but none as built as Siril. Would those arms hold her gently? She'd found him to be witty and entertaining, but could he be tender too? She really, really wanted to find out. They'd finished their meal and he'd ordered dessert, insisting that they should share the massive skillet brownie in the middle of the table, topped with drizzled chocolate and caramel syrup with a scoop of ice cream. It was the most divine thing she'd ever had. The entire meal had been wonderful.

"I love the look of bliss on your face every time you take a bite," Siril said. "I wonder if you'd make that same expression with me deep inside you."

Jennifer nearly choked on her bite of brownie. He was certainly direct. But then, she rather liked that about him. He didn't play games. Siril said exactly what he meant, whether it was outrageous or not. Perhaps part of that was him being an alien, but she suspected a lot of it was just who he was. And the more she talked to him, the more she liked him. Adult conversations were few and far between, unless she counted talking to her coworkers on her breaks. And while Lila was technically an adult now, she was still Jennifer's baby. She'd thought she had a close relationship with her daughter, one she loved, but now she was questioning everything.

She'd lived every day of her life for the last eighteen years for the daughter who had run away. Maybe it was time to take something for herself. Every night she'd gone out, she'd felt guilty for leaving her child at home. She'd worked herself to the bone, picking up as many shifts as she could, trying to give them a decent life. Now, she wondered if any of it had ever mattered to Lila, or if her daughter had only seen the things her mother *couldn't* do for her, instead of everything she gave up to give her a safe and happy home.

"You're thinking too hard," Siril said.

"Despite my best effort to raise a well-adjusted child who appreciated the things she had, I think I failed. I was just thinking that maybe my Lila left because she was so unhappy with her life here, and everything I couldn't do for her. I've sacrificed every day for eighteen years so she could have the things she needed, and I guess it wasn't enough. So, maybe it's time I do something for me."

"That sounds reasonable. What is it you want to do for yourself?"

"I want to leave this restaurant, as amazing as it's been, and instead of going right back to the Terran Station, I want to drive around for a while."

He smiled a little. "Drive around?"

"There's a human custom of making out in cars. Do you know what making out is?" she asked.

"I'm not familiar with the term."

"It means that we kiss and your hands are free to roam where they will." She smirked. "And it means I get to remove that shirt and see if that chest of yours is as impressive as it seems."

His eyebrows rose. "I think I like that plan. And is anything else allowed on this car ride?"

"We'll see. Depends on how good you are."

"Or maybe how bad?"

She giggled and covered her mouth with her hand, surprised it had slipped out. It had been a long time since she'd giggled like a young girl. Not that thirty-eight was ancient, but being with Siril made her feel younger, and she definitely felt like a desirable woman first and a mom second. Maybe being with him would be good for her. Her life had been in a rut for pretty much ever. She'd laughed and smiled more tonight than she had in ages, and it felt incredible.

Jennifer waved at their server and Siril paid for their meal. On the way to the limo, she looped her arm through his. He towered over her, but walking beside him didn't feel awkward. If anything, she felt safe. His size and strength made her feel protected, and she was able to let down her guard. As a single mom, she'd always been ever vigilant, as any woman should be. Having Siril by her side allowed her to relax and enjoy herself. She'd pity the mugger who tried to take on the sexy alien.

When they reached the limo, the driver held the door open for them. Before Siril slid into the vehicle, he requested that they drive around town for a while, and suggested that the dividing window remain closed. Jennifer felt giddy as he eased onto the seat next to her, his thigh brushing hers. The driver shut the door and a few minutes later, the limo glided forward.

Feeling brave and bold, Jennifer threw a leg across Siril

and straddled his lap. Her fingers toyed with his shirt, easing one button free, then another. She paused partway down, his chest partially exposed. There were faint scars marring his skin, but they were barely discernible. She wondered if he had marks elsewhere, or anything else missing. Obviously his cock was in perfect working order with the way he'd been talking to her in the restaurant, unless it had just been talk. She somehow doubted that, though.

"Before I strip this shirt off you, is there anything else I need to know? Is there a chunk of flesh missing out of your side or something?" she asked.

He grimaced and reached around her to bang on his lower leg with his fist. It clanged. Jennifer eased off his lap and lifted his pant leg. The silver limb surprised her, but she wasn't the least bit repulsed by it. Curious, perhaps, about what had caused him to lose the leg, but plenty of soldiers came back from war missing a limb or two. Siril was no different, even though the wars he'd waged had been in space.

"If you wish to stop, I'll understand," he said.

Jennifer slid her hand up the metal leg, beyond his knee, and came to rest on his well-muscled thigh. "Nothing about you disgusts me. You lost your leg fighting for your people, right? It's honorable. I'm only sorry that the cost of their freedom caused you so much pain."

"You aren't going to ask me to keep my pants on even during sex?" he asked.

Anger made her cheeks flush. "Who the hell made you keep your pants on?"

He shrugged, which told her it was more than one person. Bitches. Every last one them needed a good hair pulling and a slap across the face. What the hell was wrong with them? Obviously they just weren't good enough for Siril. Not that she felt worthy of being with him, but he'd been mistreated by females in his past, and she'd had shit luck with men. Maybe they would be good for each other.

Jennifer sat on her knees between his splayed legs and

finished unbuttoning his shirt. The material parted and she wasn't disappointed with the view. Reaching out, she caressed his hard chest and chiseled abs, a shiver raking her spine at having so much power at her fingertips. If he was the best at what he did, it meant he was probably the deadliest, and yet he seemed hesitant to reach for her. How could someone so powerful be so uncertain when it came time to get undressed? It touched her, and Jennifer decided she would do whatever it took to prove to Siril that he was desirable.

He leaned forward so she could pull the shirt down his arms and toss it on the seat across from them. Her fingers itched to remove more of his clothing, but that hardly seemed fair when she was still fully dressed. Jennifer removed her shirt and tossed it on top of his. Her bra was plain and she wished she had something lacy and sexy to wear for him. Her breasts overflowed from the cups and she reached behind her to pop the clasp. The garment slid down her arms and landed on the floor of the limo.

Siril watched, his gaze heated. The clenched fists at his sides said he wanted to touch her, but for some reason he refrained. She couldn't think of anything she wanted more than his hands on her body. Reaching for one of his fists, she unfurled his fingers and placed his palm over her breast. Her nipple puckered in response and a jolt of desire shot through her.

His grip was light as he explored her body, and his callused fingertips gave her goose bumps. Siril gripped her waist and lifted her, laying her down across the seat of the limo, he braced his arms on either side of her and settled between her legs. Her heart pounded in her chest, feeling like it was running a race. Slowly, his head lowered to hers. He hesitated only a moment before brushing his lips against hers. They were warm and firm, and she melted as his tongue swept inside for a taste. Siril took his time. The kiss was languid, as if he wanted to savor every moment.

Jennifer slid her hands up his arms to grip his biceps. His muscles flexed and she moaned as her pussy pulsed with need. Her panties felt soaked, and if he teased her much more, her jeans would be too. Her thighs encased his hips and she could feel the hard ridge of his cock as he pressed against her. It seemed he was proportionate everywhere, and that thought alone almost made her come. Too many layers, too many clothes. She wanted to feel all of him, skin to skin.

The limo hit a bump and they tumbled to the floor. Jennifer ended up on top of Siril once more and couldn't help but laugh. He smiled up at her, also amused by the situation. Pressing against him, she thoroughly kissed him before unsteadily climbing off. As much as he said he loved the boots, they had to come off for her jeans to do the same. The limo toppled her onto her butt, startling another laugh from her, as she tugged off one shoe then the other. Jennifer shimmied out of her jeans and panties before sliding to the floor again. Siril had eased his pants down, but seemed hesitant to remove them completely. She'd give him time and show him that he was sexy just the way he was, metal leg and all. Next time, she'd get his clothes off.

"Just so you know, it's been quite a while since I've been with anyone," Jennifer said. "So, I'm clean. I mean, I'm not carrying anything."

"I'm thoroughly tested after every mission," Siril said.

Straddling him, she reached between their bodies and held his cock as she eased down onto his length. A moan tore from her lips as he stretched her. When she'd taken all of him, she rocked her hips and splayed her hands across his abdomen. Siril's hands gripped her hips as she rode him. Every stroke was more delicious than the last, and her need became stronger. Sweat coated her skin and her breath came out in pants as she chased after the incredible sensations that were rolling through her, knowing there was more to come.

Siril groaned beneath her and she felt his cock pulse. He was close, but her orgasm was just out of reach. She needed… something.

"Touch me," she begged. "Make me come."

His hand cupped her breast and tweaked her nipple.

Shockwaves of pleasure shot to her clit, but it wasn't enough. Jennifer reached between her splayed legs and teased the bundle of nerves. So close. She rode him harder, faster. Siril pinched down on her nipple as her fingers flew over her clit, smaller tighter circles, until she was screaming out her release.

Siril gripped her hips and thrust upward, spilling himself inside of her. Thankfully she didn't have to worry about pregnancy, courtesy of a little procedure she'd had done when Lila was born.

Out of breath, and more relaxed than she'd been in forever, she collapsed onto his chest, listening to his racing heartbeat. His arms came around her and they just laid in the bottom of the limo, basking in the afterglow. The moment was perfect and she wished it could last forever.

After they'd caught their breath, they pulled their clothes back on and Siril tapped on the dividing window, asking the driver to return to the Terran Station. Jennifer eased onto the seat next to him, their hands clasped. They'd had one hell of a first date, and she couldn't imagine they would ever top it. Their first time together would always be a fond memory for her, and she hoped Siril felt the same. No words were necessary as they cuddled on the seat and enjoyed what was left of the ride. At the Terran Station, the driver opened the door and Siril slid out first, helping her out of the limo.

"I guess this is goodbye, at least for now," she said.

"You're going home?"

She nodded. "I'll be there in about fifteen to twenty minutes, depending on how many red lights I hit. Thank you for tonight."

He brushed his lips against hers. "I'll walk you to your vehicle. Even though this area is safe, you can never be too careful."

"And here I thought you believed me to be a badass who could handle herself."

"Oh, I have no doubt. I'm more worried about your attacker. I'm sure you'd land a direct hit to his balls and he'd never be the same again."

Jennifer threw back her head and laughed. "Well, if he's mugging women, then he deserves a good kick in the balls."

"True." She led him to her car and popped the locks, but she wasn't ready for the night to end just yet. Going up on tiptoe, she pulled his head down for another kiss. Her body warmed and her pussy tingled, more than ready for another round. Perhaps one night he could prove that he'd turn her legs to Jell-O. He'd done a pretty damn good job of rocking her world tonight, but the limo had limited what they could do. It made her eager to see what would happen if they were ever alone in a bedroom.

"May I pick you up in the morning?" he asked.

"Fifty-five Mulberry Lane. It's a mint green house with white trim. You'll see my car in the driveway. Just not too early. I'm not a morning person."

"You don't work tomorrow?"

"I took today and tomorrow off, not knowing what I was going to do about Lila. I'll have to go back the day after, though, or I might lose my job. Chain stores don't generally care if you have a personal crisis. They put you on the schedule and expect you to be there."

"Then I'll enjoy tomorrow with you, and do my best to convince you to return to my world with me the day after. Then you won't need your job."

She smiled, rather liking that plan.

Siril stood in the parking lot as she got into her car and drove away. As she pulled onto the street, she saw him watching her. Jennifer waved, even though she wasn't certain he could see her, then she headed for home. She'd gotten to live in another world for a short time, a place where limo rides and expensive restaurants were an everyday thing. For her, the night had been a once in a lifetime experience. She'd had the best meal she'd ever tasted, ridden in a limo for the first time, and had the most incredible sex ever. And with an alien no less. She wasn't sure anything would ever top tonight.

Her street was quiet when she got home, but getting

Jessica Coulter Smith                    Intergalactic Brides Vol. 4

out of her car, she was still ever vigilant. She wasn't exactly in the "bad" part of town, but she was on the fringes. Close enough she still dealt with drug dealers and burglars. The house she was renting had been broken into three times over the last few years, but her landlord still refused to install more secure windows or one of those security doors. Thankfully, she didn't have much of anything someone would want, but they always made a mess when they broke in.

She let herself into her house, locked the door, and flipped on the lights. Tonight hadn't gone as she'd planned. While she at least knew where Lila was, if she didn't go with Siril, she'd never see her daughter again. It still hurt, knowing that Lila had run away, had planned to never see her again. It had just been the two of them for eighteen years and now she was alone. The house didn't feel as welcoming, knowing she'd never hear her daughter talking down the hall or laughing with her friends. She'd built her life around her child, and now she had nothing to show for it.

"I hate my job. I hate this house. I hate my car. The only thing I loved about my life was Lila, and she left me." Jennifer flopped onto the couch. She pulled off her boots and tossed them onto the floor then stretched out, her head resting on a throw pillow. If there was nothing she liked about her life, what was the point? She'd liked being with Siril tonight. It was hard to picture spending the rest of her life with him, knowing so little about him, but there was nothing keeping her here.

Except Lila. If her daughter had gone to another world to escape her, how would Lila feel when Jennifer showed up anyway? Her daughter had hurt her deeply, but she still loved her and wanted what was best for her. If Lila needed to be on another planet in order to find her happiness, should Jennifer leave her alone? It was hard, thinking about never seeing her again. And lonely. So damn lonely. Even if she didn't go to another planet, it didn't mean she had to stay here. She had her money in savings. She could use it to start over somewhere -- but it wouldn't change the fact she was alone. No matter what city, state, or country she travelled to, it would still just be her. There was nothing wrong with being alone; plenty of people did it every day. But she was older now and wanted someone to share her life with. She'd never thought about what would happen when Lila grew up and moved out on her own. She'd always taken things one day at a time.

Tomorrow. She'd see Siril again tomorrow, spend more time with him, and then she'd have to give him her answer. He made her laugh. No one had made her laugh in a long time. And he'd made her feel safe. Spending time with him had been effortless, almost as if they were supposed to be together. Which was ridiculous. Jennifer didn't believe in fate, not so much anyway. She did, however, trust her instincts, and they were screaming that Siril was someone she could trust, that he'd take care of her if she let him. She'd taken care of herself for so long, having someone by her side to help during the stressful times sounded nice.

And he was sexy as hell. He looked intimidating because of his size and eye patch, which worked for him. He claimed to be the best at what he did, and she believed him. There was a dangerous vibe about him, and yet he'd been tender with her, shown her a softer side of himself. A vulnerable side. It showed how strong he was, that he'd allowed her to catch that glimpse. Not many men would show any sign of what they deemed a weakness, but he'd let her in.

She didn't know what tomorrow would bring, but she looked forward to spending more time with him. Just the thought of his arms being around her, his lips against hers, was enough to make her smile and anticipation to hum in her veins. It had been a long time since she'd reacted to someone so strongly, if ever. Was this what that fabled love at first sight felt like? She didn't kid herself into believing she loved Siril, but she definitely liked the hell out of him.

She stretched then rolled to her feet. Padding down the hall, she decided calling it a night early was the right thing to do. The sooner she went to sleep, the sooner morning would get here. And with morning would come Siril.

## Chapter Five

Siril stared at the structure in front him before surveying the neighborhood. The homes were old, their paint faded. Most of the vehicles were dented or rusted. Her driveway was cracked, but the windows of her home sparkled. She might not have much, but she seemed to take care of what she had. What would she think of his home on Zelthrane-3? It would be a palace compared to this place. He made his way up to her front door and knocked loudly, hoping she was awake. He'd waited until seven, even though he'd been awake since five this morning.

After a few minutes, he knocked again. When Jennifer still didn't answer the door, he began to worry. She was home alone. What if she'd fallen and hurt herself? Or what if someone had broken in and harmed her? Gripping the knob tight, he twisted until the lock snapped then put his shoulder against the door to break the second lock. The wood frame around the door gave a loud *crack* and the door flew open. He'd owe her a new one, but it wasn't like he couldn't afford it.

The house was even smaller than he'd imagined and he found her room easily. She was tangled amongst her bedding, her hair wild about her head and an arm flung out. Her toes peeked beneath the edge of the blanket. Relief filled him, then amusement. The woman could sleep through anything. Gripping the bottom of her bedding, he eased the covers off her body until they pooled on the floor.

She grumbled in her sleep and reached for them blindly before huffing and cuddling closer to her pillow. Siril sat on the edge of the bed and caged her body between his arms. Leaning down, he brushed his lips against hers. Jennifer hummed in her sleep and wound an arm around his neck. When he drew away, she was still dozing. With a shake of his head, he stood and then pressed his hands up and down on the mattress, shaking the bed until she jolted awake.

"What? What's..." She blinked up at him. "Siril? How did you get in my home?"

"I broke your door."

Her eyes went wide and she looked from him to the open bedroom door then back again. "You broke my door? As in the front door? It was bolted!"

He shrugged. "Not anymore."

"How do I explain to my landlord that an alien broke my door?" she demanded.

"I'll pay to replace the door. When you didn't answer, I worried something had happened to you."

"I'm fine. What time is it?" She squinted toward the window. "Why does it look like the sun is still rising?"

"Because it is."

"Seriously? You're waking me up before the sun's even all the way up?"

He frowned and looked at her window. "The sun is up. There's light outside."

Jennifer sighed and buried her head under her pillow.

Siril ran a hand up one of her shapely legs until his fingers brushed the hem of her shorts. The pillow shifted enough that she could peek from under it. He let his hand wander a little higher, a groan torn from him when he realized she didn't have on anything under the shorts. Siril adjusted himself and heard Jennifer snicker. At least she was amused by the situation. If her front door weren't broken, he'd have stripped and crawled into the bed with her. Doubtful she'd be laughing then. She'd be too busy screaming his name.

"Whatever is required for you to be ready, get up and do it," he said.

"Oohh. Bossy. Someone hasn't had their morning coffee yet."

He sighed and reminded himself that she was damn cute before turning and leaving her to get ready. He'd have used his time to explore her home, but he could stand near the front door and see pretty much everything. The kitchen and dining area were all one room. Her living room was small and only had a couch and TV. He'd been so focused yesterday on how sexy she was, and how fierce, that he hadn't noticed the tell-tale signs that she was hurting for money. Her boots lay by the couch. He bent down to retrieve one, remembering how great they'd looked on her. But now he saw the soles were well-worn and didn't have much thickness left.

Even if she didn't go to Zelthrane-3 with him, maybe she would accept a little money. Since her daughter had signed up for the bride program, she was owed some money to his way of thinking. Usually families received some cash as an apology for their loved one moving so far away, but that hadn't happened with Jennifer and her daughter. He wondered if Lila had requested the money be delivered to her account instead of her mother's. If that were the case, she was a selfish brat and her mother was better off without her.

Jennifer stumbled out of her bedroom and into a room off the hall. A door slammed and he went to check out the rest of the space. He assumed she was in the bathroom, and he'd seen her room. He was curious about the daughter's sleeping space. The room was smaller than the other bedroom, but not by much. The walls were a soft lavender and while it was obvious Jennifer had tossed the place looking for clues to her daughter's whereabouts, he now saw where most of her money had gone. The closet stood open and it was still bursting with clothes and shoes. There was a TV on the dresser and a bookshelf full of movies.

Jennifer had been wearing her shoes almost all the way through, and her daughter had all this abundance, and had still abandoned her mother. What she needed was a firm hand across her ass until she couldn't sit down. He pitied whatever male ended up with her. It was obvious that she didn't appreciate the things she was given, and would likely demand more, even if her male couldn't afford it. He'd met females like her before and wondered how she'd slipped into the program. There were personality tests to help weed out that sort.

Disgust filled him and he left the room. While he waited for Jennifer to finish, he called the Terran Station and arranged for someone to come replace her front door. He was assured someone would come by to keep an eye on the place until the new door was in place and the keys would be waiting for them at the station when they'd finished their outing. It took a while for Jennifer to finish getting ready, and by the time she was done, one of the maintenance crew from the station had arrived.

Jennifer came into the living room wearing another pair of jeans that showed off her legs, and another off the shoulder top, this time in mint green. She pulled on her boots while eyeing the new alien in her living space then came forward.

"Is he going with us?" she asked.

"No. This is Kwintex. He's going to remain here until your door is replaced, then we'll pick up your new keys from the Terran Station later."

"It's nice to meet you, Kwintex."

Kwintex smiled and winked at her. Siril hid his annoyance and reached for Jennifer, pulling her against his side. She fit perfectly, and felt so damn right pressed against him. He hoped that things went well today and she agreed to move to his world with him. He couldn't think of anything he wanted more than her as his mate. He escorted her outside to the waiting limo. She paused on her front stoop and stared at it before casting a glance around her neighborhood. There was a woman across the street, peering out around a curtain, but otherwise he didn't see anyone around.

"Something's wrong?" he asked.

"There's a limo. On my street."

"Well, I told you I was picking you up this morning."

"In a limo." She stared at it. "You couldn't have borrowed some dented, beat up piece of crap to come here? Or even something like that," she said pointing to the truck Kwintex had arrived in.

"I wasn't aware the limo would be a problem."

"They're going to think you're my sugar daddy."

"Your what?" His brow furrowed.

"You know, a guy I'm sleeping with so he'll take care of me financially."

Siril snorted. "Before last night I'd have said that was the dumbest thing I've ever heard, but I can see where having sex with you would make men want to take care of you. I've had my share of females over the years, but none compared to what we shared last night."

Her cheeks pinked. "You weren't so bad yourself. In fact, I've been looking forward to an encore. Would it be presumptuous to assume that our outing will end back at your hotel?"

He growled softly and pulled her tight against his body. "If you'd like, we can start the day there. I'm sure I could find ways to keep you entertained."

"As much as I love that idea, you promised me an outing. Do you know how long it's been since I did anything fun? Dinner and a limo ride last night topped my list of favorite things I've ever done, but I was looking forward to what you'd come up with today."

Siril pressed his lips to hers. "Then we'll go out."

She wrapped her arms around his neck and kissed him harder, deeper, then scurried off to the waiting limo. The driver opened the door for them and Siril slid into the car after Jennifer. She immediately pressed against his side, her hand on his thigh. He had to remind himself that it was one thing to undress her in the limo when it was dark outside and another to do it during the day. He didn't care if the windows were tinted. Siril wasn't about to take a chance on someone other than him seeing her without clothes. As far as he was concerned, that treat was reserved solely for him. At least, until she told him she didn't want to see him again. If she decided to remain here when he returned to Zelthrane-3, it was doubtful they would ever see each other. Not unless he took more trips to Earth between missions.

"What are you thinking about?" she asked.

"Trying to think of ways to keep seeing you even if you don't agree to leave with me tomorrow. I'm not ready for whatever this is between us to end."

"I'm not either," she said, pressing even closer.

"Do you have a preference for what we do today? The

driver has instructions for our first stop, which is breakfast. After that, we can do whatever you want."

"It's supposed to be sunny and warm today. How do you feel about the zoo?" she asked.

"That's the place where animals are kept?"

She nodded. "I haven't been since Lila was little. They have free days once a week and we'd go on the day she didn't have school. Sometimes I'd get her out an hour early and we'd spend the afternoon there."

"If you want to see the animals, that's what we'll do."

"You don't have zoos on your world?" she asked.

"No. We have a... I believe the term is zoologist? Someone who specializes in animals. On the edge of our main city, he has a place where he keeps breeding pairs when they are going extinct. He cares for them and when he feels it's safe, he releases them back into the wild until another animal needs help. He doctors them too when they are sick."

"That sounds like an interesting job. I just check out items at the dollar store, or sometimes I stock the shelves. I've worked at a few stores over the years, a coffee shop, and a diner. I guess getting to talk to people at the diner was kind of interesting, but I think I'd have much rather worked with animals."

Siril nodded. "I would imagine it's a rather calming job, as I've noticed animals have that effect on most people."

"If you hadn't become a warrior, what do you think you would have done?" she asked.

"I'm not certain. From an early age I showed an aptitude for things like battle strategy. I think I was always destined to be a warrior. I enjoy my work. I always have, but the older I get, I know I'm getting close to the council retiring me. I'll be stuck on my world training warriors until I'm too old to do even that."

Her lips turned down a little. "You don't get retirement there at like age sixty-five where you get to sit home and enjoy time with your family?"

He laughed. "No, nothing like that. We work until

we're unable."

"What if you're able to work until you're eighty but someone else can only work until they're seventy? That hardly seems fair."

"It's the way my planet works." He shrugged. "It's all we've ever known, so we're fine with it. A lot of changes have happened since your Earth females have come to my world, and I imagine over the years there will be more changes. If your Earth females are used to having their mates around in their older years, perhaps that is something the council will consider. But if none of the elders are working, how will the younger generation learn anything?"

Her brow furrowed, but she remained quiet.

The limo pulled to a stop in front of the restaurant he had requested. The Terran Station assured Siril they had the best breakfast in the entire town. He helped Jennifer out of the car and her eyes widened when she saw the sign over the café door. *Blueberry Hill.*

"We can't eat here," she said.

He paused, the door midway open. "Why not?"

"It costs too much. It was one thing for you to buy me an expensive meal once, but twice…"

"Jennifer, I have more than enough money to feed you. Now come on. I heard this was the best place for breakfast. We'll enjoy a nice meal and then go to the zoo."

"The zoo probably isn't open this early," she said.

"Then we'll improvise."

She sighed a little and allowed him to urge her into the restaurant. It didn't look all that fancy to him, but maybe anything out of her price range was considered expensive. If she'd never eaten out very often, it was doubtful she'd ever been to this place. He wanted to spoil her a little, if only she'd let him.

Getting her to order whatever she wanted took a little coaxing, but he pulled out the slip of paper in his wallet he was given when his funds were transferred to the Earth American dollars. He showed her the slip and assured her he'd barely spent any of it. Her eyes went wide and her face paled a little. She swayed in her seat, her eyes turning glassy. He worried she was going to pass out and rushed around the table to kneel beside her and hold her upright.

"Jennifer. What's wrong? Is it not enough?" he asked, having no idea what the dollar amounts of his money meant here.

"N-Not enough?" she stammered. "You have more money than anyone I've ever met. That's more than I'd make in ten years, possibly longer."

He smiled faintly. "It's only a fraction of my money, Jennifer. I transferred some funds so I'd be able to do things while I was here. I had no idea what the conversion rate would be, and I honestly didn't realize I'd transferred so much until now. I thought it was a common enough amount."

She laughed, but it was humorless and her eyes still held a glassy sheen, like she was in shock. He squeezed her hand and tried to get her to focus on him. Maybe he shouldn't have shown her how much money he had, but he didn't want her to worry that she was going to bankrupt him. He'd been assured he'd transferred enough money to have fun on his trip, but no one had told him he'd transferred too much. Judging by Jennifer's reaction, he'd overdone it quite a bit.

When she seemed to snap out of it a little, he pressed a kiss to her lips and then returned to his seat. She took several deep breaths, then gulped down her drink. Her hand shook a little as she set the glass down and he worried she wasn't over the shock of how much he'd brought with him. He knew he made good money on his world, but he hadn't realized until now just how much that was. To someone like Jennifer, who had fought so hard for how very little she had, it must seem like a fortune.

"That's what you call travel expenses?" she asked, her voice hoarse.

"I didn't know what I'd be doing while I was here, so I wanted to be prepared. When I leave, I can revert it back to my currency and the money will go back into my account.

Or I can leave it in a bank here and draw on it if I make future trips to Earth." He tipped his head a little. "Or if a rather beautiful, yet stubborn, female refuses to go to Zelthrane-3 with me, I could give the funds to her so she could have a fresh start on life here."

She reached for her glass and to take another drink, but the ice just clinked in the glass. She set it down and smoothed her hair back from her face.

"I appreciate the gesture, but I don't want your money, Siril. I might not have much, but I've earned everything I have. If we were married, it would still bother me a little to spend your money, but it would be different from you just giving me over two hundred thousand dollars because you can."

"I understand. Then I'll just have to convince you to be my mate before I leave tomorrow. The shuttle leaves at nine o'clock. You have until then to decide. After that, I'll be returning to my world, and I'm not certain when I'll have time to come back for another visit. But know that if you do decide to remain here, I *will* come back and see you. Even if it takes months or a year."

She looked stricken by his words. "You can't return before that?"

"It's not likely. I'll be sent on other missions and have more training sessions with our warriors. I stay pretty busy, but I was allowed time off since I've never taken a vacation. I'm sure I could take another one after a while, but if I make it a habit of coming here every few months, my council might become frustrated with me."

"You said you work a lot on your world. What would I do while you're off saving the planet?" she asked. "I'm used to working all the time, and I don't think I'd do well at having nothing to do."

"There are plenty of other human females on my world you could interact with. I admit that most are younger than you. It isn't typical for someone your daughter's age to get approved for the program -- most are in their early twenties. But those who entered the program when it first started are in their thirties now. You could make new friends, if you'd like. There are activities, and I've heard that more are coming soon. We have a library. If you have one of those smart phone things, there's a way to charge them on my planet and you could still access your movies and music."

Jennifer bit her lip. "I do have a smart phone, but it doesn't have anything downloaded to it. I never had the funds for games and stuff. I always let Lila get the music and movies she wanted, when I could afford something extra."

"Then we would load your phone tonight so you'd have plenty to do on my world. There's a store on Zelthrane-3 that sells solar chargers that will work with your phone, or if you have a tablet or… what's it called? An e-reader? It will charge those as well."

"I've always wanted something that would allow me to read e-books, but I could never afford one. I suppose if I was going to live my life on another planet, it would be nice to have hundreds of books at my fingertips."

Siril took a sip of his drink and set it down. Before he could say anything, the waitress arrived with their meals. The food looked and smelled incredible and he couldn't wait to try it, but even more, he couldn't wait to see Jennifer's face when she took her first bite. He loved getting to experience new things with her, and hoped she'd agree to go home with him. Showing her his world would be amazing, as she stared at everything in wide-eyed wonder.

When they were alone again, he watched her for a few minutes and then picked up the conversation where it had left off.

"If you go home with me, become my mate, I will leave instructions with the Terran Station to purchase an e-reader for you and load it with hundreds if not thousands of books. You just leave a list of some you like, and I will have them find more like them."

"And how would I get the e-reader if we've already left this planet?" she asked.

"It would arrive on one of the shuttles flying from here to my world. It might take a week or so before it would arrive, but I promise you would get one. You could use my card they gave me for purchasing things to load movies and music to your phone before we left. As many movies and songs as you'd like. You've seen my balance and I've barely touched it. We could even go to the Terran Station for a more current printout if it would make you feel better."

She shook her head. "If you've not purchased a house or a car, I doubt you've made much of a dent in your balance. I'm honestly not sure how to download stuff to my phone though. Maybe through the provider's store."

"There are Terrans at the hotel where I stay who might know how to use it. We could ask them to show us how. Or someone who works at the station might know. They have someone over in communications who I'm certain would be familiar with how Earth phones work."

Jennifer bit her lip. "I can't believe I'm seriously thinking about moving to another planet. It just seems too… incredible."

"Anything I can do to make that a definite yes? I want you with me, Jennifer. I want you as my mate, more than I've ever wanted anything. And it's not just because I'm lonely. I truly enjoy spending time with you."

She smiled a little and leaned closer. "You could always take me back to your hotel room before the zoo opens and prove that you can make me scream your name."

Siril chuckled. "I believe I already did that, but I'm open to trying again. And again. As many times as you'd like."

"Then I guess we'd better finish breakfast."

He ate another bite and watched her with amusement, as she shoveled in bites of food faster than before. It was good to see that she'd enjoyed their time together last night as much as he had, and while he knew there was more to a relationship than just sex, it couldn't be denied they had more than just a few sparks between them. When the meal was finished and he'd paid for it, they went back out to the limo and he gave the driver instructions to go to the hotel.

He couldn't wait to get Jennifer alone in his suite, and

preferably without clothes.

# Chapter Six

Jennifer stared in awe at everything around her. The hotel was grander than anywhere she'd lived before. The nearly all glass building had been one she'd passed many times, but this was her first time inside. She felt out of place, but gripped Siril's hand tight and let him lead her through the lobby. They rode the elevator up to his floor and he let her into his suite. The furnishings were white and the floors were made of wood and pale carpet. She'd be worried she'd stain something if she were here any length of time.

The door clicked shut behind them and Siril placed his hands on her waist, then slid around to her stomach and pulled her tight against his body. His lips found the sensitive skin along her neck and a shiver raked over her. She wanted him just as much as she had last night. Turning in his embrace, her lips met his, her tongue slipping inside. He tasted of syrup and berries from his breakfast. The kiss was deep and left her knees shaking, as her hands gripped him tight to stay upright.

He lifted her shirt and they broke apart long enough for the garment to be removed and dropped onto the floor. She pulled off her boots and shimmied out of her jeans. Standing in front of him in her plain bra and panties, she felt a blush rise to her cheeks. He'd seen her naked before, but in the bright light of day, she felt more exposed than before. Her underthings weren't sexy, but practical, and she hoped he wasn't disappointed.

Siril's gaze devoured her, caressing her breasts and lingering on her hips. The passion blazing in the depths of his eyes was enough to have her reaching for him. She needed him, wanted him. If he didn't take her soon, she knew she'd end up begging. He removed his clothes slowly, his gaze trained on her the entire time. When he was bare, he stood uncertainly for a moment. It was the first time she'd seen him completely naked, but the metal leg didn't bother her, if he was waiting for a reaction. When she merely smiled and held out a hand, he reached for her, removing the last of her clothes.

Siril lifted her and pressed her back against the wall, her legs going around his waist. She felt his cock brush against her and she moaned, arching against him. Jennifer wanted him, more than her next breath. The entire ride in the limo, his thigh had brushed against hers, driving her a little crazier with every mile that passed. She'd silently begged for his kiss, but he'd merely smiled at her, as if knowing what she wanted and refusing to give it to her. Siril reached between their bodies and teased her slit with the head of his cock before slowly pressing inside of her. He stretched her wide, filling her better than anyone else ever could. He felt perfect as he slid inside of her.

"So good," she murmured, her hands going to his hair. She clutched handfuls of it.

"I don't know that I can go slow," he said. "I want you too desperately."

"Then take me. As hard and fast as you want."

With a groan, he buried his face against her neck and took her with such force, her body bumped against the wall with every thrust. She would doubtless have a few bruises later, but it would be so worth it. The feel of him withdrawing nearly all the way then surging inside of her once more, had her crying out in pleasure. The room started spinning and she realized she'd forgotten to breathe. Jennifer sucked in a breath and then called out Siril's name again, her eyes sliding shut as she came, harder than ever before. Shockwaves of pleasure rocketed through her as colors burst behind her closed eyelids.

"Jennifer!" He pounded into her a few more times, his release slicking the inside of her.

Siril shook as he held her. He lifted her away from the wall and carried her into the bedroom, easing her down on the bed, withdrawing from her body in the process. He crawled in beside her and she curled against his body. Being with him felt so incredibly right, so perfect. It was almost as if they were meant to be together. It only took her a moment to realize that she'd come to a decision about her future. It lay with Siril. If he still wanted to take her to his planet as his mate, she would go willingly.

"I've been so caught up in you, I never asked you about protection. I don't know how late in life human females can have babies," Siril said.

"When I had Lila, I had my tubes tied. Of course, I didn't date a lot after that and it's been a really long time since I had sex, so it was probably pointless. But since they're tied, I can't have kids. Is that a deal breaker for being your mate? I know the big sell of the bride program is that the women agree to have children with your people."

"I had already decided that if I were lucky enough to find a mate, I wouldn't care if we had children. Just having you will be enough for me."

"I feel like I'm cheating you. I mean, I had Lila, and while things didn't turn out as I'd hoped, I did have eighteen years with her. We've had our fights, but I'd always thought she was a really great kid. I'd felt blessed to have her, until this. Right now, I'm so mad and hurt that I want to spank her ass and send her to bed without her supper. I know she's supposed to be an adult now, but she's still my baby. I miss that little girl who used to wake me up at six on Saturdays to watch morning cartoons."

Siril pressed a kiss to the top of her head. "If you go with me --"

"When," she said. "If you really want me for your mate, I've already decided I'm going with you tomorrow. I just need to go pack my things and leave my keys with the rental office."

He kissed her hard and fast, a smile spreading across his face. "I promise you won't regret it. And if you'd like, we can find Lila when we first get there. Or if you need more time, I'll show your new home to you first. We should get dressed and go to the Terran Station."

"I thought the shuttle didn't leave until tomorrow?"

"It doesn't, but I wish to petition the council to approve our mating before we leave Earth. There's no reason for them to say no. You'll need to see the doctor at the clinic first, just so I can assure them you're in good health. I'll explain that I don't care if we ever have children, as long as I have you."

He seemed so excited that Jennifer found herself smiling in return. They climbed out of bed, cleaned themselves up a little, and got dressed. Siril held her hand tight as he led her down to the lobby and out to one of the waiting limos. After giving the driver instructions, he slid in behind her and they pulled away from the curb a moment later. She was a little nervous about speaking to his council. He seemed so certain they would approve the mating, but what if they didn't? Just because he claimed to be okay with not having children didn't mean his council would feel the same way.

At the station, he practically ran for the clinic, making her laugh and try to keep up with him. The waiting room was empty and he rang a bell on the desk. A Terran wearing a white lab coat stepped out to greet them. He smiled warmly when he saw Siril.

"Since you're here with a human, does this mean you're finally taking a mate?" the doctor asked.

"Xonos, this is Jennifer, and yes, I'd like to claim her as my mate. I thought, perhaps, you could do an exam so the council wouldn't have cause to say no." Siril tugged her forward. "I'm anxious to speak with them, as the shuttle leaves in the morning."

Xonos nodded. "Follow me."

He led them down a hallway and into what looked like a mash-up of a human and alien exam room. There were gadgets she had never seen before, but the padded table was the same as every exam room she'd been in. Jennifer stood awkwardly, not knowing if she was supposed to strip and put on a gown. Xonos patted the padded table and she climbed on top, sitting nervously. What exactly would happen during an alien exam?

Xonos checked her vitals, then scanned her with some weird device, from head to toe, coming back to rest over her abdomen. Her stomach clenched as she realized he must be able to tell that her tubes were tied and she'd be unable to have children. He smiled faintly and tipped his head toward a chair in the corner.

"Why don't you sit over there a moment so I can do a more in-depth scan?" he asked.

Jennifer got off the table and walked over to the reclining chair. She eased down into it and held still as a much larger device scanned her once more, paying special attention to her abdomen. Siril had said it wouldn't matter that she couldn't have children, but the longer the doctor took to examine her, the more anxious she became. He drew several vials of blood and examined them before smiling broadly when he faced them once more.

"Well, it seems congratulations are in order, Siril. You work fast."

"Congratulations?" Jennifer asked, her brow furrowed. "Does that mean we can be mates?"

Xonos chuckled. "I'd like to see the council separate this one from his first child."

Jennifer felt the blood drain from her face and the room spun. Child? There had to be some mistake. She couldn't have children anymore. She glanced at Siril, who looked every bit as shocked as she was.

"Are you certain?" Siril asked. "A baby?"

Xonos nodded. "I don't know why you seem so surprised. I'm assuming the two of you have had sex."

"Twice," Jennifer said, her voice rasping as her throat suddenly felt as dry as a desert.

"Well, once is usually all it takes," Xonos said. "I don't understand why the two of you are so surprised."

"I had my tubes tied eighteen years ago," Jennifer said. "I'm not supposed to be able to get pregnant anymore. It's supposed to be impossible."

Xonos's eyebrows rose and he pulled out the device again, doing another scan. "It seems they must have grown back. I've heard of the procedure you had done, and it's not one hundred percent foolproof. If you'd wanted to guarantee you'd have no more children, you would have needed a hysterectomy. Or your mate would have needed to get snipped."

Her gaze met Siril's and she could tell he was equal parts surprised and happy. Right now, her heart felt like it was racing out of control and she couldn't seem to get quite enough oxygen. She'd thought she was finished raising children, but a baby? Could she go through that all over again, knowing she might lose another child when they became of age? If she was such a horrible mother to Lila, who was to say the second baby would be any different?

Siril came toward her and knelt at her feet, taking her hands in his. "I can tell you're shocked, and it's understandable. Would having a baby with me be so bad?"

"What if I'm not any good as a mother? My daughter obviously hates me. What if this baby grows up to hate me too?" She blinked at him, fighting back the tears that welled in her eyes. She didn't think she could go through the heartache again of knowing her child didn't want anything to do with her.

"This baby will be different, Jennifer. He or she will have both of us from the beginning to the end. They will have everything they need, and at least some of the things they want. You'll never have to work tirelessly from morning to night to pay the bills and feed the baby. I have more than enough money to take care of the three of us. Four of us, if Lila doesn't find a match and wants to move in with us."

Jennifer shook her head. "I love my daughter, but after what she's done, she can try to stand on her own two feet for a while. Maybe if she sees how hard it is to take care of herself, she'll appreciate all that I've done for her over the years. I thought I hadn't given her enough, but maybe I gave her too much."

"If you don't want this baby, if it's asking too much of you, it's early enough we could have the pregnancy terminated," Siril said.

She could tell it pained him to utter the words and she knew she could never take his child away from him. Jennifer shook her head and squeezed his hand. As long as he was by her side, she'd get through it. And as he said, this time she didn't have to work from sun up to sun down, trying to keep a roof over her head. If their technology was so advanced they could detect a pregnancy when it had just happened, then she would imagine they would be prepared for anything. While there were plenty of women who had babies at thirty-eight, most had probably taken better care of themselves than Jennifer had. But she would put herself in Siril's capable hands, and those of whatever doctors they had on his world.

"I want to keep the baby," she said softly. "Just... promise me you won't take any dangerous missions that will keep you away for weeks or months at a time. My last pregnancy wasn't all that easy and I'm even older now. I don't want to be left alone with no one to help if something should happen."

"You seem perfectly healthy," Xonos said. "But if you're genuinely concerned, I'm sure they can give your system a boost with some vitamins when you reach Zelthrane-3. I'll file my report immediately so the council will have access to the files. Congratulations again to both of you, on the baby and the mating."

Siril helped her out of the chair and led her out of the clinic. She wandered behind him, barely seeing where they were going as she still processed the news that she was going to have another baby. They entered what looked like a conference room but had a large screen on one wall. Siril walked over to it and punched in a series of buttons and a few moments later, an alien-looking conference room appeared on the screen with several of his people around a large table. All were dressed in black leather except for one who wore white from head to toe.

"Chief Councilor Borgoz and council members. I would like to request that a mating be approved," Siril said, getting right to the point. "Xonos said he would file his medical report immediately so you should have access to it soon."

The man in white smiled broadly. "We send you to Earth for a vacation and you return with a mate? Maybe we should have sent you years ago."

"I was very fortunate to be in the right place at the right time," Siril said. "And there's something more. Jennifer is pregnant with my child."

All of the council members broke into grins at the news and congratulated them. Jennifer felt her cheeks warm and gave them a shy smile back. From what she understood, these men were the ruling members of his society. Kind of like speaking to the president of the United States. It awed her that he spoke so easily to them. She found them a little intimidating, even on the screen, and hoped she wouldn't embarrass Siril if she ever met them in person.

"What of her other daughter?" Borgoz asked.

"She will meet with Lila when she's ready, if her daughter is still on our world. Do you know if she's found a mate?" Siril asked.

"Lila Montgomery, correct?" Borgoz asked.

"Yes," Jennifer said, speaking up for the first time.

"Miss Montgomery, your daughter hasn't found a mate as of yet. She's been here a few weeks now, and if she doesn't find one soon, we'll return her to Earth. She'll get to keep the money she was paid. Unless of course, you wish for her to live with Siril and you?"

"She's welcome in my home, if that's what Jennifer wishes," Siril said.

"No," Jennifer said. The word being harder to say than she'd thought. "I would like to see her before you send her back here, but if my daughter is old enough to enter a bride program on another planet and not say a word to me, then she's old enough to stand on her own two feet. I don't know how much you gave her, but hopefully it will be enough for her to get by while she finds a job and a place to live."

Borgoz didn't seem surprised by her response. "And will she have lodgings when she arrives there?"

"No, I'm turning in the keys to my rental tomorrow. Anything Lila left behind will be donated to charity. All she'll have is whatever she took with her or purchased while she was there. It may seem harsh, but she's not the young woman I thought her to be. Just… can someone watch out for her? Make sure she doesn't fall too far?" Jennifer asked. "She's my baby, and I love her, but she's shown me that she doesn't appreciate the things I've done for her or the life I gave her. I'm obviously not enough for her."

"Understood," Borgoz said softly. "We'll let her remain here one more week. It will give you time to meet with her, and perhaps she'll find a mate. I must admit, there are rumblings amongst those who have shown an interest in her that she's spoiled and seems a little selfish. I know that isn't easy to hear."

No, it really wasn't. She'd thought she'd raised Lila better than that. Yes, she'd given her as much as she could, but apparently it had never been enough. Jennifer had sacrificed for her daughter, and now it felt like Lila was just throwing it all away. She'd thought she'd raised a kind, loving daughter, and didn't recognize the woman Lila had become. Where had she gone so wrong?

Tears misted her eyes and her heart broke at the thought of losing her daughter. But in reality, wasn't she already gone? She'd cut Jennifer out of her life, with no expectation of ever seeing her again. Whoever Lila was now, it wasn't the sweet girl who'd begged for Fruit Loops in the morning or left fingerprints on the glass of all the windows. She wasn't the little girl who had begged relentlessly for a puppy, and had been content enough when Santa had brought her a stuffed one. What had happened to that sweet little girl?

"I'm sorry, Miss Montgomery," Borgoz said. "You are most welcome on our world. If Siril has chosen you as his mate, there must be something special about you. Your daughter, however, will not be welcome here much longer. Not unless we see some changes."

Jennifer nodded, understanding where they were coming from. And she couldn't blame them. As much as it pained her, it was time to let her little girl go. When she could speak with Lila, she'd let her know that she'd always be there for her emotionally, but that she wouldn't support her financially any longer. She leaned against Siril's side, drawing strength from him. She knew he would support her, whatever she decided. She'd never had that before. It had always just been her, and then her and Lila. Having a man around would be a big change, but she looked forward to her life with Siril.

He wasn't just *any* man after all. He was the sexiest, most badass alien in the galaxy.

She grinned a little as Siril talked a bit longer with the council. Her life was changing, and in ways she'd never imagined, but no matter what was thrown her way next, she knew she'd conquer it, just like she did everything else. One step at a time.

# Chapter Seven

Siril growled as he led Jennifer through the streets of Terran Prime. Some gawked in open curiosity, but more than one male showed her too much interest. The council had approved their mating and they were officially... what was that human term? Husband and wife? Yes, Jennifer was his wife now. He rather liked the sound of that. His arm curved around her waist as he led her through the city toward their home. He'd spent last night helping her pack her belongings. Instead of turning in her rental keys this morning, they'd left them at the Terran Station so the remainder of the belongings could be donated. Lovik assured him it would be taken care of and the keys returned to the landlord.

Jennifer stared at her surroundings in wide-eyed fascination. He wished he could see his world through her eyes. She hadn't said much since they'd disembarked the shuttle. He hoped she liked her new home. As they walked down the main thoroughfare, he pointed out some of his favorite shops and restaurants. She paused in front of the pet store, smiling at the fluffy and feathery companions inside. She hadn't had any pets in her home, and he wondered if she'd ever had one.

"What do you think so far?" he asked as they pushed through another throng of people.

"It's amazing! I can't wait to explore more."

He lightly touched her ear. "How's the implant?"

Her fingers brushed over the area. "It's fine. I'm glad you convinced me to have it done this morning before we left. Otherwise I might have missed out on a lot going on around me. And the thing in my wrist will me buy stuff?"

"Yes. It also unlocks our home. Now that we're mated, you'll have access to my funds. If you make friends and want to treat them to lunch, you just swipe your wrist across the payment screen and it will debit the funds from our account."

She grimaced. "I don't like the idea of spending your money. You worked hard for it."

"Money means nothing without my sweet mate by my side," he said with a grin.

Jennifer smiled up at him, pausing long enough to kiss him in front of everyone. He would imagine it wouldn't be long before the entire city knew he'd taken a mate. He supposed in a way he was like her Earth celebrities. Except instead of dancing, singing, or playing a part, he defended his people. Everyone knew his name, even those he'd never personally met.

"You followed me?" a voice screeched from ahead.

Siril looked around and saw a younger replica of his mate heading their way. It seemed Lila knew her mother was on Zelthrane-3. He'd hoped they would have more time before confronting her. The young girl didn't look happy to see her mother, but Jennifer stiffened her spine and waited for her daughter to come toward her.

"How did you even know I was here?" Lila demanded. "Who told?"

"No one told me," Jennifer said. "I found the empty envelope in your room from your acceptance letter and I went to the Terran Station."

"You weren't on my list." Lila's eyes narrowed. "Can't you let me have anything? All you've done my entire life is tell me I can't have this or that. Did you come here to stop me from getting married?"

Siril snorted. "From what I've heard, I don't think that would be hard to do."

She flinched when she looked up at him. "Why are you with my mother? Are you her guide? Well, you can take her right back to the shuttle. They shouldn't have even allowed her here."

Siril tried to remind himself that this was his daughter by mating, even if he did want to turn her over his knee and give her a good spanking. Someone should have tamed her smart mouth a long time ago. He couldn't believe how disrespectful she was to her mother, and in front of everyone. His arm tightened around Jennifer's waist, letting her know she wasn't alone and had his support. He would follow her lead when it came to her daughter, even if he did want to toss Lila off the planet.

"Your mother is my mate," Siril said.

Lila's eyes widened and she took a step back. "You've *moved* here? I can't even leave an entire world behind without you following me and ruining my life?"

"Enough!" Siril said with a harsh tone. "Your mother hasn't done anything wrong. We met when she came to the Terran Station to look for you. She was devastated, not knowing where you were or what had happened to you. It was selfish of you to do that to her, after all that she's sacrificed for you. I don't care that she's your mother or that you're an adult, do not ever speak to her that way again or I'll have you removed from this planet."

"You're not a council member," Lila sneered. "You can't have me removed."

A throat cleared nearby and Siril realized they had an audience.

"Actually, that's Siril. He can pretty much do whatever he pleases, and the council will go along with him. If I were you, I wouldn't anger him, or upset his mate," Kelvyk said. "And if he doesn't have you removed, my uncle is the Chief Councilor. I will be more than happy to speak to him about your behavior."

Ryoku stood at Kel's side as always, folding his arms across his black and white chest, staring Lila down. The young girl flinched and inched away a little. Siril was glad the warrior duo scared her. She needed to be scared. For some reason she didn't think she'd get into trouble for the way she was treating her mother, but Siril wasn't about to let Lila destroy her mother verbally or otherwise in front of everyone. He had too much respect for his mate to allow that.

"Why, Lila?" Jennifer asked. "I worked so damn hard to give you a place to live, clothes, shoes, all those movies you loved so much. Why do you hate me so much?"

"All of my friends were buying the latest trends and I was shopping at the thrift store. We never had money for me to see movies at the theater with everyone else, or meet them for lunch somewhere. They pitied me, made fun of me, and it's all your fault. You should have tried harder to find my father. I bet he wouldn't have let us live in poverty." Anger rolled off Lila in waves. "Do you know how embarrassing it is to tell people my mother works at the dollar store? And try explaining to your class why you're the only student who never has a birthday party? And I'm supposed to thank you for that?"

Siril took a step forward, but Jennifer reached out and placed a hand on his arm. He could see the pain in her eyes and knew that her daughter's words were tearing her apart. He could almost see her drawing armor around herself as she faced off against her daughter. The crowd was still watching them, waiting to see what would happen. He knew that how Jennifer handled this situation would determine how accepting they would be of her. His people could be very welcoming, but he didn't doubt there were expectations of the mate he chose.

Jennifer stepped away from him a little. "I'm sorry you feel I ruined your life. I was terrified when I found out I was pregnant with you. I was twenty and didn't have a clue how to take care of myself much less a baby. I didn't have support from anyone and couldn't find your father because I never learned his name. He was a one-night stand gone wrong, but once the fear eased, I realized he'd given me an incredible gift. You. I might not have had a glamorous job, but I worked damn hard to give you what I could. Your clothes might not have been new, but they were in good shape and good quality. I tried to give you the things you wanted, even if it meant I did without. Do you know how many days I only ate the meals I fixed at home and went without breakfast, lunch, or both, just so I'd have extra money for whatever toy or movie you wanted?"

Lila's jaw set and she opened her mouth, but Jennifer raised a hand to silence her.

"I worked at a thankless job, doing work I hated, just to have a steady paycheck. So I could take care of you. When I realized the men I dated didn't want anything to do with you, I stopped going out. I centered my entire world around you, this perfect little girl who had been gifted to me. It pains me to realize how selfish and spoiled you are, how entitled you are. I didn't raise you to act like this."

"Yeah, Mom. You really deserve mother of the year," Lila sneered.

Jennifer shook her head sadly. "I'm sorry you were so disappointed in the way we had to live. I'm sorry I wasn't enough for you, because you were always enough for me. I can't watch out for you anymore. You've clearly made your choice and have decided to face the world alone, and you will be alone. Anyone who hears the hatred and venom spewing from your mouth would never want you for a mate. I want you gone. You were given money for coming here. I suggest you use it to build a life for yourself. Get a job, because you're going to need one. The house, your belongings, everything left on Earth is gone now. You'll be completely on your own, just the way you wanted."

Lila looked uncertain as she stared at her mother. "What do you mean?"

"I mean that my life is here now. Yours isn't. In the weeks you've been here, no one has claimed you, and no one will after this. Your time here is done. I'm requesting that you be placed on the next shuttle back to Earth. It doesn't even have to be in Kentucky. Pick a place to start over. I'm sure they'll take you to any Terran Station on Earth."

"You can't do that."

"She can," Siril said. "And I support her decision."

"As do I," Kelvyk said.

A murmur went through the crowd and Lila must have realized everyone was against her. Her face paled and he could almost see the thoughts racing through her mind. But it was too late to take back the hurtful things she'd said, too late to turn back the clock and erase her behavior from the past few weeks. What was that Earth saying? She'd made her bed and now she had to lie in it. He'd never really understood it until now.

"I love you, Lila. I always will. Regardless of how you're treating me, you will always be my little girl." Jennifer placed a hand on her stomach. "Even when this baby arrives, they won't replace you in my affection. But I can't be around you like this. No one should have to."

"You're pregnant?" Lila sputtered.

"I lived my life for you for eighteen years," Jennifer said. "Now I'm going to live my life for me. I'm starting a new life here, with Siril. We're starting a new family, and we'd have welcomed you into our home, but I won't have someone so hateful under my roof. I hope one day you learn compassion and the value of hard work. Until that day comes, I worry about the life you'll lead. It will be a lonely path, and I wouldn't wish that on anyone."

"You're really sending me away?" Lila asked softly.

"Yes. You wanted to be an adult, start a new life. You have my blessing. It just won't be here. You can contact me anytime at one of the Terran Stations. I'll always answer when you call. But until you learn a few hard lessons, I can't... I..."

He saw Jennifer struggling and pulled her against his side.

"Your mother loves you," Siril told her. "But you threw her love away when you acted rashly. Now you have to pay the consequences. When you've grown up a little more, when you've learned those lessons she's mentioned, then perhaps we'll welcome you into our home for a visit. Maybe one day you can try living here again."

"I only received three thousand dollars for coming here and I spent half of it on new things before my trip," Lila said. "How am I supposed to survive on fifteen hundred dollars? It could take months to get a job. And where will I live?"

Siril kissed the top of his mate's head, knowing she would waver if he didn't step in. She had a tender heart, especially where her child was concerned. Siril approached his new daughter by mating and hoped he wasn't about to make a mistake. He didn't understand Earth money, but if the council had given her three thousand Earth dollars, he didn't see why he couldn't offer the same, if it gave her a little security. He knew it would keep Jennifer from worrying about her quite so much.

"This is a one-time offer. I will match the three thousand the council gave you in order for you to have a fresh start. The council will arrange for you to take a shuttle to a destination of your choosing. And will provide you with a hotel suite for one month while you find a job and start making arrangements for your new life. Once the money is gone and the time has run out, you'd better be able to stand on your own, or you will find yourself without money or lodgings. I'm only offering this as my mate cares for you a great deal and I don't want her to worry about you." Siril stared down at her. "Do I make myself clear?"

"Three thousand really isn't all that much," Lila said.

Jennifer snorted. "It's more than I brought home in two months. If you can't live off that, especially if you don't have to pay rent the first month, then there's no hope for you. I suggest you learn to live within your means."

"I will never forgive you for this," Lila said.

"Then I'll have to live with the knowledge that my daughter hates me," Jennifer said. "But I think you've been coddled too much. I'm granting your wish, Lila. You get to live a life without me."

Lila turned on her heel and stormed off.

The crowd continued to watch, and one by one, they came forward. The females offered his mate hugs and assured her that everything would work out. The males seemed impressed with her strength and resolve, and Siril couldn't be prouder of her. He'd worried that she'd cave and give Lila whatever she wanted, but she was a good mother, not giving her daughter what she wanted, but what she needed.

He'd find out where Lila was delivered once she left their world, and he would ask someone to keep an eye on her. The least he could do was give his mate peace of mind. And if Lila truly did flounder, if she failed miserably, then perhaps they could find a way to help her. Maybe not through money, but he'd think of something. There were life lessons she needed to learn, but it didn't mean she had to do it alone. Once her anger had cooled, once she realized just how hard it would be to live on her own, perhaps then she would be ready to accept a little help, and be gracious about it.

"Come, my mate. It's time to show you your new home," Siril said. "And I think you could use a little time to rest."

Jennifer nodded, seeming as if life had just drained from her. He worried that the altercation with Lila would weigh heavy on her and he was determined to keep her occupied so she wouldn't have time to fret. He'd introduce her to his friends, help her make some of her own, and show her the pleasures of living on his world, a place of no crime and no hatred. They were a peaceful people and he knew that once she settled in, she would love living here.

The crowd parted and let them pass. Jennifer walked almost in a daze the rest of the way to the house, but she perked up a little when she saw it, a smile playing around her lips.

"When you said you were taking me home, you neglected to say you slept in a palace. This place is huge." Jennifer nudged him. "Did you forget to tell me you're royalty or something?"

Siril laughed. "No, I'm not royalty, but I've been treated very well by my council and my people. If there's anything you wish to change, do it. I want this to feel like yours and not just mine. It's always just been a place for me to sleep when I'm on my world, but now I want it to feel like a home."

Jennifer kissed his cheek. "Then we'll make it into a home. I guess I don't have to ask if you have room for a nursery."

"We have five bedrooms."

She gave him a mock glare. "I am *not* having three more children."

The smile slipped from his face. "I don't care if this baby is the only one we have. I will leave that decision to you. If the pregnancy or delivery are hard on you, I will offer to get sterilized."

Jennifer kissed him on the mouth, hard and fast. "Better be careful, Siril. You'll make me fall in love with you. Then you'll never be rid of me."

His heart kicked in his chest. He couldn't think of anything he'd love more. Having Jennifer's love would complete him. Yes, he was excited about becoming a father, but none of it mattered. Not if he didn't have Jennifer. He was quickly coming to realize that she meant more to him than anything else in his life. More than his crew, his ship… more than his very life. He'd always been willing to die for his people, to keep them safe, but it was nothing compared to how he felt about Jennifer.

"I've already fallen for you," he said softly. "You don't have to say it back. I don't want you to feel pressured. But my life… it's not an easy one. I could get called away on a mission tomorrow and not come back, and I don't want to leave this world without you knowing that you're loved."

She kissed him again, softer this time. "I'll always want you to come back to me."

"Even if I lost my other leg?" he said with a smile.

"You lose your other leg and both arms, and I'd still want you to return to me. You make me happier than I've ever been before." Her hand caressed his cheek. "Now, show me my new home."

Siril escorted her inside and took her room by room, showing her how to work everything, including the Vid-comm. If he should get called away, the last thing he wanted was for his mate to be cut off from communicating with the council. They would be her only guarantee of keeping track of him. There was a Vid-comm on board his ship, but if he were in the middle of a battle, he wouldn't be able to answer her call, and he wouldn't want her to worry.

It was almost as if his council could read his thoughts. The Vid-comm lit up with a call from Borgoz.

"Please tell me you're only calling to check on my mate," Siril said.

"No. I'm afraid not. We've just received word a Destrentes ship was spotted a few clicks away and coming in fast. I need you to get to your ship and chase them into the next galaxy."

Siril knew from experience there would be no chasing. The Destrentes were a fighting race and if he went after them, there would be a battle. One he might not come home from, and the thought pained him. He'd just found his mate, he wasn't ready to say goodbye to her just yet. He'd never even had the opportunity to make love with her in his own bed.

"I'm on my way," Siril said.

The call ended and he reached for Jennifer, pulling her into his arms. "I would stay if I could, but if the Destrentes reach Zelthrane-3, there could be a lot of casualties. I will do anything to protect you and our child. If you leave the house, the Chief Councilor lives in the big house on the hill. Go there. His mate will welcome you."

Jennifer blinked against the moisture gathering in her eyes and he smoothed a thumb across her cheek.

"I'll return as soon as I can." Siril kissed her tenderly, holding her a little longer than he should have, before retrieving his weapons and racing toward his ship. He knew his crew would have already been contacted and would be waiting for him. Whether he was ready or not, they had a job to do.

# Chapter Eight

Jennifer explored her new home for what felt like hours, but her thoughts kept turning to Siril. She hadn't thought she'd spend her first night on this world alone, or that she'd be worrying about never seeing her mate again. She might have raised one fatherless baby, but she hoped to God she didn't have to do it again. At least before, she'd been able to tell herself they were better off without Lila's dad. But with Siril, she knew that wasn't the case. He would be a wonderful father, and was already an attentive mate. She would miss him horribly if something happened to him.

She gazed out the back window and saw the massive home on the hill. He'd said it belonged to the Chief Councilor. The man intimidated her a bit, but Siril had mentioned a mate. Having another woman to confide in might be nice right about now, and she could certainly use a friend. Jennifer couldn't remember the last time she'd had a true friend and she hoped she'd find one on this new world. Being a single mom had been a hard and lonely life, not that she'd ever regretted it.

Coming to a decision, she left her new home and made the long walk up the hill toward the larger house. If she'd thought Siril's was big, this one dwarfed it. She wondered how large the Chief Councilor's family was to have such a massive home. She was a little winded by the time she reached their front door and she searched for a bell. After pressing it twice, she waited patiently for someone to answer.

A woman close to her height answered, a hesitant smile on her face.

"May I help you?" she asked, her voice a soft sing-song.

Jennifer had heard that tone before and knew the woman was deaf. It had been a long time since she'd had to sign anything, having learned in elementary school when the new girl couldn't talk to anyone. She slowly signed a message to introduce herself.

"I'm Charlotte," the woman said. "And you don't have to sign. I can hear a little and I read lips."

"Siril said I could come here while he's gone. I didn't know where else to go."

Charlotte stepped back and motioned for her to enter. "Have you eaten anything today? I think if my mate had been called off to battle right after I arrived, I'd have been too nervous to eat."

"No, I haven't eaten. Not since we left Earth. It seems like forever ago."

"We were just sitting down to dinner. My daughter, Arabella, is completely deaf. You'll need to sign for her to understand you."

"Are you sure I'm not imposing?" Jennifer asked.

"I'm positive. Ever since I heard Siril was taking a mate, I've been anxious to meet you. Our mates are close friends. I'm sure we'll see a lot of each other."

Charlotte led the way through her home to a dining room. The Chief Councilor sat at the head of the table, a little girl next to him. Charlotte took a seat on his other side and Jennifer awkwardly followed her. She felt a little like she'd entered a king's domain and she didn't know the proper etiquette. Borgoz smiled at her warmly and the little girl hardly cast her a glance.

"I know this isn't how you imagined your first night here," Borgoz said. "I'm sorry I had to call Siril away, but he's our best. With some luck, he'll return by morning."

"Is it okay that I'm here? He said I could come, but..."

Borgoz waved away her concern. "You're always welcome here. I'm hoping you and Charlotte will become fast friends. There's a small handful of women she likes to keep close, and I'm sure you'll meet them soon enough. You're not alone, Jennifer."

"Thank you," she said softly and took the seat next to Charlotte.

A plate was brought out along with what looked like juice. She ate her meal quietly, listening to Charlotte and Borgoz speak. The little girl cast her curious glances, but mostly kept to herself. When the meal was over, Charlotte stood and held out a hand. Jennifer took it hesitantly and let the other woman lead her away.

"Borgoz will watch Arabella," Charlotte said. "Is there anything you need?"

"No, I… just didn't want to be alone."

"You can stay as long as you'd like, but you might want to return home in a few hours in case your mate returns. I'm sure he'll be anxious to see you, especially if he faced a hard battle. But you're welcome here as long as you wish to stay. You could even stay the night if you wanted."

"No, I'll return home before bed."

Charlotte nodded. "Would you like to watch a movie on the Vid-comm? It might help the time pass a little quicker. I could show you how to set them up so you can watch them at home too."

"We have movies here?" Jennifer asked in surprise.

"They add more all the time. Do you have a preference?"

"Something lighthearted?"

Charlotte nodded and showed her how to program the movie selections, then they settled back to enjoy the show. Jennifer only half paid attention to what was on the screen, still concerned about Siril. She wondered how many nights like this one she would pass as his mate. Not that she would change anything about him. He was a warrior and was only doing his job. She just hadn't realized how much she'd worry.

"I heard about your daughter," Charlotte said. "I'm sorry."

"You just do the best you can as a parent, but I guess sometimes it isn't enough. Hopefully, one day she'll appreciate the life I was able to give her. It breaks my heart that she hates me so much when she's been my entire world, but I can't live my life for her anymore. I'm thirty-eight and it's time I did something for myself."

"I think you'll be good for Siril. He's wanted a mate for a long time, but seems to think his looks make him unworthy," Charlotte said. "I'm glad he found you."

"Does he get called away like this often?"

"Often enough, but now that he's mated, I'm sure Borgoz will try to send others when he can. For so long, Siril has taken every mission that came his way, but it wouldn't surprise me if he started asking for more time off. Now that he has a mate, things will be different."

Jennifer placed a hand on her belly. "And a baby. I still can't believe I'm pregnant. I'd thought those days were behind me."

A wistful expression passed over Charlotte's face. "I love Arabella, but I wish we could have had more children. When I was pregnant, she had siblings, but they didn't make it. The doctor said it would be too dangerous for me to have more children, so she's an only child."

"I'm sure the two of you spoil her."

Charlotte nodded. "We do. She's a pampered princess."

"I wonder if this one will be another girl or if I'll have a boy this time?"

"It won't be long before you can find out." Charlotte smiled. "You'll have to think of names. I've noticed most of the mates around here choose Earth names for girls and Zelthranite names for boys. But maybe you'll buck tradition and reverse it."

"I got to name Lila. This is Siril's first child, and possibly his only child. Maybe I'll let him name the baby."

Charlotte giggled. "There's no telling what he'd name a baby, but it would be interesting to find out."

Thoughts of Lila sobered Jennifer. Her daughter... it was painful, knowing she might never see her again. If only Lila hadn't turned out so rotten. The sweet girl she'd been as a child still had to be in there somewhere, unless it was all a lie all along. It would have been so much fun for both of them to start a new life here. They could have talked and visited whenever they wanted, and Jennifer could have watched her grandchildren grow up. Now she'd likely never even know if she had any. At least, not Lila's children.

"She'll come around," Charlotte said, as if reading her mind. "Once she realizes how hard it is to live on her own, she'll grow up fast. It won't take long before she misses you."

"Do you think they'd ever let her come back here? After the way she's acted?"

"If she truly changes, I'm sure Borgoz could be persuaded to at least let her come for a visit. As a parent, he knows how hard it would be to be separated from his daughter, and he wouldn't wish that on anyone."

Jennifer nodded.

"Why don't we have a real girl's night?" Charlotte asked. "I have a manicure set and some new polish. We could do each other's nails while we watch TV and talk. I don't have popcorn, but I saw some potatoes in the pantry. I could ask the chef to make some French fries for us. The way he seasons them, they're so good."

"A girl's night?" Jennifer asked. She hadn't one of those in... well, probably eighteen years or more.

"It will be fun and it will keep your mind off Siril and your daughter."

"All right. And you can tell me more about what it's like living here. I lived in the same town my entire life, and now I'm suddenly on an alien planet. Siril pointed out some of the shops and restaurants when we first arrived, and I'd like to explore soon."

"If Siril isn't back tomorrow, we'll go to breakfast and enjoy a bit of shopping," Charlotte said. "I could introduce you to a few more mates if you'd like?"

"That would be really great."

"Jacie and Haven are younger, especially Haven, but they're really nice. And trust me, Jacie could use a break. She and Barimere have four children. All of them are six and have more energy than you could ever imagine. Haven's daughter is only a few months old, so I'm sure she'd like some time out of the house too."

Jennifer spent the next two hours talking with Charlotte, getting her nails painted, and making tentative plans for the next day. The time passed quickly, and she realized sooner or later, she'd have to go back to that empty house. Making her goodbyes, she went home and hoped she'd be able to sleep. Not knowing if Siril was okay was weighing heavy on her.

She busied herself, unpacking her things, and snooping through Siril's stuff. After taking a shower and putting on her pajamas, she crawled into bed and closed her eyes, but sleep wouldn't come. Was Siril missing her as much as she missed him? He'd shown her how to work the Vid-comm and had mentioned they had one on board his ship, but she didn't want to disturb him if he was planning a battle, or in the middle of a fight. The last thing she wanted to do was distract him and cause him injury or worse.

Her hand smoothed over the empty side of the bed before resting over her belly.

"Your daddy is off fighting right now, being brave and heroic. But he's going to come home to us soon. I bet he doesn't know that he can talk to you already. I know your ears aren't developed yet and you're just a little tiny pea-sized thing right now, but I'm going to talk to you every day."

She couldn't remember talking to Lila until closer to the end of her pregnancy, and then it was more so she wouldn't talk to herself. There were things she could do differently this time. With Siril's support, she could focus on her health more and in preparing for the baby. She wouldn't be so tired all the time, working ten and twelve hours, trying to save every penny for the weeks she'd have to take off. Everything wouldn't feel rushed or as scary. She'd have help this time.

Spending time with Charlotte had been great tonight, but now that she was alone, she missed Siril more than ever. Maybe they could get a pet so she wouldn't be by herself when he went on missions. His job was too important for her to ask him to give it up, even if she would feel better having him by her side every night. She wasn't that selfish. His people needed him, and she felt she knew Siril enough to know that he needed to feel useful. Being a warrior wasn't just what he did, it was who he was.

It wasn't who Siril was that was the problem. It was the fact that now she wasn't just a hard-working single mom,

Jennifer had no idea who *she* was. She'd thought she had everything figured out, knew exactly how her life would end up. And then life had thrown her a curveball and nothing was how she'd imagined it would be. It wasn't a bad thing. She loved that she'd found Siril and had so many possibilities in front of her. It was just going to be a little bit of an adjustment.

Having friends would help. She'd had fun with Charlotte tonight, and looked forward to meeting Jacie and Haven. Maybe in time, she'd feel comfortable enough to introduce herself to strangers around town and make even more friends. Being given the gift of this amazing life wasn't something she would ever take for granted. This home was far grander than anything she'd have ever been able to afford on her own. And Siril treated her so well. He seemed in tune with her every need, and genuinely listened when she spoke. He was amazing and just so…

She sighed. Just so far away.

A beeping sound made her get of bed and follow the noise. The Vid-comm was blinking and she answered it the way Siril had shown her. When his face filled the screen, tears sprang to her eyes. He looked tired, but he smiled when he saw her.

"I know it's getting late," he said. "But I couldn't go another minute without talking to you."

"I'm glad you called. I was worried I'd bother you if I called you."

He reached out and touched the screen. "I wish you'd have called. I miss you."

"I miss you too, but I didn't want to be a distraction."

He laughed a little. "I'm afraid you're a distraction whether you call me or not. You're not far from my thoughts even when I'm discussing strategies with the crew. We managed to chase the other ship a good distance away from Zelthrane-3, but Borgoz wanted them in another galaxy. If all goes well, I should be home tomorrow night."

"I spent some time with Charlotte tonight. She's going to introduce me to her friends tomorrow. She said if you weren't back yet, we'd go to breakfast and do some shopping. I'll try not to spend too much."

"Jennifer, spend whatever you wish. The amount I showed you on Earth is a pittance compared to what's in my accounts. Even if I were to retire tomorrow, we'd be okay. I'm not paid as well as the council, but damn close."

"There's no need for me to spend tons of money if I don't have to. I thought I might pick a few things for the house, to make it feel more like mine. And since half my wardrobe was useless and was left behind, I might pick up a few new outfits. Maybe something nice for when we go out to dinner or something."

Siril smiled. "Have fun with your new friends. I'm glad you aren't hiding in the house alone. I worried you wouldn't get out and explore while I was gone, and I didn't have time to introduce you to anyone before I left."

"It's a little lonely being here by myself tonight. Charlotte offered to let me stay at their house, but I wanted to be here. It didn't seem right not to sleep in our bed the first night I'm here."

"I wish I was there with you. I'll probably stay in the command center tonight, keep an eye on things. I doubt I'd sleep anyway. I'd be missing you too much."

"When you get home, you'll have to show me just how much you missed me." She smiled. "I can think of several ways we can pass the time when you get back."

"I love you, Jennifer. I need to go check on the crew, but I'll call you again tomorrow when we're getting close to home. If you need anything, go to Borgoz. He'll be happy to help you while I'm gone."

She nodded, tears misting her eyes. He reached out and touched the screen one last time before the Vid-comm went dark. Her heart ached as she realized she hadn't said the words back to him. It was possible he'd go into battle tonight or tomorrow, and she hadn't told him she loved him. It was tempting to call him back, but he'd said he had things to do.

Curling up in the chair near the garden windows, she

stared up at the moons.

At some point, she must have dozed off because hours later, the rising suns woke her. Stretching, she winced, noting her neck was stiff and ached, and her back didn't feel all that great either. Nothing a nice hot shower wouldn't cure. She didn't know what time Charlotte would come for her, but she'd be ready. And no matter how much she missed Siril, she'd smile and laugh and have a good time.

It didn't take a long time for her to get ready. Just as she was pulling on her favorite boots, the door chimed. Excitement raced through her at the idea of exploring this new world, and meeting new people. With a smile on her face, she greeted Charlotte and invited her inside.

"Jacie and Haven are meeting us at the restaurant," Charlotte said. "There's a café in town that serves human food, so I thought we'd go there. Then Abbie, she's mated to one of the councilmen, said she'd meet us at my favorite store. Borgoz mentioned you only brought one suitcase with you, so I thought you could use some more clothes."

"Siril called me last night. He told me to have a nice time and not worry about spending too much. I guess some new clothes are in order, maybe a pair or two of shoes, and I'd love to get some things for the house."

"When he returns, you should have your picture taken! They didn't have photography here until recently. One of the Zelthranites who settled on Earth requested pictures of the animals we have here. He sent a digital camera on the shuttle and it was sent back to him, so his new human son could see a bit of our world." She waved a hand. "Anyway, when the mates saw someone with a camera, they all asked about having pictures taken. One thing led to another. Our inventors came up with a way to print off digital pictures without having to send the camera back to Earth, and now there's a photography shop in town. Not many people have their own cameras, but they have a studio in the back of the shop for portraits, or you can borrow a camera for a day and take your own."

In some ways this new world was so backward and out

of touch with something as simple as family pictures, but their medical advances blew her mind. And she'd seen the car things flying overhead yesterday. It was a little funny that a race so advanced had to borrow some things from humans, like cameras and movies. What had these people done before humans came to live with them? Just worked all the time?

"Come on," Charlotte said. "We're going to have a great time today."

Jennifer made sure the door locked behind her and followed Charlotte to the café. For so early in the morning, there was quite a crowd on the streets. Or maybe they were more walkways, since their vehicles didn't use roads? Everyone smiled and waved at Charlotte, giving Jennifer curious looks. A few people who must have seen her altercation with Lila yesterday greeted her in passing. It made her feel welcome, and a part of the community, even though she'd only been here a day.

At the café, two women waited outside. One looked barely older than Lila and the other seemed a bit older. Charlotte made the introductions, and both women hugged her. A buzz of excitement filled her as they entered the café. Music played in the background, a fifties tune that made her smile.

Charlotte led the way to a booth in the back corner that was curved and plenty big enough for all four of them. They slid in and Charlotte showed her how to use the menu and then informed the table she was treating everyone this morning. Jennifer tried to protest, but Jacie snorted.

"Once she decides to do something, just let her," Jacie said. "Arguing won't do you any good. From what I've heard, she went from this soft-spoken timid woman to being a force to be reckoned with. I think we can thank our Chief Councilor for that."

Charlotte smiled. "Borgoz has been good for me."

"I think we all won the lottery by getting Zelthranite males for husbands," Haven said. "Dryden knew I was meeting you today, so when Amelia was fussy last night, he stayed up to walk with her, and he didn't hesitate to get up with her first thing this morning."

Jacie nodded. "Barimere was the same way with ours when they were little. I think he has a soft spot for Jenny though. He'd never admit to having a favorite, but she's definitely his favorite."

"Jenny?" Jennifer asked.

Jacie smiled. "It's not short for Jennifer, even though your names are similar. Jenny is special. She's different from any other child on this planet because she has Down Syndrome. Not that it's held her back from joining her two sisters and her brother. They're all really protective of her, especially Lyndir. He's only six, but he acts so much older."

"Does Jenny still have her other protector?" Charlotte asked.

Jacie laughed a little. "It's so cute. Fyro is twelve, one of the first children born after the bride program was introduced, but he's decided he's Jenny's protector. He watches over her and makes sure no one bothers her. If she's sitting alone, he'll entertain her. It's sweet watching them. We explained to him why she looks different, and how she isn't quite as developed as other six year olds. He's been really great."

"I think someone has a crush," Charlotte said. "Watch. When she's older, when they're both grown, I bet he asks permission to take her on a date."

The smile slipped from Jacie's face. "She could never have a relationship like her siblings. I know Down Syndrome people get married on Earth, but usually it's with someone just like them. She wouldn't be able to give him the kind of relationship someone else could. In some ways, she'll always be childlike. No, Jenny will probably live with me and Barimere all her life."

"And if she outlives you?" Charlotte asked softly. "Don't deny her the chance at a mate because you're worried or scared. I've seen Fyro with her. He would never push her for more than she could give. Maybe companionship would be enough for both of them. They could live a long, happy life together."

Jacie nodded.

Haven hugged Jacie and conversation switched to another topic. Jennifer was glad she'd let Charlotte talk her into coming out with them today. Not only was she not constantly thinking of Siril, but she was having a great time. Maybe they could make it a weekly thing.

"So, Jennifer," Haven said. "What's it like being mated to Siril? He seems so intimidating."

Jennifer smiled. "He's been so wonderful to me. I've smiled more since meeting him than I probably did in the last eighteen years."

"He's a sweetheart," Charlotte agreed. "Well, as long as you aren't the enemy."

The women laughed.

"All I've seen is the tender side of him," Jennifer admitted. "But he looks fierce enough that I'm sure he scares anyone who faces him in battle."

"Oh, it's not just that," Jacie said. "He's ruthless from what I've heard. Barimere gets this awed tone to his voice whenever he talks about Siril. You'd think a god lived among us."

Charlotte snorted. "A battle god. Borgoz insists peace wouldn't have reigned on this world for so long if it weren't for Siril. We owe him so much. I'm glad he's finally found a mate to make him happy."

It was odd hearing them talk about Siril like that. To her, he was just Siril. Her mate. The man she loved. It was hard for her to think about him in a battle situation. She'd done little last night other than worry about him, but even then, she hadn't pictured what he would be like on the battlefield. Pride swelled inside of her that her mate was so well thought of, and she hoped he was just as proud to have her by his side.

"I knew he was my hero," Jennifer said. "I guess I never thought about him being a hero to someone else too."

"You picked a good one," Charlotte said.

Jennifer smiled and nodded in agreement. She'd

definitely picked a good one, although it had been more like him picking her. And she'd be grateful every day for the rest of her life.

# Chapter Nine

Siril should have known that things were going too smoothly. As they'd neared the edge of the galaxy, the Destrentes ship had turned, and seemingly out of nowhere, two more ships had joined it. There was no way they were getting out of this without being boarded. The odds weren't in their favor. The C-class ships the Destrentes were using required a crew of at least eight each, but could hold a crew of twelve. So, twenty-four to thirty-six males against his screw of seven? Even if his crew used blasters, which could damage the hull of the ship if misfired, it still wasn't likely they were going to walk away without injuries and possible casualties.

"Prepare to be boarded," he announced over the system.

Opening communications with his council, he quickly relayed their coordinates and situation. "Prepare five ships and have them orbit Zelthrane-3 in case they get past us. Alert the warriors of incoming danger, but don't scare the population just yet. We'll hold them off as long as we can, and take them out if possible."

"Be careful, Siril," Councilman Larimar said.

"I always am."

He ended the connection and checked his weapons.

With the distance between his ship and theirs, he didn't worry about the docking port, but the teleportal was another matter. It could hold as many as five at a time and it wouldn't take long for every Destrentes on board those ships to enter his vessel. His heart clenched as he wondered if this would be the day he didn't return home. If that were true, Fate was a cruel bitch since he'd just found his mate.

Siril cleared his mind, set the controls to autopilot, and headed for the teleportal. He knew the rest of his crew would already be there. His blades cleared their sheaths as he gripped them tight. His boots clanged on the metal floor of the ship as he raced toward the battle. His ears picked up sounds of fighting as he neared the chamber. At least twenty Destrentes were already on board, and the teleportal lit up with more incoming.

One of his crew lay dead against the wall, the others were fighting for their lives. Siril jumped into the fray, hacking and slicing at the Destrentes. He felt the heat of a Noctu slice into his arm, the ebony blade forged in the hottest fires of Noctorin, holding the heat for decades. His skin sizzled around the wound and cauterized, but he knew it would scar. He faced the Destrentes that had attacked and went after him, his Corian blades doing some damage but not nearly enough.

The Destrentes laughed. "My skin is hard coated, Zelthranite. You'll never pierce it."

*Fuck*. The Destrentes had essentially laid a permanent blast and blade proof coating on his skin, and nothing short of a bomb would take him down. If Siril could get close enough, he could possibly blind the warrior, or damage his throat so that he couldn't breathe as easily, but every step he took was countered. The Noctu bit into him again, going deeper this time as it sliced into his side.

A wave of dizziness hit Siril, but he remained upright and went on the offensive. Coming in low, he slammed the heel of his hand against the Destrentes' knee, making the joint pop and sending the warrior to the floor. Siril leapt onto him and went for his eyes with the Corian blades, but the Destrentes was prepared for the attack. He bucked Siril off and reversed their positions, pinning him to the metal floor.

"So you want to play dirty?" the Destrentes asked. His hand clamped on Siril's side, his fingers breaking open the cauterized wound until it freely bled.

Siril ground his teeth together to keep from crying out. He brought up his knees, slamming them into the Destrentes' back, but the male barely wavered. The warrior laughed and slammed the Noctu into Siril's other side, even deeper than before. Blinding hot pain seared him, making his vision blur and the room spin. His gaze looked to his crew, hoping someone would notice he needed help. Four were now dead, and the others were barely surviving.

He briefly closed his eye and prayed that Jennifer would be all right without him, that his son or daughter would know that he loved them, even if he couldn't be there. When he opened his eye, the Destrentes had a smirk on his face. The warrior looked at the chaos around them before returning his gaze to Siril.

"All we wanted were a few women," the Destrentes said. "If you'd just left us alone, we'd have snatched your single females and we'd have left. Even we aren't cold-hearted enough to break up families."

"What single females?" Siril asked. "We have to exchange money for females to even come to our world to consider mating with our males. Our race would have died out if it weren't for the bride exchange."

"We've been watching and listening. Even a handful of single Earth females would be worth the trip. It's not like you'd miss them. You'd just get more." The Noctu hovered over his heart. "Give me one good reason to spare your life. Your crew is lost. It's just a matter of time. But everyone has heard of the revered Siril. Your life is worth something."

"I have a mate, and a child on the way. They'll be alone if I die." Siril hated admitting his weakness, but he'd do anything to return to Jennifer's side. Almost anything. He wouldn't give up the females on his planet, even the unmated ones.

The Destrentes hesitated. "You've mated?"

"Yes. Recently. She already carries my young."

The blade eased away from his heart. "Then I will spare your life, but I can't run the risk of you coming after us again. I know your planet will send others to try to wipe us out in retaliation for coming near your precious planet, but they are mere ants in an army. You… you are a different matter."

He couldn't promise to leave them alone because it wasn't his decision. If he went home and his council demanded it, he'd have to go after them again. He wouldn't lie, even to save his own life. He heard the fighting stop and knew his crew was gone. The other Destrentes gathered around, their weapons still drawn.

"What are you going to do with him?" one of them asked.

"He's going to live, but we're going to make sure he's permanently retired."

His heart stuttered and he wondered what the warrior meant by that. If they cut off his other leg, he'd just get another Corian one. If they cut off his hand, he'd replace that too. There wasn't anything they could do to him that would keep him down for long, except end his life, and the warrior had said he wouldn't do that.

The Destrentes got a calculating look. "You were going for my eyes, weren't you? Trying to blind me since you couldn't take me down?"

Siril remained mute, but horror filled him. If they took his remaining eye, he'd never get to see his child, never behold Jennifer's beauty again. He'd be unable to return to this ship, and unable to train future warriors. His life would be over and he'd be utterly useless to his people and his mate. He'd be alive, but it would only be a half life.

The Noctu rose and the warrior brought it close to his face. Siril turned his head, and closed his eye, trying to avoid the heat of the blade.

"Hold him," the warrior demanded.

Hands gripped his head and turned it while fingers pried his good eye open. More hands gripped his arms and legs, holding him completely immobile. He saw the blade drawing near and was powerless to stop it. The heat made his skin burn and his eye felt like it might explode. The warrior halted a few inches from his eye, but the heat was intense.

A film settled over his vision and the longer the blade remained near, the worse it became. Within seconds, his vision was nearly gone. He could see shapes, but little else. The heat was removed and the weight holding him down lifted. Siril remained motionless, defeated. His crew was gone. His sight was nearly gone. His life was gone. No longer could he command this ship or lead warriors. And when he returned home, his mate... Gods. He'd be helpless. She'd have to take care of him and their child.

Moisture leaked from his eyes as the last of his vision faded and the shapes blurred. Soon there was nothing but darkness. Boots clanged around him as the Destrentes left him to his fate. He had no idea how to pilot his ship home. Could he even reach the command center? If there were a way to reach his council, they could send others to aid him. He'd be humiliated, but nothing compared to being removed from duty permanently.

There was a noise to his right. "I've set your auto pilot to return this ship to your world. We'll leave your planet in peace for now, but come after us, and we will retaliate. We will kill every male who comes for us, whether they have families or not. Tell your council that the mercy we have granted you comes with a price. If they don't want their precious planet invaded, they will send us a female from each shuttle that arrives through the end of the lunar cycle. When the new moons rise, the Destrentes will offer peace to your people. But only if our terms have been met."

"Understood," Siril said.

A hand gripped his forearm and the warrior helped him stand.

"I grew up hearing stories of your exploits," the warrior said. "It would have saddened me to end your life. The great Siril. I'm sorry for the pain I've caused you, but the well-being of my people must come first."

"Who are you?" Siril asked.

"Santor."

"Heir to the Destrentes throne?" Siril asked.

"Yes. I only sought a princess to have by my side. Remember what I've said."

Siril swayed on his feet as he listened to the warrior leave. Feeling along the wall, he slowly made his way through the ship. He tried to remember the twists and turns and eventually made his way to the command center. Collapsing into a chair, he allowed the tears to fall. First was relief that he hadn't left his child without a father, and then the humiliation of returning to his people without his sight. The most feared warrior in the galaxies, and now he wouldn't even be able to walk through his home unassisted.

Lost in his thoughts, he didn't realize how much time had passed until the ship slowed and then shuddered as it landed. Siril remained seated, knowing when he didn't disembarked his people would investigate. It didn't take long before he heard voices and shouts. *They must have found the bodies.*

"Siril!" a voice called out.

"Ryoku?"

Booted steps drew near and then he heard the warrior curse. A hand lightly touched his shoulder. "What did they do to you?"

"They took my sight. They let me live, but they took away my status, my ability to care for my family, and my pride."

"Come, friend," Ryoku said softly.

The warrior helped him stand and led him off the ship. He felt the cool breeze on his face and only stumbled a few times. There were murmurs around him as those nearby realized what had happened to him. He should be grateful to be alive, and he was, but without his sight he couldn't be the great Siril anymore. He was no one. Just a washed up warrior who wasn't good for much of anything.

"Let's take him to the clinic," Kelvyk said, taking his other side.

The warriors on either side of him made sure he didn't trip and humiliate himself further. When they reached the clinic, Vyrex was on duty. He suffered through eye washes, injections, scans. None of it returned his sight to him. Reaching up, he removed his eye patch and tossed it aside. If he was blind in both eyes now, there was no point in hiding only one of them.

"Am I too scary this way? Should I wear some sort of covering over my eyes?" Siril asked.

"The dark purple has faded to a color three shades lighter than your skin. It's apparent you are sightless, but not scary. What other wounds did you suffer?" Vyrex asked.

"A Noctu slice on my arm. One that pierced both my sides."

They helped him remove his shirt and Vyrex tended to the wounds. Because the skin had cauterized on one side and his arm, there was only a need for stitches on the side that had been reopened, but Siril knew it would leave ghastly looking scars. The cauterized wound in his side would never close all the way. Would Jennifer ever be able to look at him the same way? Perhaps it was a blessing he wouldn't be able to see her reaction.

"The council needs to be notified," Siril said. "I have a message for them from the Destrentes prince."

"Wait here," Kelvyk said. "Ryoku will stay with you. I'll return with a council member or the Chief Councilor."

The room grew quiet, which was far worse than the murmuring had been. He knew they pitied him, and he hated it. He wanted to scream, to punch something. He wanted to rip apart every Destrentes warrior and bathe in their blood. But he sat quietly, adjusting to the absence of light. He'd never seen such darkness before. He blinked his eyes, but still nothing but blackness.

The minutes ticked by and after a while he heard the door open again.

"Siril," Borgoz said softly. "I'm so sorry, my friend."

"Santor said that if we don't give the Destrentes one female from each shuttle that arrives until the new moons, they will retaliate. But if we give them that offering, if we keep peace with them, they will leave our people alone. Any warrior who goes after them will be killed."

Borgoz cursed. "I can't agree to those terms without first discussing the issue with Earth's government. Do you think they would abduct them straight from Earth if we don't comply?"

"It's possible. They seem desperate."

"The council will convene tonight to discuss the matter and we'll contact Earth. Until an agreement can be made, all shuttles will be cancelled."

He heard someone snicker. "That means he's stuck with his new daughter because she's still here, raising hell for all to hear."

"Do you think Jennifer would be upset if we offered her daughter to them?" Borgoz asked.

Siril chuckled. "You'd have to ask her."

"Let's get you home to your mate," Borgoz said. "I didn't notify her after your communication came through because I didn't want to worry her more. I'll walk with you."

"You'll have to guide me since I can't see where I'm going."

"Wait a minute," Vyrex said. "You aren't as helpless as you think. Count your steps. Pay attention to the sounds around you. If you hear the animals in the pet shop, you'll know you're a few blocks from your turn to go home. In your home, keep your furniture in the same spots and learn where everything is. Just because you can't see with your eyes, doesn't mean you can't see it in your mind."

Siril nodded.

"I'll guide you home," Borgoz said. "And if you wish me to remain while you speak with your mate, I will. Or if you want privacy, I'll leave the two of you alone."

Borgoz gripped his arm and Siril faltered only a moment as they exited the clinic. The night was still, which meant it was late enough the shops were closed. He could smell food though, so it wasn't past the dinner hour. It had been early morning since he last ate and his stomach rumbled. The walk home was long, perhaps made longer since he was counting his steps as Vyrex had suggested. When they came to a stop, he knew they'd reached his home.

The door opened and he heard a muffled sob a moment before Jennifer threw herself into his arms. He held her tight, breathing in her sweet scent despite the pain from his wounds. This. This was why he was still alive. Even though he couldn't see, just holding her made everything right. Her arms slid from around his waist and she eased back a little.

"You're not wearing your eye patch," she said. "And

your other eye is different. What happened?"

Siril stood mute.

"His sight was taken from him," Borgoz said. "He has a few wounds that might be tender for a while. And he's going to need a little help getting around while he adjusts."

"You can't see?" she asked softly.

"They spared my life so I could return to you, but I'm afraid you aren't getting much of a bargain. I can no longer be a warrior or a trainer. They've forced me into early retirement." Siril swallowed hard. "If you no longer wish to be mated to me, if you'd prefer a mate who isn't as damaged, I will understand."

"Siril," she said softly, her hand sliding along his cheek. "I will always want you. I love you. Do you think I care if you have a missing finger or leg? If you can't see? I love the male that you are, and all of those things are just physical. It's your heart I fell in love with."

"I'll leave the two of you alone," Borgoz said. "If you need anything, I'll be in the council headquarters. We'll be meeting most of the night."

"Thank you," Jennifer said.

"Borgoz," Siril said. "I'm sorry I let you down."

His friend clapped him on the shoulder. "No, Siril. It is I who am sorry. If we'd left them alone, they may have stolen a few of our potential mates, but you wouldn't have lost your crew or your sight. It would have been a small price to pay."

"I don't understand," Jennifer said. "They wanted women?"

"Santor, their prince, is seeking a princess. But the other males on his planet want mates as well. It's rumored that a virus swept across their planet and killed all of their females, young and old," Siril said.

"I jokingly told Siril we should send your daughter to him," Borgoz said.

Jennifer gave a snort. "Lila would be over the moon to become a princess, but she'd probably torture the poor guy."

He felt Borgoz hesitate. "You would not be opposed to

us offering your daughter to them?"

"Talk to Lila," Jennifer said. "I bet she'd be more than happy to go with them, if she got the prince. It would make her happy, and it would solve your problem for now. As she's pointed out, she's a grown woman and can choose her own path."

"Very well. I wish the both of you a pleasant evening," Borgoz said.

Jennifer took his hand and led him inside and shut the door. He smelled food and his stomach rumbled again. She pressed against his side, near his wound but not near enough to hurt. Then her hand slid down his arm as she checked on his other wound.

"You're in rough shape," she said. "Why don't we eat, and then I'll start the shower for you? We can crawl into bed afterward and snuggle under the covers."

"That's all you have to say?" he asked. "I've lost my sight, lost who I am, and I look a little rough?"

"Siril," she said softly. "I can only imagine how it was when they took your sight from you. But the fact you're blind doesn't change who you are. All the battles you've lost and won are still part of the history of this planet. Even if you're not wielding a sword, or whatever weapon you use, you're still a warrior and will always be a warrior. Maybe you just need to be a different kind of warrior now."

He didn't understand her words, but he let her lead him to the table.

"I ordered enough for two and set the table," she said, "hoping you'd be home for dinner. I don't understand Terran cuisine yet, so I ordered from the Earth café. I had to guess at what you might like. You have a burger and fries, same as me. And there's apple pie for dessert."

"You don't see me differently?" he asked.

"Siril, shut up and eat before you make me mad. Whether you can see or not doesn't change the fact you're the guy I love and the father of this baby growing inside of me. Your son or daughter won't care if you can see or not. They'll only care that you love them and play with them.

Your arms still work, don't they?" she asked.

"Yes," he said.

"Then you can hold a baby. And assuming everything else still works, you can still make love to your wife. We have each other, and that's what matters. Even if you'd been blind when I first met you, I'd still have come here with you. I didn't agree to be your mate because you're a revered warrior. I agreed because you're a good man. You're kind, brave, and you showed me a tenderness no one had ever shown me before. That is who you are. Your eyes have nothing to do with that."

He was humbled by her response. Siril ate his food and contemplated her words. When Santor had claimed his sight, he'd thought his life was over, that it would have no meaning. He'd always been a warrior. But perhaps, instead of focusing on being a gladiator for his people, perhaps he could focus on being a mate and father. Instead of being important to everyone, he could be important to two particular people. The weight on his shoulders lifted a bit. If Jennifer had cried, if she'd made a big fuss over what he'd lost, he might have crumpled. But he should have known better. His mate was fierce and strong, and she expected the same of him.

"I'll need help," he said. "Until I'm familiar with where everything is, and we won't be able to shift things around. If everything stays in its place, Vyrex thinks I can learn to navigate the house and possibly the city unassisted. But it will take time."

"Take all the time you need," she said softly. "I'm not going anywhere."

They finished their meal and Jennifer ran a shower for him as promised. He flinched when a hand landed on his bare back as he stood under the spray and he heard the unit door shut. Her naked body pressed against him and he wished he could see her beautiful curves once more. Using his other senses, he explored her soft skin with his hands, and listened to her sighs of pleasure.

Jennifer tugged him forward until he heard her back hit

the unit wall. Her hands braced on his shoulders and she leapt, wrapping her legs around his waist. He gripped her so she wouldn't fall, and then his lips found hers. Siril kissed her hungrily, as if it were the last kiss they would ever share. His cock surged to life, hard and throbbing. Jennifer rubbed against him as the scent of her arousal teased his nose.

"I want to make you come," he said. "I want to hear you scream my name."

"I want that too."

"I'm going to set you down and I want you to stay against the wall."

He let her slide down his body and when her feet touched the floor, he knelt in front of her. His hands caressed her thighs before pushing them wide and lifting them over his shoulders. Gripping the curve of her ass, he lifted her to his mouth. The taste of her exploded on his tongue as he licked her slit. Jennifer cried out and her hands fisted in his hair. He remembered her rubbing her clit to make herself come in the limo and he sought it out with his tongue, circling the little bud. He licked, sucked, and teased as she begged him to never stop. Every time her body tensed, ready to come, he'd slow his motions and ease off, then he'd build her back up again. When he finally let her come, her juices coated his chin and her cries filled his ears. Her thighs shook and her body trembled.

Siril helped her stand and turned her to face the wall. His hand slid down her belly and teased her pussy, drawing a moan from her. She was so hot and so damn wet. Siril gripped her hips and lifted her up a bit, then slowly lowered her onto his cock, the sweet curve of her ass nestled against him. He couldn't stop the groan that slipped past his lips and thrilled in the way her pussy gripped him tight.

He pulled his hips back then slid inside of her again. He was deeper from this angle and his control was slipping. He took her slowly, every thrust drawn out to build her pleasure. Slow. Deep. His fingers teased her clit until she was begging him to fuck her hard and fast, but he maintained his pace, knowing she would come harder than ever before.

His muscles strained as he fought to control himself. His steady rhythm had her shivering and soon she was screaming his name. As her release coated his cock, he moved faster, deeper, harder until his hips were slapping against her. When she came again, he let himself go. He called out her name as spurt after spurt of hot cum filled her tight sheath. When his balls were drained, his cock buried deep in her pussy, he just held her close, his heart pounding in his chest.

"I think… I think that's the most explosive sex I've ever had," Jennifer said. "And you were worried about not seeing."

Siril chuckled a little. "It seems there are some things I can do with or without my sight. As long as I can please my mate, then nothing else matters."

"Let me catch my breath and we can try that again," she said. "I think the worry you put me through deserves at least three more orgasms."

He nipped her shoulder. "Three seems like such a paltry amount. Why don't I just keep you up all night and give you at least ten more?"

She groaned. "I don't think my body could handle ten more."

"Let's find out," he whispered in her ear.

He took her twice more in the shower before they cleaned up and retired to the bedroom. He could feel the warmth of the suns rising before he finally allowed her to rest. Sleep didn't come for him right away, but he was content. No. He was happy. If he'd thought being inside of his mate was pleasurable before, it was even better when he had to rely on his other senses. The experience was richer, more intense. And he couldn't wait to do it again. And again. He didn't see any reason for them to leave the bed for the next few days, except to eat and use the facilities. The rest of the time he planned to keep her begging for more of his cock.

Perhaps being retired wouldn't be so bad.

# Epilogue

**One Month Later**

Siril chased Jennifer around the living room, listening to her giggle as she fled. They'd already made love twice today, but that had been hours ago, and he was hungry for his mate again. His fingers brushed against her before he heard her start running the other way.

"I'm going to catch you and when I do you'll be punished for your insolent behavior," he told her with a smile.

"Oh. I'm scared. Are you going to punish me with that monster cock of yours?"

"I'll take you so damn slow you're begging for release. I'll keep you on the edge and draw it out forever."

Jennifer moaned. "You aren't playing fair."

The door chime sounded and Siril sighed, knowing his fun was ended for the moment. But once they got rid of whoever was on their doorstep, he *would* have his mate naked in their bed.

"I'll get it," Jennifer said.

Siril followed at a slower pace and arrived as the door was shutting.

"Siril, Borgoz is here to see you," she said.

"I hope I'm not interrupting anything," Borgoz said with amusement.

Siril cleared his throat and tried to discreetly readjust himself. "Not at all."

"I wondered if we could speak for a moment? I have a proposition for you."

"I'll go get some drinks for the two of you. Why don't you sit at the table for your meeting?" Jennifer suggested.

Siril led the way to the dining table and pulled out a chair. He heard Borgoz sit as well and waited for his friend to speak. Not a word was said until after Jennifer had delivered their drinks and left the room again.

"Is this something that couldn't be said in front of my mate?" Siril asked.

"I've actually spoken to Jennifer briefly about this

already, just to see if she would be open to it. I didn't want to cause strife in your mating."

"I don't understand," Siril said.

"You seem to be enjoying retirement," Borgoz said. "You're by your mate's side at all times, unless she's spending time with her friends. I wondered if you would be willing to give some of your time to your people once more."

"My days as a warrior are over," Siril said. The pain those words would have once caused didn't give him even a twinge now.

"I had something else in mind. The council and I have been in discussions the past few weeks, and with the new development with the Destrentes, we're a little overwhelmed. While Lila agreed to mate with their prince, there's still the issue of other females to contend with. The Destrentes agreed to leave us in peace if we provided females to them, and we plan to do it. Even if negotiations with Earth aren't going as well as I'd hoped. So, we've added an additional council seat. It's only a part-time position when our load is heavier than usual. Of course, the person taking that seat would be brought in on all major decisions as well. They'd have full council powers and benefits, just not as many hours away from home."

"A new council seat?"

"We want you to take the position," Borgoz said. "Jennifer said if that's what you wanted to do she would give her support. She worries you'll grow bored staying around the house. And I know you miss helping the people. This would allow you to do that and still have plenty of time at home with your family."

"Say yes," Jennifer hissed from the doorway.

Siril chuckled. "It seems I'm supposed to say yes."

"You'll do it?" Borgoz asked.

"Yes," Siril said. "I'm honored to accept the position."

"Excellent!" He heard Borgoz stand. "Our next meeting is in a week. We'll expect to see you there for at least part of it. I've promised Jennifer we won't monopolize your time."

Siril stood. "I'll see you next week."

"No," Jennifer said. "You'll see him tomorrow. Charlotte invited us for dinner."

"I stand corrected," Siril said.

Borgoz laughed. "Very well. As you were. I'll see myself out."

Jennifer moved closer. "I don't think he was fooled. He knew exactly what we were doing when he arrived."

"You know," Siril said. "This table is pretty sturdy."

"You're not taking me on the table where we eat. Just like I wouldn't let you take me on the kitchen counters."

Siril sighed. "Fine. I'll give you to the count of five to get to our bedroom and strip."

"And if I don't?" she asked.

"Then I will strip you naked where you stand when I get to five, and take you right there. And a door chime won't stop me."

"Siril."

"One."

"You're serious?" she asked.

"Two."

She squeaked and he heard her take off toward the bedroom. He followed and when he reached their room, he shut the door and stripped out of his clothes. Hearing movement across the room, he found her by the window, her soft skin bare for his enjoyment. With the afternoon suns caressing them, Siril made love to his mate. Slowly. Tenderly. Savoring every moment, and every cry of pleasure. When they were too weak to stand, he moved them over to the bed and crawled in next to her.

Jennifer curled against his side and rested her head on his shoulder. "I told you you were still a warrior."

"Because I can fuck you until your legs don't work?"

She giggled. "Well, the stamina is nice, but no... You might not be able to go into battle, but now, as part of the council, you will still be a warrior for your people."

"Did you know this would happen?" he asked.

"No. Not this specifically. But I knew you'd find a way

to help them. It's just who you are. Even if Borgoz hadn't made this offer, you'd have found another way."

He kissed her softly. "I love you."

"And I love you. I always will."

"Even though I'm not some revered badass anymore?"

Her lips met his and her hand reached for his cock. "You'll always be *my* badass. Now why don't you show me just how bad you can be?"

Siril grinned as he rolled his mate onto her back and spent the rest of the afternoon making her scream his name.

Sometimes life gave you exactly what you needed. And all he'd ever need was right there in his arms.

# Jessica Coulter Smith

Award-winning author Jessica Coulter Smith has been in love with the written word since she was a child writing her first stories in crayon. Her first romance was published in 2008, and since that time she's had over one hundred short stories, novellas, and novels published. She's particularly fond of writing paranormal and science fiction romances, but she also writes overly hot contemporary romance as Harley Wylde. Romance is an integral part of her world and Jessica firmly believes that love will find you at the right time, even if Mr. Right is literally out of this world.

More books by Jessica changelingpress.com/jessica-coulter-smith-a-144

More books by Harley changelingpress.com/harley-wylde-a-196

Dulce on Changeling: changelingpress.com/dulce-dennison-a-205

## Changeling Press E-Books

More Sci-Fi, Fantasy, Paranormal, and BDSM adventures available in E-Book format for immediate download at ChangelingPress.com -- Werewolves, Vampires, Dragons, Shapeshifters and more -- Erotic Tales from the edge of your imagination.

## What are E-Books?

E-Books, or Electronic Books, are books designed to be read in digital format -- on your desktop or laptop computer, notebook, tablet, Smart Phone, or any electronic ebook reader.

## Where can I get Changeling Press e-Books?

Changeling Press ebooks are available at ChangelingPress.com, Amazon, Barnes and Nobel, Kobo, and iTunes.

**ChangelingPress.com**